THE BROW OF THE GALLOWGATE

Doris Davidson is a retired primary school teacher living in Aberdeen. She has been writing novels since 1984, although *The Brow of the Gallowgate* was the first to be published – in 1990. Her married daughter is a Civil Servant and lives in Surrey, but her son, an art teacher, also lives in Aberdeen, and presented her with a grandson in 1987.

DORIS DAVIDSON

The Brow of
the Gallowgate

HarperCollins*Publishers*

HarperCollins*Publishers*
77–85 Fulham Palace Road,
Hammersmith, London W6 8JB

This paperback edition 1995
1 3 5 7 9 8 6 4 2

Previously published in paperback by Fontana 1990
Reprinted twice

First published in Great Britain by
Collins 1990

Copyright © Doris Davidson

The Author asserts the moral right to
be identified as the author of this work

ISBN 978-0-00-783318-4

Set in Palatino

Printed and bound in Great Britain by
Clays Ltd, St Ives plc

1925

Should he tell his family how and why Charlie had died? Or should he keep the truth to himself?

The sickness that had swept over Albert in New Zealand, when he found out what had happened, surged up in him again, as it did every time he remembered. Was it fair to place the remainder of his children under that same stress?

In any case, could he trust himself to speak about it rationally? Could he sit down, when he returned to Aberdeen, and tell them that Bella Wyness had taken her terrible revenge on the Ogilvies at last?

Thank God – and God forgive him for even thinking such a thing – that Bathie hadn't lived to see her prediction coming true.

Bathie – his own, dear Bathie, whom he had loved since the first day he saw her. Thirty-six years ago.

PART ONE

Chapter One

Just as Albert's mother ladled out his potato soup, his father came into the kitchen and glowered at him.

'What time o' night's this to be comin' hame for your supper?' he demanded. 'Your mother's got enough to do withoot waitin' a' hours o' the night to get the table cleared.'

Having had his say, Wattie Ogilvie crossed over to the fireplace and held his backside to the heat, for the outside lavatory was cold, even in May.

'A customer came into the shop just on seven.' Albert glanced up at his mother as she laid his plate down in front of him. One lock of her dark hair had escaped from its hairpin confines, giving her a rather lopsided appearance, but her eyes were twin gimlets boring into him, and he knew she hadn't been fooled by his excuse. 'I'm sorry, Mother,' he added, somewhat belatedly.

Nell's expression softened. 'Mr Duthie'll never mak' you manager, lad, even if you work twenty-four hours in the day.'

'I'm as good as manager already.' He blew on the spoonful of soup he lifted to his mouth. 'The only difference is, I'm not getting paid for it. I'm just trying to set things out better, to make it easier for him as well as for me.'

'He's an auld man, Albert. He'll nae change after forty year.'

'That's the whole point, Mother. It maybe worked fine for him forty years ago, but this is 1889.'

His rheumaticky knees refusing to bend with him, Wattie sat down with a thump. 'You tak' ower muckle

7

on yoursel', Albert. Let the man run his place the way he wants.'

Nell looked from one to the other as Albert lapsed into offended silence. They were so like each other, the two of them, their natures as well as their looks. Wattie's skin was weatherbeaten from being at the fishing since he was a laddie, but, apart from that, Albert was nearly his dead spit – red hair parted in the middle, round healthy faces and moustaches even brighter than their heads – though Albert's was less bushy than his father's. But Wattie had a fine beard, while his son's clean-shaven chin showed an attractive cleft, making him look younger than he really was.

Nell took the boiled beef out of the soup pot at the side of the range. 'Belle's been anxious for you to come in.' The spaniel rose from the hearthrug at the mention of her name, and Albert patted her head affectionately. 'Just five minutes, Belle, and I'll take you out.'

When he finished his second course, which his mother had dished onto his empty soup plate, he lifted his jacket and cap and went out without a word, and Nell turned to her husband.

'I'm worried about him, Wattie. He's goin' to get a real sair he'rt if Mr Duthie doesna mak' him the manager.'

'He's nae a bairn, Nell. He's near twenty-four.'

'He'd maybe be mair content if he took a wife. Walter and Jimmy were wed lang afore they were his age, and they're happy enough, even though they're baith fishin' oot o' Grimsby.'

'Albert's aye been different,' Wattie reminded her. 'Aye wantin' what he canna get.'

Their youngest son strode along the street, angry at his parents for believing that his ambition was to be manager of Joseph Duthie's grocery shop. It was his own shop he wanted, but they'd think he was mad if they knew that.

It wouldn't be right to set up in Torry in opposition to his present employer, of course, but he could go to another district of Aberdeen, so he always kept one eye open for a suitable property when he took Belle out. He

8

had not yet come across anything he liked, and perhaps it was just as well, for he'd feel frustrated at not having the money to buy it. But there was no harm in looking.

Belle padded along beside him, sniffing in the gutter and squatting occasionally in a token gesture, so he spoke to her, as he often did. 'I know my mother thinks it's time I took a wife, but I'll not think about that for a while yet. You're the only lass for me, Belle.'

He'd walked out with a few girls since he'd been old enough to take an interest in them, but not one of them had caused his sap to rise, nor made his heart beat any faster. They'd all been common, ignorant lassies, and they'd disgusted him with their blatant attempts to trap him into marriage. He recalled the one time he had been roused, when he was only seventeen. The girl had been on holiday in Aberdeen, living with her auntie next door to the shop, and he'd asked her out after she'd hinted that she was willing. She'd been a bonnie wee thing and he'd felt kind of drawn to her.

They'd walked towards the sea, then along the coast, and he'd unexpectedly wondered what it would be like to bed her. The urge in him had grown quickly, and he'd taken her, with no preliminaries, on a grassy bank at the side of the road. It had been over in a flash, and he'd felt rather let down that there was nothing more to it, though the girl had seemed pleased enough. He'd been glad when she went back to Glasgow the following day, for she hadn't meant a thing to him, and he'd been very relieved that she hadn't written afterwards to tell him that she was in the family way.

He'd never touched another lassie. It wasn't worth the worry, and most of his leisure hours were spent in trying to broaden his knowledge. Having left school at twelve, he'd felt he needed more education before he would amount to anything, so for years he'd gone to the public library every Wednesday afternoon, his half day off. He'd been little more than a dogsbody to Mr Duthie when he first started working, but he'd known he was destined for much better things, and he'd grown certain of it as he grew older. It was entirely up to himself, for nobody got anything without having to work for it.

He was practically in charge of Mr Duthie's shop now, but when all was said and done, he was still only an assistant, still single and still rather disgruntled with his life.

A wife would only complicate things, though, for she'd be forever on at him to buy new clothes for herself and for any bairns they might spawn, so he was far better off without one. Especially since she might turn out like his brothers' wives, who thought about nothing but themselves.

'We'll take a look round Ferryhill on Sunday,' he remarked to Belle. 'I've heard it's a nice area.'

Bathia Johnstone gave a little giggle when she thought of how clever she had been in asking for a dog for her birthday. Of course, her father had been against it, but she'd won him round like she always did.

She had never been allowed to go out on her own before, but here she was, this lovely spring Sunday afternoon, taking Spanny to the Duthie Park, where she would surely meet some boys of her own age. The only boys she knew, the sons of her father's friends, were so namby-pamby they weren't any fun, but real boys, ordinary boys, would have more spirit. She might even meet her fate amongst them, and be transported away from her present dull existence. She had read all about the facts of life, so she would never give any coarse philanderer the chance to seduce her – although it might be rather enjoyable if one tried . . .

Standing still for a moment to let Spanny inspect a tree, Bathia became aware that a young man was coming towards her – a tall, slim man with a very handsome face. His jacket was rough and didn't match his baggy trousers, but she felt that she could learn to like him a lot. And when she saw that his dog was a spaniel like hers, she took it as a good omen.

He seemed to be deep in thought, however, so how could she make him notice her? It was really quite unladylike, but when he was almost abreast of her, she

10

gave a discreet little cough to draw his attention. His head jerked up, revealing an attractive cleft in his chin, and he smiled when he lifted his shapeless cap. The bright red hair, parted in the middle, came as a surprise to her, but she recognized the naked admiration in his dark eyes as he walked past.

When she went to bed that night, she couldn't stop thinking about the red-headed stranger, and wished fervently that girls could speak to a man without waiting to be introduced.

Albert's dream that night was not about his shop, and in the morning, his mind was made up. He didn't know her name, or anything about her, but he did know that the girl he'd smiled at was the only one with whom he would ever want to share his life, however long it took for him to find her again.

He haunted the Duthie Park every night that week, but without success. So when he entered the gates the following Sunday afternoon his expectations were low. He'd been all the way round once and was finishing his second circuit when he saw her coming towards him, and the hammering of his heart made him awkward and self-conscious. He hadn't planned how he would approach her, but luck seemed to be on his side, because her little puppy sidled up to sniff round Belle.

The girl bestowed her dazzling smile on him again, so he removed his cap and said, tentatively, 'Our dogs seem to have introduced themselves, maybe we should do the same. My name is Albert Ogilvie.'

She held out a gloved hand. 'I'm Bathia Johnstone.'

Her voice was low and sweet, and he hesitated for only a second. 'Would you . . . er . . . allow me to accompany you on your walk, Miss Johnstone?' He held his breath in case she thought him too presumptuous.

'I'd be delighted, Mr Ogilvie.'

Her acquiescent smile made Albert think of dawn breaking on a clear summer morning, lighting up the whole world, and he turned back with her, praying that Belle wouldn't baulk at a third journey round the Park.

11

But his dog was running around quite happily with the puppy.

Albert found himself tongue-tied, but the girl broke the silence before it became uncomfortable.

'What's your dog's name, Mr Ogilvie?'

'Belle. She's nearly six. Quite old, really.'

'She's beautiful.'

They walked on a few more steps, then Bathia asked, 'Do you work at all, Mr Ogilvie?'

'Yes, I'm afraid I have to work for my living. I serve in a grocer's shop in Torry.' Albert wished that he could have told her he was the owner of the shop, but it was better to stick to the truth. 'I've been there since I left school when I was twelve, and I'm nearly twenty-four now.'

'Twenty-four? You don't look it, Mr Ogilvie. You have a very young face. I'll be seventeen on my next birthday.' She laughed suddenly, a little silvery trill that made Albert's heart thump, and sealed his fate for ever. 'To be quite honest, I've just been sixteen for about ten days,' she confessed. 'Would you have known that's all I was? Does my face give me away?'

'You've got a perfect face, Miss Johnstone.' He had never paid any girl a compliment before, but she was perfect, every bit of her, from the shining brown ringlets under her bonnet right down to her dainty kid-shod feet.

She looked up at him coquettishly. 'I like your moustache, Mr Ogilvie. Oh, do you think it forward of me, saying that?'

'Oh, no. I think you're . . . perfect.' Why couldn't he have found a different word this time? She'd think he didn't have any vocabulary, when he'd spent years trying to build one up.

Her delighted laugh dispelled his fears. 'I'm not perfect. My mother says my father spoils me by giving me everything I want. He would never let me go out alone, though, but I fooled him, because I asked for a dog for my birthday, knowing he would say I'd have to exercise it.' Looking away demurely, she added, 'I may as well admit, too, that I've been coming to the park every afternoon since last Sunday, hoping I'd see you again.'

'I work during the week, but I've been coming here every night looking for you.'

'Oh.' She sounded pleasantly surprised. 'I was afraid to come at night, but if you were here to protect me . . .'

'I'll be here every night.' He noticed, with a pang of guilt, that Belle was flagging a little. 'I'll have to be getting home now, though. I think Belle's a bit tired, for we've been right round the park twice already.'

She halted abruptly and bent down to pat his dog. 'Poor Belle, we've exhausted you. We're turning back now, Spanny.'

'There's no need for you to cut your walk short, Miss Johnstone,' Albert said, hastily.

'I want to go back with you. I enjoy your company.'

Her candour was fresh and gratifying. There was no guile about her, and none of the simpering, false modesty of the other girls he knew. They walked slowly back the way they'd come with no awkward silences – Bathia seemed to have the knack of drawing Albert out, and listened with interest to his little anecdotes about the customers he served.

They had left the park before he realized that he'd been monopolizing the conversation. 'I'm sorry, Miss Johnstone. You'll be tired of hearing about the shop, for you must be accustomed to doing much more interesting things than me.'

Wrinkling her small, turned-up nose, she said, 'I don't do anything at all, really. My father says I don't have to work, so I play the piano, write letters to my aunts, embroider, read books.' She came to a halt beside two granite pillars at the foot of a short flight of stone steps. 'Here's where I live.'

Albert's eyes widened with dismay as he looked up at the large mansion, for there was no hope of him ever being allowed to court a girl who lived here. 'Your father must be a very rich man, Miss Johnstone,' he said sadly. 'Our house would fit six times into this place.'

'He's a banker, Bank of Scotland, you know. I suppose he is quite rich, I'd never really thought about it. Well,

13

goodbye, Mr Ogilvie, and I'll see you tomorrow night, won't I?'

Albert's heart sank so quickly, he felt sick. 'Maybe we shouldn't see each other any more. I'm sure your father wouldn't approve of you meeting a grocer's assistant.'

She tossed her ringlets. 'He doesn't need to know.' Then her eyes darkened with doubt. 'Don't you want to meet me?'

'Yes, I do, but . . . '

'Well, there's no reason not to. Please?'

His doubts drowned in the depths of her beseeching eyes. 'I don't finish till seven, but I could be at the park gates at half past, if that's not too late for you?'

'Until half past seven tomorrow, then.' She ran gaily up the steps and waved to him from the top, then turned to pass through the imposing doorway.

Albert's feet executed a joyful skip. 'Oh, Belle, I'm sure she likes me, and she's absolutely . . . perfect. It's the only word for her.'

It was. The delicate oval face, the swelling bosom, the nipped-in waist, the rounded curves of her hips before the fullness of her skirt hid them. How he'd love to . . . God, what was he thinking? He didn't believe he would ever have enough courage to kiss her sweet, tempting lips, never mind anything more intimate.

Bathia Johnstone filled his dreams again. She looked so fragile, but it was clear that she'd a mind of her own, and what was wrong with that? It only made him love her more.

At the breakfast table the following morning, Albert did his best to appear nonchalant. 'I won't be needing any supper tonight, Mother, for I'm meeting . . . somebody at half past seven and I'll have to hurry.'

His blushing excitement wasn't lost on Nell, who was only too pleased to think that her youngest son had found a girl. At last she'd have grandchildren. Her other daughters-in-law were barren – by choice or otherwise, she wasn't sure.

She said nothing to her husband, who was having to miss a fishing trip because of a badly cut hand, and

14

who would only tease her for counting her chickens before they were hatched. Wattie was a great one for teasing, but it was all in good fun, and she never bore him any grudge for the things he said. He was a good man, and if Albert was half as good to the girl he wed, the lassie would have no complaints.

His mind fully occupied with the most beautiful girl in the world, Albert could hardly wait until it was time to shut the shop, and locked up at three minutes to seven – something he'd never done before – then ran all the way home.

Having been warned by Nell, Wattie made no comment until his son rushed out again. 'He's put on his Sunday suit. It must be a lassie, and it looks like he's smitten real bad.'

When he came to the park gates, Albert was relieved to find that Bathia hadn't yet arrived – it gave him a chance to get his breath back. When she did appear, and the two dogs were let off the leash, she turned to him apologetically.

'I hope you haven't been waiting long, Mr Ogilvie?'

'Just a minute or so,' he replied, truthfully.

'My father said it was too late for me to be going out, but I reminded him that it wouldn't be dark for some time yet, so he gave in. It would have been awful if you'd been left waiting, and wondering why I didn't come.'

It would have been worse than awful, Albert thought. It would have broken his heart if he'd believed she hadn't wanted to keep her promise. After answering some questions about his job, he shyly told her of his ambition to have his own shop, at which she grew very excited and made a few suggestions which he stored away in his mind, just in case.

She became so carried away that he was forced to bring her back to earth. 'It's only a dream, remember. I can't see me ever having my own shop.'

'Don't be so pessimistic, Albert. Oh!' She coloured and looked confused. 'I'm sorry, Mr Ogilvie, I shouldn't have called you that.'

15

Hearing his Christian name on her lips came as such a surprise that he was every bit as confused as she was, and mumbled, 'It's all right.'

'I always think of you as Albert, you see, and it just sort of slipped out.'

'I don't mind, Miss Johnstone.'

'Miss Johnstone,' she said, scornfully. 'I'm sure you could say Bathia, if you really wanted to.'

'I do want to, and nothing would give me greater pleasure, Miss John . . . er . . . Bathia.'

'What I was going to say, Albert, was that you shouldn't think you can never have your own shop. If you believe enough in something, it's bound to come true one day.'

They had been walking for more than thirty minutes, with Albert describing some of the shops he'd come across in his search, and why they weren't suitable, when she interrupted. 'I think I'd better go home now, before it gets too dark, but I'll see you again tomorrow?'

He hesitated, wondering if it was fair to her to continue with these meetings. 'We shouldn't . . . your father . . . '

'You don't need to worry about him – I always get round my father.' She chuckled engagingly. 'Please, Albert?'

Even if he'd wanted to, he hadn't the willpower to refuse her. 'Half past seven, then.' Looking down at her upturned face, he had a great longing to kiss her, but was afraid that he would scare her off altogether if he did.

When they parted at the granite pillars, she said, 'Until tomorrow, then, Albert.'

On Tuesday night, they arranged to meet on the Wednesday afternoon, since it was Albert's half day. Bathia was far more important to him than sitting poring over dry-as-dust books in the public library.

This time, they had longer of each other's company, and after walking round for a little while, they sat on a bench for a good hour and a half, discussing whatever came into their heads, and laughing at the least little thing.

Albert had to restrain himself from kissing her, her

16

lips looked so sweet and inviting. He could never be so familiar with her, not for a long time yet, and it would be all the sweeter for waiting.

Their assignations continued in the same manner all that week, and it wasn't until the following Monday that Bathia took matters into her own hands. They'd been talking outside her home for a few minutes when she suddenly stood on tiptoe and kissed his cheek, then, without waiting to see his reactions, she whirled round and went up the steps and into the house.

'Oh, God, Belle,' Albert said, softly. 'Is one of my dreams going to come true? The best dream I've ever had?'

In bed, he couldn't sleep for remembering the soft touch of her lips, and he pictured himself kissing her, very tenderly at first, then more and more passionately until he could . . . No, no! She was far too fragile and genteel ever to let him do what he felt like doing at that moment. His coarse thoughts disgusted him, and he would have felt better if he'd known that Bathia's mind was working on much the same lines. She longed for Albert to kiss her, to embrace her, to caress her, to . . . love her properly.

When they met the next night, they were both slightly ill-at-ease, trying to ignore the desires building up inside them, and, after a long silence, they spoke together.

'Bathia . . . '

'Albert . . . '

Glancing at each other, they both laughed nervously. 'You first.' Albert's voice sounded gravelly in his own ears.

'I was going to ask if you thought it was terrible of me to kiss you last night, when we've known each other for such a short time.' Her husky voice was almost a whisper.

'No, I . . . '

'I couldn't help it, Albert. I just felt like kissing you. Could you ever bring yourself . . . ? Have you ever wanted . . . ?'

'I want to kiss you right now,' he muttered, feeling like a callow schoolboy. She had awakened feelings the

17

depth of which he hadn't known he possessed, and he was rather afraid of setting them loose.

'You have my permission, Albert.'

He meant to be gentle, but her innocent, yet seductive, response unleashed the emotions he'd been repressing. He crushed her against him, and his mouth covered hers hungrily.

When he let her go, he moaned, 'Oh, Bathie, Bathie.'

The distortion of her name was a form of endearment, how he'd thought of her every night – it seemed to suit her – so he was relieved when she gave a little mew of pleasure.

'Bathie? Yes, I like that, Albert.'

She lay against him and held up her face, but he said, roughly, 'No, Bathie, I mustn't . . . It makes me . . . '

'Makes you what, Albert?'

'It makes me want to do something I shouldn't.' A pulse was beating at his jaw, and he held himself away from her, not wanting her to feel how much he needed her. 'Something a man shouldn't do to a girl till they're married.'

'Married?' Her eyes widened in wonder, then a shy smile stole across her face. 'Is that a proposal, Albert?'

Before he could either confirm or deny it, she whispered, 'If it is – and I hope it is – I accept with pleasure.'

Burying his face in her soft, fragrant hair, he murmured, 'Dearest Bathie, I want you to be my wife more than anything else in the world, but I'm sure I'm not the kind of man your father would want as your husband, and he'd move heaven and earth to prevent it. Can't you see how difficult it would be?'

'I'm sixteen, and he can't stop us.'

How innocent and trusting she was, Albert thought, his heart almost bursting with love. He said, recklessly, 'No, he can't stop us, but I'll come home with you this very minute to ask his permission.'

Although his stomach churned more and more as they came nearer her house, his resolve didn't waver. However much her father was against it, he meant to make Bathie his wife.

When they reached the stone pillars, she gripped his hand much tighter. 'Don't let my father intimidate you, Albert, dear. His bark is much worse than his bite.'

This didn't make him feel any easier about the coming ordeal, but he smiled bravely. 'Let me do all the talking.'

'I love you, Albert Ogilvie,' she whispered, then pulled him up the steps and through the front door.

'Father, Mother,' she began, quietly, when they went into the large elegant room, 'I've brought someone to see you, and he's got something very important to ask you.'

Of the two astonished faces which turned towards them, Arthur Johnstone's was first to change expression, when he saw Albert holding Belle's lead with one hand and Bathia's arm with the other. His brows descended abruptly, almost overhanging his nose, his eyes hardened and his nostrils flared. 'And who is this . . . person?' he demanded icily.

It didn't bode well for the young man, but he strove to answer calmly. 'My name is Albert Ogilvie, Mr Johnstone. I love your daughter, and I want to marry her.'

Arthur's shocked splutterings made no sense, so Albert repeated, 'I want to marry Bathie – with your permission, preferably, but without it, if I have to.'

The older man's face turned rapidly purple, causing his wife to stand up in alarm. 'Are you all right, Arthur?'

'No, I am not!' he shouted. 'An absolute stranger walks into my house and says he is going to marry my daughter, and you ask me if I am all right? God in heaven, Henrietta . . . ' He stopped to take a deep breath, then addressed the girl in a slightly less violent manner. 'What is the meaning of this, Bathia?'

Before she could answer, Albert gave her arm a warning squeeze and said, firmly, 'I love her, Mr Johnstone, and she loves me, that's all that needs to be said.'

'No, by God, it is not all that needs to be said.' Arthur was breathing heavily, as if every word were an effort, and his flinty eyes were fixed on Albert.

Henrietta Johnstone touched her husband's arm. 'You must calm down. It is not good for you to get in such a state.'

Ignoring her completely, he burst out, 'Who are you, what are you, and how do you come to be on such familiar terms with my daughter?' His voice had risen angrily once more, and his chest was heaving with violent emotion.

Keeping his eyes on the great cord throbbing at the man's high-winged collar, Albert said, clearly and deliberately, 'I serve in a grocer's shop in Torry, my father's a fisherman, and we live in a tenement in Market Street. I'll be twenty-four years old next month, and I met Bathie when we were both out walking our dogs. Is that all you need to know?'

Henrietta gasped at his audacity in speaking in such a manner to her husband, and Arthur snarled, 'She has had that dog for less than three weeks, so you must have known her before that.'

'No, we smiled at each other two weeks last Sunday, then we met accidentally the next Sunday and walked in the park together, and we've been meeting every day since.' Albert felt nowhere near as bold as he sounded, but he carried on. 'That's exactly how long I've known Bathie, Mr Johnstone, but I knew she was the only girl for me as soon as I saw her.'

Arthur was rendered speechless, but Bathie shook Albert's hand off her arm and ran to her father's side. 'I love Albert, Father. I love him with all my heart.'

Arthur snorted in derision. 'What do you know about love? You are only a child still, and you have never met any other men. I have shielded you all your life from this type of person.' He looked at Albert as if he were the lowest creature in God's creation. 'He is only after you for your money.'

'He didn't know I had any money, honestly,' Bathie cried, desperately. 'He didn't know you were a banker, either, and when he found out, he tried to make me stop seeing him.'

Grunting, Arthur searched feverishly for some other argument to put forward, and the ensuing deathly silence was broken only by the loud tick of the ormolu clock on the high marble mantelshelf. The three minutes that

20

elapsed seemed like an eternity to Albert, who felt like grabbing the girl's hand and running out with her, but her father was an influential man and could surely make life unpleasant for them if they went against him. The young man would have faced anything for Bathie, so it was for her sake that he waited. If Mr Johnstone was not prepared to see reason, then they'd leave, but only then, for Albert didn't mean to drive a wedge between Bathie and her parents if he could avoid it.

Arthur's eyes narrowed calculatingly, and he turned to the young upstart again. 'Would you still be prepared to marry Bathia if I told you she would come to you penniless?' Pushing his daughter away when she tried to interrupt, he carried on, relentlessly. 'Could you provide for her properly on what you earn? You, a common assistant to a grocer? A nothing?' The cold contempt he felt was quite clear.

'I want Bathie if she comes to me with just the clothes she stands up in,' Albert declared. 'I can't promise to keep her as well as you've done, but she'll not starve with me, nor go naked.'

Henrietta gasped again, and Arthur turned triumphantly to the girl. 'Now do you see how common he is? He has given himself away by the foul things he thinks. It is only your body he wants, Bathia, and you are not going to marry him. That is my final word.'

Bathie's eyes were blazing now, like her father's, but she bit her lip and adopted the coaxing tone which usually won him round. 'Please don't say no, Father, because I won't be able to live without Albert.'

He shoved her aside roughly. 'You have survived without him for sixteen years.' His harsh voice held no compassion. 'When you meet a man who is suitable for you, and who comes to me first to ask my permission to court you, I will give you my blessing, but meantime, you stay under my protection. You are obviously not to be trusted to behave in an adult manner.'

Bathie burst into tears, and Albert went to comfort her. 'I can understand how your father feels,' he said, quietly. 'I'm no catch for a girl like you, but if love me

21

enough to wait for me, I'll come back for you in a year or so, a successful man.' He hadn't the faintest idea of how he could fulfil his promise, but he had uttered it in all sincerity.

'I'm not going to wait for you, Albert. Take me away with you now – I don't care about money or about anything except you.' Her mouth quivered as she laid her head on his shoulder, and he placed his arm round her.

Looking up helplessly, he met Arthur Johnstone's tortured eyes. 'I'm sorry. I can see you're trying to protect Bathie, but you've nothing to fear from me. I know this has been a great shock to you and your wife, so I'll leave you now to give you a chance to consider the matter.'

'Don't go, Albert.' Bathie pulled the sleeve of his jacket. 'I don't want to live if I can't be with you, and my father won't change his mind. You don't know him like I do.'

'I must go,' he said, gently. 'Your mother and father have the right to discuss it and decide what's best for you, but I'll come back tomorrow night for their answer.'

'It won't make any difference,' she persisted, 'and I can't wait until tomorrow to know what's going to happen.'

'It's better this way. If your father's still against our marriage when I come back, I'll take you away with me, if you still want me to.' Removing her hand from his arm, he turned towards the door. 'Come on, Belle, we're going home now.'

His legs carried him outside without buckling, but he was forced to lean against one of the pillars at the foot of the steps for a few seconds, wondering how he could have had the temerity to say those things to Bathie and her father.

'I must have been mad asking her to be my wife,' he said to Belle, who looked up at him with her head on one side. 'No, I wasn't mad. It's the most sensible thing I've ever done.'

But had he been wise in leaving her house when he did? It gave her, as well as her parents, time to think, and what if she changed her mind about him? Or if her father sent her away somewhere before he went back? God Almighty! He might never see her again, and he might just as well throw himself into the Dee now and be done with it.

His agony was eased by a more comforting thought. Bathie wouldn't be easily swayed, and she truly loved him, he was sure of that, just as he was sure that she was the only girl for him. His pace, which had become very slow and despondent, quickened now, and he arrived at Market Street with a much lighter heart than when he left Ferryhill.

As soon as the front door closed behind Albert, Arthur Johnstone vented his spleen on his daughter. 'Now do you understand why I would never let you go out unaccompanied before?' he thundered. 'It was to save you being taken in by the first man who made advances to you. You are so gullible, I knew it was bound to happen if there was no one with you to prevent it. My God, he cannot even say your name properly.'

'Leave the child alone, Arthur!' Henrietta's face was red with the effort it had taken to stand up to her husband. 'She is upset enough as it is. Bathia, you may go to bed now.'

'I have not finished with her yet.' The banker caught the venom in his wife's eyes, and some of his pomposity went out of him. 'Very well, Bathia. Do as your mother says, but do not think that the matter is over. We will continue with it in the morning.'

The girl, weeping hopelessly now, trailed out with her head drooping, too emotionally exhausted to argue any more, and convinced that her life would be ruined for ever because of her wicked father.

As she watched Bathia go, Henrietta's heart went out to her daughter. She felt determined the girl should not miss her chance for happiness as she had done.

A way to thwart her husband occurred to her then, but the idea was so repugnant she decided not to implement it unless it became absolutely necessary, so she waited for him to speak first.

Arthur sat, hunched forward, elbows on knees, his dark head resting on his hands. The dangerous colour that had suffused his face earlier had faded, and only a small circle of red in each cheek remained to show how badly he had been affected by the unexpected events of the last fifteen minutes.

When he straightened up, his top lip curled grotesquely. 'It was not so clever of that *person* to leave when he did.'

'I think he was being honourable, leaving us to talk it over without any interference from him.'

'Honourable? Pah! His kind do not know the meaning of the word. Well, he has given me the opportunity to get Bathia out of his clutches. I will send her to my sister in Edinburgh in the morning, and she can stay there until she forgets him.'

'She will never forget him, whatever you do. Can't you see she loves him too much? And . . . ' Henrietta's eyes glittered defiantly. 'And besides, I thought he was rather nice.'

'Rather nice?' he sneered. 'An ignorant lout like that?'

'He is far from ignorant, Arthur. He has obviously tried to better himself, and his speech is quite educated, not coarse or rough like most of the working men I have heard.'

'So he has taken you in, too?'

'He did not try to take anyone in.' She was annoyed and exasperated by her husband's pigheadedness. 'He seems honest and genuine, a far better person than most of the young men Bathia knows, the sickly, mealy-mouthed sons of your colleagues, who would not recognize truth if it hit them in the face.'

The dark colour began to creep up his neck again, but she carried on stubbornly. 'He loves her, and I am quite sure he would look after her in the best way he can.'

'He will not have the chance!' Arthur shouted. 'What can you be thinking of, Henrietta? I thought you would have wanted better for your only child. I certainly do! What kind of life would she have with a common grocer's assistant?'

The time had come for Henrietta to tell him the plain, unvarnished truth, whatever the consequences, so she said, very quietly, 'A better kind of life than I have had.'

'What does that mean?' Arthur sat up indignantly.

'She would have a man who would do anything to please her, not a man like you, who rides roughshod over everyone he comes in contact with. She would be loved and cherished, and treated with all the respect you have never shown me.'

Very much taken aback by her outburst, her husband opened his mouth to defend himself, but was given no chance to say anything. Henrietta was in full flow and would not be silenced. After all, he had been asking for this for a very long time, and he deserved every last word.

'I have put up with your vile behaviour for twenty years, Arthur Johnstone. I have closed my eyes to you sneaking off into bed with every maid I've ever had. I was hurt at first, but eventually I stopped caring, and let you share my bed only because I did not want Bathia to find out what was going on.' The memory of the years of degradation she had suffered made Henrietta continue relentlessly. 'You have never loved anyone but yourself, and you are only against this marriage because you cannot face having a grocer's assistant as a son-in-law. That would make you a laughing stock in the eyes of your banking fraternity.'

Her voice had risen hysterically and her bosom heaved as she stopped and looked at her husband over her pince-nez. His shoulders had sagged, he was regarding her as if he couldn't believe what he'd heard, and his mouth was opening and closing like a fish's. She wondered if she had gone too far, but it was too late to stop now. This threat to her daughter's happiness had been the spur she needed to make her repay him for the shameful way in which he had treated her. She took a long, deep breath. 'The money Bathia inherited from her grandmother is only in trust until she is twenty-one, then she can do what she likes with it. In the meantime, I intend to give them what my mother left me, and that should be enough to let them live decently until she comes of age.'

Desperate that he would never spoil her daughter's life as he had spoiled hers, Henrietta issued her ultimatum. 'One last thing, Arthur. If you persist in forbidding the marriage, I will leave you, and your precious banking colleagues will laugh at you behind your back for the rest of your days. Perhaps then you will wish that you had been more honourable.'

His shocked eyes met hers briefly before he bowed his head again, obviously deep in thought. Henrietta waited, feeling sure that he would order her out of the house when he recovered. Afraid that his anger would be uncontrollable, she braced herself to defend her rash threats.

But when he did look up, his face was stamped with defeat. 'Henrietta,' he murmured, 'I am sorry. For what I did to you, and for what I almost did to Bathia. I see now that my love for her has been selfish, but I honestly meant it for the best, to save any harm befalling her.' Looking down at his hands, he added, 'I must admit, however, that Albert Ogilvie certainly does not seem to be an ordinary working-class man.'

When his wife still remained silent, he scratched his chin in embarrassment. 'I can offer no excuse for what I did to you, except to remind you that I only turned to those girls because you persistently refused me, but I assure you that it will never happen again. You have made me feel thoroughly ashamed, and the only way I can redeem myself, it seems, is to give my consent to this marriage, although I make it quite clear to you that I do not altogether approve.'

His wife's tensed backbone felt like jelly now that the crisis was over, so it was a minute before she pulled herself forward on her chair and stood up.

'What are you going to do, Henrietta?' Arthur sounded anxious and apprehensive. 'I have agreed to what you want, and what Bathia wants, and there is nothing more, is there? What else did you expect me to do?'

Stifling a flash of triumph at his new insecurity, she

found herself pitying him. 'I am going upstairs to tell Bathia that she has your permission to marry the man she loves. She probably hates you at this minute for your heartlessness, and she should be told as soon as possible that you have changed your mind. That way, we can all sleep peacefully tonight.'

Chapter Two

Nell could see that her son was troubled, but she knew better than to ask any questions. Instead, she set his plate of porridge and his bowl of milk in front of him, then sat down to sup her own, her spirits sinking at his obvious lack of appetite. When he pushed his plate away after only one mouthful, she could hold back her curiosity no longer.

'Is somethin' botherin' you, Albert?'

He hesitated. It was an ideal time for him to confide in his mother, with his father back at sea, but, superstitiously, he felt that speaking about it might bring bad luck, and his expectations were low enough without that. 'There's nothing bothering me,' he said, at last. 'I'm feeling a bit low, that's all.'

Suspecting that he'd quarrelled with the lassie he'd been seeing, Nell's heart went out to him, but she said nothing.

'I'll stop on in the shop this afternoon,' Albert muttered as he went out, 'but I'll be home about six for my supper.'

He wouldn't have time to think that morning, but it being half day, he couldn't face his mother's silent curiosity from dinner-time until it was time to go to Ferryhill. It was better to stay in the shop and do some tidying up.

All forenoon he was somewhat distracted, and several of the women customers remarked that he must be in love, which he didn't trouble to deny. He locked the door thankfully at one o'clock, and spent the next few hours arranging and rearranging the shelves.

When he got home, he ate his supper hungrily, not having had any breakfast or dinner, and his mother was pleased that his appetite had returned. She was even more pleased when she saw that he changed his clothes after he washed himself – his romance surely wasn't over, after all.

On his way out, Albert said, 'I might not be so late in coming back tonight, it just depends.' He knew it would set her puzzling, but he would tell her everything when he got home again, whatever the outcome might be. He didn't intend giving Bathie up without a struggle, so, while he was walking, he went over in his mind answers to any possible objections Mr Johnstone might raise. The man was bound to be disappointed that his daughter wanted to marry a working-class man, but he couldn't possibly understand how deeply in love they were, and Albert would have to prove it to him.

He took the stone steps two at a time, and pulled the bell vigorously, his courage ebbing somewhat when he heard footsteps nearing the door.

The immaculate little maid who opened it eyed him up and down before she said, incredulously, 'Mr Ogilvie?' When Albert nodded, her icy manner thawed a little. 'Mr Johnstone's expecting you in the drawing room.'

As he followed her along the wide, tiled floor, Albert reflected wryly that she was more the type of girl he should be thinking of marrying – a servant, not a banker's daughter – but he walked boldly through the door she held open for him.

The faint suggestion of a smile on Arthur Johnstone's face doused any hopes the young man had nurtured. Bathie's father appeared to be rather too pleased with himself – had he sent her away already?

'Sit down, Mr Ogilvie. I thought it would be better to see you alone, so that we can talk freely. My wife and I have discussed the matter and . . . '

During the man's short pause. Albert clenched his hands by his sides and prepared to do battle. ' . . . and we have decided to give our permission for you to marry our daughter.'

The wind taken completely out of his sails, Albert stared in disbelief for a few moments, but this dapper figure, this banker with his business suit and business manner, would never make a joke about anything, especially anything as serious as this. It must be true.

'You mean, you don't object to me marrying Bathie, now?'

Arthur's mouth twisted as he flicked an imaginary speck off his trousers. 'I would not go as far as to say that, but I have . . . er . . . been made to understand that you love her, and . . . '

'I do love her,' Albert interrupted eagerly. 'I told you that last night, and I'll worship her till the day I die. I'll make sure she never wants for anything, supposing I've to work night and day to provide for her.'

'There will be no need for you to do that. As you no doubt gathered last night, when my mother-in-law passed away she left quite a considerable sum in trust for Bathia. She cannot touch this until she is twenty-one, but . . . '

'I don't want her money. I'll work for her . . . '

Arthur continued as if Albert hadn't spoken. 'Meantime, my wife intends to place at your disposal all that her mother left her, and you will be at liberty to draw on it at any time, if the need should arise. Of course, when Bathia reaches her majority, you will have sufficient funds to work on.' Reddening a little, he hurried on. 'I am afraid that I was narrow-minded and bigoted about your occupation, but I apologize now for what I said. It was quite uncalled for.'

'I thought some terrible things about you, as well,' Albert said, frankly. 'But it takes a big man to admit he's wrong, and I admire you for it. There's just one thing, though. I want none of Bathie's money, nor her mother's. I mean to provide for my own wife, for that's how I was brought up to think.'

Again, a faint smile lifted the edges of Mr Johnstone's mouth. 'And I admire you for that, Mr Ogilvie, but I ask for your assurance that you will care for Bathia, and look after her for the rest of her life, to the best of your ability.'

'You have my word on that.'

'Then I give you my blessing.' Arthur Johnstone shook hands with his future son-in-law, then went to the door to call for his wife and daughter to join them.

They appeared almost immediately and Bathie ran across the room to perch on the arm of Albert's chair, laughing at his bemused expression. 'I couldn't believe it at first, either, Albert, but it's true. We can be married as soon as you like.'

Arthur gave a little cough. 'We will have to discuss it a little further, Bathia. I mean to provide you with a wedding you will never forget. After all, you are my only daughter, and this is the only chance I will have, but it will take some time to organize fully, so I would suggest that you leave it until next year. In the spring, perhaps?'

'Oh, no, Father. We can't wait all that time. I don't want a big wedding, do you, Albert?' She turned anxiously.

'I'd prefer a quiet ceremony,' he admitted, 'but I'm quite willing to agree to what your father says.'

Arthur inclined his head in acknowledgement of this. 'Your parents may have some suggestions to make, and my wife will require a list of all the guests they wish to invite.'

Henrietta spoke for the first time. 'Ask them to come to tea on Sunday so that we can discuss it.'

Misgivings suddenly setting in, Albert agreed to pass on her invitation, and after another half-hour spent listening uncomfortably to Arthur's talk of wedding guests, he made his excuses and left. Now that his dream was nearing fulfilment, he wished that it was all over.

His mother and father wouldn't feel easy at a grand wedding, he knew that, and he wouldn't himself, if it was as grand as Arthur Johnstone was planning, but if that was the only way he'd get Bathie, they'd all have to put up with it.

Nell raised her head from the seaboot stocking she

was darning when her son came in, but waited for him to speak.

'I'll take Belle out in a wee while,' he began. 'I didn't take her with me before, because . . . Oh, I'd better tell you everything. I met this girl, a couple of weeks ago, and . . . well, it was love at first sight, Mother. I used to think that was a lot of nonsense, but it happened to us, and we're going to get married, whenever her father gets the wedding arranged.'

'Oh, Albert, I'm right pleased about that.' Nell laid down her darning needle and clasped her hands together with joy. 'I've prayed for you to settle doon wi' a nice lassie, an' I'm sure she must be a nice lassie, seein' you took to her so quick – I just wish you'd tell't me afore. What's her folk sayin' aboot you askin' her so sudden?'

'Well, her father's a banker, and he . . . '

'A banker? He hadna been very pleased aboot it?'

'No, he wasn't.' Albert sighed deeply. 'He refused his permission last night, and I said I'd leave him to speak it over with his wife. I don't know what made him change his mind, but he agreed tonight, and he's wanting to give Bathie a big send-off. Father and you are invited there for tea on Sunday, to discuss the plans.'

Nell's smiling face had fallen. 'Are you sure you ken what you're doin', Albert? A banker's lassie? You canna keep her like she's been used to, so you'll nae ha'e a smooth path to tread, an' . . . oh, laddie, I'm sorry for you.'

'You needn't be sorry for me. I'm very happy about it, or I will be, once the wedding's past. You'll love Bathie, Mother, she's not a bit like you'd think a banker's daughter would be. She'll not fuss about not being kept in the same manner, for she's a sensible lass, friendly, and easy to speak to, and real bonnie, and . . . she loves me, Mother, as much as I love her.'

'Well, well.' Nell looked a lot happier. 'I dinna ken what your father's goin' to say aboot this when he comes hame on Friday. He gets tongue-tied among ony kind o' folk that's nae fisher folk, but a banker? That'll put the fear o' death in him, an' he'll be sittin' there like a fish oot o' water.'

31

'He'll just have to do the best he can.' Albert bent down to pat the spaniel. 'Aye, Belle, we'll go our walk now.'

The worries beset him again as soon as he went outside. How would Arthur Johnstone react when he met his daughter's future in-laws? Would the sight of them, shabbily dressed and uncomfortable with strangers, make him change his mind? Would he back down and cancel his permission?

Albert felt very disloyal to his parents, but he knew that they had nothing in common with the Johnstones, and that they were incapable of putting on a show for anybody's benefit. It was another hurdle to get over before he could make Bathie his, but it would have to be negotiated.

On Thursday night, when he visited Ferryhill again, Albert was pleasantly surprised by the warmth of the welcome he received. Bathie's father seemed to set himself out to be amiable, and there was no trace of condescension in his manner whatsoever.

With her severe hairstyle, and the pince-nez on her long sharp nose, Mrs Johnstone had given the impression of being a very haughty woman, and her plain face had made Albert think that Bathie's beauty must be inherited from some earlier generation, but today, she, too, couldn't have been more friendly.

'Bathia insists on a quiet church wedding followed by a special meal here, and, although my husband and I would have preferred it otherwise, we have bowed to her wishes. She will be attended by her cousin from Edinburgh, and no doubt you will want to choose one of your own friends as groomsman.'

Quickly running over his acquaintances in his mind, Albert decided that John Benzies might stand up with him, for they'd been at school together, and had been quite close until John had married – Albert having done duty as groomsman at that time – but they had always remained friends.

He became conscious that Bathie's eyes were resting

on him lovingly. 'We won't have to wait so long now, Albert, so you can arrange the date with the Reverend Mitchell of Ferryhill Church, for as soon as he can manage.'

'I would suggest that you should not be too hasty,' Arthur remarked. 'If you set the date for some time in August, it will give Bathia's mother time to order a wedding gown made, also it will give us all time to become accustomed to the idea.'

'But this is only May, Father,' Bathie began, and stopped when she saw his slight frown.

'There is no need for any unseemly haste,' he told her. 'Marry in haste, repent at leisure.'

'I'll go to see the minister tomorrow night.' Albert sensed an undercurrent of resentment in the man's manner now. 'I'll make it the beginning of September, Mr Johnstone, or later than that, if you'd prefer it. I'm quite willing to wait for as long as you think necessary.'

'Unfortunately, it seems Bathia is not willing to wait,' Arthur said, dryly. 'She is still a child, with a child's need for things to be done immediately after she thinks of them.'

Henrietta saved the situation by rising out of her seat. 'Arthur, I'd like you to come up to the attic with me to move one of the trunks. I'm sure I know which one holds my wedding gown and headdress and veil, and they could be made ready for Bathia if she liked.'

Her husband's broad brow creased. 'Could this not wait until another day?'

'No, it could not. They may need to be altered to fit her and it might take some time.'

Henrietta held the door open for him, and Albert thought that he was seeing things when she turned back briefly after her husband walked through. Surely she couldn't have winked? Bathie's low giggle made him glance at her.

'Mother's not as formidable as she looks, Albert, dear. She understands that we would like to be alone.'

He felt embarrassed. What was he expected to do? He couldn't kiss his betrothed, not here in this house, with her parents upstairs, yet she was waiting expectantly.

She slid along the couch nearer to him, so he planted a light kiss on her brow, but she raised her face, her lovely glistening lips coming within an inch of his, and he couldn't help himself. Their kiss was long and gentle, and when he drew back, she sighed contentedly.

'Just think, Albert. In another two or three months, we'll be husband and wife. It'll be fun, won't it?'

As he bent to kiss her again, he reflected that her father was right. She was only a child, with a child's rosy outlook on life, and he must protect her. His love for her almost choked him. His sap, unfortunately, chose that moment to rise and he broke away from her abruptly.

'Bathie.' His voice was husky with desire, and he had to clear his throat before he could continue. 'I'll have to rent a house, nothing expensive, maybe only two rooms in a tenement.'

'I've never been inside a tenement.' Her trilling laugh made his passion almost unbearable. 'Oh, it's going to be a great adventure, Albert. Just you and I in our own tiny home, doing whatever we feel like doing, whenever we feel like doing it, and no one to tell us we shouldn't be doing it.'

Moaning, he pulled her hair tight back off her face to nuzzle her ear. 'Oh, Bathie, what am I going to do with you? It won't all be fun. There's the cooking and washing, and all the other housework – I can't afford a maid – and sometimes you'll be so tired you'll be glad to crawl into your bed.'

Her face had sobered during his little homily, but a twinkle came into her bright eyes as she said, 'I'll be glad to crawl into my bed every night, as long as you're there, too.'

He knew he startled her when he jumped to his feet and stuck his hand deep down in his trouser pocket, but it was the only thing he could do to tether the rearing beast that had gone almost out of control at her innocent remark.

After a minute's silence, Bathie looked up at him somewhat repentantly. 'Have I made you angry, Albert? I'm sorry, I didn't mean to.'

'You didn't make me angry, my dear. You made me so happy I couldn't bear it.' He turned round from the fireside and his breath caught in his throat. She was so lovely, sitting up straight, with her hands splayed out on the couch on each side of her. He believed he could span her tiny waist with his hands, and the contour of her hips wasn't altogether hidden by her long black skirt, which had ridden up to reveal her slender ankles.

Her cream-coloured blouse had a narrow strip of black velvet over the frills high at her neck, making her skin look even creamier than the silky material. The ribbon, with its ends crossed and hanging down on to her bosom, was fixed with a brooch set with several small gemstones, the reds exactly matching the colour of her parted lips, and the blues the same deep shade as her wide eyes, made even wider by their fringe of sooty lashes.

She made a picture that any artist would give a ransom to capture on canvas, Albert mused, yearning with love, and it came as something of a relief when he heard Henrietta's heels clicking along the tiled hall before the door opened.

'I can get at the trunk much more easily now,' she said brightly. 'So you and I can start looking through it, Bathia, as soon as you like.'

'Tomorrow, Mother?' the girl said, eagerly.

Albert noticed that she was a little flushed, and wondered guiltily if her parents would realize that they'd been kissing. Mr Johnstone's eyes seemed to be fixed on him accusingly, but when Bathie's mother turned to him she was smiling.

'My husband tells me that you do not wish to accept the money I meant to offer you?'

'Oh, no.' Albert wondered if he could safely remove his hand from his pocket, and decided that he'd better wait. 'I want to start as I mean to go on, supporting my own wife.'

'A very laudable resolve, but rather impractical.'

Bathie jumped up and slid her arm through his, the touch of her legs against him making him glad that he still had his beast under restraint. 'Yes, we want to stand

35

on our own two feet,' she declared, then giggled. 'Four feet, I mean.'

Her father snorted. 'You are just as impractical as he is. Neither of you has the least idea of what it takes to run a household.'

'Our expenses won't be anywhere near as high as yours,' Albert said. 'I was just telling Bathie it would have to be two rooms in a tenement, and . . . '

'A tenement? You cannot seriously expect my daughter to live in a tenement?' Arthur's horror couldn't have been greater if the young man had suggested that they live in a cave.

'I'd love to live in a tenement,' Bathie cried. 'It's all that Albert can afford, and it will be our home.'

'But you are accustomed to . . . ', Arthur began, but subsided when Henrietta frowned at him.

'I believe some tenements can be quite comfortable,' she said, firmly. 'A home is what you make it, after all.'

'We'll make a marvellous home, Mother.' Bathie hugged Albert's arm. 'And when we're settled in properly, you can come to visit us, and I'm sure you won't find any faults.'

At that moment, the little maid wheeled in a trolley set with delicate gold-rimmed china. A plate of dainty sandwiches sat beside the solid silver tea service, and Albert's spirits, and his passion, plunged rapidly downwards, for he could never provide Bathie with anything like this – only earthenware dishes like his mother's, and no fancy silver, either.

He sat down, both hands free to accept the damask napkin which the young servant handed him. Was this whole thing a mistake? Should like marry like, and not attempt to break the class barriers? He became acutely conscious of how cheap and shoddy his Sunday suit looked in comparison to Mr Johnstone's, and Mrs Johnstone's frock was far more elegant and stylish than anything his mother had ever possessed. Should he bow out now? Mr Johnstone would be more than pleased if he did, he was sure, but when he stole a furtive glance at Bathie, he knew he couldn't give her up.

She had never looked disapproving of what he wore, and he believed that she didn't care about it, in any case. She loved him, and love could work miracles, so it could surely make a success of their marriage.

When Wattie Ogilvie arrived home from the sea on Friday night and learned of Albert's forthcoming nuptials, he was almost as much against the idea as Bathie's father had been.

'It doesna work when you wed oot o' your class, Albert,' he said. 'I've seen it happen time an' time again. The lassie thinks it's great at first, to be keepin' a hoose and lookin' after a man, but she soon gets tired o' it, an' then it's back to father so she can get whatever she asks for.'

'Bathie's not like that.' Albert went on the defensive at once. 'She understands that we won't have much money.'

'Mind you, if it had been the other way roon',' Wattie continued, 'it would ha'e stood a better chance. A workin'-class lassie can easy learn to be a lady, but a lady doesna want to learn how to be a workin' man's wife. An' you dinna ken her weel enough yet, that's another thing.'

'I know her well enough to love her,' Albert protested. 'And I'm sure she loves me.'

'Ach, leave the laddie be, Wattie,' Nell put in, sharply. 'She's the lass he wants, and it's him that'll ha'e to bide wi' her, so you'll just ha'e to haud your tongue.'

Her husband let out a roar of laughter. 'That's put me in my place, hasn't it, Nell? Maybe you're right, at that. We've a' to mak' oor ain way in life, and sort oot oor ain mistakes. So! When are we gettin' to meet this Bathie?'

'You and Mother are invited to Ferryhill on Sunday.'

'An' you'll need to be on your best behaviour,' Nell added, caustically. 'Nane o' your foul jokes in front o' the lassie's folk, for we dinna want to gi'e them a bad impression.'

Wattie picked up his newspaper, and took his pipe

37

from his pocket. 'They'll ha'e to tak' me as I am,' he said, as he struck a match. 'I'm ower auld to change.'

'Fine do I ken that.' Nell glanced at Albert and grinned.

Chapter Three

After setting the wedding for the beginning of September, Albert's next priority was finding a house to rent, so he asked several of his customers if they knew of anything, but none of them did. Then, late one Saturday evening, after Joseph Duthie had appeared, to check the takings and give his employee his weekly wage, a rather stout, oldish woman came hurrying in and asked for half a pound of syrup.

'How's the rheumatism, Mrs Nutten?' Albert asked as he took the small jar she held out, for she was a regular, though she couldn't afford to buy much, being on her own.

'Och, it comes an' goes wi' the weather,' she smiled, watching him hold the container under the big barrel and turn the tap to one side. 'I heard you were lookin' for a hoose, Albert, an' my sister says there's ane goin' above her.'

In his excitement, Albert almost let the thick, sticky syrup overflow the jar, but turned the tap off just in time. 'Where is it, Mrs Nutten?'

'King Street, four rooms on the first floor, an' the lobby and the stairs are aye kept spotless.'

He could see that she was delighted to be in a position to do someone a favour, but his wages would never run to four rooms in King Street, and he couldn't hide his disappointment.

'It's very good of you to think about me, Mrs Nutten,' he said, carefully, 'but I couldn't afford four rooms.'

The woman was also disappointed, but she understood his problem only too well. 'Aye, it's a big rent – my sister's man has a good job an' they can weel afford it.

I'll keep my ears open for you.'

'Thank you very much, Mrs Nutten. Now, were you needing anything else today?'

'I'll tak' my usual two ounce o' pandrops, it's my treat to mysel' on a Saturday night.'

He weighed out the peppermint sweets, giving her good measure and a few extra, and when she had paid for her purchases and left, he took a clean damp cloth to wipe the mouth of the tap on the syrup barrel.

'I didn't know you were looking for a house, Albert.' Mr Duthie had come through from the back shop and was looking at the young man questioningly through his thick glasses.

'It was just arranged on Wednesday.' Albert blushed as he spoke, for it felt strange to tell anyone about his forthcoming marriage. It had been bad enough telling his own parents.

The old man's eyebrows shot up. 'Are you getting wed?'

Albert laughed self-consciously. 'Aye, that's right.'

Thumping him on the back, Mr Duthie cried, 'That's grand news, but there's no need for you to look for a house – that is, if you're not in too big a hurry.'

'The wedding's not till the beginning of September.'

'That's fine, then. One of my houses on the top floor's being given up on the twenty-eighth day of July. Old Mrs Duncan's moving to her daughter's.'

Albert could hardly take it in at first, then he said, 'Oh, that would be ideal, for I'd be above the shop.'

'It's only two little rooms, mind, but I believe they're quite comfortable.'

'It's the very thing I was looking for.'

Mr Duthie seemed to be considering something else. He stood gazing into space for a moment, then smiled. 'I've been thinking about this for a good while now, Albert, but single men aren't as dependable as married men.' Not comprehending what his employer was trying to say, Albert waited for enlightenment. 'But now you'll be settling down with a wife, you'll be needing more money.' This was even better, Albert thought. A house handed to him on a plate, and extra money to keep it going. 'So, if you're not scared to take on the responsibility,' the old man went on, 'I'll make you the manager of my shop. You'll get your wages up, of course, and I'll leave the whole running of the place to you. I'll not interfere, whatever you decide to do to improve it. I can't be fairer than that.'

'Mr Duthie, I can't tell you how much I appreciate all this.' Albert could feel himself trembling with gratitude.

'Ach, it's what I should have done years ago, but, as I said, you were single, and I was maybe a bit over-cautious. Now, I'll charge you a small rent for the house, for I don't believe in young folk having things made too easy for them, and if you bring your lass to see me, maybe the night before the wedding, I'll tell her the rules of the tenement, for I must be sure my property's looked after properly.'

Albert shook his head and lifted his eyes briefly to the ceiling. 'I don't know how to thank you, Mr Duthie.'

'Just carry on the way you've been doing, lad, that'll be thanks enough for me.' A sadness came into the man's eyes as he paused. 'I envy you, Albert, just starting out on marriage, and I hope you'll be as happy as I was till my wife passed on.'

The weeks passed slowly for Albert, but far too quickly for Nell Ogilvie. The visit to the Johnstones' house had been a terrifying ordeal for her, and she was dreading having to go back there after the wedding service, which was how it had been arranged.

Even in her best dress, she'd felt dowdy on the brocaded couch in the splendour of the huge drawing room with all its richly-coloured mahogany furniture. Mrs Johnstone's ornaments looked tasteful and expensive, although Nell wasn't aware that most of them were very old and valuable pieces, handed down through several generations of Henrietta's family.

Wattie had said he'd felt 'a wee bit oot o' place', though it wasn't so bad for a man, and Nell's main worry now was what she would wear to the wedding.

By scrimping from the time she was told about it, she'd saved a wee bit, and she hoped to have enough by September to buy the dark blue bombazine she'd seen in a gown shop in Union Street.

Her husband had told her that he might buy himself a new suit, so they shouldn't look so out of place this time, and Bathie Johnstone shouldn't feel ashamed of her new in-laws. Not that she seemed to be that kind of lassie, Nell reflected happily, a bonnie, open-faced little thing, it was clear her heart was set on Albert as much as his was set on her.

At Ferryhill, the main consideration was also clothes. Henrietta's dressmaker had come to fit the delicate old wedding dress on Bathia, and it only needed a few slight alterations, apart from the hem having to be taken up.

Bathie had been impressed when her mother had first taken it out of the trunk, and was absolutely delighted when the alterations were completed. The dressmaker had laundered it before she brought it back, and neither Henrietta nor her daughter could believe that it was the same twenty-year old gown. From being a rather dingy greyish colour, it had been transformed into shimmering fairy-tale ivory, the pin tucks on the bodice entirely creaseless, the tulle overlay of the skirt falling in graceful folds.

When her daughter tried it on, she looked so beautiful and virginal that Henrietta was almost choked by the lump which rose in her throat. Had she done the right thing in forcing Arthur to agree to this marriage? Bathia was only sixteen. Would she be prepared for what would happen to her on her wedding night, or would she be horrified by her husband's lust – as she herself had been? Henrietta's thoughts came to an abrupt, slightly guilty halt. Albert Ogilvie may be only a grocer's assistant, but he was a proper gentleman, and would never harm his wife in any way. Just the same, as a mother, it was her duty to prepare the girl a little.

About three weeks before the wedding, when Arthur's new suit was delivered by his tailor, he, too had renewed

41

misgivings about this step his daughter was about to take. She was an innocent child, and the man she was marrying was eight years older, a working man who had probably had experience of women of a very different kind.

Recalling how his wife's maidservants had been more than willing to let him possess them, he could feel a need building up, a need to have a woman, but he had promised Henrietta . . . Dare he suggest to her . . . ? Was it possible that she would relent, after all these years, and be a proper wife to him again? He still thought very fondly of her – even loved her, he supposed – and it was her duty to satisfy his needs, but he would have to be careful not to demand too much too quickly.

On the afternoon of the 28th July, Joseph Duthie came into the shop and handed Albert the keys for the house on the top floor of his property.

'There you are, then, lad, it's all yours now. It won't need much furniture, being so small, and I've a few bits and pieces I'd be quite glad to be rid of. I can hardly move about for all the things my wife . . . If you come up when you close the shop, I'll let you pick whatever you want.'

For a man who didn't believe in young folk getting things too easily, Albert thought, the grocer was being more than generous. 'Thank you, Mr Duthie, that'll be a big help.'

He discovered, later, that it was more than a help, it was practically all he'd need, for the old man pressed him to take so many items that it seemed to Albert that all he would have to buy was a bed.

Bathie had demanded to see the house as soon as he was given the keys, but he said she'd have to wait until he made it ready for her. He spent his evenings washing down the walls and scrubbing and polishing the oilcloth which the previous tenant had left on the floors.

When that was finished, he asked his friend John to help him carry Mr Duthie's contributions up from the first floor, also to move the chest of drawers his mother had said he could take with him. During the time that he was setting everything up, he went to see Bathie only on his half days.

'I'm sure you'll love it,' he told her, on the Wednesday before the wedding, 'but if you don't like the way I've done it, we can shift things about once we're in.'

'We've been very lucky to receive so many lovely gifts.'

Nell and Wattie had given them two pairs of sheets and a pair of pillows, and although Bathie's parents' main gift was a bone-china tea set, silver tea service and cutlery, Henrietta was always handing over little items she thought they might need.

Albert was very touched by the small wedding gifts his customers brought in – pillow cases, dish towels, butter and jam dishes, even a hand-embroidered tablecloth – but the women all said that they were only showing their gratitude for the friendly way he had served them over the years.

On Friday, the eve of the wedding, Bathie called at the shop just before seven, to be taken up to see Mr Duthie, as he had requested. The old man was astonished to discover how dainty and well-spoken she was, and felt rather embarrassed at having to tell her the washing rota and rules of his tenement, but she nodded and absorbed everything gravely, then thanked him for all he had done for them. By the time the young couple left his house, Joseph Duthie was as much her slave as Albert was.

She begged to be taken up to see their own two rooms, but Albert steadfastly refused. 'I want to carry you over the threshold as a bride, my love.'

That made her giggle delightedly. 'You're quite romantic, Albert, though nobody would think it to look at you. That's part of why I love you, you know, because you keep springing surprises on me.'

'Surprises?'

'Asking me to marry you so suddenly, standing up to my father, and now this.' She looked up at him as he opened the street door. 'In less than seventeen hours I'll be your wife, Albert.'

'I can hardly wait.' They said it together and laughed hilariously, then he said, seriously, 'I'll make you happy, Bathie. You'll never regret being my wife, I swear.'

'I know I won't, Albert, dear, never as long as I live.'

Chapter Four

On the morning of the wedding, Albert rose much earlier than usual. He'd been too excited to sleep very well, but he didn't feel in the least bit tired, and his blood pounded in his veins each time he thought that in six hours . . . five hours . . . four hours, he and Bathie would be united in holy matrimony.

He took Belle out for a walk to let his parents have privacy to bathe in front of the kitchen range, but returned in plenty of time to make himself ready. After filling the zinc bath from the pail which had been left heating on the fire, he stepped in gingerly.

It was very hot, so he hopped from one foot to the other for a few moments, then eased himself down, gasping as first his backside, then his genitals, came in contact with the near-scalding liquid. Lathering himself with the carbolic soap, it crossed his mind that the next time he took a bath, it would be in his own home. Quickly rinsing off the soap, he stood on the hearthrug to dry himself with the large towel his mother had laid out for him.

In just over an hour, he reflected as he rubbed himself vigorously, Bathie and he would be making their vows in the sight of God, and she would belong to him for ever, just as he would belong to her.

Arthur Johnstone watched his daughter standing before the altar. She looked so beautiful, so happy, so vulnerable, that his love for her almost overwhelmed him, and he ran his finger round the inside of his stiff, high collar to ease his Adam's apple. It seemed only yesterday that she had been a tiny infant, wrapped in swaddling clothes, and grasping his finger when he held it out to her.

Henrietta had been a good mother and had suckled their daughter for almost nine months, but during that time she had never allowed him to touch her at all. Afterwards, she had succumbed grudgingly to him only about once a month, as if she were bestowing a great favour on him.

Bathia had been about a year and a half, he recalled, when he had first been tempted to stray. Their maid at that time had been a buxom fifteen-year-old, whose well-developed body had made her appear much older, and who had an equally well-developed appetite for men. His wife had retired early one night, saying that she felt slightly unwell, as she so often did, and he had been sitting in the drawing room going over some of the bank's papers when the girl – he couldn't even remember her name now – had come in with a cup of hot milk for him.

'If the mistress isna able,' she had said, softly, 'I'm quite willin'.'

It had taken him a minute to realise what she meant, but it had took less than a minute for his body to respond to her offer once he did understand. He had gone up to her room in the attics where she had undressed slowly, nearly driving him mad with desire. That had been the first time he had ever experienced the thrill of a woman climaxing at exactly the same time as he did, for Henrietta had never, as far as he was aware, let herself reach that point at all.

Henrietta. His mind jumped back to the present, and he glanced round at his wife guiltily, but she was dabbing her eyes with a dainty lace handkerchief, caring about nothing except that her lamb was leaving the fold.

At that moment, the Reverend Mitchell looked up. 'Who giveth this woman to this man?' he intoned.

Stepping forward, Arthur took the bride's hand and placed it in Albert's, his eyes filling with tears for the baby, the toddler, the schoolgirl, the young woman, who was leaving his jurisdiction for ever. His only daughter.

His Bathia. No, he thought mournfully, she was Albert Ogilvie's now.

His duty over, Arthur went to sit beside his wife, who grasped his hand and squeezed it sympathetically. He did love her, he realized now, and she had shown more affection for him lately than she had ever done before. Perhaps the improvement in their own relationship would help to make up for the loss of their daughter.

As the bride and groom, followed by the two attendants, made their way through to the vestry to sign the marriage register, Arthur recognized the conclusion of the ceremony. Bathia and Albert had finally been pronounced husband and wife, for better for worse, for richer for poorer, until death did them part.

A weight seemed to lift from him and he leaned back against the wooden pew. It was not the wedding he had ever envisaged for his only child, but when she reappeared, looking so radiant on her new husband's arm, he had no regrets, and he found himself – unexpectedly, for he was not a man given to such a thing – praying that she would have no regrets, either.

Nell Ogilvie was so happy that she couldn't help weeping. Albert looked very handsome in his new suit, his face shining and wearing an expression of pure rapture she had never seen in him before, and Bathie . . . Oh, words couldn't describe how lovely Bathie was. Her wedding gown – her mother's, Albert had said – was a perfect creation of lace and tulle, and the headdress, low on her forehead, with a beaded band round it, covered all her hair except for a few curly tendrils.

This young lady would make Albert a good wife, for there was that tilt to her chin which told of a determination to overcome all obstacles. The only thing was – would she be strong enough to bear children? She looked so fragile, as if a puff of wind would blow her away.

When her new daughter-in-law came over and kissed her warmly, Nell's already full heart was in danger of bursting.

'Thank you for giving me Albert,' the bride whispered, then turned to Wattie and kissed his cheek, before going across to her own parents.

Bathie was a very thoughtful lassie, Nell decided, and it was God's blessing that Albert had won her, for it must have taken some doing for him to persuade her father.

Back at the Johnstones' house, the mood was one of gaiety and a slight relief. Nell felt more at ease this time in her new bombazine dress, which wasn't outshone by the blue taffeta Bathie's mother was wearing, and Wattie looked every bit as smart as Mr Johnstone.

Bathie's father seemed to be more free in his manner than he'd been the first time they'd met, and her mother set herself out to include them in every bit of the conversation. Albert's friend John was a bit overcome by all the grandeur, but the bridesmaid was a little chatterbox, so the meal passed very well, and after they moved to the drawing room it seemed no time at all before Albert said they should be leaving.

Nell sensed that Wattie was going to make some kind of ribald remark at this, so she poked his leg with her knee, hoping that no one would notice. He had opened his mouth, and now looked at his wife in hurt surprise, mouth still gaping.

'I'll go up and change out of my wedding gown,' Bathie said, 'and if you're ready to go when I come down, Mr and Mrs Ogilvie, we can walk together as far as Market Street.'

'Two Mr and Mrs Ogilvies,' Nell laughed, loving the girl more and more by the minute.

Before she could stop him, Wattie remarked, 'I'll change wives wi' you ony time, Albert, lad. A young Mrs Ogilvie would suit me fine, for a change would kittle me up an' put a bit o' lead in my pencil.'

He winked to show everyone that he was joking, but Nell shook her head reprovingly. 'He's a great tease,' she told Henrietta, who looked shocked at the man's coarseness, but now smiled a trifle uncomfortably. 'Folk that dinna ken him must think he's terrible,' Nell went on, 'but it's just the way he aye is, an' he doesna mean onythin' by it.'

She did not seem at all put out, her eyes turned affectionately on her husband, and Henrietta wished that she and Arthur had that kind of easy relationship, although theirs had improved a great deal lately. It was funny how adversity often brought a husband and wife closer together, and she had better make sure never to refuse Arthur again.

Chapter Five

The white damask cloth set off the delicately patterned china, the silver cutlery gleamed in the sunlight streaming in through the tall narrow window, the crystal condiment set glittered as if it were encrusted with diamonds, and Bathie Ogilvie nodded with satisfaction.

This was their first breakfast together, and she was still tingling, outside and inside, from Albert's love-making, which had more than fulfilled her rather vague dreams. She had laughed when her mother tried to tell her what she should expect, and had said that she knew all about it, but she had discovered last night that she'd been wrong.

The book she'd read had said that, at first, the female partner would experience much pain and bleeding, but would have to endure it as her wifely duty. Whoever had written that couldn't have enjoyed it, Bathie thought, but she had. She'd been slightly apprehensive when Albert came into the bedroom last night, but when he kissed her, more ardently than he'd ever done before, she'd found herself wanting more.

Then, when his hands had slid down from her neck to her bosom, and he'd started to caress her nipples, great shafts of delight had shot downwards, making her aware of the stirring in her private parts.

There *had* been pain at first, but it had been quite bearable, and Albert had been so gentle that the discomfort had soon been forgotten. She'd been conscious only of the thrill of it, growing stronger and stronger until she was practically desperate with the need for release.

She couldn't describe, even in her thoughts, how she'd felt when that release finally exploded inside her like a blinding flash, but she knew that it had happened at exactly the same time for Albert.

She must stop thinking about it. It was most unseemly, and Albert would think her very unladylike if he ever found out how much she had enjoyed it. He was so considerate that he'd even tried to stop her from rising first this morning.

'I'll get up today,' he'd said. 'I can't have you lighting the fire and making porridge for me on the morning after our wedding night, even if it is Sunday.'

She'd planted a kiss on his brow. 'No, thank you anyway, but I want to be a real wife to you from the very start, Albert, dear.'

Washing himself in the bowl of hot water she'd brought through to the bedroom, Albert was musing over how perfectly everything had worked out for them; Mrs Duncan deciding to move out of her house, and Mr Duthie offering it to him. And if that wasn't enough, giving him the furniture and all the other odds and ends he needed to make a decent home. It was providential, that's what it was.

Being officially made manager, with quite a substantial increase in wages, had also been a godsend, for now he'd a wife to keep, as well as himself. He groped for the towel, his eyes full of soap, and dried himself quickly before he pulled his shirt over his head.

He struggled with his collar stud for a moment, then sat down on the bed – there was no room for a chair here, even if they'd had one – to put on his boots. The sight of Bathie's nightgown, flung carelessly over the rumpled bedclothes, made him flush with the memory of his passion of the night before. Thankfully, it had been nothing like his awful, sordid first experience with the girl from Glasgow. It had confirmed to both of them the full extent of their love for each other.

He'd let her come through to the bedroom first, to

save her the embarrassment of undressing in front of him, and had put on his new nightshirt in the kitchen. He'd been accustomed to sleeping in his woollen linder and long drawers before, but had felt he should show some respect for his bride. She'd looked so beautiful when he joined her, so young and innocent, that he'd hesitated to get into bed beside her. She was only a child, and what he was about to do would change her for ever.

'Are you scared, Albert?' she'd whispered. 'Because I am, just a little bit, but I'm very happy.' Then she'd turned the covers back, inviting him in, and he'd lain down at her side, trembling like an aspen leaf in a breeze.

'I'm the happiest man in the world,' he'd breathed, as he slid his arm round her, and the feel of her softness through the thin cotton gown had set him on fire . . .

Oh, God. The memory of last night had set his sap rising again, and he couldn't go through to Bathie and ask her to go back to bed. She'd think he was an animal, with animal lusts he couldn't control . . . and maybe he was. But he had controlled them last night to a large extent, and had been gentle and tender with her, guiding her through her initiation until he could feel that she was ready for the final thrust which would let them reach the heights together. She hadn't said she enjoyed it, but he was sure that she had.

He stood up hastily, and looked through the window at the small square of grass three floors below. This was where Bathie would have to hang the clothes she washed on Thursday, which was their turn for the wash-house and the drying-green. Poor Bathie. She'd likely never had to wash any clothes in her life before, but she hadn't appeared too upset when Mr Duthie explained the situation to her.

When he felt calmer, Albert went into the kitchen, where Bathie dished up his porridge, waiting for his opinion before she filled a plate for herself. Lumpy and over-salted though it was, he assured her that it was the best he'd ever tasted, and she chuckled with pleasure. It wasn't until she tasted her own that she realized he'd been gallantly untruthful.

'Ugh!' She screwed up her face in disgust, and spat the porridge back into her plate. 'It's awful. I'm sorry, Albert, I can't cook. I've never been told how, and I've never seen anyone . . . ' A tear spilled on to her cheek, so he rose and took her in his arms. 'Bathie, my love. You'll learn as you go along. Stop crying, for it breaks my heart to see you. It doesn't matter. We can throw the porridge out and toast some bread instead.'

Drying her eyes with her new apron, she looked up at him with such a pitiful expression that he just had to kiss her.

In the forenoon, they took the two dogs out for a long walk, after Bathie made sure that the fire was burning well enough to cook the small piece of mutton and potatoes that were huddled together as if for warmth in the centre of a huge roasting tin, another gift from Henrietta.

The aroma of cooking welcomed them when they returned, and Bathie ran to open the oven door. 'I thought I could smell something burning, but it looks just right.'

The meat was delicious, and the fresh air having given them an appetite, they did full justice to their first course. The second course, however, was another disaster.

'It's my fault this time,' Albert said, ruefully. 'I told you to put in two handfuls of rice, for that's what my mother did, but maybe she used more milk, or didn't bake it so long.'

Instead of dissolving into tears, as she'd done in the morning, and as he half expected her to, Bathie surprised him by eyeing the solid black mass in the pie dish and bursting into peals of laughter. It was so infectious that he couldn't help joining in, and soon they were holding on to each other, almost hysterical about this second culinary catastrophe.

'Oh, goodness,' she gasped, after a few minutes. 'It's going to be great fun being married, if we don't die of hunger.'

He sat down on one of the armchairs and pulled her on to his knee. The seat was anything but comfortable, but he wouldn't have noticed if he'd been sitting on a bed of nails.

Running her finger round his ear, she whispered, 'You've got very nice ears, for a man, did you know that, Albert?'

Desire for her flooded up in him again, but he couldn't ask her to go back to bed, so he said, 'We've still all the dishes to wash, we'd better get started.'

By the time they had cleared up and put everything away, the fire was low and had to be stoked, then Albert dozed off in spite of himself, having had little sleep for two nights.

When he woke up, he apologized for his bad manners, but Bathie laughed. 'I fell asleep, too.'

'I've been thinking,' Albert said later, while they were eating cheese and oatcakes. 'We don't want your folk to know about our problem with the cooking, but I'm sure my mother would be glad to show you what to do.'

'I'll go to see her tomorrow, then, when you're in the shop, but I hope she won't think it terrible of me being so ignorant. I feel bad enough about it already.'

'You won't take long to learn, I'm sure.'

'I hope not. I want to prove to them I'm not useless.'

He poured her another cup of tea. 'Nobody could say you're useless, my love. My life would be empty without you.'

Chapter Six

Their first guests, a few weeks later, were Wattie and Nell Ogilvie, because Bathie wanted to have Albert's mother's seal of approval on her cooking before she dared to ask her own parents to eat in the little tenement house.

After the meal was over, Wattie leaned back and patted his ever-enlarging stomach. 'That was just grand, Bathie, lass. You'll be as good a cook as Albert's mother afore we ken where we are.'

The girl stole a glance at her mother-in-law, who gave her a little secret smile. Bathie was very grateful to Nell for the cookery lessons, although she'd been mystified, at first, by instructions like, 'Add a wee puckle salt', or, 'Rub in a good daud o' butter', or, 'Shak' in a han'fu' o' floor'. Such were Albert's mother's recipes.

'You'll get to ken by the look o' things,' Nell had told her, one day. 'You'll get the hang o't in nae time.'

She *had* got the hang of it in no time, Bathie reflected, now, and set herself out to entertain her guests.

When they were leaving, she was very surprised when Wattie laid his rough hand on her shoulder. 'I must tell you this, lass, though it goes against the grain to admit I was wrong. You've proved me a liar, an' I'm real pleased aboot it.'

Seeing her surprise, he explained. 'I tell't Albert that a banker's lassie would never learn how to be a workin' man's wife, but, by God, you have.'

Bathie's cheeks were red with pleasure. 'Thank you, Mr Ogilvie.'

'An' we'll ha'e nane o' this Mr Ogilvie business.' Wattie's dark eyes twinkled. 'If you canna bring yoursel' to say Father, you could aye say Wattie.'

'Thank you,' Bathie repeated, sure that she could never bring herself to call her father-in-law that. From the time she'd learned to talk, she'd been taught never to address her elders by their Christian names.

Nell also had something to say. 'I'm real pleased Albert ken't what he wanted. He waited a lang time afore he took a wife, but he couldna ha'e picked a finer. An' never mind what Wattie says. I ken you could never ca' him by his first name, for you've been brought up better than that, but the problem winna exist in a wee while.' She smiled as she went out.

Bathie turned to Albert. 'What did your mother mean?'

He lifted his shoulders in an expressive shrug. 'I didn't understand her, either, so we'd better wait and see.'

When the Johnstones came, the following Sunday, Arthur

was dismayed by the size of the tiny rooms, but his mind was set at rest by Albert's prowess as a host, especially while the two women remained talking in the bedroom.

The young man asked some pertinent questions about the bank and about banking in general, and seemed to be content to listen as Arthur expounded on the new system he'd introduced and how it worked.

When the women came through, Bathie sliced the silverside and cut up the Yorkshire Pudding as if she had done it for years. The roast potatoes were exactly how her father liked them – crispy on the outside and mealy in the centre – and he asked for a second helping. Albert was glad that his wife's efforts were being appreciated, and helped her to clear away the dirty plates, ready for the next course, smiling at her as she removed the pie dish from the oven.

The rice pudding was creamy, and the grated nutmeg Nell had told her to sprinkle on top made it deliciously different.

Arthur wiped his mouth and remarked, 'If anyone had told me, even on your wedding day, that you could cook like this, Bathia, I would have told him he was mad.'

'You have picked it up very quickly.' Henrietta smiled indulgently. 'Cooking is something I have never attempted.'

Bathie caught Albert's eye and laughed. 'Albert's mother gave me some lessons, so you've really her to thank.'

Arthur rose to occupy one of the armchairs by the fire – originally Joseph Duthie's. The springs almost pierced his trousers, but he remained sitting, genial and uncomplaining, until his wife said that it was time they went home.

He waited until Bathie brought in their coats, then stood up. 'As Albert knows, I do not hesitate to admit it if I have been wrong, and I can say, now, that I have been pleasantly surprised at how well he has provided for you. I can honestly state that I am happy, and proud, to have him as a son-in-law.'

Bathie went over to kiss him, and Albert mumbled, 'Thank you, Mr Johnstone. I never thought I'd hear you saying that.'

On the way home, Arthur was rather thoughtful. 'Albert Ogilvie is rather a fine young man, you know, and I am quite sure, now, that he really does love Bathia.'

His wife smiled. 'Of course he does, I never doubted it, and she will have no cause to regret marrying him.'

She was pleased that their own marriage had improved, and that he had stopped ogling young Hannah, the current maid. Telling him exactly how she felt about him had made him turn over a new leaf, and she did not object to his amorous overtures to her now, either. She had been so young when Bathia was born that his lust had repelled her, but she should have known where it would lead. A man must have an outlet for his needs, and if his own wife was not willing, what else could he have done except turn to those girls who were?

With their house to themselves again, Bathie and Albert were tidying up before going to bed.

'I think everything was satisfactory, don't you?' she said, blissfully. 'They seemed to enjoy my cooking.'

'They were really surprised you were managing so well.'

'I had to prove it to them.' Bathie sat down. 'Albert,' she murmured, after a minute, 'I'm going to have a child.'

He almost dropped the teapot he was filling for one last cup before they went to bed. 'What?'

'I wasn't sure at first, but I've never . . . missed before.' Her cheeks flamed as she turned her face away from him.

It had crossed his mind to wonder why she hadn't been bothered with 'the curse', as he'd heard other men calling it, but he'd never once thought that this was the reason.

'Are you not pleased about it, Albert?' His wife was looking at him anxiously now.

Laying the brown china teapot down so quickly that some of the newly-made tea spilled on to the hob, he took her in his arms and almost squeezed the breath out of her. 'There's not a happier man in the whole of Aberdeen.'

His reassurance was all she needed, and she kissed him with such ardour that he led her into the bedroom without remembering about the tea he'd just made.

Long after Bathie was asleep, however, he lay worrying. He should be happy. He *was* happy. But their house was hardly big enough for the two of them, never mind an infant as well. He should have been more careful, though he loved her so much everything else went out of his head when he was inside her.

He'd have to provide her with better accommodation, even though it would mean more work for her, and he'd never be able to afford a maid. For that matter, he couldn't see himself ever being in a position to afford a bigger house, either.

The moon was full, shining like daylight through the thin curtains, and Bathie's lovely dark hair – she'd taken to pinning it up after the wedding, but let it down at nights – was spread over the pillow, making her look like a schoolgirl. Poor Bathie. What could he do to make up to her?

When at last he fell asleep, his old dream returned, but with an added impossibility. His shop would need to have a large house attached, to accommodate his family, for he meant to have more than one, and with enough room for a live-in maid. He couldn't expect his wife to look after his children and keep a big house as well.

All the next day, he turned the problem over in his mind when he had a chance, and came to his decision just before closing time. There was only one thing for him to do, and he'd do it without telling his wife. He wouldn't need to rush at it just yet – everything must be well planned out – and, much as the first step went against the grain, it would have to be taken before he could go any further.

It was a week later before he had the opportunity to put his plan into action. Seeing his employer going past the window, he ran out. 'I've a favour to ask you, Mr Duthie.'

The old man looked rather surprised – Albert had

never asked him for anything before – but he nodded kindly. 'Aye, if it's in my power, lad.'

'Could you take over the shop for a half day, some time? There's something I want to do, and I don't want Bathie to know anything about it.'

A frown corrugated Joseph Duthie's already furrowed brow. 'You're not keeping secrets from her, are you?'

'It's something I want to get for her, Mr Duthie, and I want to have it all cut and dried before I tell her.'

'Ah, that's different. When were you wanting off?'

'Whenever suits you. There's no desperate hurry, and it'll maybe just take an hour or so.'

'Well, let me see, now.' The old man scratched the side of his face with his gnarled forefinger. 'I'm going to London the day after tomorrow to see my son, and I've still my case to pack and a few things to attend to. It's not worth going all that distance unless I stop for a month, so I'll not be back till the first day of December. Is the second too late?'

'The second of December will do fine, thank you.' Albert would have preferred it to be sooner than that, in case he lost his nerve, but it couldn't be helped.

He began looking at shops again when Bathie and he took the dogs out, going a different route each time, but she was completely unaware of what was in his mind.

She was still very happy being a housewife, cleaning and cooking for her husband, and ever since her mother-in-law had shown her how to knit socks, as well as sew, she'd occupied what spare time she had by keeping Albert supplied with them. Lately, however, she'd started making some tiny garments, which was far more exciting.

When she told her mother about the expected child, Henrietta's thin face had grown even longer. 'Already, Bathia? It wasn't . . . conceived . . . before the wedding, was it?'

Nothing could detract from Bathie's joy, and she gave a little laugh. 'It might have been conceived on the wedding night, Mother, but it certainly wasn't before. Albert's an honourable man, and he never did anything out of place.'

She noticed, with great amusement, that neither her father nor her mother ever mentioned it when they were visiting after that, nor when she and Albert visited them.

Albert's parents, on the other hand, had been delighted at the news, although they didn't seem to be very surprised.

'I just ken't it.' Nell sounded happily triumphant. 'Didn't I tell you, Wattie, there was a bairn on the road?'

'She can tell when a lassie's expectin' afore the lassie kens hersel'.' Wattie winked fondly at his wife.

'D'you mind, Bathie, I tell't you, the night he said to ca' him Wattie, that the problem wouldna exist in a wee while?' Nell laughed. 'I ken't what was in the wind, you see.'

Rather bewildered, Bathie was also dismayed that her condition had been noticed so early, but what did it matter? It would soon be obvious to all and sundry.

Every time she saw her in-laws now, they asked her how she was keeping, although she was actually blooming with health and happiness. This, of course, was a great relief to Albert, who had heard stories of women suffering terrible bouts of morning sickness when they were carrying.

When Joseph Duthie came to relieve him on the second of December, Albert strode purposefully to Ferryhill.

Henrietta was taken very much aback when her maid showed him in. 'There's nothing wrong with Bathia, I hope?'

'No, no, she couldn't be better. I've something to ask you, Mrs Johnstone.' He always addressed Bathie's parents formally, and they had never told him to do otherwise.

Now that he was actually there, he didn't know how to begin. To his mind, what he was about to say could be interpreted as an admission of failure, a complete reversal of what he had vowed to Bathie's father before his marriage, and he was more than half afraid that Mrs Johnstone would despise him for it – her husband certainly would – but he had to carry on, for Bathie's sake.

He cleared his throat nervously and Henrietta took pity on him. 'It must be very important since you have taken time off your work to come here. Would you like a cup of tea?'

'It is important to me, but I'd rather not bother with tea, if you don't mind, for I want to get it over as soon as I can. I'm finding it very difficult, Mrs Johnstone, so I must ask you to bear with me and let me finish before you say anything.'

Her smile faded slightly, and he began slowly. 'As you know, Bathie's expecting, and our house just isn't big enough for three.' He held up his hand as she opened her mouth. 'I know I told you before that I wanted none of your money, but I'm . . . climbing down and asking if . . . '

She interrupted before he could stop her. 'You are asking if I will give you the money my mother left me, after all.'

Dropping his eyes, he twirled his flat cap in his hands. 'Yes,' he admitted. 'That is what I was going to ask.' The tips of his ears were red with shame, but her laugh made him look up in surprise.

'You are about three weeks too late, Albert.'

This made his whole face colour, and his mouth went dry with bitter disappointment, for she had been his only hope.

'After Bathia told me of her condition, I asked Arthur to open a bank account in your name, Albert, and I have already transferred that money into it. I was certain that, however independent you were, you would want to buy a decent house for your wife and child. So it is there for you to use whenever you want it.' She sat back and regarded his astonished face with faint amusement.

It was an anticlimax to all the long hours of painful deliberation, and he felt rather cheated. It shouldn't have come this easy. 'But it's Bathie you should have opened that account for, not me,' he said, after a long silence.

Henrietta's voice was still gently kind. 'As you are aware, Bathia's own money will come to her when she is twenty-one, and she need never know about this. The arrangement is strictly between us, Albert.'

'She'll have to know, for I couldn't keep a thing like that a secret from her.'

'I fail to see why not.'

'She'll know I couldn't buy a house on what I make, though I have saved a wee bit since Mr Duthie gave me my wages up.' He fell silent again, stroking his chin as he considered, then his troubled face cleared. 'I'll accept your generosity on one condition, Mrs Johnstone.'

'And what is your one condition?'

'That you let me pay it back, though it takes me years.'

The woman removed her pince-nez and rubbed the bridge of her nose. 'And if I don't agree to that condition?'

'Then I'll have to try somewhere else.'

'Oh, Albert Ogilvie, I'm very glad that Bathia found you.' His face lit up. 'Then you agree to my condition?'

'I meant to buy a house, but I knew you would not accept it, and this was the only way I could think of to help you.'

'Thank you for your kind intentions, but I still consider it as a loan.'

Henrietta raised her eyebrows. 'I thought you would want to know how much money is available to you.'

'As long as there's enough to buy a decent-sized house, I don't see the need for . . . '

'There's three thousand pounds, Albert.' His reaction was not quite what she'd hoped for.

'Three thou . . . ?' he faltered, consternation clouding his eyes. 'I can't take all that, I'd never be able to repay it.'

She felt a little irritated. 'Take as much as you need, then, and remember, in less than five years, Bathie will have control of the two thousand pounds presently in trust for her.'

Albert's head was spinning in a struggle between his natural proud thrift and his determination to give his wife the best house possible. Also, at the back of his mind, a little voice was telling him that he could buy a house *and* a shop if he had three thousand pounds at his disposal. The profits he'd make from his own business would enable him to repay the loan all the quicker.

Studying him, Henrietta could almost read his thoughts. 'Money begets money, you know,' she said, softly.

He clasped his hands together to steady them. 'I don't know what to say. I've dreamed about having my own shop ever since I started working for Joseph Duthie, but I never . . . '

'There you are, then.' Henrietta stood up as a signal that the discussion was terminated. 'You can buy your shop, as well as a house, with the . . . loan.'

So overcome with gratitude that he forgot to thank her properly, he walked back to Torry in a daze. Dreaming was one thing, but having that dream within his reach was strangely disquieting.

He entered by the side door and exchanged his jacket for his long white apron before he went through to the front shop where his employer was counting change into a woman's hand. The old man's genial smile disappeared as soon as the customer went out, and his lined face bore signs of great anxiety when he faced his manager.

'You're back, are you, Albert? I've something to tell you, and I don't know where to begin. I hope you can understand, but I've thought and thought about it, and it was my son made me see it was the only thing I could do.'

Slightly puzzled, and not particularly interested in anything outside his own situation, Albert waited.

'It's like this. I'm wearing on for seventy, and since my wife died there's nothing to keep me in Torry except the shop. Joe's been at me for years to sell up and go to London, but I couldn't bring myself to do it. I've spent my whole life here, but when I was down there this time, he said he'd be a lot happier if I was where he could see I was eating properly.'

He made a sucking noise with his tongue. 'I'm not even bothering much nowadays, and there'll come a time . . . If I sell, I'd have a bit of money, so I could pay him for my keep.'

'You'd be a lot better with your son.' Albert felt quite pleased for the old man. 'Blood's thicker than water, and you'd have somebody to look after you if you took ill.'

'Aye.' There was a long pause. 'It's just . . . you'll be out of a job, Albert, and maybe out of a house, as well, if the new man wants it for some of his own relations. I'll have to sell everything, tenement and all. I know it must be an awful shock to you, and I've had some sleepless nights over it.'

'Don't worry yourself about me,' Albert assured him. 'We're going to be looking for a bigger house, anyway, for we've started our family, and I'll easily get another job.'

Mr Duthie's face cleared so suddenly, it was like the sun bursting through after a shower of rain. 'So little Bathie's expecting? That's one bit of good news, at any rate.' He hesitated for a moment. 'Well, I'd better be off. I'll have to think about clearing out my house and making up my mind what I want to take with me when I go to London. Joe hasn't got room for all my stuff.'

A worrying thought struck Albert then. 'When were you thinking of selling up, Mr Duthie?'

'Oh, I think I'll leave it till after the winter. The beginning of the summer, more like. When's Bathie due?'

'The last week of May, but . . . '

'It'll not be before that, Albert, so you'll have plenty of time to find another house, and another job.' Patting the young man's shoulder, he went into the back shop for his coat and hat.

When he was left on his own, Albert marvelled at the strange coincidence. Here was he, with the wherewithal to buy a shop, and there was Joseph Duthie, wanting to sell his. But this little place wasn't what he'd pictured in his dreams. Even the three rooms that the old man would leave vacant on the first floor weren't what Albert had in mind for his family.

They'd certainly be better than the two tiny rooms he and Bathie occupied at present, and he'd be helping Mr Duthie out if he bought this property, but it wasn't what he wanted. It would be like breaking faith with himself if he knuckled under and used his mother-in-law's loan for that.

At seven, he locked up thoughtfully. Was it wise to break away, or should he accept what fate seemed to be offering him? Anyway, it was Bathie who should have been given that money, so he'd leave it to her to make the decision.

All through supper, he tried to think how to broach the subject, and was still puzzling when he sat down by the fire.

'You're very quiet, Albert.' Bathie had positioned herself on the rug in front of him, with her elbow on his knee. 'Is there anything wrong? Don't be afraid to say if there is.'

He shifted a little, to avoid the spring that was digging into his left hip, then said, slowly, 'Not exactly wrong, but I'd better tell you about it, my love.'

She interrupted his recital only once. 'You should have told me what you meant to do.'

When he came to an end, he looked down at her pensive face. 'It's like fate meant me to buy this place, but . . . '

'But the shop downstairs isn't what you dreamt about? Albert, I look at it in a different way from you. I think, from the way it happened, that fate meant you to buy what you wanted, and just gave you a little push by telling you that you'd be out of a job and a house when Mr Duthie sold up.'

'So you don't think I'm reaching for the moon?'

'It's not reaching for the moon when you have the money to make your dream come true, and Mother won't expect it back.'

'She'll have it paid back, every penny of it,' he declared loudly. 'I don't want your father sneering at me for having to go cap in hand to them, not after what I said before.'

'He wouldn't. He's not as bad as you think, Albert, and he quite likes you, now that he knows you better.'

'Bathie, you're the best wife in the whole world.'

'I know.' She gave a little giggle. 'But you're not the best husband in the world.' Kissing his hand as his face fell, she added softly, 'You're the best husband that ever lived, Albert, dear.'

Chapter Seven

'It just doesn't exist,' Albert lamented, when they returned home one Sunday about three weeks later. 'I'd better just forget my dream and offer to buy the place downstairs.'

'It's still only December,' Bathie chided him, gently. 'Some of the shops we've looked at were quite good, and remember, you can afford to alter one to suit you.'

Her husband ran his fingers through his hair, two tufts springing on to his forehead like horns, one on each side of his middle parting. 'No, Bathie. If I don't get the right feeling about it, it's no use. And it's got to have a big enough house attached to it, that's another thing.'

'You'll find it, Albert dear.' Bathie had seen nothing amiss with several of the properties they'd looked at, but she respected her husband's expectations.

Her own thoughts had been concentrated on preparing for Hogmanay, which was drawing nearer. She'd wanted to invite the two sets of parents to a New Year's Day meal, but had found opposition to her plan from more than one direction.

In addition to Albert and his mother, her own mother had been very much against the idea. 'There is not room for six people in your kitchen,' Henrietta had told her. 'And it's too much work for you, in your condition. You must come here.'

'But Albert's mother and father . . . '

'We will invite them, too.'

'Ach, we're only common folk,' Wattie protested, when his son passed on Henrietta's invitation. 'We canna mix wi' the likes o' the Johnstones.'

'They're quite friendly, really,' Albert said, earnestly. 'They want it to be a proper family gathering, and Bathie'll be disappointed if you don't go.'

Nell frowned, then glanced at her husband hopefully. 'I can hardly wear the same frock I had on at the weddin'.'

64

Wattie struggled with his thrifty conscience, but the thought of bonnie little Bathie being disappointed was too much for him. 'I daresay I could let you ha'e you a pound or two to buy a new ane,' he offered.

The New Year celebration went off very well. Arthur Johnstone had been schooled by his wife not to talk about the bank, and he discovered that Wattie Ogilvie was actually quite a character, in his own droll way.

Her dark hair shining like silk shot with faint traces of silver, Nell wore her new grey dress with ribbons across the bodice, and as she looked across at her husband, in the new shirt she'd also been able to buy out of the money he'd given her, she felt that they could hold their heads up beside the Johnstones, or anybody else, for that matter.

Her usual reserve in the presence of her 'betters' being completely forgotten, she exchanged views with Henrietta on the problems of raising a family, and told her how it felt to be a fisherman's wife when great storms were raging.

'I'll be glad when he gi'es it up,' she smiled, 'though he gets under my feet sometimes, even now, when he's at hame.'

Henrietta listened, with great interest. She'd never come in contact with anyone like Nell before, and was realizing how narrow her own life had been.

It gave Bathie great pleasure to see the two sets of parents getting on so well together, and her cup of happiness would have overflowed if it hadn't been for Albert.

Arthur Johnstone had been very generous with the whisky, so he and Wattie were now laughing hilariously as they recounted some slightly risqué jokes to each other, but the spirits seemed to have had the opposite effect on Albert, who had withdrawn into himself and was obviously in a state of melancholia.

The two mothers, having sipped a little port, were smiling indulgently at their husbands, although Nell was praying that Wattie wouldn't disgrace her by coming out with some of the crude stories he bandied about with the other fisher folk.

Bathie slipped her hand into Albert's. 'Cheer up,' she whispered. 'Our mothers and fathers will think we've had a quarrel. Everything'll work out, you'll see.'

He turned towards her. 'I'm sorry, it must be the whisky that's making me feel like this. You're right. It's a new year, and a new beginning. Though 1889 was the best year ever for me, for that's when I found you.'

The Ogilvies all shook hands with the Johnstones and wished them Happy New Year when they left. Albert and Bathie walked as far as the foot of Market Street with his parents, then carried on over the Victoria Bridge into Torry.

When they arrived home, Albert took Belle and Spanny outside for a few minutes before he joined Bathie in their bed. He gripped her breasts with more insistence than usual, making her cry out as his nails dug into her flesh, and she had to fight down a rising tide of nausea at the smell of whisky on his breath. Within seconds, he was on top of her, but to her great relief, he rolled off again almost immediately.

'My cock winna rise,' he mumbled, reverting, in his drunken state, to the common speech he'd overcome years before.

Bathie listened to his deep, steady breathing with a touch of wry amusement, and before long, she, too, fell asleep.

In the morning, Albert had no recollection of most of the previous evening, and when his wife told him what he'd done when they'd gone to bed, he was mortified.

'Oh, my God, Bathie, I'm sorry. It was the drink speaking, and I'll never touch another drop, Bathie, I swear.'

She smiled. 'We'll see, Albert, we'll see.'

The weeks flew past for Albert, unable to find his dream, but dragged for his wife, who was finding her condition rather cumbersome. Her belly felt huge, and her breasts were heavy and tender. She stopped going out in daylight, imagining that everyone was looking at her and laughing. She'd had to let out the laces on her stays and the waistbands of her skirts, and she was only just into her seventh month. What would she be like by the time her child came into the world?

'I love the way you look,' Albert said gravely, when she voiced her fears one night. 'There's something, I can't explain it, but carrying a child has made you even more beautiful to me. Let me feel my son, Bathie.'

It was a request he often made since she told him about the infant's movements, so she let him run his hand slowly over her bulging belly until he took a shuddering breath and let his arm drop.

'Oh, Bathie. This is torture for me.'

He seemed very irritated when he couldn't get his arm into the twisted sleeve of his nightshirt, and his obvious need of her made her realize that he was frustrated at not being able to make love to her, although it was Albert, himself, who had decided to stop, a few weeks earlier.

He lay down next to her, with his hands under his head, and she assumed that he was thinking about his still fruitless search for a suitable property, but she was wrong.

'You know, Bathie,' he said, after a few minutes, and never taking his eyes off the ceiling, 'I went for years without taking a woman, though you maybe find that hard to believe.'

'I do believe you, Albert.'

'I only had one once, when I was just a laddie, to see what it was like, and it meant nothing to me. Yet here I am, hardly able to keep my hands off you. My sap rises every time I look at you, and I'm starting to fear you wakened the beast inside me, the beast that must have been there all along.'

'You're blethering.' She used one of the expressions which she'd heard Nell often using to Wattie.

'No, I'm serious, and if you ever think I'm behaving like an animal, I want you to tell me.'

'If you're worried about the time you had too much to drink, you never really did anything bad.'

'I can feel there's an animal in me, Bathie, and I'm feared I'll disgust you some day.' He changed position and turned away from her, and she lay wide awake wondering how it would feel to be treated roughly.

The next day being a Wednesday, Albert took the dogs out in the afternoon to let Bathie have a rest. She didn't doze off, as she often did, but lay thinking of the terrible scene there had been when she'd taken him home with her, smiling at the memory of how he'd stood up for himself. But she'd never discovered what had made her father climb down the way he did.

She'd been in bed for less than ten minutes, weeping her heart out, when her mother had come up to tell her that he'd changed his mind and was now agreeable to the marriage, so what on earth could have happened during those few minutes? She hadn't thought it strange at the time; she'd been so filled with happiness she could think only of Albert, but what had her mother said to her father? She was quite sure that it was Henrietta who had talked him round, but how?

After puzzling for a minute, Bathie gave up. She would never know, and perhaps it was just as well. She used to have a strange feeling that things weren't plain sailing between her mother and father, but since that night, they seemed to be much happier and more affectionate towards each other.

Her thoughts turned to Albert's proposal, and a peculiar disquiet assailed her. He'd kissed her, then said he couldn't kiss her again, because he was afraid he'd do something he shouldn't be doing until they were married. That was all he'd said, and she had jumped to her own conclusion. What if she'd misunderstood his intentions? Perhaps he hadn't been proposing after all, but leading up to doing what he said he shouldn't?

Was that the only reason he'd wanted to marry her? Her stomach lurched, then she pulled herself together. She was being stupid. Of course he'd wanted to marry her, and not only for that. He loved her as much as she loved him, and their matings were a natural outcome of their love.

Chapter Eight

The potatoes were boiling on one side of the hob, the pot of stew and vegetables was bubbling on the other, when Albert burst in, excitement shining from his dark brown eyes, his red hair ruffled and falling over his brow.

Bathie looked up from setting the table. 'What is it? You look like you lost a ha'penny and found half a crown.'

'I feel like it, and all,' he crowed. 'I've found it! The perfect property. The house has nine rooms, and the shop'll do, though the whole place needs some attention.'

'Nine rooms? Oh, Albert, that's much too big for us.'

'We'll need nine rooms by the time we've finished, Bathie.' His voice was pitched rather high. 'I never mentioned it before, but listen. My name starts with A, and yours starts with B, and it came to me, when you first told me about the child, that we could carry on through the alphabet. That's my new ambition.'

'Oh, Albert.' Consternation made her eyebrows meet. 'Not twenty-six children? You surely can't mean that?'

'No, no. We'll have as many as we can, starting with C, of course, seeing we're A and B already. What d'you say, Bathie? Think of the pleasure we'll have just from making them, for a start.'

She turned a deep rose. She always felt guilty when she thought of how much she enjoyed their couplings, because it was really something a decent woman should never admit, not even to herself.

'It would be silly to have just three of us in nine rooms when we could have a proper family.'

'Yes, Albert,' she murmured. 'I often used to wish that I'd had brothers and sisters – it wasn't much fun being an only child – so I'd like to have lots of children.'

'Come with me to see the house tonight, my love, for you're going to love it as much as me, I promise.'

After suppertime, Bathie put on her baggiest coat, to hide her condition as much as possible, although nobody would see her in the darkness outside, and set off arm-in-arm with her husband to an, as yet, undisclosed destination.

'Where is it?' she asked anxiously, after they'd crossed the Victoria Bridge and were going along South Market Street.

'Wait and see, my love,' was all that Albert would say.

They walked alongside the docks, and on up Market Street itself, where Albert had been born and raised, then he led her across Union Street, Bathie's heart sinking when they turned left into Broad Street.

'Is it much farther? I can't walk very far, not just now.'

He halted at once. 'I'm sorry, my love, I've been too anxious for you to see the place and tell me what you think.'

He didn't need to tell her that, she thought. It had been obvious from the minute he'd burst into the house, but how far did he still expect her to walk?

He allowed her to lean against a wall for a short time, then said, 'Are you ready to carry on?'

The short respite had helped her a little, so he took her arm again, to walk her past Marischal College into the Gallowgate. She hoped that this wasn't where Albert had found his ideal property, because it had once been the road to the Gallows and was now old and very run down. She couldn't be happy living here.

But at the top of the hill, he stopped and pointed proudly to a tall building. 'This is it, Bathie, on the very brow of the Gallowgate. We'll be able to look down both ways, and feel like we own everything we can see.'

Her first dismayed thought was that they would have to climb a steep hill whichever way they came, then she felt bitterly disappointed that Albert would even consider such a place. Standing in the middle of the uneven street, she tried to see what he found so attractive about it, because it didn't appeal to her in the slightest. The whole building, which had seen better days, comprised three shops – a confectioner, one standing empty and a shoemaker – and although the empty one was the largest,

70

it wasn't nearly as impressive as many of the others they'd looked at before.

'The house is over the shops,' he said, 'and I've got the key, so you can see what it's like inside.'

She followed him through a dark close, between the empty shop and the shoemaker, and they emerged into an open quadrangle with an iron staircase to their left, leading up, she presumed, to the house which had taken Albert's fancy.

He was already at the top when she placed her foot on the first step, but she stopped to take a look around her. The moon showed several doors off the open area, and she wondered what was behind them, but Albert was saying, 'Come on, Bathie,' so she made her way laboriously upwards.

Her heavy feet clanked on the metal, and when she passed through the door Albert was holding open for her, her spirits sank even lower at the sight of another flight of stairs.

'Oh, Albert,' she gasped. 'What a lot of steps.'

'You should be used to stairs, my love, after being on the top floor of a tenement.'

'This is different,' she told him, but left it at that, and went on ahead of him, trying to ignore the dank, musty smell that grew stronger in her nostrils with each step she took.

'It must have been empty for a long time,' she remarked, when they both stood on the first-floor landing.

'Aye, I suppose it would be difficult to sell, with the three shops included, but once it's all been aired and done up, it'll look much better, I promise.'

His cheerful eagerness surprised Bathie. She knew that his heart had been set on a house with a lot of rooms, but this place wasn't even habitable, and the shop below . . . surely it wasn't what Albert had dreamt of for so long?

Opening one of the four doors on the landing, she entered a large room with a torn blind at the window, and when she crossed to pull it up, she found that she was looking down into the eerie quadrangle.

It wasn't a very inspiring outlook, she thought sadly, and turned to have a look at the room itself. The moonlight was now streaming in over her shoulder, and, unexpectedly, she could sense what Albert must have felt. She scarcely noticed the dark patches on the walls, nor the rusting steel on the huge range, for there was an indefinable something about the room that touched her and warmed her heart.

'I like it,' she said, simply.

Albert beamed. 'I told you.'

A connecting door led into the next room, which was just as large, and just as seedy, as the kitchen, but it had a low fireplace under the high wooden mantelshelf.

'They're very big rooms,' she murmured, but she wasn't criticizing, for the magic of the house had taken her over, too.

'It's what we're going to need, and they're all connected with each other, as well as opening on to the landing,' her husband informed her, in barely repressed excitement.

The idea of being able to walk from one room to another so easily appealed to her, and she sighed with contentment after they'd seen the other two.

'There's a friendliness about the whole place.'

Albert squeezed her arm. 'I'm glad you feel it as well, Bathie. We'll go upstairs to see the rest, now.'

She climbed the next flight of stairs with lighter feet, not expecting to see anything very impressive, but the three rooms here were only fractionally smaller than the four below, and, again, they all had fireplaces.

Her surprise turned to amazement when she heaved herself up the last narrow flight to the attics. Even these two rooms were much larger than the two poky rooms in the tenement, and they, too, had fireplaces. By this time, she felt she could go no farther without a rest, so she sank down on the top step.

Albert squatted on the landing behind her. 'It doesn't look much just now, but once I've finished, it'll be a home fit for a princess. Fit for you, Bathie, for you're my princess.'

He still had the power to turn her heart to jelly, even after nearly eight months of marriage. 'I can picture it, Albert, dear,' she said, softly. 'I can see it filled with our children, and our children's children.'

'Aye.' His hand slid round her neck. 'We'll have to buy new furniture, for what we have will be lost in this place, but I'll see to everything.'

They remained there for some time, planning what they would need to buy, until Albert rose stiffly and rubbed his leg. Then he helped his wife to her feet and placed his hand under her elbow, to begin a slow and careful descent.

When they emerged from the house door, he locked it and went in front of her while they negotiated the outside stairs. By the time they reached the bottom, they were both out of breath and had to stand and rest for a minute.

'What are all the other doors for?' Bathie swept her hand out in a wide arc.

'That's our own wash-house, that's the WC, that's a store for the shoemaker, one for the empty . . . my shop, and one for the sweetie shop.' He indicated as appropriate. 'There's some that aren't used, but I'll find a use for them, no doubt.'

His face assumed a look of great satisfaction. 'I'll be taking in rent from the other two shops, of course, and . . . Bathie, the sign above the middle shop's going to read "Albert Ogilvie, Licensed Grocer", and maybe, one day, "And Sons".'

Bathie had to ask, 'It's not exactly what you dreamt about, though. Are you sure this is what you really want?'

Her anxious expression made him laugh. 'It's maybe not the shop of my dreams at this very minute, but I can see the possibilities, and thanks to your mother, I don't have to worry about the expense. It was the house I liked, though.'

She lifted her face up. 'It'll be heaven living here.'

Bending his head, he kissed her. 'It'll always be heaven for me, wherever I am, as long as I've got you, Bathie.'

'And for me, as long as I have you.'

Linking arms, they walked through the close on to the granite setts of the Gallowgate again.

While the renovations and alterations were being carried out, Albert refused to discuss their progress, and, any time Bathie asked, he replied, 'It'll all be ready before the end of May, and that's all you need to bother your pretty head about.'

As the weeks passed, she had to loosen her stays even further, until she could hardly fasten the laces. But she kept in good health, and finished sewing four pairs of curtains – which was all that Albert had allowed her to do – and all the baby's layette, with time to spare. She'd stopped enquiring about the house, it only made her husband frown, so she was extremely surprised when he came home one night and informed her that they'd be moving the following week.

'But that'll only be the first week in May,' she gasped.

'Aye, well, but the builder's men have been going at it for all they're worth, and they've made a right good job of it. You'll hardly be able to believe it when you see it, Bathie, for they've worked a miracle. They've done everything you could think of, and things you'd never think of, so the place looks like a palace now. They even hung up your curtains for you.'

She hadn't noticed that he'd removed the box she'd stored them in, and felt a momentary flash of anger at him for not telling her. She'd wanted to choose the rooms each pair would be hung in, and he'd taken even that pleasure away from her.

Albert sensed what was going through her mind. 'It's better that you haven't got the work of it, lass. You've got to be careful, and look after yourself, for I don't want anything to happen to my first son.'

She let her breath out slowly. What did it matter which set of curtains went where? They were all beautiful.

'I've ordered Wordie's cart to be here on Saturday at ten,' Albert went on, relieved that she hadn't made a fuss. 'So we'll have to pack everything in the evenings.

Mr Duthie's giving me some tea chests, and he says I can stop work this Friday. I told him I'd just take Saturday off and work all next week, for the new man takes over his shop the following Monday, but he said it would be better if I'd a week to organize my own place, so it's all worked out fine.'

On Saturday, after all their belongings had been loaded, Bathie was lifted on to the cart by the two leather-aproned carters, and when they reached her new home, an exhilarated Albert came running to help her climb down.

'I'll get them to take all that stuff up to the attics,' he told her, 'till we make up our minds what we're going to do with them. The first floor's all furnished.'

When they reached the kitchen door, he pushed it open with a flourish. 'What d'you think of it now, Bathie?'

He'd been correct in saying that she would hardly be able to believe what she saw. A wide Welsh dresser sat along one wall and a long pine table stood in the centre of the floor, with six chairs tucked under it. A cupboard had been built in at each side of the range – now burnished to a high degree, and with a bright fire burning in it – and shelves were fitted between the doors to the landing and to the next room.

The walls were wood-panelled halfway up and painted white above that, and the previously damp, neglected room now threw out an immediate welcome. Bathie's legs gave way, and she sat down heavily on one of the wooden-armed chairs in front of the cupboards at the fireside.

'What's wrong, my love?' Albert sounded concerned.

'Nothing's wrong, I'm . . . I'm just overcome.' Tears trickled down her cheeks. 'I couldn't have planned it better myself.'

'I wanted to have everything just right for you.'

'It is, it is! Oh, Albert, you're so good to me.' She took her handkerchief out of her bag and wiped her eyes. 'Just give me time to come to myself, then I'll look at the other rooms.'

'This is the dining room,' he told her proudly, when they went through the connecting door from the kitchen.

'We won't be using it all the time, of course, it's just for when we have visitors.'

She'd thought he could give her no more surprises, but this was almost a replica of the dining room in the house in Ferryhill, from the marble fireplace right down to the geranium sitting at the window. The walnut table and six chairs were placed in the middle of the room, and a tall sideboard took up almost the whole of one wall.

Bathie's eyes returned to the delicate crocheted centre-piece on the table. 'Where did you buy that, Albert? It's just exactly what the table needed.'

His smile was smug. 'I didn't buy it. My mother made it for us, when I told her the table needed something.'

Determined not to show him how much Nell's handiwork had touched her, she turned to admire the brass fender round the fire, flanked by a set of brass fire-irons to the right, and a brass scuttle and log box to the left.

'They're real Persian rugs on the floor,' Albert boasted. 'They'll last us for the rest of our lives.'

'It's all very elegant,' she managed to say, in spite of being choked with emotion at his thoughtfulness. 'It must have cost an awful lot.'

'A bit, but not as much as you'd think.'

In the parlour, there were two comfortable-looking horsehair armchairs and a couch, all covered in brown hide. A small mahogany table stood at one end of the couch, and there was even a whatnot in the corner for her knick-knacks.

Another table, at the window, taller and on a pedestal, held a large aspidistra, and the low fire was glowing, with a padded fenderstool round the front, a wooden coal scuttle and log box tucked into one corner, and a steel poker and tongs in the other.

Bathie let her eyes roam round, speechless for a moment, then she whispered, 'I don't know what to say. It's perfect.'

'Aye, I made a good job of things, didn't I?'

His pride was excusable, Bathie thought. 'Oh, Albert, I love you,' she said, as he led her into the bedroom.

She gasped with delight when she saw the huge double bed, with brass rails and knobs, covered by a white bedspread whose fringes touched the floor. 'Did you make up the bed, Albert?'

'I did that. I'm not useless at housework, but it's not man's work, and that's the last time I'll ever make it.'

She had to agree. It was only proper.

'There's a wardrobe each, and two chests of drawers, as well, and the joiners put in two presses.' He opened one of the cupboard doors to show her the shelves.

'You've thought about everything.' Bathie was more overcome than ever, but did her best not to break down, in case she spoiled his pleasure. 'You're a good man, Albert.'

'I'll always be a good man to you, my love. But you're tired. Why don't you have a lie down for a while, till I go and see if our dinner's ready.'

'Dinner? Have you been cooking as well?'

His gingery eyebrows lifted. 'Oh, no. I'm not starting to cook. I asked Mrs Wyness, from a few doors down, if she'd make something for us.' He gave an embarrassed laugh. 'Well, it was her that offered, really, when she heard we were moving in today. I've engaged her to attend at your confinement, for she's a midwife, and she's a really fine woman.'

A faint stab of jealousy touched Bathie's heart. Surely Albert wasn't interested in another woman? 'What's she like?'

'She's fat and she's forty if she's a day.' His open laugh made his wife feel much better. 'And I've employed her oldest daughter, Mary, to come and help you with the housework. She's just thirteen, but her mother says she's a grand wee worker.'

'A maid, as well as all this?' But Bathie took his advice, and lay down and closed her eyes, barely conscious of the feet still tramping up and down the stairs, as the removal men carried their old furniture up to the attics.

At one o'clock exactly, Albert shook his wife gently. 'You'd better get up now, Bathie. Our dinner's all set out in the kitchen, and we don't want to let it get cold.

There's soup first, then a lamb stew, and it all smells very good.'

As they ate, he told her, 'That's everything finished, and the carters took the tea chests back to Mr Duthie. You'll have nothing to do except make our supper, and Mary Wyness'll be here in the morning to help you sort things out.'

'I could easily manage on my own,' Bathie protested, wishing that he'd let her do something for herself.

Ignoring her, he went on. 'You're not to do any heavy lifting, that's what Mary's to be here for, but if you like, I'll give you a hand later on to unpack the using china, then we should have an early night, for it's been a long day.'

After they washed Mrs Wyness's dishes, and before they started to unpack their own, Albert said, 'Would you like to see the nursery I've made ready? I didn't want to take you up there when the carters were still going up and down.'

'A nursery upstairs? But that's too far away from our bedroom?' Bathie remarked, anxiously, as she lumbered up the stairs. 'I wouldn't hear the baby crying in the night.'

'Just wait.' Albert turned one of the brass handles on the middle landing, then stood back expectantly.

The nursery was all in white, like their own room, but with little blue flowers on the wallpaper and curtains. The wooden crib was painted white, and the quilt and pillow case were covered with the same material as the curtains. Even the pure white blankets were bound with blue floral ribbon.

'My mother made everything for in here,' Albert explained. 'She was determined to do it, and I couldn't tell her you'd likely want to do it yourself. She meant it for the best, and she's made a grand job, and saved you all the work of it, into the bargain, so I hope you're not angry, my love.'

She had felt a little resentful at first, but common sense made her summon up a smile. 'I'm not angry. I'm very grateful to her for wanting to do it.'

Relieved, he pulled her round to face the other way. 'She gave us that, as well.'

'That' turned out to be an old cradle, which was sitting behind the door, looking quite incongruous in the white room.

'It's what she had for my brothers and me.' Albert looked at her apologetically. 'My father says he'll paint it white for you if you want to use it. We could keep it in our room till the infant grows out of it, then we could transfer him up here to the crib, and I'll make the room next door ready for a live-in nursemaid, so you wouldn't have to worry about him crying through the night. But you don't have to use the cradle if you don't want it.'

Bathie set it rocking with her foot. 'I'd like to use it for our son, Albert, and I'd like it left just the way it is. Your mother and father are both very thoughtful.'

'They love you as much as me . . . well, nearly as much.' With a boyish grin, he slid his arm round where her waist should have been. 'That's why we've done all this for you.'

'I'm so happy I could cry,' she whispered.

'We didn't mean to make you cry, my love, but I'm glad you're happy about everything. We did it to save you work.'.

'I know, Albert, dear.'

As she went downstairs, she thanked God for her husband, and for Nell and Wattie Ogilvie.

By half past eight, Bathie was so tired that she was glad to go to bed, and she suspected that Albert felt the same. When he did join her, she burrowed as close as she could to him, and he turned towards her at once.

'I'll be glad when you can get back to being a proper wife to me, for the last two months have been purgatory.'

She did know that, and thought none the less of him for admitting it.

Albert's parents arrived the following afternoon to inspect the house, and were loud in praise of it.

'It's like a palace,' Nell exclaimed. 'The rooms are that big you near expect to see the Queen hersel' come walkin' in.'

'Will you nae feel lost in a place this size?' Wattie's eyes twinkled. 'Just the two o' you, well . . . three o' you? But I must say, it's real bonnie.'

'Albert chose all the furniture and set everything out himself.' Bathie was very proud of her husband, even though she still felt a little piqued at being allowed no say.

Always sensitive to other people's emotions, Nell said, 'You can change things round once you're on your feet again, if you want to. I canna get ower how good it was o' your mother lendin' Albert a' that money to let him buy this place.'

Suddenly wistful, she added, 'I only wish I could ha'e helped a bit, as weel.'

'You did help,' Bathie said, hastily. 'You crocheted that lovely table centre in the dining room, and Albert said you sewed all the cushion covers here as well as everything for the nursery. They're all really beautiful, and you must have spent hours making them.'

'Aye, weel.' Nell was embarrassed. 'It's a' I could do.'

Wattie turned to his son. 'I'd like fine to tak' a look at the shop, to see what kind o' job you made o' that.'

Albert could scarcely hide his excitement as he led the way out, and Nell glanced conspiratorially at Bathie. 'They're like a couple o' bairns wi' a new toy.'

Bathie grinned. 'Yes, Albert's been dying to show off his shop, although he hasn't got his stock in yet.'

'How are you, though, after the upheaval o' the flittin'?'

'I was really tired last night, but I felt better this morning. I just wish this was all over.' Bathie patted her extended belly ruefully.

'Aye, the waitin' gets worse the nearer your time comes, but there's nae that lang to go noo.' Nell paused, then added, 'Would you like me to come an' bide wi' you when the bairn's born, just till you get back on your feet? It would be nae bother to me, an' I could sleep on your sofa seein' you've only got the one bed.'

Bathie seemed flustered. 'It's very good of you to offer, but Albert has asked Mrs Wyness to attend at my confinement, and I'll have her daughter Mary here every day.'

Understanding that she was afraid of offending her own mother, Nell nodded. 'Weel, if you need me, just let me ken.'

'Thank you. I'll remember that.'

'He's made a grand job o' the shop,' Wattie informed his wife when he returned, sitting down as Mary Wyness brought in a tea tray. 'She's a nice wee lassie,' he observed, after the girl withdrew, then lifted a buttered scone from the plate and put it all in his mouth, laughing at Nell's frowned reprimand.

'Mary made the scones this afternoon,' Bathie told him. 'I hope they're all right.' She waited anxiously for his approval.

'Light's a feather.' He helped himself to another.

The Johnstones were more reserved in their praise when they called in the evening. After they'd been shown all three floors, Arthur took up his stance in front of the parlour fire. 'I was rather taken aback at the area you chose, Albert, and the outside of your property did nothing to dispel my fears, but you have made a fine home here.'

'Thank you, Mr Johnstone.' Albert's face was wreathed in smiles. 'If you'd like to see the shop, I'll take you down now.'

When they went out, Henrietta looked searchingly at her daughter. 'Are you sure you will be happy here, Bathia?'

'I couldn't be happier.'

'I was not altogether happy about it being the Gallowgate, but . . . oh, I suppose everything will work out for the best. What arrangements have been made for the birth?'

'Mrs Wyness, Mary's mother, is to be attending me . . . '

'Mrs Wyness? Is she a qualified midwife?'

Amused, Bathie said, 'I don't know if she's qualified, but she told Albert that there hasn't been a baby round

81

here in the past fifteen years that she hasn't brought into the world.'

Henrietta radiated strong disapproval. 'I'd have thought that Albert would have engaged someone more suitable. I can still remember how ill I was when you were born. I needed a nurse with me day and night . . . ' She stopped, shaking her head. 'I suppose I shouldn't interfere. Albert and you are both so independent. However, I can't help worrying about how you will manage afterwards. Do you wish me to come and live here for two weeks, until you feel stronger?'

The idea of her coping in the kitchen or sickroom was so incongruous that Bathie couldn't help smiling. 'No, Mother, but thank you just the same. Albert's mother offered to come and look after me, too, but you know yourself that I'm very healthy, so it won't take me long to recover. Anyway, I'll have Mary and I'm quite sure she'll manage.'

Looking slightly relieved, Henrietta changed the subject. 'I wish you would make Albert understand that I do not expect him to pay any of that money back.'

'I'm not even going to try. He's proud and independent, and I like him that way.'

The thin eyebrows rose. 'Only like him?'

'I love him, Mother – more and more every day.'

At ten past ten on Tuesday morning, Mary noticed that her mistress halted on her way out of the kitchen, then carried on after a moment. 'Have your pains started, Mrs Ogilvie?' she called out, solicitously.

Bathie turned round. 'I think so. I was having twinges all night, but they're getting worse now.'

'How often are they comin'?'

'I haven't noticed.'

Mary tutted loudly. 'We'll ha'e to time them, then.'

Feeling rather like a goldfish in a bowl, Bathie sat in the kitchen with Mary's eyes fixed on her, until the severe pains forced her to stand up and walk about, and she wondered if the child would be born without Mrs Wyness being there.

Then Mary said, quietly, 'I'd better get Ma now. Just you go through an' put on your goonie an' get into your bed.'

Bathie waddled obediently into the bedroom, and wasn't quite undressed when the girl returned with her mother. While Mary helped her employer to put on her nightdress, Mrs Wyness took a rubber sheet out of her holdall and spread it on the bed, talking all the time.

'Noo, a'thing's fine, jist tak' it easy an' dinna start pushin' just yet. I ken you'll be a bittie feared, but there's nothing to be feared at. It's God's way o' bringin' bairns into the world, an' even the Queen's to go through the same.' She straightened up and looked round. 'Are you ready? Into the bed wi' you, then, an' tak' this.' From the pocket of her voluminous overall, she produced a flat pebble, worn smooth by the sea, and handed it to Bathie as she lay down. 'Bite on that if the pains get ower bad.'

Seeing Bathie's expression of distaste, she added, 'It's quite clean, for I scrubbed it mysel'.'

For the next few hours, Mrs Wyness wiped her patient's brow and kept up a steady flow of encouragement, but Bathie could concentrate only on what was happening inside her body, as her bones were wrenched open by the child leaving her womb.

When Albert came up at dinnertime, Mary said, 'Ma's ben wi' Mrs Ogilvie, an' you'll ha'e to bide here.'

'I want to see my wife.' Albert's stomach was churning at the thought of what Bathie was going through.

'You'd just be in the road, an' they're managin' fine. It's nae place for a man.'

He could see that it was useless to argue. 'Come and tell me as soon as it's over,' he ordered as he went out.

'Go canny now,' Mrs Wyness was saying to Bathie. 'Nae ower fast – easy, now.'

In spite of her previous intention not to avail herself of the 'comforter', Bathie bit on the stone until she thought her teeth must snap and the whole of her insides would be prised out, but just when she imagined she could bear no more, Mrs Wyness's voice reached her again.

'It's near here. One last push an' I'll ha'e it.'

Along with the push, Bathie gave a long low-pitched scream, then suddenly the child emerged with a plop, rather like a cork coming out of a bottle.

'It's a boy,' announced the midwife with great glee. 'That should mak' your man happy.'

'Yes,' Bathie whispered. 'Albert wanted a son.'

'It's a boy, an' Mrs Ogilvie's sleepin' noo,' Mary told Albert, when she ran down to the shop, adding, 'but Ma says it was touch an' go for a while.'

This last piece of information failed to register with Albert, whose brain was occupied with thinking of a suitable name for his son, but when he went up for his supper an hour or so later, Bathie's sleeping face looked so white that Mary's words came back to him: Ma says it was touch an' go for a while.

God, had the woman meant that his wife had almost died?

Forgetting all about the infant, Albert spun round and ran down the stairs, telling an astonished Mary, as he passed the open kitchen door, 'I'll be back in a minute.'

Past the shoemaker's shop he ran, into the next close and up the stairs to the first floor of the tenement. When Mrs Wyness answered his loud knock, he was scarcely able to speak.

'What ails you, Mr Ogilvie?' she said in alarm. 'Is it your wife? Has something happened to her?'

'Did . . . you . . . expect something . . . to happen?' His words were punctuated by gasps for breath.

'No, it was just seein' you here.'

'What did . . . you mean . . . when you told Mary . . . it was touch and go for a while. Did my wife . . . nearly die?'

'Mercy, what gi'ed you that idea? I was tryin' to save her bein' torn, that's a'.'

'Oh.' Albert's relief made him stagger, and he clutched at the doorpost for a moment. 'She looked so white, and I . . . '

'She lost a lot o' blood, but she's fine. Maybe you'd better get the doctor for the next bairn, though.'

84

'Any special doctor?' Albert wasn't thinking of another child just yet, but it was better to be prepared.

'Weel, auld Dr Thomson retired a year or so ago. He was very good at a birth. But they tell me the new man's every bit as good. McKenzie, I think his name is, though I've never needed him for onythin' mysel'.'

'Dr McKenzie? I'll keep him in mind, for we'd better have a family doctor. Thank you very much, and I'll settle up with you now, Mrs Wyness.'

'What did you think o' your son?' she asked, as he handed her the half crown she had told him she charged. His stricken face made her laugh. 'Dinna tell me you havena even looked at him yet?'

'I was worried about my wife,' he excused himself.

'Aye.' She nodded her head, still untidy from the past few hours' work, and brushed away some wisps of fair hair from her eyes. 'Love's a terrible thing. Puts a'thing else oot o' your mind.' Her smiling eyes were a little wistful as she watched him going down the stairs, and she waited until he reached the bottom before she closed her door.

His wife was still asleep when Albert arrived back, so he was able to give the tiny red-faced mite in the cradle his full attention. His first son's head was covered with black down – he was surely going to take after Bathie – but what would life hold in store for Charles Ogilvie?

He had chosen the name Charles because it was strong and had character, and would need no other Christian names along with it. Charles Ogilvie had a ring of importance, he felt, a good Scottish name.

Bending over the cradle, Albert's heart swelled with pride. 'You'll be taking over the shop one day, little Charlie,' he whispered. 'You and your brothers.'

Chapter Nine

Nearly a year had passed and the grocer's shop was thriving, with Bathie serving for an hour or so whenever

Albert had to visit the wholesalers to replenish his stocks. She also spent some time every evening checking his takings, and wrote up his books once a week.

Little Mary Wyness, less than five feet tall in her shoes, kept the house shining like a new pin, and had shaped up well as a cook. She doted on eleven-month-old Charlie, and was looking forward to the next arrival, due shortly.

'I think we'll make Mary nursemaid,' Albert told his wife one evening. 'She can fairly keep wee Charlie in order, and we can get another lassie for the cleaning and cooking. I'll have a word with Mrs Wyness, for I think young Jeannie's due to leave the school at summer, but we could likely get her off before that. It'd be best if she started as soon as she can, so Mary can train her up before our second son's born.'

Bathie smiled to herself. Albert was always so sure of himself, and if he said this baby would be another son, it would definitely be another son. He'd even chosen the name.

'I think Donald sounds right,' he'd said, a few days ago. 'We'll maybe not get right down the alphabet, but we're doing our best,' he'd added, quite seriously, and had been rather offended when she laughed.

Within two weeks, he'd arranged for Mary's sister to leave school, and had made another of the rooms on the middle floor ready, next to the, as yet, unused nursery, as a bedroom for Mary. 'It'll be better if she sleeps here, so she can hear Charlie if he cries through the night,' he'd explained.

Their first child had almost outgrown the old cradle in their bedroom, so he would be going into the crib upstairs when the new baby was born.

Jeannie Wyness learned her duties quickly and was every bit as diligent as her sister, so Bathie had little to occupy her time other than making sure that the layette she'd used for her firstborn was in a presentable enough state to be used again. Fortunately, everything was ready in good time, because little Donald Ogilvie made his premature debut only a week after the new housemaid started.

Although Dr McKenzie had been asked to attend, young Jeannie alerted her mother when she was sent to fetch him, so Mrs Wyness was also present, if only as a spectator.

'It wasna so bad this time,' she remarked to Bathie when the doctor left. 'You just shot it oot like a hen layin' eggs.'

Bathie smiled weakly. 'It's just as well – Mr Ogilvie wants a big family.'

'Men are aye the same. They get a' the pleasure an' none o' the pain. I'm tellin' you, if the men had to gi'e birth, there'd only be one bairn in every family.'

When Albert came up at six o'clock for his supper, he was in high spirits. 'I'm glad Donald gave you no problems, and I think we'll have another son before we start making daughters.'

'I'll do my best.' His wife still felt exhausted, and her soreness wouldn't let her dwell too long on the prospect of producing any more babies. As Mrs Wyness had said, it was all right for the men.

When Mary brought Charlie in to say goodnight, he looked with interest at the new brother in his mother's arms, then touched her exposed breast curiously, and Bathie wished that she'd had time to cover herself up.

'Give Mother a kiss, Charlie.'

He was a good wee soul, Bathie reflected as Mary whisked him off, and she hoped that the one she was changing to the other side would give her as little trouble.

As the little mouth fixed on her again, she thought, if the Queen could give Prince Albert nine – or was it ten? – children, surely Bathia Ogilvie could do the same for his namesake, and she'd many child-bearing years ahead of her yet.

When her husband came through again, the baby had fallen asleep, and Albert leaned over to stroke her nipple.

Bathie sighed contentedly. 'Be careful of the baby.'

Without a word, he picked up the infant, laid him in his wooden cradle and turned back to his wife to lift her heavy breast in his hand.

'Oh, Bathie, I can hardly wait,' he murmured, then bent his head to her and suckled, while she caressed his ginger head and longed for the next few weeks to pass.

It would have been difficult to judge who was the most embarrassed when young Jeannie came in, but Albert was first to recover.

'Haven't you learned yet to knock at doors before you come barging in?' he demanded angrily.

'I . . . I'm sorry, Mr Ogilvie. I didna ken you were here.'

Seeing how upset the girl was, Bathie said, hastily, 'It's all right, Jeannie. Mr Ogilvie didn't mean to shout at you, but remember to knock in future.'

'Yes, Mrs Ogilvie. I came through to put the bairn in his cradle, but . . . '

'I've done it, Jeannie.' Albert was already regretting losing his temper. 'He fell asleep at his feed. If you've tidied everything up, you can get off home.'

'Yes, Mr Ogilvie.' She closed the door quietly.

'After I shut the shop tonight, I'm going to make up some quarters and half-pounds of tea, and maybe some cheese and ham. It'll help when there's a few customers in at one time,' he explained. 'I think I'm going to have to employ somebody to help me in the shop, though, for I've hardly time to do anything but serve. I shouldn't complain, for it's meant that my debt to your mother's being reduced all the quicker.'

'You've done well in your first year, Albert.'

He stood up. 'I'll try not to be late, Bathie, but you know I lose all track of the time when I'm working. I'll tell Mary to come down and sit with you when Jeannie goes home.'

'No, no. Mary needs some rest, now Charlie's sleeping. I'll be all right on my own.'

There was no sound in the house when he went out, and only the occasional clip-clop of horses' hooves as a cart went over the Gallowgate, or the ring of tacketty boots as a weary workman made his way home, broke the silence. Bathie closed her eyes. Life was good, she mused. She'd never thought, when she married Albert Ogilvie less than two years ago, that she'd ever be living in a fine house like this, with two maids, or that he'd have his own shop and be considering employing an assistant. He'd turned out to be a proper businessman.

And she still loved him – his red hair and thick bright moustache, waxed at the ends now, his hands strong but gentle on her body. She ran her own hands lightly over her belly. He gave her so much pleasure, it was little enough that she gave him as many children as he wanted.

When Mary woke her up with a cup of cocoa, Bathie opened her eyes with a start. She hadn't realized she'd been asleep, but felt quite refreshed from it. 'Is Charlie sleeping?'

'He's got an awfu' cough, an' I rubbed him wi' wintergreen, but it hasna done much good.' Mary looked rather concerned.

'Give him a spoonful of honey in hot water. That should help to stop the tickle.'

It seemed only five minutes later, although the clock showed almost half an hour, when Mary burst in, her face anxious. 'He's worse, Mrs Ogilvie. He's drawing back when he's coughin' noo, an' I think it's the croup or the kink host.'

The kink host – whooping cough – was just as serious as croup, so Bathie threw back the bedclothes in alarm and swung her feet on to the floor. Her legs wobbled a bit when she stood up, and she could feel the blood surging out between them, but she steadied herself against the bed for a minute.

By the time she struggled up to the middle floor, Charlie was fighting for breath. 'Tell Mr Ogilvie,' she instructed the terrified fourteen-year-old, 'then run for a doctor. The nearest doctor, it doesn't need to be Dr McKenzie, if there's one nearer than him.'

Mary's feet could scarcely have touched the stairs, and neither could Albert's, for he was with his wife in seconds.

'What's wrong with Charlie?' he puffed as he came through the door. 'That girl was jabbering . . . ' He drew breath sharply when he caught sight of the boy. 'My God, he's near blue in the face. Can you not do something for him, Bathie?'

She shook her head and leaned against him weakly. 'Oh, Albert, he's going to die.' She burst into hysterical sobs. 'My little Charlie's going to die.'

'My son's not going to die, I won't have it.' Albert bent over to pick Charlie up, but halted midway.

Bathie's head jerked up. 'What is it?'

'I remember my mother's neighbour's baby having croup, years ago, and the doctor told them they should have wrapped his throat with something hot.' Albert turned to his ashen-faced wife. 'Bathie, go down and fill a basin with boiling water, and get . . . ' His eyes darkened. 'God Almighty! You shouldn't be out of your bed. Sit there and I'll go and get the stuff myself.'

Before he reached the door, however, they could hear determined feet ascending the stairs, then a breathless Mrs Wyness came in, Mary having gone to her mother to find out who was the nearest doctor.

'I've put Jeannie to get Dr McKenzie,' the woman told them. 'You're better wi' the doctor you ken, an' I'll manage mysel' till he comes. I took Mary back wi' me, an' I've got her fillin' a basin wi' boilin' water for a fomentation.'

She pulled a strip of flannelette out of her apron pocket. 'It's a bit o' an auld sheet,' she explained, 'but it's clean.'

'Thank God you're here.' Albert stood back from the crib. 'He seems a wee bit easier now, but . . . '

'Aye, it comes in spasms.' The woman was rolling up her sleeves when her eldest daughter carried in a steaming basin.

'Where d'you want this, Ma?'

'Just lay't doon there aside me on the floor, Mary, an' go back an' put the kettle on the fire again. We'll persevere wi' this till the doctor comes.'

Poor little Charlie started to cough again and Bathie stood up from the low, nursing chair where she'd collapsed.

'You should be in your bed.' Mrs Wyness's voice was gentle, but firm. 'It's just hours since you gave birth, an' you'll start haemorrhagin' if you dinna watch. Tak' her doon, Mr Ogilvie, I'll manage fine here. I've done this afore.'

Holding her arm, Albert led his protesting wife away, exclaiming, when he saw the telltale stain spreading over her nightdress, 'Oh, Bathie, my love, you must rest. I can't lose you, for that would be the finish of me.'

'I'll need some big towels,' she whispered, through teeth chattering with fear for her child. 'And a clean gown.'

He left her at the side of their bed and hurried off to fetch them, his heart aching with worry for her as much as for his son.

'Go to Charlie, he needs you,' she said when he came back.

Torn between his duty as a husband and his duty as a father, he stood uncertainly until she gestured impatiently to him to leave her. 'Go on, Albert. I'm not moving till you go.'

About ten minutes later, Jeannie burst into the house with the doctor, who had brought her back in his small pony trap.

'Up here!' commanded Albert from the middle landing.

Mrs Wyness stood aside while the doctor examined his small patient, then realized that her daughter was hovering in the doorway.

'Jeannie, you go doon an' see to Mrs Ogilvie. Me an' the doctor'll manage fine, withoot you standin' there gapin'.'

The stooping man smiled briefly. 'We'll give him a mustard bath first, then something to inhale. It's a blessing that this good lady's been here,' he added to Albert.

Mrs Wyness lifted her head again. 'Tell Mary to mak' up a mustard bath, an' to be quick about it,' she shouted after her daughter.

By the time Jeannie presented herself to help, Bathie had stripped off the blood-sodden nightdress and was holding on to the bedpost in her weakness.

'Oh, Mrs Ogilvie, what are you doin' up?' The girl rushed to cover her mistress's nakedness, and took in the situation when she saw the soiled nightgown lying on the floor. 'See what you've done, you've started 'haemorrhagin',' she accused. 'You'd nae business gettin' oot o' your bed.'

In a few minutes, Bathie was tucked up with the towels packed round her where they were needed. 'Thank you, Jeannie. I went up to Charlie, but your mother sent me away the very minute she arrived.'

'An' so she should've.' Jeannie turned to look in the cradle, where young Donald was waving his fists in the air and opening and closing his mouth. 'This wee lamb's needin' to be fed, an' what your milk's goin' to be like wi' this excitement, I'm feared to think.'

Picking up the infant, she handed him to his mother, who obediently unfastened her buttons. 'I'll go ben an' see if Mary's needin' ony help, but I'll be right back.'

When she went out, Bathie closed her eyes, feeling the pulling suction of the child's mouth, and wondering what was going on upstairs.

'Mary says the doctor's steamin' Charlie now,' Jeannie informed her gravely when she returned. 'And he's goin' to gi'e him some ipecac to mak' him bring up the stuff that's blockin' his tubes.'

Her son was in capable hands, but Bathie couldn't banish the iciness that had come upon her, and she shivered violently.

Jeannie recognized the sign of delayed shock, and came over to the bed. 'I'll change the bairn's hippens to let you get peace for a minute, Mrs Ogilvie, but he'll need the other side afore he'll sleep.'

Bathie wished desperately that she could see Charlie, but realized that she could not climb the stairs again. Every movement she made started a renewed draining of her womb, and there was nothing she could do except pray.

Dear God, please don't take my Charlie. I'll go to church every week for the rest of my life, if you'll spare him. Are you punishing me because I enjoy Albert so much? No, you're a kinder God than that, so I'll have as many children as Albert wants, and I'll bring all of them up to be good Christians. Please God, let me keep Charlie. Amen.

She felt calmer after that, until another thought occurred to her – maybe God would change His mind and take her instead of Charlie? She mulled over this for a moment, then concluded sadly that she'd be sorry to leave her husband and her two sons, but she'd go if she had to.

She jumped as heavy feet came careering down from above, wondering who it was, and dreading what he or she might have to tell her.

'He's going to be all right, Bathie!' Albert shouted. 'He's vomited up all the muck and the doctor says he should sleep for hours, but I'll stay with him all night, just in case.'

He stopped, his breathless excitement changing to alarm. 'You look like death, Bathie. Are you still . . . ?'

'I'm fine, Albert, and much better now I know Charlie's out of danger. I'm just tired and I was worried about him.'

Kissing her cheek, he said gently, 'You shouldn't have gone up there, no matter how worried you were. I'll get Mary to sit with you tonight, seeing I'll be in the nursery with Charlie, so you'll have nothing more to worry about.'

Dr McKenzie poked his head round the door. 'I'll be off, then, Mr Ogilvie. I shouldn't think there will be any complications, but just let me know if you need me again.'

Albert spun round. 'Doctor, I wonder if you'd take a look at my wife, seeing you're here. She's been bleeding badly.'

The man approached the bed and felt Bathie's pulse. 'It's a bit fast, but it's not surprising with the worry you've had. Are you still haemorrhaging?'

'No, it was only when I went up to see Charlie.'

'You went upstairs? You're a very silly woman. I quite understand your anxiety, but I hope you haven't done yourself any permanent damage. Remember, absolute bed rest!'

'I'll make sure of that. Thank you, Doctor,' Albert sighed with relief.

Left alone with his wife, Albert kissed her ice-cold brow. 'I hope I never have to put in another evening like this, Bathie. You'd better lie down and sleep now.'

'I'm in the middle of feeding Donald. You'd better tell Jeannie to bring him back.'

'Indeed and I'll not. She can give him some cow's milk. It'll not do him any harm for once.'

Bathie fell asleep almost immediately, and heard nothing of the continued commotion. Mrs Wyness had made Jeannie light the boiler, and it was after four in the morning before mother and daughter hung all the sheets and gowns over the ropes in the wash-house and went home, absolutely worn out.

Chapter Ten

'Mother, Mary's crying and I don't know why. None of us have been doing anything bad, not even Ellie.'

'All right, Charlie.' Bathie laid down her knitting with a resigned sigh. 'Tell her to come and see me.' She was glad that Jeannie had gone out with the two dogs to buy some butcher's meat, and wouldn't be there to inhibit her sister. She'd no idea what was wrong with Mary, but it shouldn't be anything too difficult to sort out.

When the weeping girl appeared, Bathie said, 'Sit down, Mary, and tell me why you're crying.'

'I . . . I'm s . . . sorry, I didna want to bother you, Mrs Ogilvie.' The girl lifted a corner of her long white apron to wipe her eyes. 'There's nothin' you can do.'

'Nothing I can do? Let me be the judge of that. Tell me what's wrong. It can't be that bad.'

'It is, it's awfu' bad, an' I canna tell you.'

Irritation made Bathie snap. 'I'm not waiting all day.'

'Promise you'll nae tell Ma?'

'I won't promise anything. Tell me this minute.'

'I . . . I'm . . . in the family way.' It came out in a rush at last, and Mary's eyes, streaming though they were, opened wide with the fear of what her employer would say.

'Oh.' Bathie was taken completely aback. She hadn't had the least inkling of this, although she knew that Mary had a young man who took her out on her evenings off. 'And Willie doesn't want to marry you, is that it?'

'It's n . . . nae W . . . Willie's.' Mary's sobs turned to howls.

'Stop that noise. You'd better tell me before Jeannie comes back. I take it she doesn't know?'

Mary gulped. 'No, she doesna. It was like this. Me an' Willie had an awfu' row, about nothin', really, you ken how it is. Ony road, I ran away from him, an' I was comin' back here when I met this lad I used to go to the school wi'. He could see I was upset an' he said he'd walk hame wi' me for it was pitch dark, an' I was that pleased to ha'e company, an' I was that mad at Willie, I let Davie kiss me.'

She paused, then whispered, 'When we came in through the close, he started . . . touchin' me, an' I liked it, for Willie's never did it, so when he asked if there was a place we could be out o' sight, I took him in the wash-house.'

'I see.' Bathie decided to let this indiscretion pass. 'Then he forced himself on you, was that it?'

'He didna ha'e to do much forcin'.' Mary looked ashamed. 'It was my very first time an' I liked it.' She blinked. 'Is that terrible for me to be sayin'?'

Bathie smiled. 'Some women might think so, Mary, but I'll let you into a secret – I like it, too.'

'Do you?' Mary looked astonished, but slightly happier. 'My Ma aye says she'd to shut her eyes an' think about somethin' else every time my Da wanted it, an' I thought you'd be the same, bein' a lady.'

Hiding her amusement, Bathie said, 'All women aren't made the same. We're not supposed to enjoy it, but I don't see why we shouldn't. Have you told this Davie . . . ?'

'He doesna believe he's the first man that ever touched me, an' he says it must be Willie's, but, Mrs Ogilvie, Willie's a good laddie, an' he's never laid a finger on me.'

'How far on are you?'

'Five month, so it's nae use tryin' to get rid o' it. I bought a little bottle o' gin, awa' at the beginning, and tried drinkin' that, but nothin' happened, an' I tried takin' castor oil, an' that didna work either. I'm ower far gone now, it would be like murder, wouldn't it, for the bairn'll be formed an' everything? Oh, what's goin' to happen to me?'

Gritting her teeth, Bathie considered. 'Do you love Davie, or do you still love Willie?'

'I still love Willie, an' I've made up wi' him again, but I canna tell him.'

'I think you should, and if he wants to stop seeing you, you'll just have to accept it. But if he loves you enough . . . who knows? He might forgive you.'

'What about Ma?'

'I maybe shouldn't say this, but I think you should tell Willie before you tell your mother. I'm sure she'll look after you if he won't, but give him the chance first. You're not the only girl who's ever made a mistake, and you won't be the last. Now, go and wash your face and get back to my children. You can tell Willie tonight – I'll let you have the evening off – and everything's going to sort itself out, so stop worrying.'

'Thank you, Mrs Ogilvie. I was that upset, I couldna think straight.'

After supper, Bathie told Albert about the plight in which their nursemaid had landed herself.

'I'd never have thought Mary had it in her, the little devil.' He laughed for a moment, then added, 'We can keep her on, if she wants. It wouldn't bother me if she had her own bairn in the house.'

'Oh, Albert, that's good of you. I was frightened to suggest it, in case you wouldn't agree.'

'Frightened? Of me?' He looked somewhat hurt.

'No, no. Frightened for what it would do to Mary if I built up her hopes, then had to let her down. I've given her the evening off to go and tell her Willie, so I'll have to put the children to bed myself.'

'Get Jeannie to stay on, she wouldn't mind, I'm sure.'

'I want to do it myself, Albert. I don't often get the chance to be with them at bedtime.'

Her face sobered suddenly, her blue eyes clouding. 'Were you terribly disappointed that Ellie wasn't a boy?'

'For a minute, that's all. I love my daughter, she looks such an angel, with her red curly hair and big blue eyes, but I don't think Charlie and Donnie ever got in as much trouble as she's done, and she's not two yet.'

'Maybe this one'll be another boy,' Bathie murmured. 'It's funny to think that I'm five months gone, the same as Mary.'

'Aye, that's a coincidence, and I'm just as pleased about this one as I was about the first three, Bathie, but are you sure everything's all right?'

'Yes, quite sure. Dr McKenzie has examined me.'

After settling her three children for the night, Bathie sat down with her knitting in front of the fireguard in the nursery. She knew that her miscarriage, earlier in the year, had been the cause of Albert's concern. It was also why she had consulted the doctor so early in this latest pregnancy, but it was well past the dangerous third month now, and she hoped, for Albert's sake, that it would be another boy.

One of Ellie's kind was enough. She'd arrived a month too soon, and had been difficult ever since birth. She often threw tantrums, and led poor Mary a merry dance at times. When Dr McKenzie had held Ellie up after she was born, he'd remarked, 'She's got a determined chin, this one. She's going to want to be boss.'

She certainly had, for all her tender age, and Charlie and Donnie usually ended up by giving in to her. Yes, her mother decided, Eleanor Ogilvie was going to go through life knowing what she wanted, and making sure she got it.

It was just after ten o'clock when Mary came in, her face glowing. 'Willie's goin' to gi'e the bairn his name,' she burst out. 'He says he'd never asked me to wed him afore, for he wanted to save up a bit first.'

'He's a sensible lad, anyway,' smiled Bathie.

'Would you like to meet him, Mrs Ogilvie? I tell't him to wait ootside in the close.'

'Bring him in.' Bathie did want to meet the young man who was willing to take on another man's child, and who had never laid a finger on Mary in the two years they'd been courting, so she rolled up her knitting and went downstairs.

Willie Dunbar was very shy, but his eyes were earnest as he said, 'I'll never do anything to harm Mary, Mrs Ogilvie, and I'll look on the child as my own.'

He looked at his sweetheart with so much compassion and love that Bathie's heart contracted with sympathy for them. They were both so young and they were having to start off with two disadvantages – a shortage of money and an unplanned child. She realized, with a start, that she'd been a year younger than Mary when she married Albert, but, of course, he'd been twenty-four.

Well, there was nothing she could do to help Mary and Willie about the child, but she made up her mind to give them some of her own money as a wedding present.

Albert came in just as Willie was leaving, and the whole thing had to be told over again. He was pleased that Willie was going to stand by Mary, and he had some more good news.

'I was thinking, when I was in the shop filling up the shelves, we've two attics that are never used. Would you be willing to carry on as nursemaid, Mary, if I let you have them? You can sit rent-free, for they're no use to us, and, in any case, I'm not wanting to make money out of you.'

Mary's eyes were glistening by the time he had finished speaking, and she turned to Willie. 'Did I nae tell you they were good folk? The best in the whole world.' She looked at Albert again. 'I dinna ken how to thank you, Mr Ogilvie, but I promise I'll work harder than I ever did, an' . . . '

'You work hard enough, lass.' Albert's laugh was tinged with embarrassment. 'And, Bathie, I was thinking. Mary and Willie won't need to buy any furniture, for they can use that old stuff of ours, it's still up there, gathering dust.'

Willie had been silent since Albert came in, and seemed to have difficulty now in speaking. 'There's no way I can thank you, but I'll do any jobs you're needin' done about the house.'

'He finishes servin' his time as a joiner in a month,' Mary put in, 'but he can put his hand to onythin'.'

'I'll be getting the best side of the bargain, then,' Albert joked to Bathie, who was almost as overcome with his philanthropy as Mary and Willie. 'Well, that's settled,' he carried on. 'You can arrange your wedding for as soon as you like, for we'll get the place ready for you within a few weeks. Now, Mary, I think you and Willie should go and tell your mother everything, but don't stay too long.'

When the excited couple went out, he remarked, 'It's as well to have those two attics used, to save them getting damp, so it's them that's doing us the favour really.'

Willie fitted some shelves in the attics for his bride-to-be, Bathie ran up some curtains and cushion covers on the box-topped sewing machine she'd bought the previous year, while Mary hand-stitched a fine layette for her expected child.

Two-year-old Ellie, with her father's red hair but her mother's blue eyes, seemed to know Bathie was busy, and didn't pester her as much as she usually did. Occasionally, however, the curly red head would pop round the door and the piping voice would proclaim, 'Challie and Donnie won't let me play wiss 'em.'

Bathie would lift her eyes momentarily from whatever she was sewing. 'Tell them Mother says they've to let you play, whatever it is they're playing at . . . and tell Mary to make sure that they do.'

Mary's mother and Bella, her youngest sister, Willie's parents and Albert and Bathie were the only people present in Greyfriars Church when Mary became Mrs William Dunbar.

Mary had insisted that Mr and Mrs Ogilvie must be there, and Jeannie had been a little put out at first at not being allowed to go, but acting nursemaid, even for only a morning, was such an honour that she soon forgot her grievance.

Bathie's eyes were moist as she watched the bride and groom being joined together; Mary radiant in the blue dress which Bathie had helped her to make, and Willie, uncomfortable in his hard-starched collar and stiff new suit.

'This brings back memories,' she whispered to Albert.

He squeezed her hand. 'You were a lot bonnier than Mary.'

She'd wanted to lend her nursemaid the beautiful white lacy dress and veil she'd worn herself, but he had flatly refused to allow it. 'I want that kept for our Ellie.'

'She's only two, Albert, and Mary would look after it.'

'No, Bathie,' he'd answered firmly. 'And that's final.'

She'd had no option but to give in, but felt sad that Mary had been deprived of wearing a proper wedding gown, although she might not have got into it anyway, being six months gone.

Mrs Wyness had prepared a special meal, which she'd left in the care of her sister, Mrs Lindsay, until they came back from church, and while they were dishing it up, Albert poured out the port wine he'd provided to toast the bride and groom.

After a few glasses, Mrs Lindsay started telling some rather crude stories which caused Bathie to blush, and Mary and Willie to look embarrassed, but Mrs Wyness roared with laughter, and was soon joined by Albert, who had kept his old promise and was drinking lemonade. But, taken all in all, it was a good celebration.

It was nearly three o'clock before Bathie and Albert could get away, and her head was spinning with the effects of the two glasses of port she'd drunk, but she felt at peace with the world as they walked the short distance to their close.

'I'll change out of my finery and get back to the shop,' Albert was saying, when the house door opened and Jeannie came flying down to meet them, her eyes popping and her fair hair streaming out behind her.

'I thought you'd never come,' she gasped.

His happy face changed. 'What's wrong?'

'It's Ellie. She was climbing on the top of the chest o' drawers in the boys' room, an' . . . '

'Out of my way, girl!' Albert pushed past her and ran up the two inside flights, with Jeannie close behind him babbling, 'It wasna my fault, it wasna my fault.'

Bathie's heart, as well as her head, was reeling by the time she reached the middle floor, and she leaned against the nursery door weakly, the scene before her etching itself on her brain.

Ellie was lying unconscious on Donnie's bed, her face waxen and a huge, purpling lump protruding from her forehead. Albert was on his knees, feeling for a pulse. Jeannie was standing at the end of the bed with her knuckles in her mouth and her shoulders hunched up. Donnie was beside the fireplace, anxiously watching his father's movements, while Charlie was sheltering fearfully behind him. Belle and Spanny were cowering in the far corner, as if they sensed that something terrible had happened.

Not one of them was aware of Bathie standing just inside the door, her heart in her mouth, unable to move.

'She's still breathing,' Albert said quietly, 'but her heart's quite faint.' He slipped his arms under his daughter and gently lifted her up. 'The quickest thing would be for me to take her to the Children's Hospital at Castlehill myself.'

He carried his precious bundle to the door. 'Look after your mistress, Jeannie. I'll speak to you when I come back.'

Although obviously very upset and apprehensive, the girl turned to take hold of Bathie's arm, and led her over to the rocking chair by the fire. 'Is there anything I can do for you, Mrs Ogilvie? Would you like a cup of tea to steady your nerves? Ma says hot, sweet tea's best for that.'

'Yes, please.' Bathie's teeth were chattering now, and her voice was scarcely audible. 'I'll be all right in a little while, it's just the shock.'

When Jeannie ran out, three-year-old Donnie sidled over to his mother, his round face white and his brown eyes full of fear. 'Is Ellie going to die?'

'Oh no! She's not going to die.' Bathie was reassuring herself as much as her son. 'Your father won't let anything like that happen to her.'

'He's angry at Jeannie, but it was all Charlie's fault.'

Bathie patted his ginger head affectionately, then saw that Charlie was standing at her other side.

101

'I didn't mean for her to fall down.' His blue eyes were huge circles, and his teeth were biting into his bottom lip. 'I just said she couldn't get on top of the wardrobe from where she was, but she likes to show she's not scared at anything, so she jumped, and hit her head on the chest of drawers.'

Picturing what had happened, Bathie could feel a terrible pain gripping her heart and a pounding at her temples, but she couldn't give way. Tears would solve nothing, in any case, and would just alarm her sons. There was only one thing to do.

Placing her arms round both boys, and drawing them close, she said, very softly, 'Dear God, please let Ellie get better. She's not really a bad girl, just headstrong, and Charlie didn't mean it.'

'No, God, I didn't, but I'm sorry, and I'll never do it again.' Charlie buried his face in Bathie's side.

'God understands,' she murmured. 'Now we'll all say amen.'

As the little chorus went up, Jeannie came in with a tray and echoed, 'Amen.'

The tea did help, and Bathie felt calmer as she said, 'Why didn't you send someone to tell us about it, Jeannie?'

The girl grew agitated again. 'Oh, Mrs Ogilvie, it wasna lang afore you came back, but I was feared to leave her, an' Charlie was feared he'd get a row, an' . . . Oh, I just couldna think.' She hesitated, then burst out, 'What'll Mr Ogilvie say? Will he gi'e me the sack?'

Bathie sighed. 'I'll try to make him see it wasn't your fault, Jeannie, but I can't promise anything.'

Even the boys were quiet over the next hour, and although Bathie insisted that the girl make something to eat at five o'clock, she had to force herself to swallow a few mouthfuls before her sons would touch what was laid in front of them. Jeannie, however, didn't eat a thing.

When a haggard Albert returned from Castlehill alone, just after half past six, his wife's blood ran cold, but he smiled as reassuringly as he could.

'She's got concussion, but they'll let her home tomorrow.'

'Thank God.' Bathie and Jeannie spoke together.

'I told George Pirie I'd be down in a minute to let him go home, for he hasn't had any dinner or supper yet, but I'll have to change my clothes first. I can't serve with my dickie on, for the customers would die laughing.'

'Albert, it wasn't Jeannie's fault.' Bathie had to make it quite clear to him.

'No, I suppose it wasn't,' he answered wryly. 'I'd time to think about it when I was sitting waiting at the hospital, and I know Ellie won't listen to anybody. Don't worry, Jeannie, I'm not blaming you for what happened.'

'Thank you, Mr Ogilvie.' His unexpected kindness released the anxiety the girl had been suppressing, so she thumped down on a chair and let herself go by wailing loudly as she rocked backwards and forwards.

'I'll leave you to cope with her, Bathie.' Albert went out hastily.

His wife thought it best to let her little maid cry her tension out, and was relieved when Jeannie raised her head after a few minutes. 'I'll put the boys to their beds, Mrs Ogilvie.'

'Wash them and take them out to the lavatory first, then. I'll let you do everything, because I'm very tired.' Bathie went into her bedroom, and, as she lay on the bed, she found her mind going over the events of the day. It had started off so happily; dressing for the wedding, the peace of the ceremony, the hilarity in Mrs Wyness's house. She felt thoroughly ashamed that she had never once wondered how Jeannie was coping with the three children. She wouldn't feel easy about leaving them again, and soon there would be a fourth one to worry about.

But Mary would be there, once her own baby was born, and she seemed to have a steadying influence on the wayward Ellie. Poor little Ellie. It would be good to have her home again and up to all her little tricks.

Bathie dozed off, and didn't hear the two boys coming in until Donnie touched her hand. 'Good night, Mother.'

'Good night, my pet.' She sat up. 'Charlie, there's no need for you to look so sorry for yourself. You couldn't help what happened, any more than Jeannie could, but for goodness sake don't tell Ellie to do anything like that again.'

He ran over to kiss her cheek. 'I promise. Good night, Mother.' He made no move to leave, and realizing that there was still something on his mind, she lifted her eyebrows.

'Do you really like Ellie best?'

'Whatever gave you that idea?' She couldn't tell him that *he* was her favourite, her eldest son, born out of the wanton passion of the first days of her marriage.

'Ellie said you liked her best because she's a girl.'

'I love you all exactly the same, Charlie, boy or girl,' she said firmly, and brushed the top of his head with her lips.

His worried, shining-clean face lit up. 'That's what I told her,' he squealed delightedly as he ran out.

Chapter Eleven

For some time after the two infants were born, Jeannie Wyness had been kept very busy. Florence Ogilvie and William Dunbar, both dark like their mothers and fair-skinned like their fathers – had meant a lot of extra work for her. Willie wasn't really the father of Mary's child, of course, but he'd been just as excited as if he had been.

As she waited at the corner of Nelson Street, Jeannie was thinking that she was getting her reward now, the last laugh. Robbie Park might never have asked her out if he hadn't felt sorry for her. He'd always been very friendly, ever since Mr Ogilvie had taken him on after George Pirie had left to go to another job, but it had all started when she'd told him that her sister and Mrs Ogilvie were back on their feet and that she was having her first night off in weeks.

Robbie had come straight out with it. 'Maybe you'd like to come oot wi' me? We could tak' a walk, if it's still fine.'

She'd never been out with a boy before, but she'd liked him ever since she first saw him, and he'd told her, just last night, that he'd felt the same about her. She hadn't told her mother that she was meeting him in case she put a stop to it, and Ma still thought she was working every night. That's why they had to meet in Nelson Street, for fear of being seen.

Jeannie turned with a faster-beating heart as Robbie Park touched her arm. 'You're late,' she accused.

'Sorry, but somebody came in at the last minute and kept me speaking.' He tucked her arm through his, as they walked along the street.

Jeannie was so intent on looking up at her young man, that she didn't see her mother coming towards them, and jumped in alarm when Mrs Wyness let out an angry roar.

'You sleekit besom, an' here's me thinkin' the Ogilvies had ta'en advantage o' you, never lettin' you get a night aff. I'd ha'e sorted you oot if I'd ken't you were meetin' a lad.'

It was Robbie who answered. 'Mrs Wyness, did you never sneak out to meet a lad when you were young?'

'Mony's the time, but . . .' She stopped, then gave a loud chuckle. 'Ach weel, I suppose it's a' right, as lang as you mind she's only fifteen.'

'Ma, Robbie says he wants me to be . . . his steady lass,' Jeannie confided, proudly, looking even younger than she was.

Her mother's face straightened abruptly. 'How lang have you two been meetin' in secret?'

'Just a week, Mrs Wyness,' Robbie said, and added, shyly, 'I've been oot wi' other lassies, but I never felt like this aboot them. It's only Jeannie I want.'

His earnest face won her round. 'See an' nae jump the gun, then. One o' my lassies ha'ein' to get wed's enough.'

Jeannie was afraid that her mother's forthright speech would upset the boy, but he grinned. 'I'll nae jump the gun.'

Next morning, Bathie took her little maid aside. 'I've never had a chance to thank you before, but I want you to take this to show how much I appreciate all you've done to help recently.'

Jeannie accepted the envelope her employer handed her, but said, 'You didna ha'e to gi'e me onything, Mrs Ogilvie, for I was happy to do it. I'll be pleased to oblige ony time.'

When she opened the envelope, she was so overcome by the five pound note she found inside that she ran up to the nursery to have a weep, and Mary was as affected by Bathie's generosity as she was.

Later on, Jeannie told her sister what had happened the night before, and was rather annoyed when Mary told her not to let Robbie go too far.

'You didna stop that Davie when he went the whole way wi' you,' she said indignantly.

'Aye, an' look where it got me,' Mary retorted, regretting having told Jeannie that Willie wasn't the father of her child. 'An' if the same thing happens to you, you maybe winna be so lucky as me. My Willie stood by me, would Robbie Park stand by you if he lands you the same?'

Bathie was quite pleased when she learned that Robbie and Jeannie were walking out. He was a decent young man, and the girl would come to no harm with him, she was quite sure.

Robbie stuck rigidly to his promise to Mrs Wyness not to 'jump the gun', and Jeannie began to feel rather hurt that he did nothing more than just kissing and cuddling. She sometimes thought that he couldn't like her as much as he swore he did, then some sixth sense told her that he was having to hold himself back from what he really wanted to do, and that made her feel much happier. He'd let himself go one day.

For over six months, Jeannie Wyness and Robbie Park met once or twice every week, and Mary eventually stopped asking her sister, 'Did Robbie try onythin' last night?' She could tell by Jeannie's indignantly innocent face that he hadn't, and was glad that the boy was as honourable as he looked.

Albert teased his young assistant by asking, every now and then, when the wedding bells would be ringing, but Robbie took it all in good part, and it was assumed by everyone that he and Jeannie were only walking out together, and that there was nothing serious in it.

It was on Jeannie's sixteenth birthday that things took a different turn. Bathie had given the girl a lovely, fine lawn blouse as a gift, and she looked so beautiful in it that Robbie lost control, forgot his promise and let his emotions run away with him. His kisses became demanding, his hands caressed her until she could hardly breathe for the thrill of it, and she didn't even think about stopping him.

When it was over, Robbie whispered, 'Oh, Jeannie, I was goin' to say I was sorry, but I canna. I've been wantin' to do that for weeks, an' what's mair, 'I want you to say you'll wed me, as soon as I've saved up enough. That is, if your mother winna be against it.'

'Ma likes you, Robbie, an' I'll wed you whenever you like.'

'It'll nae be for a while yet, of course,' he murmured, somewhat shy now. 'I was thinkin' we could go to New Zealand, for my cousin's been there for over a year, an' he says there's a lot o' good jobs. What do you think?'

'Oh.' Jeannie's happiness ebbed rapidly. 'New Zealand? Oh, Robbie, that's awa' at the other side o' the world.'

He smiled. 'Aye, it'll be a great adventure.'

'I'd like to go,' she said, rather uncertainly, 'but it's a terrible distance, an' I dinna want to leave Ma.'

His arm tightened round her. 'Your Ma'll aye have Mary an' Bella, an' you needna be feared, Jeannie, for I'll look after you. Do you nae want to be wi' me?'

She could feel love for him surging up in her again, and it *would* be a great adventure. 'Aye,' she said, family ties forgotten, 'I want to be wi' you, Robbie, for ever an' ever.'

Although Mrs Wyness was rather sad at the thought of her middle daughter going so far away, she wasn't against the wedding. It wouldn't happen for a long time yet, Mary would always be near, and young Bella was still at home.

Albert was very pleased when his assistant informed him that Jeannie had promised to marry him. 'That's great news. She'll make you a fine wife. When's the happy day to be?'

Robbie shrugged. 'Nae for a good while. I'm wantin' to go to New Zealand, an' I'll have to save up enough money for oor fares, so it'll be a year or so afore we can tie the knot.'

The romance in Albert's soul was aroused now, so, after a moment's thought, he said, 'Find a house, and I'll lend you enough to buy some second-hand furniture, then you could be married as soon as you like.'

'Oh, no, Mr Ogilvie, I couldna let you do that.' Robbie looked quite embarrassed at the very thought of it.

'I was thinking about giving you your wages up,' Albert went on, recognizing in Robbie the same streak of independence that he'd had himself when he wanted to marry Bathie. 'So that would help you to save for your fares all the quicker.'

'We're quite prepared to wait,' Robbie said doggedly. 'I only tell't you for I couldna keep it to mysel' ony langer.'

'You're getting a rise, in any case.' Albert was just as determined as the younger man. 'Starting this Saturday.'

'Well, thank you very much.' Robbie's eyes grew wistful. 'Maybe New Zealand's just a dream, though.'

'If you want it badly enough, it'll come true one day, as my wife used to say.' Albert recalled how his own dream had been fulfilled by his mother-in-law's persistence.

Her loan was almost two thirds repaid, and would soon all be squared, at the rate his profits were rising. Of course, Bathie had come into her own money almost a year ago and had offered to pay it, but it was up to him to settle his debt to Mrs Johnstone. He also wanted to do something to help Jeannie and Robbie, and he didn't intend to let his wife use any of her inheritance for that, either.

A few weeks later, however, Jeannie had a very disquieting piece of news to give her young man. 'We'll nae be able to wait to get wed,' she told him, keeping her eyes on his face. 'I'm goin' to ha'e your bairn. I'm two months gone.'

He looked at her in disbelief for a moment, then said, 'I'll wed you as soon as I can, for I've saved a wee bit since Mr Ogilvie gi'ed me my wages up. I'm sorry this has happened, though, for I wanted to gi'e you a better life in New Zealand.'

'I'll be happy wi' you, wherever we are.'

When they told their respective families, Robbie's father, a fish market porter, gave them a few pounds to help them out, and Mrs Wyness, although disappointed that Jeannie had been just as sinful as Mary, gave them as much as she could spare. Jeannie, of course, still had the five pounds that Bathie had given her for her hard work after the two confinements.

Robbie hadn't intended letting his employer know about this latest development, but Mary told Bathie, and Bathie told her husband, as the young man might have guessed.

'Poor Jeannie,' Albert said. 'Robbie wanted them to go to New Zealand, where there's better opportunities, but once the bairn comes, he'll not have the same chance to save.'

Bathie didn't take time to consider, and it was little enough to ask. 'They got some money from Robbie's father, and from Mrs Wyness, but they still haven't enough to pay their passage. Albert, will you let me give them the rest of their fares as a wedding present?'

Seeing his slight frown, she added, 'Please, Albert? For my sake, as much as for theirs?'

He laughed softly. 'Bathie, when you look at me like that, how can I refuse you? But you're not to use your own money. For your sake, my love, I'll give them half their fares . . . '

'Oh, thank you, Albert dear. I knew you'd understand, but will that be enough?'

' . . . and for my own sake, I'll give them the other half. Will that satisfy you?' His eyes twinkled mischievously.

Her radiant smile answered him, before she moved to kiss his cheek. 'Oh, Albert, I'm glad I married you.'

'I've never been anything else but glad I married you. That's the main reason I wanted to help Jeannie and Robbie, like your mother helped me.'

'I want to see their faces when you tell them.' Bathie was almost jumping with excitement. 'Invite Robbie to tea on Sunday. Oh, Albert, I can hardly wait, can you?'

He grinned. 'You're still a bairn at heart, Bathie lass, and I hope you never change.'

'I'm nearly twenty two,' she protested, then burst out laughing along with him.

On Saturday night, when the Johnstones visited, Henrietta went straight upstairs to see her four grandchildren before they went to bed, and came back shaking her head. 'That Ellie is a bright one,' she said. 'She refused to kiss me until I gave her the sweets she knew I had.'

'She knows what she wants, right enough,' Albert agreed.

'The same as her mother.' Arthur glanced fondly at his daughter. 'Bathia was always determined to have her own way.'

Henrietta sat down on the long couch. 'I am glad she had her own way over Albert,' she remarked, 'otherwise we would never have had Charlie, nor Donnie, nor Ellie, nor little Flo, and think what we would have missed.'

Making a wry face, Arthur said, 'C, D, E, F, and A and B to start with? Are you going down the alphabet, Albert?'

'Aye, that's right.' Albert laughed self-consciously. 'As many Ogilvies as we can, though I doubt if we'll ever reach Z.'

'I should hope not!' Henrietta looked scandalized.

'He's teasing, Mother.' Bathie felt uncomfortable about it, however, so she changed the subject. 'Mrs Wyness is going to have another wedding on her hands, soon. Jeannie's going to be married to the boy who works for Albert.'

As she'd hoped, the conversation turned to discussing the match, and then to the opportunities which the young couple would have in New Zealand, and nothing more was said about Albert's procreative intentions.

On Sunday afternoon, Jeannie's eyes almost fell out of her head when Robbie Park arrived with his best suit on and said he'd been invited to tea. She was even more taken aback when Bathie told her to take her place at the table with them, and sat on heckle pins while she watched her mistress dishing up.

As soon as the meal was over, Albert stopped Jeannie from rising to clear the table. 'Stay where you are, lass, I've something to tell you both.'

'I canna let you do that,' Robbie declared when he learned of Albert's plan.

A smile played on his employer's lips. 'I knew you'd say that, for I was the same myself once. But, Robbie, it's Jeannie and your bairn you have to think of, as well as your own pride. I was nearly in the same position myself, a few years back, and I wouldn't be where I am today if I hadn't backed down. Take the money as a wedding present, along with my wish for a better future for you. I'll be offended if you don't.'

Looking at Jeannie, who nodded with tears in her eyes, Robbie said, after a very slight pause, 'Well, I don't know how to thank you, Mr Ogilvie, for I thought my dream was lost for ever, but I'll never forget you for this.'

'You could name the bairn after me, if you like,' Albert joked, as he stood up and slapped Robbie on the back.

'I'm glad it's all settled,' Bathie said, with a catch in her throat. 'You'd better see about booking your passage quickly, so you can be in New Zealand before the baby comes. I'm going to miss Jeannie, and I'm sure Albert's going to miss Robbie, but we want you to be happy – as happy as we've been.'

Jeannie could hold back her tears no longer, and rushed upstairs to tell Mary about her good fortune, while Albert looked sheepishly at his wife, who was beaming happily. In another few minutes, however, when the sisters entered the kitchen, with their long aprons held to their streaming eyes, Bathie couldn't keep from weeping with happiness,

111

too, and stood up to place her arms round the two overcome girls.

Albert burst out laughing. 'Robbie, lad, it's time we left. Come through to the parlour with me, and I'll give you a wee dram to celebrate. We'll get Willie Dunbar down, as well, for us men have to stick together.'

When the women recovered, their tongues went twenty to the dozen as they cleared the table and washed the dishes. The other two smiled to each other as Jeannie prattled on about what she would do once she had her own house in New Zealand, until Mary realized that her sister would shortly be going to live at the other side of the world, and the tears began to flow again.

When the kitchen door burst open, they all jumped round in surprise, wondering who had come in so unceremoniously, and both Bathie and Mary took an anxious step forward when they saw Ellie standing there in her long white nightgown.

'Mozzer,' the little figure announced, loudly, and not in the least ashamed about it, 'Ellie pee'da bed.'

Chapter Twelve

'Ellie's pulling Spanny's tail again, Mother.' Seven-year-old Donnie's outraged expression made Bathie want to laugh, but she maintained a straight face as she followed him upstairs.

She could hear the chaos in the nursery now, but wasn't prepared for what met her eyes when she went in. Ellie, her red curls streaming out, was whooping as she whirled round and round like a dervish, while the dog she held by the tail howled like a banshee.

Flo and Will, Mary's son, both three years old now, were crouched together on the floor holding hands, their blue eyes wide with terror, and Gracie, only two, was bawling loudly. Charlie, who was oldest, and should have known better, was adding to the din by screaming at Ellie to stop.

Bathie's first thought was, where on earth was Mary? This wouldn't be happening if the nursemaid had been doing her duty. Then she took a deep breath and roared, as loudly as she could, 'Stop this noise! At once!'

Her voice floated away in the merciless cacophony, and Donnie picked his drum up off the floor and held it out to her, but the hollow booming she produced on it had no better result. Striding across the room, she grabbed her eldest daughter by the shoulders, and at last the spinning girl came to a halt.

When Ellie saw who was holding her, she dropped Spanny, who shot out like a streak of greased lightning, and all the noise ceased abruptly as the other children held their breaths to see what would happen next.

Bathie's temper had risen. She couldn't remember ever having been so angry before, and without being aware of what she was doing, she swung her hand against Ellie's cheek with full force. She had never hit any of her children before, and, immediately she felt her palm stinging, she was horrified and repentant. She wanted to gather the shocked little girl into her arms, and assure her that Mother didn't mean it, but knew that any advantage she'd gained would be lost if she did.

The stricken blue eyes stared into hers, then the five-year-old lowered her eyelids and a tear trickled slowly down from one corner, although she remained stubbornly silent.

Bathie steeled her heart. 'Ellie, this is to be the end of you tormenting that dog! And I want to hear no more about you misbehaving. Do you understand?'

Waiting until the girl acknowledged this, she walked to the door, then turned. 'The rest of you – tidy up!'

She leaned against the wall of the landing, then sighed and bent down to pick up the poor spaniel, which was cowering on the landing, its mournful eyes fixed on her in dumb appeal.

'Poor Spanny,' she crooned, ruffling his long silky ears. 'You've been missing Belle, haven't you?'

The other dog had died four weeks previously, a fat old lady, at the age of fourteen, and Wattie Ogilvie, in

113

a vain effort to comfort his grieving grandchildren, had been all for giving them another dog, a puppy to grow up with them, but Bathie had refused.

'There's a big enough menagerie in our house with Spanny and Ellie,' she'd told him. 'That girl's worse than any puppy.'

'But they need two dogs,' he'd protested. 'They've aye had two dogs, an' . . . '

Nell had interrupted him. 'Bathie's right, Wattie. It's you that should ha'e a dog, to mak' you walk a bit more. You've put on that much weight since you gi'ed up your work, you'll soon be ower fat to sit doon.'

'Maybe I will, then. I'd ha'e somebody that loved me, instead o' a woman that moans at me from morn to night.' He dug his wife in the ribs with his elbow, and winked to Bathie.

Bathie had known he was only joking, anyway, because there were not a more loving husband and wife in the world than Wattie and Nell Ogilvie . . . except for Albert and herself.

Setting Spanny on the floor again, she went downstairs to the kitchen, where Bella Wyness, Mary's youngest sister, was peeling potatoes. Bathie regarded her silently for a moment, fervently wishing that Jeannie hadn't gone off to New Zealand, because she felt, somehow, though she didn't know why, that this girl was going to cause trouble. It was something about the way she looked at you.

'Bella, have you any idea where Mary might be? I can't find her anywhere, and Ellie's been misbehaving again.'

'Aye, Mrs Ogilvie. She'd to run down to Littlejohn Street wi' her man's dinner piece, for he forgot to tak' it wi' him when he went oot in the mornin'.'

Anger rose up in Bathie again at the insolence in her maid's face, but she said, in a controlled voice, 'She didn't mean the children to be left on their own, surely?'

Bella's eyes slid away. 'She tell't me to keep an eye on them, but I havena had time, for I'd my ain work. She said she wouldna be long, so she should be back in a minute, ony road.'

Fortunately for Bella, Mary came running in breathlessly but she looked apprehensive when she saw Bathie's grim face. 'I'm sorry, Mrs Ogilvie, but Willie went awa' withoot . . . '

'Bella told me.'

The cold voice was like a death knell to Mary. 'Did Bella nae go up? Did something terrible happen? Oh, I'm sorry, Mrs Ogilvie . . . '

Bathie's anger evaporated. It wasn't Mary's fault that her sister hadn't done what she was told. 'Yes, something did happen, but nothing terrible. Just let me know in future if you have to go out. Bella can't be depended on.'

'Yes, Mrs Ogilvie.' Mary shot a venomous glance at her sister before she disappeared up the stairs to read the riot act to her charges.

Bathie kept watching Bella – who was fully aware of the scrutiny, but kept wielding the vegetable knife – then she went through to the parlour, still quite shaken. She couldn't put her finger on it, but there was something about this sister of Mary's that made her flesh creep.

When Mrs Wyness had suggested her youngest daughter as a replacement for Jeannie, Bella hadn't been quite thirteen, and had seemed to be a quiet, hard-working girl like her sisters. As time went on, however, there had been signs of something odd smouldering under her subservient manner, and her deep brown eyes, unusual in one so fair, now looked out between dark lashes in a most disturbing manner.

Her figure had changed, too, and from being a skinny, scraggy child, she had developed into a voluptuous fifteen-year-old, who quite clearly wore no restricting undergarments. Her breasts were like balloons, swinging when she moved, and Bathie had caught Albert, and even young Charlie, staring at them sometimes with fascination.

It would be a blessing if Bella would give cause for her to be dismissed, Bathie reflected, but today's episode wasn't enough, and there was nothing else about the girl's work that could be faulted – only her insolent manner and the way she looked at Albert. But a sense

115

of some impending calamity, a foreboding of evil, made Bathie pray that her husband wouldn't succumb to Bella's obvious charms.

At dinnertime, when she told him how she had dealt with Ellie's escapade, she was rather peeved when he laughed.

'Our little Ellie's turning out to be a bit of a problem, and she deserved that smack, so don't worry your bonnie head about it, my love.'

'But if Bella had done what Mary told her, it wouldn't have happened at all.'

He frowned. 'Bella's a bit of a problem, as well. She bothers me sometimes, with that look of hers. It's like she was looking right down inside you.' If only she'd been sure that was all that bothered him, his wife would have felt easier in her mind, but she shrugged off her fears in the belief that, being a bit under the weather, she was imagining them. She hadn't felt really well since her second miscarriage, ten months previously.

That afternoon, when the younger children were having a nap, and Charlie and Donnie were outside playing with a ball in the quadrangle at the back, Mary knocked on the parlour door and went in looking rather worried.

'Excuse me, Mrs Ogilvie, but I've somethin' to tell you.'

'I hope it's something good, like a baby on the way,' Bathie smiled. 'You've fallen away behind me, you know. I've had Gracie since I had Flo, and you've still only got Will.' She'd thought that her nursemaid had been too quiet over the past few weeks, but this would explain it.

'No, it's nothin' like that, and afore I go ony further, I'm sorry about what happened this mornin'.'

'It's all right. I was angry at the time, but with Ellie and Bella, not with you. It was your duty to your husband . . . '

'That wasna why I went out, Mrs Ogilvie. I just tell't Bella that to save her askin' ony questions.'

Her thin face bore such fear that Bathie was alarmed. 'Why did you leave the children, then?'

'It's . . . I was . . . Oh, I'd better tell you the truth. Willie's made up his mind to emigrate. It's Jeannie's letters,

116

you see, aye speakin' about the grand hoose they've got in Wanganui, and the fine job her Robbie has. That's what's made Willie want to go. He canna see us gettin' out o' the bit here, an' he's gettin' ower-ambitious.'

'There's nothing wrong in a man having ambition, Mary. It's good that Willie wants to better himself.'

'Aye, well, but he's signed the papers, an' we'd to go for an interview this mornin', the two o' us, to see if they'll tak' us in New Zealand. I should ha'e tell't you about it afore, but I was worried in case you'd think we werena grateful for what you an' Mr Ogilvie did for us.'

'We didn't think you'd stop in our attics for ever. I'm happy for you, although I'm sorry I'll be losing you.' Bathie knew what would be expected of her, and tried desperately to find an excuse to turn the suggestion down when Mary made it.

'Bella would like my job, Mrs Ogilvie. She just needs a firm hand, an' she's good wi' the bairns . . . honest.'

Mary's trusting eyes won her mistress over, against her better judgement. 'All right, Mary, I'll give Bella a try, but she'll be out straight away if she doesn't give satisfaction.'

'Oh, thank you, I'll tell her that, an' if you let me show her how things have to be done afore I leave, I'll mak' sure she kens everything outside in.'

'In that case, it's a housemaid I'll have to find.'

The whole thing had obviously been well planned-out beforehand, presumably with Mrs Wyness's help, because the girl burst out, 'My cousin, Maggie, that's Ma's sister's lassie, she's lookin' for a place, an' she'd suit you fine.'

So fourteen-year-old Maggie Lindsay started working for the Ogilvies on the following Monday morning, and Bella went upstairs to the middle floor with her sister to commence her training as nursemaid, although her mistress was anything but happy about the whole affair.

'Remember, you'll have to sleep here when Mary leaves,' Bathie warned Bella, 'so you can listen for Gracie and Flo, in case they waken up in the night.'

'Aye, Mrs Ogilvie, I ken that, an' I'm quite willin'.' The girl's smouldering eyes were serious for once.

In just over four weeks, Mary was bidding her employers, and her charges, a tearful farewell.

'Remember to let us know how you get on,' Bathie told her. 'We don't want to lose touch with you.' She regarded the girl as one of the family, she'd been with them so long, ever since they'd moved into the house in the Gallowgate.

'I promise I'll write.' Mary wiped her streaming eyes.

Willie Dunbar had been standing behind his wife, but now he stepped forward and cleared his throat. 'I have to thank you very much for giving us a home for the past three years, Mr and Mrs Ogilvie. You gave me the chance to save enough to take this step, and I'll always be grateful to you for it.'

Albert, embarrassed, gave a short laugh. 'Forget about it, lad. It was for my own benefit as much as yours, and you saved me a lot with all the jobs you did about the place. I'd have had to pay another tradesman, if you hadn't been here, for I can't even put a nail in straight.'

Their slightly hysterical laughter faded away when Charlie came running in. 'The cart's here, Mary.'

Gulping loudly, she said, 'I'm sorry at ha'ein' to leave a' the bairns. Charlie, Donnie, Ellie – aye, even Ellie, though she had me runnin' roon' in circles sometimes – Flo an' wee Gracie.' She turned now to her sister. 'Mind and work hard for Mrs Ogilvie, Bella, for she'll write an' tell me if you've been . . . ' Her tears choked her, and she grasped her son by the shoulder. 'Come on, then, Will. We'll ha'e to leave now, or we'll be missin' the train.'

Little Will had been holding Flo's hand – they'd been inseparable since the day they were born – but he let it go sadly and accompanied his mother out, while his father lifted their large trunk and swung it on to his shoulder.

'Good luck!' called Albert.

Walking after the children, who were heading for the parlour window to watch the departure, Bathie said, somewhat shakily, 'Mary's been like a younger sister to me for eight years, I'm really going to miss her, Albert.'

'You'll have Bella.'

His wife's trembling lips tightened suddenly, but, as she glanced at the weeping girl standing behind the children, an unexpected pity surged up in her. This was a sad parting for her, too. Bathie stood up, in an attempt to take all their minds off what was happening. 'It's quite sunny today, Bella. I think you could take the children out for an hour or so.'

Taking the two youngest girls by the hand, Bella led them upstairs to put on their coats, while the other three children trailed behind, strangely quiet.

When the school opened the following Monday, after the long summer holidays, life returned to normal, and Bella was left with only two children to look after during the forenoons and afternoons, because five-year-old Ellie started in the infant class at Porthill School, just across the road.

Bella's youthful exuberance made her bored with being tied to the house for six evenings a week, so she tried to think of ways to cheer herself up. Aware that her large bosom excited men, and that Mrs Ogilvie watched her husband when they were all in the kitchen together, she set herself out to attract him. It would be a feather in her cap if he fell for her, and one in the eye for the stuck-up mistress.

Unfortunately, he didn't respond to the sly glances she bestowed on him, glances with the promise of delights to come. Once or twice he touched her breasts in passing, whether on purpose or accidentally, she wasn't sure, but nothing more than that, and she grew frustrated because her own desires had been kindled and because her wiles weren't working.

When Bathie went to bed early one night with a very bad headache, Bella took full advantage of the golden opportunity. As soon as she heard Albert coming up from the shop, she crept down from the middle floor, and, knowing that her thin nightgown hid very little, she had deliberately left off her wrapper. If he saw her like this, she thought, he wouldn't be able to resist her now.

In her bare feet, she tiptoed across the kitchen floor to where he was standing at the sink, then pushed her arm past him to take the kettle out of his hands, brushing against him closely in the process.

'Let me do that for you, Mr Ogilvie,' she whispered, as seductively as she could, when he turned round in surprise.

'You don't need to bother.'

His voice was slightly husky, and she was aware that he couldn't keep his eyes off her erect nipples.

'It's nae bother, an' I want to do something for you, Mr Ogilvie, for you've aye been awfu' kind to me, an' I like you an awfu' lot.' She fluttered her long lashes, and added, softly, 'I'd do onything for you. Onything you wanted.'

Relinquishing the kettle, he turned hastily away from her, muttering, 'I'll go through and ask if my wife wants some tea.'

'I looked in, and she's sleepin',' she lied.

Thwarted of his means of escape, he moved towards the table to sit down, but the girl turned round after she'd set the kettle on the fire, and crossed to stand at his side.

He didn't look up into her face, but, when she leaned forward, he couldn't avoid seeing down the front of her gown, and the swinging breasts with their hard pink tips made him lose his self control. But as soon as his fingers closed round them, he came to his senses and dropped his hands.

'Get back upstairs, you shameless besom,' he ordered. 'For my wife's sake I'll not sack you this time, but if you try anything like this again, you will be out of a job.'

'I didna mean ony harm,' she muttered, but her eyes filled with hate as she straightened up and stalked out.

Bathie had worried about Ellie behaving herself at school, but the girl settled in surprisingly quickly – it was Charlie who created the problem. At first, his mother assumed that he was outgrowing his strength – at eight, he was almost as tall as she was – but as the weeks passed, his eyes becoming dull and sunken, her alarm made her ask Bella about him.

'Is Charlie sleeping all right? He always looks so tired and pale.' She was dismayed to see Bella's eyes sliding away.

'He's aye sleepin' when I look in at him.'

Bathie felt that Bella wasn't telling the truth, so she tackled the boy himself when he came home. 'Are you worried about something at school, Charlie?'

'No, Mother. There's nothing worrying me.'

Bathie was horrified when he wouldn't meet her eyes. It was so like the way Bella acted that it was frightening, but she didn't pursue it. She'd try to find out from Donnie, who seemed normal enough, and often observed quite a lot in his own way. More than he was meant to, at times.

At the first opportunity, she cornered her second son. 'Do you know what's wrong with Charlie?'

Donnie looked at her candidly. 'I didn't know there was anything wrong with him, Mother, but you should ask Bella. She goes into his bed nearly every night, so maybe he's told her what it is.'

Bathie's heart almost stopped beating at the implication of this. 'Goes into his bed? Right into his bed?'

'Yes, she comes in and takes off her nightgown and goes in beside Charlie. I've seen her lots of times, but she's never there when I waken up in the morning.'

'Thank you for telling me, Donnie.' She kept her voice as steady as she could, to avoid transmitting her disgust to him.

'Is that all, Mother? I want to finish reading a story.'

'That's all. No, tell Charlie I want to see him.'

'Don't tell him what I said about Bella, because he doesn't know I've seen her.'

'It's all right, Donnie. Just do as I ask.'

God in heaven, what should she do? How could she deal with this without leaving scars on her son's mind? Looking up when Charlie came in, her heart went out to him, having to cope with emotions he knew nothing about.

'Sit down beside me, dear. There's something I have to ask you, and don't be afraid to tell me the truth.'

121

He hesitated for a moment, then sat down, his head bowed.

'Charlie, you told me there was nothing worrying you, but that wasn't true, was it?' She prayed that he could tell her that Donnie was mistaken, or dreaming, or making it up.

When Charlie didn't answer, she braced herself to ask. 'It's . . . Bella, isn't it?'

His dark head jerked up. 'What about Bella?'

Bathie plunged in. 'Does she come into your bed?'

His face turned crimson. 'Who told you?'

'Never mind who told me. It's true, isn't it?'

'Yes, it's true, but I can't speak about it.'

'Why not?'

'She said she'd kill me if I told anybody.'

'She won't kill you, because I'm going to send her away. You'd better tell me, Charlie.' Bathie's voice was urgent.

'It wasn't so bad the first time.' He looked hopelessly at his mother, pleading with her not to interrupt. 'She came into our room and I wasn't sleeping because it was the day Mary went away and I was . . . crying.'

That was months ago, Bathie thought. Had this been going on all that time without her being aware of it?

'She came over to me, and knelt down on the floor and put her arms round me . . . like you used to do when I was little.'

The pressure round his mother's heart eased, fractionally. Was this all there was to it? Had Bella just been comforting him because he'd lost Mary, and easing her own sadness, too?

But Charlie wasn't finished. 'She said she was cold, and she came under the blankets with me and cuddled me tight until I stopped crying. Then she went away.'

Bathie held her breath. She sensed that there was more to come. Much more. She hated having to upset the boy by making him talk about it, but she had to know everything.

'She didn't come back until the night you went to bed early, remember? And she wakened me up, and came

122

in beside me again. Then she gave me great big sloppy kisses, and asked me if I liked them. I didn't, but I was scared, so I said I did, and she kept on and on at it nearly all night.'

He paused, his distaste for what had happened showing plainly on his face. 'I don't think she came the next night, but when she came again, she said it was too hot with two of us under the blankets, and she took off her nightgown before she got in beside me, then she made me take off my nightshirt.'

Bile was rising in Bathie's mouth, but she had to ask. 'Did she do anything to you, besides just kissing you?'

'She made me touch her . . . ' He pointed shyly to his mother's bosom. 'She got all excited and her breath was hot and coming fast, especially when she started rubbing my . . . ' Embarrassment made him stop.

'What else did she do? You must tell me everything, or else I can't send her away.'

'That was all for a start, but the next time she came, she made me put my hand between her legs, at the same time as she was rubbing me, and . . . Mother, my . . . you know . . . grew big.' He sounded astonished, remembering about it.

Bathie didn't want to hear any more, and what Charlie had told her already would enable her to get rid of Bella Wyness. It was her duty to soothe her son now.

He was still agitated. 'Why did it grow big when she rubbed it, Mother? I felt I was doing something wrong and I was ashamed, but I didn't know why it was wrong.'

'You didn't do anything wrong, my pet. Any boy, or man, will grow big if a woman rubs him there. It's how you're made, but you won't understand about it properly till you're older. What Bella did was very bad, but it wasn't your fault, and you must never breathe a word about it to anybody else. I'm sorry I had to make you tell me, but now I can make her go away for good, and she can't touch you ever again.'

His eyes still regarded her anxiously. 'I grow big now when I rub it myself. You see, I liked how it felt.'

His honesty disconcerted her. 'Charlie, it was wrong when she did it, and it's not very nice to do it yourself.'

'I'll try not to do it again. I was worried when I thought I was doing something wrong with Bella, and I'm glad you say I wasn't.'

'Off you go, Charlie, and we'll never speak about this again, I promise.'

Bathie started to shake with fury when he left. She'd been sure, all along, that Bella meant trouble, but it had been Albert she'd worried about, not Charlie. The filthy, perverted trollop! How could she do that to an eight-year-old boy? Not much wonder the child looked ill, having that on his conscience and being terrified to tell anybody about it.

Waiting until she felt more composed, she went through to the kitchen. 'Maggie, go upstairs and tell Bella I want to see her in the parlour.' She trusted that her voice sounded fairly normal. 'I want you to stay with the children until I come up.'

Bella presented herself to Bathie only a minute later, giving her mistress little time to plan what she would say. 'You wanted to see me, Mrs Ogilvie?'

The girl's swagger, and her old insolent manner, almost made Bathie lose her self control, but she swallowed several times and said quietly, 'Bella, as from this very moment, I am terminating your employment.'

'Terminatin' . . . ? You mean, you're gi'ein' me the sack?'

'I'm sure you know why. I am absolutely disgusted, and I only wish I'd known sooner what was going on.'

A sneer crossed the sensual face. 'Charlie's been tellin' tales, has he? He's a little devil, that ane.'

'You're the devil, Bella. I want you to pack your things and go, and I mean to tell your mother why I've put you out.'

'You canna tell Ma! She'd knock the livin' daylights out o' me. What was the harm in lettin' the laddie feel my tits? He's nae so innocent as you think, ony road, for you shoulda seen the size his cock grew when I . . . '

'That's enough! Go, right now!' Bathie's insides were churning so much it was an effort to speak. 'And if you ever mention this to anyone, I'll . . . I'll strangle you with my own hands.'

The girl sidled towards the door. 'He's goin' to be a right ane in six or seven year. The lassies'll ha'e to watch theirsel's wi' Charlie Ogilvie.' She fired a parting shot. 'An' he kens where to put it, for I showed him.'

She flounced out, but the last glimpse of her face, filled with hatred and vindictiveness, galvanized her mistress into action. The filthy slut might just go to the nursery and take her spite out on Charlie for telling the truth about her.

Bathie hurried up the stairs and heaved a great sigh of relief when she saw Maggie Lindsay reading a story to Flo and Gracie, who were both sitting in her lap with their eyes fixed intently on the page. Ellie was on the floor, colouring some pictures in a picture book, and Charlie and Donnie were beside her, playing with their train set.

Maggie looked up, smiling. 'Will I go down now and see to the supper, Mrs Ogilvie?'

'No, I want you to take over as nursemaid.'

'Me, the nursemaid?' Maggie's eyes popped and her voice squeaked with excitement, making the two little girls look up at her in surprise. 'Oh, Mrs Ogilvie, it's what I've aye wanted, but what aboot Bella? She'll ha'e somethin' to say if I took her job.'

'Bella will have nothing to say about it. She's leaving us in a few minutes, and she won't ever be coming back, so you don't have to worry about her.'

Maggie was full of curiosity about why her cousin was leaving, but she just said, 'Thank you very much, Mrs Ogilvie.'

'I'll go down and see to the supper myself after Bella goes, and we'll sort out what's to be done after we've eaten. I'll have to find another girl to take your place downstairs.'

Bella came out of the next room at that moment, but swept past Bathie with her head in the air, her face scarlet.

Listening until the outside door banged, Bathie said, 'Charlie, Donnie, Ellie, I want you to have your supper up here tonight, so you'll have to help Maggie to carry the things up. I want to speak to your father alone.'

When Albert came up from the shop, her repressed emotions could be held back no longer, and he could hardly understand what she was trying to tell him through her wild sobs. When he did, his face went turkey-red.

'Good God! I should have sacked her when . . . ' He stopped abruptly as he realized that it was probably his refusal of Bella that had made her do this out of spite. 'I'll go down and tan the bloody hide off that bitch right now,' he shouted.

Shocked out of her hysterical weeping, his wife jumped up in alarm. 'No, Albert, let it be. I've sacked her, and Maggie's going to take over as nursemaid. Everything'll settle down and be back to normal in a little while.'

His face was dark. 'Will our Charlie be back to normal in a little while? That's the problem.'

The same thing was worrying Bathie, but she reassured her husband. 'He's young, Albert. He'll soon forget.'

'I hope so. Maybe it's best put behind us.'

She was glad that her husband had simmered down, but she knew that neither of them would ever forget what Bella Wyness had done, even if Charlie could.

PART TWO

Chapter Thirteen

'1900, a new century, Bathie, and we've started it well. Our sixth child.' Albert Ogilvie looked proudly down at his wife, his heart contracting at the sight of her dark silken hair, damp with perspiration, spread out over the pillow.

'I couldn't have timed it better if I'd tried, could I?'

Bathie's smile was weak, for her labour, although quite short, had been harrowing beyond belief. The pains had begun just before eleven on Hogmanay, strong and quick, and she had been more than glad of Dr McKenzie's quiet encouragement as they had built up to the crescendo of the actual birth just as the chimes of the Town House clock rang out midnight.

'But I'm sorry I haven't given you another son, Albert.' Her blue eyes were luminous and apologetic.

He lifted her hand reverently. 'I'm quite happy to have another daughter. Truly, Bathie.'

The doctor stepped forward. 'She needs to sleep now.'

Albert laid the limp hand back on the counterpane and straightened up. 'Right, come through to the parlour and I'll give you your New Year.'

Gavin McKenzie, about a year or so younger than Albert, followed him through and sat down by the fire. As his host handed him a full glass of whisky, he looked up. 'Are you not having one yourself?'

'No, I swore to Bathie, years ago, I'd never touch it.'

'Well, here's your health, Albert, and all your family's.' The doctor took a good sip, shuddered, then gulped some air to cool the fire burning all the way down his gullet. 'This is a grand drop of whisky, man.'

'It's eighteen-year-old malt. I get a bottle in, now and then, to take up to the house for visitors. My father-in-law's the man for downing that stuff, in spite of his wife putting on a face that would sour the milk in every dairy in Aberdeen.'

Dr McKenzie laughed. 'Women never like to see a man enjoying himself with a good drink, do they? My wife's the same.' He paused, then said, hesitantly, 'I have something to say to you, Albert, but I'm finding it difficult.'

'Out with it, Gavin. We've known each other for at least nine years. You weren't here for Charlie's birth, that was Mrs Wyness, but you've seen all the rest of my children into the world, so there's no need to worry about what you say to me.'

'Well, I think it's time you stopped having children.'

A frown of annoyance crossed Albert's face. 'It's not up to you to tell me when to stop, good friend though you are. Bathie agreed with me, when we started, that we'd have a big family, and she . . . ' He sat up, suddenly angry. 'The number of children my wife and I have is nobody's business except ours, as long as we can look after them all properly.'

'It's Bathie I'm concerned about.' The doctor's voice was quiet, but decisive. 'Her health is deteriorating after six confinements. Each one has been that much more difficult than the one before, and with the two previous miscarriages she's had, I strongly advise you to . . . '

'I never realized.' Albert ran his fingers through his fading red hair. 'She's not dangerously ill, is she?'

'I wouldn't go as far as say that, but she's much more delicate than she was when I attended her first.'

'This'll be the last, then,' Albert said, grimly. 'I'll never touch her again, I promise.'

A flicker of amusement came into Gavin McKenzie's tired grey eyes as he stood up. 'It's hardly necessary to promise that – just be more careful. I'll come in again tomorrow.'

'Thank you, Gavin. You said what you did with the best of intentions, and it couldn't have been easy.' Albert saw the other man to the top of the outside stairs, then went back and eased the bedroom door open, just a crack.

He thought he'd made no sound, but Bathie murmured, 'Is that you, Albert?'

His stomach muscles knotted. 'Aye, my love, it's me, and Bathie, I'm sorry I've been so coarse.'

She shook her head slightly, in contradiction, but he carried on. 'I should never have planted six – no, eight – bairns inside you and caused you so much pain, and I hope you can forgive me. I'm deeply sorry, Bathie.'

Her eyes, which had closed a moment before, flew open. 'You've nothing to be sorry for, Albert. I wanted them as much as you, so don't blame yourself.' She stopped to regain her breath. 'We're at H now, so can we call this one Henrietta, after my mother?'

'I was going to suggest the very same thing,' he said, in astonishment. 'We've good cause to be grateful to your mother.'

'I'm glad you feel like that, too. I thought you might have wanted to call her Helen, after your own mother, and I wouldn't really mind, because she's been very good to us, too.'

'I can't deny that it did cross my mind, Bathie, and she'd be very pleased if we did name this one for her, but I thought again. We wouldn't be where we are today if it hadn't been for your mother, so it'll be Henrietta.'

'That's settled, then.' Bathie relaxed and closed her eyes again, and Albert waited until he was sure that she was asleep before he went back to the parlour.

He'd better not share the bed with her tonight. He had to have time to consider what Gavin McKenzie had said, but how could he be expected to think about being careful when he was enjoying Bathie? He'd been waiting for the day she'd be fit to be a proper wife to him again, for he still worshipped her, but he didn't want to endanger her health. He'd just have to leave her alone until he learned how to control himself.

Lifting the poker, he stirred the dying coals, then set it back inside the fender. He undid his spaver buttons, slid his braces down, then slipped his trousers off and laid them over the back of a chair. After pulling his shirt over his head, he lay down on the couch, reflecting that it felt queer to be sleeping in his drawers and linder again, after eleven years.

Annie Lindsay had been told to take New Year's Day off, but went in anyway, for the mistress was too near her time to be doing any cooking or cleaning. The kitchen had been left spotless when the girl had gone home the previous evening, so she was surprised that it was in such disorder. She heaved a resigned sigh as she attacked the grey cinders with the poker, then raked them out on to a newspaper. When the fire was burning properly, it crossed her mind that she should see to the fire in the parlour as well, before Mr Ogilvie or his wife came through.

It was surprising that neither of them was up yet, but maybe they'd had visitors seeing in the New Year with them, and hadn't got to their bed until the early hours. Having gone through the dining room to the parlour, she made straight for the window to draw back the curtains, then went over to kneel at the fireplace.

As she wielded the poker vigorously, a movement behind her made her whip round in alarm, and she fell sideways to land sprawled out on the Persian rug with her legs in the air.

'Oh, Mr Ogilvie,' she gasped. 'What a fright you gi'ed me, for I didna ken you were sleepin' on the couch.'

Albert raised his tousled head and looked blank for a moment, trying to remember where he was, then he smiled. 'I'm sorry, Annie. My wife gave birth at midnight, so I slept here to let her have some proper rest.'

He swung his feet to the floor, meaning to help the girl up, and blinked in astonishment when she gave a little scream, scrambled up and ran out. What on earth was wrong with her? It took him a moment to realize that he was only wearing his linder and drawers. Poor little Annie had been shocked out of her wits, for she'd likely never seen a man in his underclothes before.

Grinning, he pulled on his trousers, then shouted, 'You can come through now, lassie, I've got on my breeks.'

Her face was pink when she returned, and she couldn't look at him, but devilment made him joke. 'It would have been worse if I hadn't had on my drawers.' Much worse, he realized wryly, for his sap had risen at the sight of her bare thighs when she fell over.

She turned scarlet, ignored the remark and rattled the poker amongst the cinders as if her very life depended on it.

Albert went through to the bedroom, where Bathie was still asleep. Just looking at her in the bed, he could feel his sap rising even further and was ashamed at himself for being such a beast. First Annie, though he wasn't attracted to her in the least, and now his wife, not long out of labour.

He hadn't had release for months, that was the trouble, and, Gavin McKenzie's warning coming back to him, he wondered if he'd ever feel safe to mount his wife again.

When Albert's parents 'first-footed' them that afternoon, Nell turned on her son as soon as she came through from seeing Bathie. 'She doesna look weel, Albert. You're makin' her ha'e ower mony bairns – that's eight, coontin' the two she lost, an' she's only a wee bit slip o' a thing. You'll ha'e to be mair careful and think aboot her, for a change.'

'I swear there'll be no more, Mother, for Gavin McKenzie said the very same.' Albert felt that enough had been said, and changed the subject. 'I hope you're not offended that we're going to name the infant Henrietta, but Bathie's mother lent me the money to buy this property and start my business.'

'I'm nae a bit offended, son. Bathie explained it, an' I'm pleased it was her idea an' you agreed. Henrietta Johnstone's a fine woman.' Nell paused, then added, 'You'll nae be able to name a bairn for ony o' the grandfathers, that's one thing.'

Seeing Albert's puzzled expression, she went on, 'You were the A, so Arthur Johnstone's out, an' your father's Walter, an' you'll surely never reach W?'

131

He felt angry for a moment, then, catching her twinkling eyes, he laughed heartily. 'No, I'll never have an Arthur nor a Walter. W's a bit too far down the alphabet for me to attempt, especially now.' He made a face. 'When did you find out what I was trying to do with their names?'

'I think it was when Ellie was born, though I never said onythin'. I thought to mysel', Charles, Donald, Eleanor, that's C, D, E, an' it flashed through my mind that you were an A an' Bathie was a B. It's been interesting seeing what names you chose, though – Florence, Grace and now Henrietta.'

She looked as if she might start lecturing him again, so Albert was thankful when his father joined them, having taken Spanny out for a walk.

'It's time we were awa', Wattie.'

'You're welcome to have your supper,' Albert offered.

'No, no. There's enough upheaval in this hoose the day, withoot us makin' mair work. Wattie, stop fussin' wi' that dog, you've your ain dog to feed at hame.'

Her husband patted Spanny's head and stood up, stiffly. 'You can smell my Nellie, can't you, lad?'

Looking at Albert, Nell gave a small chuckle. 'At least I got a dog named for me. That's aye somethin'.'

She walked through to the bedroom to bid Bathie goodbye. 'Tak' care o' yoursel', lass, an' dinna try to get on to your feet ower fast, for this bairn's ta'en a lot mair oot o' you than you think. Maggie an' Annie are runnin' the hoose like clockwork, so you've nae need to be up.'

'Oh, Grandma, I'll soon be as fit as a fiddle.' But Bathie lay back against the pillows weakly as soon as she said it.

The Johnstones arrived after suppertime, and Henrietta couldn't hide the pleasure she felt on hearing the baby's name.

'It was very thoughtful of you, Albert. Thank you.'

Handing her a small glass of sherry, he said, 'It's the only way we could thank you properly for all you did for us.'

Arthur raised the large glass of whisky he'd been given. 'May 1900 bring happiness and prosperity to you and all your family, Albert. And good health,' he added.

Henrietta's smile faded. 'I thought Bathia was looking quite ill, Albert.'

'It is not twenty-four hours since the child was born,' her husband reminded her. 'She has not had time to recover.'

'I am well aware of that, but I hope this will be the last one, Albert, because Bathia is not as strong as you think.'

Albert nodded. 'It's definitely the last one.'

Unexpectedly, it was Arthur who stepped in to save his son-in-law a further homily. 'Were you very busy in the shop yesterday?'

'It was like Paddy's Market.' Albert rose to fill Arthur's empty glass. 'We were packed out with folk, right to eleven at night. Then I closed the door, because Maggie came to tell me Bathie's pains had started.'

'It was not a long labour, then?' Henrietta sounded very surprised. 'Bathia said that the baby was born at midnight.'

'An hour.' He couldn't tell them of his wife's terrible ordeal during those sixty minutes. It had riven him apart just listening to her screams. Gavin McKenzie had put him out of the room eventually, and had told Maggie to see that he stayed in the kitchen.

He lifted his head with a start when Arthur spoke his name, and was rather disconcerted by the look in his father-in-law's eyes.

'Henrietta has gone through to speak to Bathia again.'

Arthur accepted another very large whisky and took a few sips, then decided to say what was on his mind and shifted his gaze to a large vase on the mantelpiece. 'Albert, I do not relish telling you this, but I, too, am very disturbed by the number of Bathia's pregnancies. You seem to be a stallion, but my daughter is not a brood mare.'

'The doctor told me to be careful, but I forget everything when I'm inside her.' Albert stopped, looking ashamed. 'I'm sorry, I shouldn't be saying anything like that to you.'

Still keeping his eyes averted, Arthur's slurring voice became little more than a whisper. 'Perhaps it would be better for you if you . . . found another outlet for your needs.'

Albert found it difficult to believe what the man seemed to be suggesting. 'Are you saying I should take a mistress? My God, I never thought I'd hear you telling me that.' After a moment's pause, he asked, 'Did you have a mistress? Is that why Bathie was an only child?'

Arthur's pained eyes met his briefly. 'I didn't take just one mistress. Henrietta used to be a frigid woman, but she had a succession of maids who were quite willing to oblige me.'

Great God, Albert thought. What could he say to that? What was he expected to say? It was disgusting to think that this man – a respectable banker, a pillar of society, Bathie's father – had bedded his wife's servants, but he wouldn't be saying these things if he hadn't had too much to drink.

'Mind you,' Arthur continued, 'I have not availed myself of any of them for some years, because my wife . . . ' A little flustered, and perhaps regretting what he'd already said, he went on, 'My wife came to her senses and now grants me my conjugal rights, though she does not excite me nearly as much as her servants did.'

Looking at the thin, dapper man with barely concealed contempt, Albert suddenly recalled how very near he'd come to bedding Bella Wyness. If Bathie had ever refused him, he'd have taken Bella with no qualms, and if the brazen hussy had stayed much longer beside him that night, he'd have done it anyway, qualms or not. His eyes softened. If Henrietta had refused Arthur as he'd said, it wasn't surprising that he'd found his comfort with her maids.

If the man was as drunk as he appeared to be, though, he would have no recollection of this conversation when he was sober, and Albert had no intention of reminding him.

When Annie brought in a tray, Arthur smirked to Albert, as if to say, 'What about this one?'

Frowning, Albert shook his head. Annie's bare thighs had certainly made his sap rise a little, but that was

134

only because he'd been in an emotional state anyway. He'd never given a thought to her charms, or lack of them, at any other time. He was very relieved when Henrietta came through again, even when she looked reprovingly at him through her new steel-rimmed spectacles.

'You'd better make sure that Bathia takes things easy, Albert,' she said. 'She seems to have had a very bad time, and she is definitely not fit to . . . ' Colouring, she hurried on. 'She is not fit to do anything for a long time. I hope you understand what I am trying to tell you.'

Her meaning was quite clear, and he wondered what she would say if he told her that her husband had serviced her maids when she refused him, but perhaps she knew. Henrietta may have been frigid, but she wasn't stupid. She must have known what was going on, so why hadn't she stopped it?

'I understand,' he murmured, 'and I'll remember.'

When his wife announced that it was time to leave, Arthur staggered to his feet and reeled towards the door. 'Remember what I told you, Albert.' He laid his forefinger on the side of his nose and leered at the younger man.

'You are drunk.' Henrietta glared at her husband, then turned to Albert. 'I hope he has not been saying anything out of place. When drink is in, wit is out.'

'He was giving me a little lecture, that's all.'

'Hmmm.' She gripped her husband's arm. 'We will walk home, to try to clear your head.'

Grinning foolishly, Arthur let himself be led out, and Albert went behind him to steady him on the stairs.

'Your father's a bit drunk,' he told Bathie when he went into the bedroom.

'You shouldn't have given him so much whisky.'

Albert could see that she was trying to assess if he, too, had been drinking. 'No, Bathie, I didn't join him,' he said quietly. 'I haven't broken my promise to you. Now, do you want me to sleep on the couch tonight again, my love?'

'No, I want you beside me. Is Annie still here?'

'She left before your mother and father went home. Did you want something, for I'll get it, whatever it is.'

'I just wondered if she'd gone. I told her not to come in today at all, but she's a good girl.'

'Aye, she's a good girl.'

And he wasn't going to make her otherwise, Albert thought, no matter what Arthur Johnstone said.

Chapter Fourteen

The Boer War was over, King Edward the Seventh was on the throne, but life in the house on the brow of the Gallowgate carried on as usual.

Albert Ogilvie, who had never been a very religious man, now accompanied his wife to church every Sunday, although Bathie had a faint suspicion that he only went because he was proud to be seen out with his family.

At twelve, brown-haired Charlie – almost as tall as his father, and very serious – looked quite grown up in his Sunday suit. Donnie, carrot-topped like Albert had been, was inclined to be stocky, even at eleven, but had a twinkle in his eyes.

Nine-year-old Ellie had the makings of a real beauty, her hair darker and more auburn than it used to be, and curling in ringlets round her determined, chubby little face. Flo, two years younger than Ellie, and as dark as Charlie, had a sweet shyness, but Gracie, coming up for five, was quiet and serious, her hair, like her personality, rather mousey and uninteresting.

There was one other girl, not yet old enough to be out with the family. Hetty, born just as the new century began, had been left in the care of Maggie Lindsay, whose special favourite she was, the mistress having been so ill after she'd been born.

The Ogilvies made an arresting picture as they came out of Greyfriars Church, Albert and Bathie leading, the three girls just behind them and the two boys bringing up the rear.

The long points of Albert's waxed moustache gave him a somewhat military appearance, accentuated by his erect bearing, which also minimized his suggestion of a paunch.

Except for a slight broadening of the hips, hidden under her fashionable full peplum, Bathie had the same trim figure as on the day she was married. Her large feathered hat, which matched her dark blue coat, became her very well, and she had found a little milliner to make several in the same style, but in different colours and with different trimmings. There were a few touches of silver in her dark, coiled hair, but, far from ageing her, they seemed to give her an almost youthful air.

As they made their way up the hill, this Sunday morning in 1902, Charlie told his brother twice to hurry up, because Donnie, tired and drawn, was dragging his feet, and seemed to be finding difficulty in matching his step to Charlie's.

Ellie, as usual, was bossing her two sisters. 'Flo, take your hands out of your pockets and stop scuffling your boots. You'll lose your hymn book, Gracie, if you don't watch.'

Albert glanced behind and smiled affectionately. Of his six children, Ellie was still the one he loved most.

'Hetty was a bit fretty when we came out,' Bathie remarked anxiously. 'I hope she's not sickening for something.'

'It'll just be a touch of the cold,' Albert comforted.

'One of the boys in my class is off with the mumps just now.' The voice from behind proved that Ellie was listening to what her parents were saying.

'My goodness, but Hetty's just two. Isn't that too young to be catching mumps?' Bathie sounded quite concerned.

Surprised that she hadn't reprimanded Ellie for butting in, but realizing that she was worried about Hetty, Albert said, 'I don't know, but it's more serious for boys than girls.' His new high collar seemed to be tighter than his old ones, so he put his hand up to pull it away from his Adam's apple.

'Why's the mumps more serious for boys than girls?' It was Ellie again, and her father answered without thinking.

'I've heard it makes them sterile.'

'Albert!' Bathie was horrified. 'You shouldn't be saying things like that to the child.'

He looked repentant. 'I'm sorry.' Lowering his voice, he added, 'But she won't understand what it means.'

'You know Ellie,' Bathie whispered back. 'She'll not stop till she finds out.'

Sure enough, the question came. 'What's sterile, Father?'

'It's something you're too young to understand.'

'Are you sterile?'

Shocked as she was, Bathie couldn't help feeling amused. 'No, your father's anything but sterile, Ellie.'

Albert's proud smile faded when his daughter persisted, 'But why does the mumps make boys sterile? Have Charlie and Donnie ever had them? Are *they* sterile?'

'Ellie, you've been told before not to pester your father with questions.' Bathie tried to be stern, but unfortunately, she caught Albert's eye, and they burst out laughing.

When Flo piped up, 'What's a mump?', her parents almost choked, much to the disapproval of two passing women.

Tapping Ellie's shoulder, Charlie said, 'Why are Mother and Father laughing like that?'

She turned an exasperated face to him. 'I don't know. Flo and me were only asking about the mumps, and I don't think that's very funny.'

Disappointed that it wasn't anything more interesting, he boasted, 'There's three boys in my class off with the mumps.'

His words stopped Bathie's laughter and she turned round in dismay. 'Three boys in your class, as well, Charlie?'

'Yes, and Donnie told me two had them in his class, didn't you, Donnie?' When he looked round and saw that his brother was lagging behind, he added, 'I think he's got them, and all.'

Bathie's hand flew up to her mouth in alarm. 'Donnie!' she called. 'Come here so I can look at you.'

The boy made a visible effort, but his eyes were listless when he reached her, so she took off her glove and felt his forehead. 'Oh, Albert,' she moaned. 'He's burning up.'

'Get him home, then, and I'll go for the doctor.'

'I'll go, Father.' Charlie was feeling guilty for having been irritable with his brother before.

'D'you know where he lives?' When his son nodded, Albert said, 'Off you go, then, and be quick. I'll carry Donnie.' He swung the boy up in his arms as Charlie ran off.

By the time Albert reached the house, his burden felt like a lead weight, and he had to give in after he'd negotiated the outside stairs and the first flight inside. 'You'll have to go up the rest yourself, I'm afraid, lad,' he gasped, depositing Donnie on the first-floor landing.

Hearing them on the stairs, Maggie Lindsay came out of the nursery carrying Hetty – a hot, restless Hetty – but she halted when she caught sight of the equally hot Donnie. 'Oh, Mrs Ogilvie, is Donnie fevered, an' all? Hetty was that bad I made Annie go for the doctor.'

Now that Bathie's fears were confirmed, she bustled about giving orders. 'Ellie, take Flo and Gracie into your bedroom and keep them amused. Albert, help Donnie to get undressed and put him to bed. Maggie, go and make sure there's boiling water, and I'll wash Hetty and put on her nightgown.'

When the little girl was back in bed, Bathie sat down to get her breath back. Thank God for Maggie Lindsay. She had proved to be a good nursemaid, even though she'd had to take over the job at a minute's notice almost five years before.

The girl who'd been hired as housemaid at that time had been willing but clumsy, and it had come as a great relief to them all when she'd told them, less than six months after she'd started, that she would have to leave because her mother was going to have another baby, and wanted her at home. Maggie had approached Bathie shyly. 'If you're needin' a maid, Mrs Ogilvie, my sister Annie would like the job fine.'

'Oh, thank goodness,' Bathie had exclaimed. 'Tell her to start as soon as she can.'

Annie Lindsay had turned up the following morning, very timid and apprehensive, and for a while Bathie had regretted engaging her. Once the girl gained confidence, however, she turned out to be a good cook, and kept the house spotless. She was a younger edition of Maggie – fair hair, large blue eyes, sturdy body – and nothing seemed to put her out of her stride.

It was over four years since Annie had joined them, and she had worked like a slave before and after Hetty's birth on the first of January, 1900.

The crash of the outside door broke into Bathie's reverie, and she jumped as Gavin McKenzie came pounding up the stairs.

'Which one is it, Bathie?' he puffed.

'It's Hetty, and Donnie, as well.'

While the doctor was examining the little girl, Bathie said, 'The children were telling me that some of their class-mates had mumps. Is that what it is?'

His expression was grave when he straightened up. 'It's more serious than that, I'm afraid. She's got scarlet fever, and I could guarantee that's what Donnie'll have, too.'

He moved swiftly through to the boys' room, and, after a few minutes, replaced his stethoscope in his bag. 'Wrap them both up, I'll have to take them to the fever hospital.'

'Oh, no, doctor.' Bathie stepped forward. 'You can't take them away. Hetty's just a baby.'

'She's highly infectious, and you don't want to risk any more of your children catching it, do you?'

'Oh, no, but couldn't we keep the rest well away from them?' She wrung her hands in agitation.

Albert's arm went round her. 'Look, my love, if Gavin says they've to go to hospital, that's all there is to it.'

Maggie had already enveloped Hetty in a thick blanket, so Bathie sadly did the same to Donnie. 'You've to go to hospital to help you to get better,' she told him shakily, 'but it'll only be for a little while, and I'll come to see you every day.'

He was too weak to protest, and his mother's heart ached when she saw the pathetic figure being carried downstairs by Albert, while the doctor bore the small bundle that was Hetty.

Maggie pushed her gently towards the stairs and followed her down. 'You should go to your bed, Mrs Ogilvie, you look fair done in. Annie!' she shouted to her sister. 'Make a cup of tea for the mistress – good an' strong, mind.'

Having stood idle since the doctor brought her back in his trap, the young girl was glad of something to do, and Bathie allowed Maggie to help her to take off her dress, but refused to take off any of her petticoats. 'I'm only going to lie down for a minute, I'm just a bit upset.' She sat down suddenly on the edge of the bed, proving to both of them just how upset she was.

The nursemaid waited until Bathie drank the tea. 'Have a wee rest now, me an' Annie'll strip all the bairns' beds, an' fumigate them. I'll light the washhouse boiler afore I go to my bed, so's it'll be ready first thing the morn.'

She withdrew quietly, and Bathie thought ruefully that it was senseless making herself ill. Hetty and Donnie would be well looked after, but she prayed that the others hadn't been infected. Apart from colds, and Charlie's baby croup, this was the first illness which had affected any of her family. There had been the time when Ellie knocked herself unconscious, of course, but this was different.

Inexplicably, her thoughts turned to Mary Wyness, her first nursemaid, who had kept the promise she'd made on the day she left, and had written every Christmas with news of her family. Willie Dunbar was now second in charge of a joinery business in Wanganui, but there was no sign yet of a little sister or brother for young Will, who had been born in the Gallowgate on the same day as Flo.

Mary's sister, Jeannie, had two children, and her husband, Robbie Park, was now manager of the largest grocery store in the same town. They lived only a short distance away from the Dunbars, and Mary often sent photographs of them all in the garden of one or other of the houses.

When Mrs Wyness had found out why Bathie had dismissed her youngest daughter, she'd taken Bella off to New Zealand, too, in an attempt to give the girl a fresh start.

'I'm that ashamed,' she'd explained to Bathie, 'I'll never be able to trust her again, the sleekit besom.'

But her own health had given way not very long after they arrived in Wanganui, and she had passed away six months later.

For three years, Mary hadn't mentioned Bella in any of her letters, then she'd written, 'I've got Bella off my hands at last. Ma would have turned in her grave at some of the carry-ons she's had, but the man that's married her will keep her in about. God knows what he saw in her, for he knew what like she was, but he'll stand no nonsense from her. He's got a grand business and a fine house with servants, so she landed on her feet, after all.'

Bathie felt her gut twisting at the memory of what Bella Wyness had done to Charlie. Charlie? Great God, where on earth was Charlie? She hadn't seen him since he'd run off to fetch the doctor for Donnie, but Annie must have been there long before him.

The doctor's wife would surely have told the boy that her husband was already on his way, and he should have been home by this time. Something must have happened to him.

In great agitation, Bathie jumped out of bed and ran on to the landing. 'Annie!' she shouted. 'Have you seen Charlie?'

The girl came to the kitchen door. 'Is he nae up in the nursery wi' the lassies?'

'I don't think so, but go up and see, will you?'

Bathie had just pulled on a skirt and blouse when Annie came running back. 'He's nae there, Mrs Ogilvie, an' Maggie hasna seen him since you came back fae the kirk.'

'Oh, dear God!' Bathie's fingers could hardly cope with her small buttons. 'He went to get Dr McKenzie for Donnie, and he hasn't come back.'

'Maybe Mrs McKenzie didna ken the doctor had came here, and she'd tell't Charlie to wait. Will I run back an' see?'

'Yes, please, Annie, as quickly as you can.'

Maggie came downstairs as the outside door closed after her sister. 'Have you found Charlie yet, Mrs Ogilvie? Ellie was tellin' me he went for the doctor, an' all.'

'We didn't know you'd sent Annie,' Bathie explained, 'and he said he knew where to go, but I should never have let him go on his own.'

'He'll come to nae harm. He's got a good Scots tongue in his heid, an' he'd ask somebody if he found himsel' lost.'

Bathie doubted if Charlie would approach a stranger – he was very shy, and might wander about until he dropped – so she was glad when Albert walked in.

His first words were, 'They'll be fine, Bathie. There's no need for you to look so tragic.'

Her brain was concentrating on one thing, and his words meant nothing. 'Charlie's missing,' she burst out.

'Missing? What do you mean, missing?'

'He never came back from the doctor's, and Annie's gone to see if he's still with Mrs McKenzie.' Leaning against him, she wept softly.

He looked at Maggie helplessly for a moment, then thrust his wife aside. 'I'll have to go out and look for him myself, Bathie. I can't just sit here waiting for him to turn up.'

'All right.' Her hands were tight balls against her chest.

'I'll have a look in Mounthooly, for he might have gone up there by mistake, and Maggie, will you go down the other way on to Union Street? If he was lost, he could have taken a few wrong turnings. You'll have to stay with the girls, Bathie, and when Annie comes back, tell her to go down Innes Street on to Loch Street, round the back, just in case.'

The slam of the outside door as he and Maggie both went out, was followed by Ellie's voice drifting plaintively down the stairs. 'Mother, when are we getting our dinner? We're all starving up here.'

Pulling herself together, Bathie called back. 'You can come down now. I'm sure it's been ready for ages.'

In the kitchen, she carved the roast beef and dished up the vegetables, relieved that they hadn't spoiled with sitting on top of the range for so long.

Ellie sniffed appreciatively when she ushered in her two sisters. 'That smells good. But where's Maggie?' Her puzzled expression deepened as she looked round the kitchen. 'Where's everybody gone? I can't find Charlie anywhere, either. And why've we had to wait so long for our dinner? Flo and Gracie and me thought we were never going to get it.'

'They've all had to go out, but you three can have yours just now, and I'll wait for Father.' The very thought of eating made Bathie's stomach cramp. 'Set the table for yourselves, Ellie, there's a good girl.'

Annie returned while the girls were still eating. 'The doctor's wife never seen Charlie at all, so he musta got lost afore he even got there.'

Fighting down her mounting hysteria, Bathie passed on Albert's instructions, and Annie went out again obediently, but Ellie fastened on to the girl's last few words.

'Is Charlie lost, Mother?'

Fragile nerves made Bathie snap. 'You heard what Annie said, so stop asking.' She regretted her sharpness when she saw Ellie biting her lip to stop it quivering.

The girl didn't touch the rest of her dinner, which was most unusual, but waited until Flo and Gracie were finished before she stood up. 'Come upstairs with me,' she ordered them. 'Mother wants some peace.'

As her daughters made for the door, Bathie said, softly, 'Thank you, Ellie, dear.'

Clearing the dishes, it struck her that a good, strong cup of tea might buck her up, but her actions were slow when she moved over to rinse out the teapot, and it took a great effort to lift the tea caddy down from the mantelshelf.

It was almost half past three, a good hour after Annie had gone out again, before Bathie heard voices and feet on the outside stairs and ran to the kitchen door with her arms held out, sure that one of the searchers had found Charlie. Her smile faded when she saw that it was Maggie, accompanied by a tall policeman, who removed his helmet when he entered.

'Charlie's not . . . ?' she gasped, anxiously.

'I havena seen him.' Maggie shook her head sadly. 'This bobby came oot when I was passin' Lodge Walk, so I tell't him aboot Charlie, an' he came to see if the bairn had come back.'

The uniformed man stepped forward. 'I'd be glad if you could give me a description of the boy and the clothes he was wearing. Anything that would help us to identify him.'

He noted down the details as Bathie gave them, then said, 'When did you see him last?'

'About twenty past twelve.'

The iron band round Bathie's heart was easing a little. She felt that she could place her trust in this man, ordinary constable though he was, for his round healthy face was full of concern and his eyes full of compassion. 'He went to get the doctor for my other son, when we were coming home from church,' she told him.

'Where's your doctor's house? That should give us some idea of where to start looking.'

'It's in Froghall, off the Spital, but he never reached there.' Bathie's hands clutched nervously at her skirt.

'He could have missed the turning, and if he'd kept on walking, he'd have . . . ' The policeman halted, then said briskly, 'We'll find him, so try not to worry.'

Maggie took off her coat when the policeman left. 'Have you had ony dinner yet, Mrs Ogilvie?'

'I gave the girls theirs, but I just had a cup of tea.'

'That was a good while ago, I'll be bound, so I'll mak' you another cup, but I'd best go up the stair first, to see what mischief Ellie's been up to.'

'She knows Charlie's lost, and realizes how worried I am, and she's kept Flo and Gracie upstairs ever since.'

'Well I never, but I'll go up just the same.'

Maggie looked surprised when she returned. 'She's readin' to them, would you credit? There's hope for oor Ellie yet.'

'They might be needing something to drink, too, for it's quite a while since they had anything.'

'I said I'd tak' up milk an' biscuits once we've had oor ain cuppie.'

They had just sat down to drink their 'cuppie' when Annie came running in. 'Is Charlie back yet?' She sank breathlessly on to a chair, the hope in her eyes fading at the grave expression on the other two women's faces.

'The bobbies are goin' to be lookin' for him.' Maggie poured out another cup of tea.

Lifting it thoughtfully, Annie said, 'What a thing for this to happen the same day as your other two got the fever, Mrs Ogilvie. It's right enough what they say aboot troubles never comin' single, isn't it?'

Her other two! Disgust at herself almost overwhelmed Bathie. She hadn't given a thought to Hetty and Donnie since she'd realized that Charlie was missing. She'd forgotten that Albert had taken them to hospital, and hadn't even asked about them when he came back.

Frowning at her sister for upsetting the mistress, Maggie said, 'Dinna fret yoursel' aboot Donnie an' Hetty, Mrs Ogilvie. They're in the right place, an' the nurses in the fever hospital are used wi' little bairns.'

Annie tried to redeem herself. 'Aye, they get them to stop greetin' for their ma in nae time.'

Had Hetty and Donnie been crying because their mother wasn't there? Poor lambs, and their mother had forgotten all about them. Every inch of Bathie's tense body turned ice-cold, but she forced herself to say something, anything, to stop herself from breaking down altogether. 'Have you any idea how long they'll be kept in the fever hospital, Maggie?'

'I think it's aboot six weeks or so, dependin' how bad they've got it, but they'll nae be let oot till they're clear o' the infection, in case they smit the rest of the family.'

'I'll go to see them as soon as Charlie's been found.'

Maggie's sorrowful eyes narrowed with pity. 'You'll nae get inside, mind. They just let you look at them through the window, for fear you catch it, an' all.'

'They'll have to let me in when I say I'm their mother.' Bathie was indignant now.

'It's the rules, Mrs Ogilvie, so dinna get upset.'

Not get upset? Bathie had believed that she couldn't feel worse than she'd done over the past few hours, but this was a further catastrophe. She'd never dreamt that she would be kept from hugging her sick children in hospital, but at least, she *would* see them, if only through a window. Would she ever see Charlie again?

At half past five, Albert dragged his aching feet up the outside stairs. 'Has he . . . ?' His shoulders sagged when he saw the worry still stamped on their faces.

Although her first inclination had been to run to her husband for comfort, Bathie remained seated – he looked in need of comfort himself. 'The police are looking for him now, Albert, so sit down and have something to eat.'

Annie jumped to her feet. 'Aye, Mr Ogilvie, you look fair dead beat. I'm makin' some scrambled eggs for the lassies, but if you want, I'll easy heat up some o' the beef an' vegies.'

'Thank you, Annie, but I'm not hungry.' The hopelessness in his voice dismayed them. 'A cup of tea's all I want.'

The noise of the metal whisk, as Annie beat the eggs in a bowl, was the only sound in the kitchen for a time, but when the mixture was poured into the pan, Maggie stood up.

'I'll set a tray to tak' their supper up.'

Albert disappeared into the parlour, leaving his wife to wonder what he intended to do, and when he returned, she was amazed to see him holding a bottle of brandy in his hand.

'I think we'd all be the better for a drop of this,' he said. 'God knows how long we'll have to wait, so we'll maybe have a long night in front of us, and brandy's the best thing to steady our nerves.'

Bathie had never tasted brandy before, and she'd no doubt that Maggie and Annie hadn't, either, but one glass wouldn't do them any harm. Nor Albert, she reflected compassionately, as long as he stuck to only one.

'Just a small glass each, then,' she told him.

Later, while Annie tidied up, Maggie went upstairs to make sure that her remaining charges were ready for bed, and Albert went outside to fill the coal scuttles for the kitchen, the parlour and the nursery.

When they were all seated again, Bathie said, 'You'd better go home, Annie, when you're finished there. Your mother will be worrying about you.'

'I'm not goin' oot o' this hoose till I see young Charlie back, safe an' sound,' Annie retorted, hands on her hips and feet planted wide-apart on the floor.

It was heartwarming to Albert that the little housemaid was just as concerned for Charlie's safety as the rest of them. 'So be it, but we'd all be more comfortable in the parlour.'

They left Annie stoking up the range – 'We'll maybe need a puckle cups o' tea to see us through' – and went into the other room, where Bathie half collapsed into one of the easy chairs. Maggie waited politely for Albert to seat himself on the other one before she sat down on the couch, but he couldn't settle, and paced backwards and forwards by the window.

Bathie lifted her head. 'Please stop that, Albert, you're only making things worse. And Maggie, sit down, for goodness sake, you've been on the go the whole day.'

When Annie came in, she sat beside her sister, placing herself, like Maggie, on the edge of the seat, because she felt ill-at-ease sitting down in the parlour.

The ornate clock on the mantelpiece ticked away minutes which seemed like hours, and at nine o'clock, Annie cleared her throat. 'I'll see if the lassies are sleepin'.'

Her quiet words rang through the silence, the click of the door, as she closed it, echoing like a rifle report in a still clearing, as Maggie murmured, 'She's needin' something to do.'

Albert jumped to his feet. 'I can't stand this, Bathie. It's my duty as a father to be out looking for Charlie.'

'He's my son, too,' Bathie said, softly. 'Let me come with you this time, Albert. Please?'

The anguish on her face made up his mind. 'Only if you promise to come home the minute you feel tired.'

She was already exhausted, but nodded. 'I promise. Wait till I get my coat.' When she came back, her face grey and huge dark shadows framing her sunken eyes, he almost put his foot down and ordered her to stay in the house, but her set, determined mouth made him bite back the words.

Instead, he said, 'We're leaving you in charge, Maggie, and if Charlie does happen to come back, see that he gets something to eat and a hot bath, before he goes to bed.'

'You can depend on me, Mr Ogilvie.'

He strode down the Gallowgate so quickly that Bathie had a stitch in her side before they arrived at Froghall, where Albert had been heading although she hadn't realized it. He halted outside Dr McKenzie's house.

She was glad of the chance to get her breath back, but couldn't see the point of wasting time by asking the doctor if he'd seen Charlie. He'd have brought him home, if he had.

'It's no use going in there,' she gasped.

'Gavin's got a trap. He could cover a lot more ground than we can on our feet.'

'You can't ask him to go out looking.' She was surprised that her husband could even suggest it.

'I'm sure he'd be very pleased at being asked.' Albert opened the gate and Bathie followed him up the curving path.

Gavin McKenzie didn't wait to be asked. As soon as he opened the door, he said, 'My wife told me your maid was here looking for Charlie, but I thought he'd have turned up by this time. Look, I'll harness my shelty and start looking, too.'

He disappeared into the house, but a minute or so later, his wife came out to speak to them. 'The boy

149

never reached here,' she said, sympathetically. 'Gavin says he still hasn't come home, but I hope you find him soon.'

'Thank you.' Bathie's teeth were chattering now, with cold or fear, or both, she couldn't really tell.

Albert gripped her arm as they heard the pony and trap coming round the side of the house. 'Gavin, I'd be obliged if you'd take Bathie with you, for she's too tired and upset to carry on walking, but she won't give in. I'll carry on looking by myself.'

Bathie accepted the doctor's outstretched hand to help her up into the little cart. What was the good of arguing?

For almost three-quarters of an hour, the pony plodded round side streets in ever-widening circles, without any sign of her son, and Bathie dug her teeth into her lower lip to stop herself from bursting into tears.

At last, the doctor said, 'I think we should go straight on for a while. If Charlie missed Froghall, and went on up the Spital, he'd have come to the River Don eventually. I don't want to alarm you, Bathie, but we have to face facts.'

Her senses were so numb, now, that nothing could affect her any more. 'All right,' she whispered. 'Whatever you think's best.'

The young constable had stopped himself from warning her about this, she realized. He hadn't wanted to alarm her by hinting that Charlie might have . . . drowned in the treacherous currents of the Don. She closed her mind to the possibility.

Their eyes searched from side to side as they went slowly along, but in vain. There were few people about this late on a Sunday, and the drizzle had turned to steady rain, making sure that no one went out unless it was necessary.

Occasionally, they saw a figure, shoulders hunched against the weather, and stopped to ask if he or she had seen a boy wandering about on his own.

The answer was always no.

Chapter Fifteen

'It's nae use upsettin' yoursel' like this, Mary.' Jeannie Park, née Wyness, patted her sister's heaving shoulders sympathetically. 'It winna bring Willie back, an' you've young Will to think aboot.'

'I ken, but . . . oh, I wish we'd never came to Wanganui. If we hadna left Aberdeen, Willie would still be alive. Joiners never have to clim' aboot on roofs o' granite-built hooses.'

Mary Dunbar, also née Wyness, started a renewed bout of weeping, making Robbie Park shake his head briefly at his wife, who ignored the warning.

'It's a blessin' Willie didna live, Mary,' she carried on. 'The doctor at the hospital tell't Robbie that he'd ha'e been a vegetable, his heid was that damaged when he fell.'

Robbie stepped forward and gripped her arm. 'Jeannie,' he said firmly, 'that's enough.'

His wife's words, instead of upsetting Mary further as he'd fearfully expected, seemed to fortify the bereaved woman.

'I'm bein' selfish.' Mary held her sodden handkerchief to her eyes. 'I'm thinkin' o' mysel', when I should be gratefu' Willie didna ha'e to suffer.' Gulping, she carried on. 'It was just that sudden, an' it's goin' to tak' a lang time for me to get used to it.'

Jeannie couldn't help shooting a small glance of triumph at her husband, who acknowledged it with a slight shrug. 'I'll mak' another pot o' tea,' she said, 'then we'll be gettin' hame.'

As she walked away, her other sister, Bella, moved over to speak to the new widow. 'Matt and I won't wait for tea, Mary.'

'It was good o' you both to come.' As Mary looked up, she marvelled for the hundredth time at the change Matthew Potter had wrought in Bella.

The youngest Wyness was now a poised, well-spoken woman, with no trace of the guttural Aberdeen accent in which her sisters spoke to each other. Her simple black dress looked expensive, but in very good taste, her blonde hair was drawn back in an elegant chignon and no one who hadn't known her before could possibly have guessed the kind of person she'd been when she first arrived in New Zealand.

Beckoning her husband over, Bella took hold of his arm possessively. 'I was saying that we'd have to leave, Matt.'

'We don't have to go just yet.'

'You usually can't wait to get back to your office.'

'They'll manage without me. I have something to discuss with Mary when everyone else goes.' His bright eyes dimmed as he turned sympathetically to the woman in black.

'Oh, as you like, then.' Bella looked displeased, but went over to speak to the man who had been Willie Dunbar's employer and who was still shocked at what had happened.

Matt bent his head to his sister-in-law. 'I'm afraid Bella's still quite easily bored,' he apologized.

Mary nodded. 'You've worked wonders wi' her, though.'

'I can't say it's because she loves me,' he said, somewhat ruefully, 'just my money. I used to think, at one time, that my love for her would be enough to change her completely, but I must admit that I've been disillusioned over the years. One-sided love isn't enough for a marriage, and fades with neglect.'

'She must care for you a bit,' Mary protested, 'for she wouldna stop on wi' you if she didna.'

He smiled, but was prevented from saying anything more by Jeannie's entrance.

'Sit doon, everybody, so I can hand roon' the cups.'

While the mourners were thus occupied, Mary studied Matt. He was tall and very handsome, with a strong jaw and piercing blue eyes, and he was a lot better than her sister deserved. She wondered idly what he wanted to discuss with her. If he was going to offer money, she'd refuse, for she wasn't going to be a beggar even if she hadn't two bawbees to rub together, and her poor man had always made a point of being independent.

Just look how Mr Ogilvie'd had to persist until Willie agreed to take the two attics in the Gallowgate. Oh, they'd been good days, happy days, there. She often had a little weep when she remembered the bairns she'd looked after – Charlie and Donnie, Ellie and little Flo, born the same day as her Will.

She and Jeannie often reminisced about that day. Dr McKenzie and their mother had been running round in circles attending to the two confinements. Poor Ma. She hadn't lasted long after she came to New Zealand, and she'd flatly refused to tell them what had made her leave Aberdeen.

Mary had the suspicion that it was something that Bella had done, but she couldn't imagine what would have been bad enough to make Mrs Ogilvie give her the sack. It couldn't have been anything to do with the bairns; surely Bella would never have neglected them?

Had she tried to come between Mr and Mrs Ogilvie, like she'd done with so many men and their wives here? She'd not have managed to do it anyway, for the master would never have been unfaithful to the mistress, that was one thing sure. He loved her too much for that.

Heaving a sigh as she reflected that she still looked on them as master and mistress, Mary knew that she would likely never know the truth, so she should stop worrying about it. Bella was settled now, and Matt made sure she behaved herself.

She came out of her reverie with a start when Jeannie removed the cup from her hand. 'Leave the dishes, it'll be somethin' to keep me busy when you all go.'

'Are you sure?' Jeannie regarded her closely. 'It would let me get away quicker, for I dinna like leavin' the bairns ower lang, though Betty said there was nae hurry.'

Betty was the Parks' next door neighbour, and had offered to look after their two children, and young Will Dunbar, until they came back from the funeral.

'Aye, I'm sure,' Mary said firmly, 'so awa' you go hame. I'm fine now, an' Bella an' Matt's stoppin' on a wee while.'

'Oh?' Jeannie couldn't hide her astonishment. 'I wonder what Bella's up to? Nothin' good, I bet.'

'It was Matt said he'd something he wanted to discuss wi' me, but I've nae idea what.'

'You can tell me the morn, when I tak' Will back.' Jeannie hesitated for a moment. 'If he offers you money, tak' it, for he can weel afford it.'

She whisked away before her sister could say anything, and within a few minutes, only three people remained in the small bungalow. Bella smoothed her skirt carefully before she sat down on the other side of the stove, while Matt drew a chair up beside his sister-in-law.

'Now, Mary,' he began, softly, 'I've been thinking this over ever since I heard of Willie's accident, so it's not a spur-of-the-moment decision. I suppose there isn't . . . ?' He paused, as if unsure of how to phrase his question. 'I suppose he didn't have much savings?'

Permitting herself a slight smile, Mary said, 'None at all, hardly, after paying for this house, but if you're goin' to suggest givin' me money, you needna bother. I'll not take it.'

The man smiled now. 'I knew you wouldn't, that's why I'm not offering you any. I want you to sell up here, and come to live with Bella and me.' He shook his head and frowned to stop her protest. 'Just hear me out. Will would be company for Martin – like an older brother – and I'd see that he had a good education. My house is big enough for all of us – you could have your own little flat – and if you want to keep your Scottish independence, I could let you have a job in my factory.'

'You might have asked what I thought, before you said anything to Mary.' The interruption came from Bella, whose face had darkened the minute she heard what was in his mind.

'This has nothing to do with you, Bella,' he said sharply. 'It is between your sister and me.'

'My sister!' she hissed. 'Do you think I want all our friends to see the kind of sister I have?'

'Bella!'

She ignored him. 'A joiner's wife, who still speaks broad Aberdeen and hasn't any decent clothes to wear?'

Mary turned to her angrily. 'Dinna fight ower me, for I've nae intentions o' disgracin' you in front o' your friends. I'll never leave this place, but if I did, it's Aberdeen I'd go, Bella, nae your fine hoose.'

'It's my house,' Matt said grimly. 'And I'll have whoever I bloody well . . . '

'No, Matt.' Mary touched his arm lightly. 'I'm not sellin' the house Willie provided for me. He maybe didna live to give me the better life he wanted for me, but he did buy this hoose, an' my memories o' him are here. I'll find a job, an' look after my son the best I can. I'm very grateful for what you meant to do, but I'd prefer to sort things out for mysel'.'

'You're a stubborn woman, Mary, and I only wish your sister had half your integrity.' Matt stood up and held her hand for several seconds, then turned away abruptly. 'I'll bring the car to the gate, Bella.'

'I'll be out in a minute, Matt.'

When he closed the door, Bella took the seat he'd vacated, her eyes as hard as the granite which had built most of her native city. 'You think you're very clever, don't you, Mary?' she sneered. 'I can see you have your eye on Matt, and I wouldn't be surprised if he thought he was attracted to you, but I'm telling you – forget it. He's mine!'

Mary, whose breath had been taken away by this completely unexpected and unprovoked attack, waited a moment, then said, quietly, 'I'm nae wantin' your man, Bella. I had the best man in the world till he was ta'en awa' from me five days ago.'

Bella gave a low snigger. 'You're so sure of yourself, aren't you, but let me tell you this. I nearly took him away from you years ago.'

Through frozen lips, Mary murmured, 'What d'you mean?'

'I mean I had Willie up to fever pitch for weeks wanting me, before I let him take me.' She laughed at Mary's gasp of disbelief. 'Yes, your dear husband took me, in the bed he shared with you, on the nights you stayed with Jeannie when she had her second child.'

'It's nae true!'

'It is true, and he'd have left you in a minute, and taken me away with him, if I hadn't met Matt. I liked the idea of being a rich man's wife, you see – beautiful clothes, a lovely house and servants to attend to my every need. That's why you still had your precious Willie.'

Bella's contorted face, so close to hers, incensed Mary so much that she swung her hand up and slapped it. 'You're a liar, an' I dinna believe you. My Willie would never . . . '

'You can think what you like.' Rubbing her stinging cheek, Bella stood up. 'But you'll never know for sure, will you?' She strode out and banged the door behind her.

Shaking violently, Mary leaned back. It couldn't be true – she'd have noticed if Willie had taken a fancy to Bella. He'd been a good, loving husband and a good father to young Will, just as he'd promised. He'd been disappointed that she hadn't given him a child of his own, but surely that wouldn't have made him take her sister? No, Bella had been lying, she'd aye been a dab hand at that. She must have been jealous because Matt had made that offer.

Bella had done some terrible things in her life, but to tell a lie like that, and to come out with it on the day of Willie's funeral, that must be the worst thing she'd ever done.

Of course, she took after their father, who'd walked out and left his wife with a young family to bring up on her own, the rotten devil. She'd been a troublemaker from the time she learned to speak, and she would never change.

Aye, Mary thought, grimly, Bella Wyness would carry on causing trouble till the very day she died.

Chapter Sixteen

It was after one-fifteen on Monday morning when Gavin McKenzie took Bathie back to the Gallowgate. She was almost dropping with anxiety and fatigue, but refused to go to bed when Maggie Lindsay told her that was where she belonged.

'I couldn't sleep.' Her voice broke. 'It's thirteen hours now. Something terrible must have happened to Charlie.'

The others in the room believed the same, but Maggie did her utmost to sound hopeful. 'Maybe some kind soul saw him wanderin' about, an' took him in oot o' the rain.'

Gavin nodded. 'You'll collapse if you don't take a rest, Bathie. I'll leave you a sleeping powder.' Knowing the state she was in, he had come prepared.

'No, no.' Bathie sat up in alarm. 'I don't want to be asleep when they bring Charlie home.' Dead or alive, came the unwelcome thought, and her heart palpitated madly.

Her vehemence dared him to argue, so he laid the folded paper containing the sedative on the table, with a meaningful glance at Maggie. 'I'll go now, then, but I'll call back in the morning . . . well, later on, to see if there's any news.' He laid his hand on Bathie's shoulder and crossed to the door.

'Thank you, doctor, and I'm very grateful that you gave up your own sore-needed rest.' Bathie smiled tremulously.

'He's a right good man,' Maggie observed, when he went clattering down the outside steps. 'An' you should tak' this sleepin' pooder. You'll ruin your health if you dinna rest.'

'My health'll be ruined, anyway, if I lose Charlie.' The long, anxious hours had taken their toll on Bathie, and she put her hands up to her face and burst into uncontrollable weeping.

When Annie moved to comfort her, Maggie restrained her. 'It's best to let her greet it out,' she whispered.

'She'll feel better for it after, but you could gi'e her a drop o' brandy.'

When Bathie's hysterical sobbing did eventually tail off, Annie laid a small glass on the occasional table beside her. 'Drink that, Mrs Ogilvie, it'll be good for you.'

At twenty minutes to three, Albert came stumbling in, saw immediately that there was still no word of Charlie, and sank blindly into his armchair. Then, lowering his head, he covered his face with his hands as though he'd given up all hope.

His wife jumped up to go to him, the waiting having given her a chance to recover slightly from her own exhaustion. 'The police will find him, Albert, I'm sure. They know the places to look, where somebody might take shelter from the weather.'

A loud knock on the outside door made them all look at each other, and Maggie jumped up to answer it. She returned with another young constable, who took off his hat and cleared his throat when he entered the room.

Albert was on his feet again. 'Is there any news?'

'I'm sorry, sir. I was sent to find out if the boy had come home himself. They're still searching.'

'Thank you.' Albert's body seemed to cave in again. 'I'm not long back myself.'

'You should all try to get some sleep,' the constable said, kindly. 'You look as if you could drop any minute. We are doing all we can, and we'll let you know as soon as we . . . '

'Yes, I know, and I'm very grateful.' Albert's head fell forward again in his despair.

'Have you time for a cuppie o' tea to heat you up?' Annie asked the young man. 'The kettle's boilin' on the range.'

'No, thank you, I'd better go back.'

He left four people to what could be a long vigil.

The grey light of dawn trickled in through the undrawn curtains. Albert had spent the best part of the last four hours looking out into the street below, and praying for a miracle. He'd been dozing in his chair for about half an hour, when he made the short pilgrimage across the room once more, and was amazed that he'd been able to sleep at all.

He took up his stance again, but after only a few seconds, he felt his wife's presence beside him, and turned and buried his head on her shoulder. 'Oh, Bathie,' he groaned. 'I can't bear it much longer.'

She stroked his untidy hair. 'It'll be all right, Albert. I can feel it now. Charlie's going to come home, I'm sure.'

Their soft voices woke Maggie, who prodded her sister. 'Annie, get some breakfast made, an' I'll attend to the lassies.'

Albert and Bathie had just washed their faces in the kitchen when they heard footsteps coming up from the close.

Grabbing the towel from his wife, Albert ran to the door, drying his face as he went, with Bathie close behind him, water dripping from her hands.

What they beheld, when the door was opened, made her cry out, 'He's not dead, is he?'

The policeman who was carrying Charlie smiled broadly. 'No, ma'am. He's just sleeping.'

Charlie's eyes fluttered. 'I'm sorry I got lost, Mother.'

Bathie opened her arms and threw them round her son when the constable set him down on the landing. 'Oh, Charlie. My dear, dear, Charlie.'

His own eyes moist, Albert watched his wife's tearful reunion with their son for a moment before he turned to the two policemen. 'I don't know how to thank you. You've done a grand job. Where did you find him?'

'He'd been sheltering in an old hut beside the Don, that's why we didn't see him before, and it was lucky we went back when we did, because he was just coming up on to the road, and he could have wandered far enough again.'

'Thank God! Thank God you found him.' Reaction to all the walking and worry caught up with Albert suddenly, and he staggered over to his chair.

159

Maggie and Annie gently took the boy from his mother and half carried him upstairs, Bathie following them, her joy at having her son home making her forget to thank his rescuers.

'We'll be away now, then,' one of the constables remarked. 'I don't think the boy has come to any harm – nothing that a good few hours' sleep won't cure.'

Albert himself was asleep before they reached the mouth of the close.

By the time Donnie and Hetty, pale and quiet, were allowed home, Maggie and Dan Munro – the policeman she'd met outside his headquarters at Lodge Walk – had been keeping company for over five weeks, and even inquisitive Ellie had lost interest in what they did when they were out.

The convalescing children were tearful at first, but Hetty soon began dishing out orders. Her sisters did all she asked until the novelty of having her home again wore off, then Hetty decided that it wasn't much fun being in bed any more.

Donnie took much longer to recover, and didn't return to school for another three weeks. He had shot up so much in height, during his recuperation, that Bathie had to let all his trousers down, and even then they were hardly long enough.

The Johnstones and the elder Ogilvies had all come to see Hetty and Donnie after they came out of hospital, and Henrietta and Nell had both been pleased that Bathie showed no signs of being pregnant again. Albert had learned his lesson, and long may he remember it.

When Donnie went back to school, Bathie felt that life was back to normal, but her complacency received a bitter blow the following day. She did wonder why Mary was writing to her in the autumn, but had no premonition about the news the letter contained, and Albert was alarmed to see her running into the shop at half past nine, with tears streaming down her face.

'My God, Bathie!' he exclaimed, leaving the customer he was serving. 'What's happened? Has one of the children . . . ?'

Dumbly, she handed him the letter.

'Oh, poor Mary,' he said, in a moment. 'And poor Willie.'

'I can hardly take it in,' wailed his wife. 'They were so happy with their life, and now . . . '

He placed an arm round her. 'Don't upset yourself, Bathie. There's nothing you can do, anyway. It's a terrible tragedy, but Mary seems to have come to terms with it.'

That was what had upset Bathie as much as anything, the calm way Mary had written about her husband's death. But, of course, she'd waited a few weeks before she wrote the letter, so perhaps it had taken her that long to 'come to terms with it', as Albert expressed it.

When she went back upstairs, Bathie closeted herself in the parlour, and had a long weep for Willie, whom she had come to regard very fondly when the Dunbars were living up in the attics. Then she wrote a letter of sympathy to his widow, reflecting as she did so that all the sympathy in the world wouldn't give Mary back her husband.

Chapter Seventeen

It took Dan Munro a whole twelve months to bring himself to ask Maggie Lindsay to marry him.

'I'd have said yes, if he'd asked me afore,' the girl told her mistress the morning after the proposal, 'but he's kept me waitin' ower lang.'

Bathie recalled how impatient she'd been at having to wait for three months until she could wed Albert, but she said, 'A year's not very long.'

'Well, it's been ower lang for me, so I'm goin' to keep him waitin' now. I said I'd gi'e him my answer in three months.'

'Three months? Oh, Maggie, he mightn't wait three months for you. Are you sure you know what you're doing?'

'He'll wait.' Maggie's smile was a little secretive. She was quite sure, for she'd watched him changing from a bashful young man, timid about touching her at all, even to kiss her, to a man desperate to possess her. At first, she'd been hurt when he broke away from her after a few minutes, but it had slowly dawned on her that he wanted more than kissing.

Oh yes, Dan would wait, but if she got any inkling that he was cooling off, she'd let him know she was willing to wed him as soon as he liked. She wasn't going to let her chance slip through her fingers through her own pettiness.

Bathie thought that Maggie was being stupid, and, to help the romance on a little, she told the girl she could ask Dan into the house on one or two of the evenings she wasn't off-duty. At least it would give the boy less time to transfer his attention to another girl who might be willing to marry him.

Ellie was very curious about Maggie's romance, but Bathie stopped the flow of questions by saying, 'When you start going out with boys, you won't like people asking you about it, so leave Maggie in peace, for goodness sake.'

Seeing Charlie grinning, Ellie flared up. 'You just love to see other people getting a row, don't you? And I don't know why it's always me that gets it.'

'It's always you that keeps asking things,' he retorted. 'I wish you'd shut up, for a change.'

'I wish you'd shut up and leave me alone.'

Albert folded his newspaper noisily. 'I wish the pair of you would shut up and stop your arguing.'

At the end of the three months, it came as no surprise to any of them when Maggie announced that she'd agreed to marry Dan Munro. They were all happy for her, although her sister felt a bit left out of things.

'I dinna think I'll ever get a lad,' she remarked to Ellie, sadly, when the girl asked her if she was interested in anyone.

'I don't see why not. You're pretty enough.'

Annie simpered. 'Oh weel, maybe some day.'

The day came sooner than she anticipated. She had been asked to be Maggie's bridesmaid, although it was just a quiet wedding, so Bathie had bought a remnant of blue taffeta at a sale, and the resulting creation transformed Annie into a lovely young woman, Albert even commenting on the difference.

'The best man'll take a fancy to you,' he joked. 'It'll maybe be your wedding next.'

Bathie hoped that he was wrong, because the young girl she'd employed to take over from Annie, who had been promoted to nursemaid when Maggie left, didn't seem to be very bright.

But Albert wasn't wrong. Bill Niven, a policeman friend of Dan's, asked Annie out, and there was a new romance to be discussed by the young Ogilvies.

Phoebe, the new general maid, was not very particular with the cleaning, and her cooking was diabolical.

'I can't eat this,' Ellie announced one day, pushing her plate away from her in disgust.

As Ellie could usually stomach anything, this was truly a disaster, so Bathie had a quiet talk with Phoebe later.

'I'm doin' my best,' the girl said, looking surly.

'I'm afraid your best isn't good enough, and unless your cooking improves, I'll have to look for another maid.' Bathie didn't say anything about the state of the house – that could come later, if necessary, and she hated complaining.

For a few days, the meals were a little more appetizing, and then Phoebe came running into the parlour in tears.

Bathie looked up in concern. 'What's wrong?'

'The mutton's burnt to a cinder,' the girl sobbed, 'an' the tatties are boiled dry. I shoulda tell't you I couldna cook.'

Remembering her own first attempts, Bathie knew how she must feel, and said gently, 'Would you like me to show you how to do things properly?'

'Would you?'

Over the next few weeks, the mistress schooled her maid, trying to be as patient as Nell Ogilvie had been with her, but although Phoebe's cooking did improve slightly, it still left a lot to be desired.

'Do you want me to tell her to go?' Albert said, one day, struggling to chew an underdone pork chop. 'I know you don't want to do it, but we can't go on like this.'

'Wait another week,' Bathie pleaded. 'She is trying.'

'She's trying my patience,' he remarked, dryly.

He didn't have to sack the girl, however, because Phoebe came in one morning and asked to speak to Bathie alone.

In the parlour, she said, 'I'm sorry, Mrs Ogilvie, but I'll ha'e to hand in my notice.'

Bathie's heart leapt, but she kept her joy from her voice. 'Has something happened, Phoebe? Have any of my children been upsetting you?' It could only have been Ellie, she thought.

'No, it's nothing here. My Da an' Ma have fell oot, an' my Ma's takin' us back to Elgin, that's where her folk are.'

'I'm sorry about that, and I'm sorry you'll be leaving us.' Bathie felt rather hypocritical, but what else could she say?

When Annie learned about Phoebe's imminent departure, she said, 'You needna bother lookin' for onybody else, for I'll easy manage the cookin' an' cleanin' as weel. Hetty's nae a baby now, and the other five dinna need me.'

Feeling a great weight lifting from her shoulders, Bathie smiled. 'I'll give you a hand, so we should manage quite well between the two of us.'

The whole family was delighted with this arrangement, and poor Phoebe's departure went almost unnoticed.

Annie was still 'going steady' with Bill Niven, and there was no word of anything serious in it yet, so Bathie banished to the back of her mind the thought that there would come a day, in the not too distant future, when the only maid she had would also be leaving. She would worry about that when the time came.

Chapter Eighteen

The gaslight flickered a little in the draught from the door, and Bathie lifted her head to smile at Albert as he came in, his lined face and sandy hair, which had once been so fiery red, making her heart fill with love for him.

'You look tired, Albert. Sit down and put your feet up.' Her own feet were resting on the opposite end of the padded fender stool. 'You should take it easier now you have Charlie and Donnie helping in the shop. You said yourself they'd a way with the customers.'

'They have that,' he admitted. 'And they can slice the ham and the cheese as good as I can myself, but the shop's my whole life, Bathie, you know that. I'd be lost sitting about the house like a woman.'

She was one woman who had no time to sit about, Bathie thought ruefully, not since Annie had left to be married to Bill Niven, her policeman. The romance hadn't been altogether smooth, both of them having stubborn natures and refusing to climb down when they fell out over anything, but it must have been true love, for they always made it up in the end.

Bill hadn't exactly proposed, according to Annie. 'I ken't he'd been tryin' to say somethin' for weeks,' she giggled, 'but he couldna come oot wi' it, so I played a wee trick on him.'

'A wee trick?' Bathie had been intrigued.

'I tell't him another lad had asked me oot, an' I was fair ta'en wi' him, an' you shoulda seen Bill's face.' She gave another low giggle at the memory of it.

'That was rather cruel, wasn't it?'

'I ken, but it worked. He hummed an' hawed, then he says he didna like the idea. "That's a shame," I says, "but there's nothin' you can do aboot it, if I want to go." Mind you, I was a bittie feared he would tell me he didna care.'

'It would have served you right if he had.' Bathie had felt quite indignant. 'But he didn't?'

'No, he stood a minute, pluckin' up his courage, I suppose, an' then he says, "If you were my wife I would soon put a stop to this," an' I looked at him an' says, "If I was your wife, I wouldna want to go." That's when he kissed me like he'd never done afore, an' I tell't him the truth.'

'What did he say to that?'

'He says, "So I'll set the date, then?"' Annie had laughed with delight. 'He's goin' to see the minister the night.'

Remembering, Bathie smiled to herself. Bill Niven had set the date, and had seemed happy enough about it the next time he'd called at the house, joking to Albert that Annie was a little torment, and had put the noose round his neck. He'd looked at Annie then, with so much love in his eyes, that they had all known that the marriage would be a success.

After Annie left, Bathie had employed a young girl to help in the house, but had found her stealing money out of her purse one day, and had given her a week's notice.

The next girl had spent most of the time avoiding work of any kind, and had quickly followed her predecessor. It was after her dismissal that Bathie had decided to take over the whole running of the household herself, and she felt years younger. She hadn't time to think about herself, although she sometimes tumbled into bed at night 'dirt done', as Nell Ogilvie would have put it.

There wasn't the same work in the house, anyway, since Albert had insisted on having the gas put in – no oil lamps to fill and keep trimmed, and the kitchen range didn't have to be kept burning all year round for cooking, not when there was a gas stove.

Now, with Ellie newly fourteen, and Flo coming up for twelve, she made them help with the dish-washing and tidying up, and after an initial grumbling period, they'd both knuckled down. In fact, they were quite a big help, and saw to their younger sisters, as well. Flo, especially, was very good, and supervised ten-year-old Gracie and Hetty, who was seven, when they were getting ready for school. Ellie and Hetty shared a room, Flo and Gracie were together and, of course, Charlie and Donnie had the room they'd had since they were first moved out of the nursery. It was all very convenient. The only thing that Bathie regretted was that Hetty had been the last of her children. After all, she would be thirty-five next birthday, and there weren't many fertile years left.

There had been no more traumas like the time Charlie had been lost and Donnie and Hetty had contracted scarlet fever, thank God, the only sad event being the death of Spanny a year before. The spaniel had been seventeen years old, of course, and had been failing for some time, so Bathie had been rather expecting it, but the children had been inconsolable for days. That was why she had firmly refused to allow them another pet.

She glanced at her husband again, at the dark hollows in his cheeks, his general appearance of ageing, but Albert wasn't an old man. He was hardly forty-three, a man at the prime of life, and her stomach turned over at the thought of what her life would be without him. He often said that the shop was his whole life, but Albert was hers.

He'd been half dozing, and looked up in surprise when she sat on the arm of his chair, but quickly slipped his arm round her waist. 'You can still make my sap rise, Bathie.'

She blushed like a young thing. He always came out with things like that at the most unexpected times, although she should be used to it. 'Albert Ogilvie, you're a terrible tease.'

'I'm not teasing, I mean it, and I wish we could . . . ' He'd been about to say he wished they could make more bairns, but had recalled the doctor's words on the day of Hetty's birth.

Well, he had been careful – though it had been difficult to remember to stop on the rare occasions he'd allowed himself to make love to his wife – but Gavin's warning had been seven years ago, and Bathie was surely fully recovered by this time. She was the picture of health, looking down at him with her lovely blue eyes, still as full of life as they were when he'd met her first, the same wavy dark hair, though it wasn't in the bonnie ringlets it was then, and had a sprinkling of silver through it.

Gavin McKenzie couldn't expect him to spend the rest of his life thinking, even before he mounted her, that he'd have to come out of his wife at the crucial second.

He threw caution to the wind, his thoughts firing his desire. 'We started going through the alphabet, but we've only reached H, it's maybe time we tried to carry on.'

Bathie could feel a stirring in her loins, and hoped that Albert meant what he was saying. She'd wondered, at first, and with a touch of disappointment, why he had stopped so abruptly when he was at the height of his passion, but had eventually realized that he was afraid he'd make her pregnant. Something must have made him change his mind, or did he think another child would rejuvenate him?

His free hand slid over her flat stomach. 'Women were made to bear children, my love, and it's a shame to waste what the good Lord blessed you with.'

Sliding his hand up to cup her breast, he moaned, 'I still go mad wanting you, and I've held myself back too long.'

She leaned down to kiss his brow, her own need building up inside her. 'Charlie and Donnie aren't home yet, Albert,' she murmured. 'We can't go to bed just now.'

'They won't be in for a while.' He removed his arm from her waist. 'Do I have to take you here on the floor?'

She was shocked at his coarseness, but followed him into the bedroom, where he undressed her, cursing under his breath when some of her tiny buttons proved stubborn.

'Turn off the gas, Albert,' she whispered, shy with him because of his unseemly haste.

'The gas stays on,' he said harshly. 'I've never seen you standing in front of me naked.' His emotions, as well as his manhood, were rampant now, and he gave himself up to them.

168

As the last of her garments fell to the floor, he said, 'You've aye made me do it in the dark, when I was wanting to see you ready for me, and wanting me as much as I wanted you.'

As she attempted to go under the blankets, he barked, 'No, don't go covering yourself up. Let me look at you properly.'

His fingers fumbled with his own buttons now, and she stood, ashamed of her nakedness, until he let his trousers fall, together with his drawers, and stepped out of them.

Her face flamed at the sight of his huge organ, but she couldn't take her eyes off it, and her shame increased.

At last, she dragged her eyes up, past his broad chest, covered with reddish hair, past the pulse beating at his neck, to his face, contorted with passion, and Mary Wyness's words – spoken so many years ago – came into her head: 'My Ma aye says she'd to shut her eyes an' think aboot somethin' else every time my Da wanted it.'

If Mary's father had acted like this, Bathie thought, she wasn't surprised that Mrs Wyness had shut her eyes, and she must have been glad when he walked out on her.

Albert, blissfully unaware of what was going through his wife's mind, grabbed her shoulders to swivel her round against the wall, then pressed in between her thighs. 'You've always been so passive, Bathie, and never let me see if you got any pleasure. Did you not like what I did to you?'

'Yes,' she faltered. 'I did like it. I liked it very much, Albert, but it's not a woman's place to show pleasure, and I don't very much care for what you're doing at this moment.'

His laugh was brutal. 'We'll do it my way for a change, with the light on so I can see you, and standing up or lying down, Bathie, you're going to show me you like it.'

Her involuntary expression of disgust enraged him. 'I used to think I should try another woman, just to see what a whore did, but I respected you. I even thought

169

about trying Bella Wyness. She made it quite clear she was willing, and she just turned to Charlie when I stopped short of obliging her.'

'Stopped short?' Bella's name evoked hateful memories, but she hadn't known that Albert was involved with the girl. 'Did you . . . touch her, is that what you mean?'

'She was asking for it, swinging her paps at me whenever I passed, so I tickled them up a few times. But one night she came down to the kitchen in her gown, and just about asked me to take her, and I very nearly did.'

Sickened, she tried to push him away, but he was much too strong. 'I loved you, Bathie, and I never laid her on her back, though it took all the willpower I had to refuse her.'

She stopped struggling – whatever it was that had got into Albert tonight must be temporary. He practically threw her across the bed, and she shuddered as he forced himself in. As he pounded into her, she thought about Mrs Wyness, dead these many years. In a short time, however, she felt herself responding to him, and was more ashamed and angry than ever.

When he released her, she felt sore and bruised, but it was her pride that had been hurt more than anything, and she began to weep quietly as she slipped her nightdress on.

Albert's rough manner changed just as abruptly as it had started. 'Oh God, Bathie,' he groaned. 'I'm sorry. I told you once there was a beast inside me, and I can't explain why it came out tonight. Maybe I was too tired to fight it, but I should never have told you about . . . Bella. She never meant anything to me, just a bit of fun.'

His dark eyes were contrite as he took her hand. 'Bathie, say you forgive me, for everything?'

She shook her head miserably. 'I can't, Albert. I thought it wasn't ladylike to show pleasure, and I thought you'd know.'

'Please, Bathie? I know you're disgusted with me, but some men are like that all the time.'

When she didn't answer, he pulled on his nightshirt and went to the door. 'I'll leave you to come to yourself.'

She lay shivering when he went out. Not that she was cold – her whole body felt on fire – but because he had been disappointed in her, and if he'd nearly had a bit of fun with Bella Wyness, all those years ago, it was her own fault. Her gorge had risen at the very mention of the slut's name, and this was another sin, almost as bad, that the girl had committed, but at least Albert had had the grace not to give in to his passion that night, and she should be thankful for that.

Hearing voices in the kitchen, she wondered which of their sons had come home. They went twice a week to the gymnastic club in the Porthill Hall, which had been built across the Gallowgate from them a few years before, but they never came home together. They would go their separate ways; with their own friends, for they weren't old enough to be meeting girls.

Her anger and disgust at her husband was abating. She'd been lucky that he hadn't acted that way before, and she was sure that he would never repeat what had almost amounted to rape. It would be best, though, if she gave him no cause to do anything like that again, so she would show him her pleasure in future, and let him study her naked body, even let him have the gas on if he wanted, for it was a wife's duty to fulfil her husband's needs, after all.

Swinging her feet on to the mat, she put on her wrapper and went through to the kitchen. Donnie was speaking to his father, but fired with new determination she broke in, 'Are you coming to bed, Albert?'

Charlie had met Vena Bruce after club. He usually gave her a light kiss when he left her, and he rather liked it, but sometimes, when he went to bed after he'd seen her home, he'd dreamt about kissing her properly, and had been surprised that his drawers were sticky when he woke up in the morning.

Tonight, however, after overhearing two of the older boys speaking about their 'wet dreams', he'd realized that that was what happened to him, and had made up his mind, there and then, to give Vena a real kiss,

171

to see if the wet stickiness would occur when he was awake.

The only place he knew where they wouldn't be disturbed was in his own back yard, where they'd have the choice of three stores to go inside. He'd been rather afraid that she might refuse, but she seemed quite willing when he suggested it, and they'd walked about a bit until he was sure that Donnie would be home before he took her back up the Gallowgate.

There was no sign of anyone as he led the girl through the close, and his fingers seemed all thumbs when he opened the unlocked hasp on the first store they came to. Closing the door behind them, and knowing that its own weight would make it swing open, he found a stick to jam it, then grabbed Vena and kissed her quickly.

'Oh, Charlie,' she giggled, 'you're doin' it ower rough. It's like this.' She put her arms round his neck and melted her supple body against him, her lips meeting his in a long, lingering kiss, her tongue poking between his teeth.

When she stopped, his first real thought was that there was no wetness in his drawers, then he felt a strange power surging up inside him, and remembered Bella Wyness. His shame hadn't let him think about her for years, but now he was growing big and hard like he'd done with her. 'Let me feel your tits,' he muttered, using Bella's words.

Vena helped him to unfasten her buttons, and as soon as his hands came in contact with her warm velvet skin, he began to tremble, the firm roundness of her young breasts, and the hardening of her nipples when he squeezed them, making his own hardness increase to an unbearable degree.

As Bella Wyness had informed Bathie at the time, 'He kens where to put it,' so Charlie took Vena Bruce at almost the same time as his father was taking his mother, the only difference being that Vena was willing and more than cooperative.

With his desperate need, and his inexperience, it was over in a few seconds, but he knew now what his

172

previous wetness had meant, and although he'd gone soft, it wasn't long before he responded to Vena's low moaning to do it again.

After seeing her back to Nelson Street, he felt his heart swelling with pride at what he'd achieved, and crept up to the middle floor when he arrived home, very relieved that there was no one about to see his excitement.

Donnie opened his eyes when his brother went into their room. 'You're late tonight, Charlie. Where have you been?'

Almost beside himself with delight, Charlie sat down on the edge of his brother's bed. 'Not all that far away.'

He hadn't meant to tell anybody, but he couldn't help it, and the words came tumbling out of him as he described every minute of the time he'd spent with Vena in graphic detail.

'And, God, Donnie, it was . . . ' He was stuck for a word to describe the ecstasy he'd felt. 'It was just wonderful.' It was inadequate, but it was all he could think of.

He lay awake long after Donnie had fallen asleep. What he'd done with Vena had felt so natural that it had banished all the shame of what Bella Wyness had made him do. He'd only been seven or eight at that time, of course, too young to understand, but if he'd known then what he knew now, he'd have done all that she wanted him to do and not felt as guilty as he'd done ever since.

There were no words to describe the thrill of entering a girl. Their bodies were made to excite, made to receive, made to satisfy. Christ! It was standing up again at the thought of Vena's young, flexible body. Wait till tomorrow night – he'd have her screaming for more, not just whimpering.

That eventful hour was bound to have repercussions. Five weeks later, both Bathie Ogilvie and Vena Bruce informed the men concerned that their passion had resulted in the making of a child. The reactions were completely different.

Albert's pleasure was tempered by apprehension at what Gavin McKenzie might say about it, in spite of

173

Bathie being as strong as a horse now. He had bitterly regretted the way he had treated his wife that night, but after she took to letting him know when she wanted him, and how much she enjoyed him, even taking the initiative at times, he believed that he'd done the right thing, after all. He felt better than he'd done over all the years he'd been afraid to make love to her. This news that he was to be a father again was just what he needed to give him a new lease of life.

Charlie's reception of the same information from Vena was exactly the opposite. 'Oh, God,' he whispered in dismay. 'What are we going to do about it?'

She looked at him scornfully. 'You'll ha'e to marry me, Charlie, that's what you've to do about it.'

He hadn't known that what he'd done to her would have this result – Albert having shirked his duty as a father – but he would have died rather than admit his ignorance to this girl, who was much more worldly-wise than he was, he knew that. He was quite unable to cope with his tangled emotions. His body desired her, his heart told him he loved her, but his brain warned him that he'd be in trouble if his parents found out. They would never approve of Vena as a daughter-in-law.

'I can't afford to marry you,' he blustered.

She smiled confidently. 'Your Da'll gi'e you mair wages.'

'Are you absolutely sure you're . . . ?'

'Goin' to ha'e a bairn?' She finished his question, then banished his faint hope. 'Aye. I've never been late afore.'

Charlie had no idea what she meant. All that registered with him was that there was no escape from the nightmare, and he racked his brain trying to think who could advise him what to do. He'd no older brother to confide in, Donnie would know less than he did himself, and the boys at the gymnastic club would laugh if he asked them. Wait, though – there was Billy Gammack. He was three years older and should know all the ins and outs – no, that was an unfortunate turn of phrase.

'Are we goin' to be standin' here all night?' Vena's voice intruded on his deliberations. 'Are you nae takin' me into your Da's store again? It's good in there, Charlie, for naebody can see what we're doin'.'

His heart fluttered, then almost stopped. 'I don't want to be making any more babies,' he muttered.

To his discomfiture, she burst out laughing. 'God, you really dinna ken onythin' aboot it. Once the bairn's started, you'll nae mak' another, suppose you did it sixty times.'

But his libido had undergone a thorough dowsing, and he wasn't capable of doing it once, never mind sixty times. 'I don't feel like it tonight,' he mumbled, shame-facedly.

'Suit yoursel', then. There's plenty o' lads that'll jump at the chance.' She turned away and flounced off.

Charlie ran after her. 'I'm sorry. I need time to think.'

She stopped, then smiled. 'I'll meet you the morn's night after the club.'

Billy Gammack didn't laugh when Charlie told him. 'You should have been careful, Charlie, lad. If you'd come out in time, your shot wouldn't have got inside her.'

Charlie began to understand the biological truth. 'It's too late now, and my father'll kill me if he finds out.'

'If she's not far gone, you could get somebody to stop it.'

'Are there people who do that?'

'It's against the law, of course, and it's a bit dangerous, but maybe she knows somebody herself.'

Charlie didn't mind about breaking the law, but he wanted nothing to do with anything that could endanger Vena's life. 'I'll just have to tell my father, I suppose.'

As soon as Charlie met her, Vena said, 'My Ma's boilin' at you. She says you'll ha'e to marry me, an' if you havena tell't your Da by the weekend, she's goin' to go to the shop an' tell him hersel', in front o' a' his customers.'

'I'll tell him, Vena, honestly.' Her moist red lips and her rounded curves were driving him mad again, so, since he knew it would make no difference how often he made love to her now, he took her arm and walked her towards the Links, hoping against hope that they wouldn't be seen there.

'Are we nae goin' into your Da's store the night?'

'I don't want to risk my father seeing us before I have a chance to speak to him.' The truth was, he was afraid he'd fail her, so close to his home, with all he had on his mind.

'It'll nae hide for lang, ye ken,' she taunted.

He knew that. When he was younger, he'd often wondered why his mother sometimes grew fat, then went thin again after a new baby came along. When he'd asked her about it, she'd told him that babies came out of their mothers' stomachs, but what she should have told him, he reflected ruefully, was how they got there in the first place.

He forgot his worries in the thrills of making love to Vena, and, after he'd seen her home, he was sure that he wanted to marry her, whatever his father might say. He loved her, and she loved him, and that was all that counted, especially with a baby on the way.

His courage ebbed as he was climbing the outside stairs, and he found himself praying that he wouldn't see anyone when he went in, but both his parents were sitting in the kitchen, talking over a cup of tea.

He couldn't bring himself to say anything in front of his mother, and waited, somewhat impatiently, for her to go to bed.

At last, she stood up. 'Goodnight, Charlie. You won't be long, will you, Albert?'

'I'll be through in a minute.' Albert was smoking the pipe he'd taken to using, but never in the bedroom.

Charlie wanted no interruption, so, as soon as the door closed behind her, he said, 'Father, I've something to tell you. Is Donnie home yet?'

'Half an hour ago.' Albert's eyes twinkled. 'Is it a lass that keeps you out?'

'Yes.' Charlie was glad of the opening. 'That's what I want to speak to you about, Father.'

'You'll be wanting to know the facts of life. Is that it?'

'No, I think I've found them out for myself.'

'The lads at the club have been saying things, have they, and you're not sure if they've been pulling your leg?'

'It's not that. I've been . . . I didn't know . . . '

Albert's brows had shot down, and the genial smile had been wiped from his face. 'Are you trying to tell me you've put a lassie in the family way?'

'I didn't know that's what would happen when I . . . did it.' The boy's eyes were fixed fearfully on his father.

Albert took his fist hard down on the table. 'Christ, Charlie. Have you no bloody sense? You must have known.'

'No, I'm telling you the truth. It was a terrible shock when Vena told me.'

'Vena? Vena who? Where does she come from?' Albert suddenly recalled Arthur Johnstone's face, purple with anger, and tried to keep himself under control.

'She's Vena Bruce, and she lives in Nelson Street.'

'What does her father work at?'

'She hasn't got a father.' She had told him that once, when he had asked her the same question.

'He's dead, is he? Well, her mother should have told her to respect her body.'

'She says we'll have to get married now.'

'Does she, though?' Albert couldn't keep the sarcasm out of his voice. 'How old is she, anyway?'

'She's sixteen, the same as me, and the same age as Mother said she was when she married you.'

Albert let this pass. 'Do you want to marry her?'

Charlie met his father's stony eyes without flinching. 'I wouldn't mind.' He didn't want to sound too eager.

'Wouldn't mind? That sounds damned lukewarm to me. Do you love her enough to live with her for the rest of your life?'

'I couldn't live without her,' Charlie said, simply.

Albert sighed. This wasn't what he wanted for his eldest son, and he could fully understand how Bathie's father had felt all those years ago, but maybe this was his own fault for not warning the boy. And it wasn't as bad as it might have been, seeing Charlie loved the girl, but it was bad enough.

'Have you considered what marriage would mean?' he said, more kindly. 'Where you would live, what you would live on?'

'Couldn't you give me more wages?'

Albert's fingers massaged his chin, thoughtfully. The boy's wages weren't big enough to rent a house, never mind support a wife and child, so there was only one thing to do.

'I could, and I suppose you could have the attics,' he said, slowly, 'but God knows what your mother's going to say about all this.'

It had been his father's reaction that Charlie had been dreading, and it hadn't been too bad, after all, but his mother! She'd despise him for what he'd done.

'How far on's this Vena?'

'About five weeks, I think.'

'Good God! The same as your mother.'

'Is Mother going to have another . . . ?' Charlie's gorge rose as he pictured his father doing to her what he'd done to Vena. A horrifying thought struck him, and he braced himself to ask, 'Did you and Mother have to get married?'

'No, we did not!' Albert's voice rose indignantly. 'I respected your mother – I still do – and I never touched her till our wedding night.'

'Will you tell Mother about Vena, please, for I can't face her?' The boy felt he'd had enough for one night.

'I'll tell her when I go through. Get upstairs to your bed now, and pray she doesn't miscarry from the shock of it.'

In his single bed, in the room he shared with Donnie, Charlie couldn't get over how lightly he'd got off so far. His father had surprised him by his eventual calm acceptance of the situation, but his mother might be more difficult. Still, his father would likely talk her round, and he'd likely offer to pay for the wedding, under the circumstances.

Vena would be delighted about the attics, and he could hardly wait until they were installed in their own little love nest, away from the rest of his family.

All things considered, Charlie thought contentedly, it had turned out quite well for him after all.

Chapter Nineteen

At ten past nine in the shop the next morning, Albert drew Charlie aside. 'I promised your mother I'd send you up as soon as the young ones went to school.'

Charlie's heart sank. His mother had said nothing during breakfast, but she'd been biding her time. He went slowly out of the side door into the close, then up the iron stairs.

When he stood in the kitchen, waiting apprehensively, Bathie said, 'Sit down, Charlie, for goodness sake.'

He sat on the edge of one of the wooden chairs, his knees knocking, his heart palpitating. 'You want to speak . . . ?'

'You know what I want to speak about, Charlie. I was shocked last night when I learned about . . . what you've done to . . . What's the girl's name?'

'Vena. Vena Bruce. We love each other.'

Bathie looked at him keenly. 'Isn't it more a case of you loving the idea of being in love with her, this free and easy girl who allowed you to have your way with her?'

The rather old-fashioned phrase annoyed him, and he tried to forget the memory of Vena helping him to undo her buttons, and then pleading with him to take her again. 'I . . . I forced her to do it,' he blustered.

'Is she a nice girl? Is she a *nice* nice girl?'

He doubted if his mother would think so, but said firmly, 'Of course she's a nice girl, and we're going to get married, no matter what you say. Father's not against it, for he told me we could have the attics.'

'He told me, too, and I must say I was very surprised.' Bathie paused for a moment. 'You'd better ask her to come to supper on Sunday, so we can get to know her.'

They'd all have to meet Vena some time, and he wasn't so blind as to think they'd approve of her, but it was his life.

'All right,' he said reluctantly, 'I'll ask her, but I don't know if she'll come. She won't like being put ˜on display for you all to gape at and criticize.'

'Is she a bit shy?' Bathie appeared to be pleased about this, so he didn't correct her.

He'd made no arangements to meet the girl that night, but he couldn't wait to tell her what had happened, and went to Nelson Street to pass on the invitation. When the door was thrown open, he stared in amazement at the woman he presumed must be Vena's mother.

An enormous mass of fat, her skin was pock-marked, her greasy lank hair hung untidily round her shoulders, her face and hands were filthy. The torn apron she was wearing was stained with gravy, or something brown, and her collar had bits of egg on it. She was by far the most revolting woman he had ever seen.

She looked at him expectantly, waiting for him to state his business, and he tried not to show his revulsion. 'Is Vena in, please? It's Charlie Ogilvie.'

'She's nae in, the now. She's . . . eh . . . away seein' her auntie, but she shouldna be lang. Come in an' wait.'

Smirking broadly, she led him into an equally revolting room, where three young children, with nothing covering their nether regions, were squatting on the bare boards of the floor. He let his eyes travel no farther, afraid of what he might see.

Mrs Bruce rushed over to a rickety, wooden rocking chair, with a dark-stained cushion. 'So you're Charlie Ogilvie, are you? Well, you can sit here, if you wait till I gi'e it a wipe. The littlest ane pee'd on it a wee while ago.'

'No, thank you,' he said, hastily. 'I prefer to stand.'

'Suit yoursel'.' She stopped the desultory rubbing, and set her own ample posterior on the chair, her piercing blue eyes squinting up at him. 'Are you intendin' to stand by my Vena now you've got her in a mess?'

It hit him in the face, like a douche of cold water, that this . . . creature would be his mother-in-law if he agreed, but he couldn't do anything about that. 'Yes, I want to marry her, and my father says we can have the two rooms in our attics.'

'Well, now.' She seemed satisfied with that. 'So you've tell't your Da, have you?'

'I told him last night.'

While she rocked gently backwards and forwards, mulling over her daughter's good fortune, Charlie tried to think of something to say to break the overpowering silence. The three children were gazing open-mouthed at him, and he wondered what kind of man their father had been. He must have been glad to get away from this lot.

'How long is it since your husband died, Mrs Bruce?'

She let out a blood-curdling cackle. 'My husband? That's a good ane. I've never had a husband.'

'But . . . I thought . . . you've got four children?'

She threw back her head, her roar of laughter making the cracked window rattle. 'I've got five bairns, by five different fathers. Mina's awa' oot, but she's the auldest.' His shocked face made her stop to laugh once more, then she wiped her eyes and shook her head. 'I wasna so lucky as Vena, though, for nane o' them would admit the bairn was his. I wasna even sure mysel', whiles.' She gave another cackle and winked lewdly.

The opening of the door came as a lifeline to Charlie, but when Vena came in, she seemed embarrassed to find him there.

'I was oot wi' Lily, next door,' she volunteered. 'We took a walk to the Brig o' Balgownie.'

'My mother's invited you to supper on Sunday,' he told her, 'so I'll come down for you about five, if that's all right?'

'Aye, that'll be a' right wi' you, Vena, won't it?' the woman prompted.

Vena nodded. 'I'll be waitin' for you at five, Charlie.'

'I'll have to go now.' He felt he couldn't spend another minute in the stench of the horrible room.

'I'll walk up the road a bit wi' ye.' Vena took his arm, possessively. 'I'll nae be long, Ma.'

As soon as they were outside, she said, 'You'll ha'e to excuse Ma an' the state o' the kitchen, but she's had a hard struggle to keep things goin'.'

'Yes, of course,' he answered politely, taking deep breaths of air into his suffering lungs.

'Was your Ma angry when you tell't her aboot me?'

'Not really, and Father says we can have the two attic rooms to live in, so everything's turning out fine.'

'He'll ha'e to pay for the weddin', for Ma canna afford onything like that.' She chuckled suddenly. 'Will he buy me a white dress, Charlie? I've aye dreamed aboot gettin' married in white since I saw a paintin' o' a bride when I was little.'

'He might. We'll ask him on Sunday.'

In bed, Charlie couldn't get the squalor of the Bruces' home out of his mind. Would Vena degenerate into a fat hag like her mother? No, no, it was unthinkable, and the girl would have a husband and a nice home, even if the rooms were small and next to the roof. She'd keep herself clean and tidy for him, and with his mother's example to follow, she'd soon forget her upbringing.

He was almost asleep when two voices floated into his semi-consciousness.

'She's awa' to see her auntie.'

'I was oot wi' Lily, next door, and we took a walk to the Brig o' Balgownie.'

His befogged brain couldn't cope with the discrepancy, so he gave up trying, and what did it matter, anyway? She'd been out with a friend, not another boy.

On the Sunday afternoon, when Charlie ushered Vena Bruce in, Bathie's mind instantly flashed back to Bella Wyness. This simpering girl had the same voluptuous figure, the same full lips, the same calculating look in her eyes, even the same fair hair. Was this what had attracted Charlie?

She forced a smile and said, 'I'm very pleased to meet you, Vena. Sit there, next to Donnie.'

Albert's welcome was also a trifle forced, and he watched her closely. She wasn't the type of daughter-in-law he'd hoped for, but if she made Charlie happy . . .

Donnie had seen Vena before, waiting outside the club for Charlie, but he couldn't help conjuring up a picture of what Charlie had told him they'd done in the back store, and found himself with an unfamiliar erection. He

182

knew what it meant, because Charlie had explained it to him, and Albert, carrying out his fatherly duty somewhat belatedly, had told him what could happen when a boy's passions got the better of him.

The warmth of Vena's leg pressing against his, whether accidentally or on purpose, made him feel even worse, and all he wanted was to get away from the thrill of it, so he excused himself from the table as soon as possible and went up to the room he shared with his brother.

Ellie, unusually quiet, had taken in every word of the polite conversation, but nothing had given her a clue as to why this common-looking girl had been invited to supper. She knew better than to ask her mother, whose expression was far from happy, and decided to ask Donnie. After she washed the dishes, the girl went to help her young sisters make ready for bed, while Bathie went through to the parlour.

Vena was sitting very close to Charlie on the couch, her leg rubbing against his, and his mother wished that she could tell him what a mistake he was making, but knew that he would resent any interference from her.

As the conversation appeared to be flagging, she said, 'Is it a long time since your father died, Vena?' and was surprised by the wary look in the big blue eyes.

'Aye, it's a good few year ago now.'

Knowing this to be untrue, Charlie stole a glance at her but she conveniently avoided his eyes, so he turned back to his father, to ask the all-important question.

'Vena's mother can't pay for the wedding,' he began, very cautiously. 'She's brought up five children . . . '

'But it won't be a big wedding,' Albert interrupted. 'Just a little get-together after the ceremony in the house here, and I'm quite prepared to pay for that.'

'Vena wants a white wedding, Father, so will you buy the wedding gown for her as well . . . please?' Charlie was quaking, but he'd have done anything to please his future bride.

Albert frowned. 'A white dress means purity, Charlie, and Vena . . . ' What he was inferring was quite clear.

Bathie had been thinking it over. 'Nobody needs to

183

know that Vena's . . . Let them have a white wedding, Albert, and that would save people's tongues wagging.'

'They'll wag all the more when the bairn's born.'

'When it arrives, we can say it's premature. Seven-month babies are quite common.'

The flicker of alarm in Vena's eyes was gone so quickly that Bathie believed she must have imagined it.

'I suppose you're right,' Albert conceded. 'You're my oldest son, Charlie, and I don't grudge what I'll have to spend. My wife'll go with you to choose your gown, Vena, and you can have your white wedding in the kirk, if it makes you happy.'

'Oh, thank you, Mr Ogilvie.' Vena looked up at him coyly, from under fluttering eyelashes.

Bathie resolved to keep the brazen hussy firmly in her place. She didn't want Albert to be tempted again, especially by Charlie's bride.

Upstairs, after she'd seen her sisters settled for the night, Ellie went through to ask if Donnie knew why Vena Bruce had been invited to supper, but her eyes widened when she saw what her scarlet-faced brother was doing before he feverishly buttoned up his trousers.

'Why don't you knock before you come bursting in?'

'What's that?' She pointed to the big bulge he was trying to cover with his hand.

His colour deepened even further. 'Never you mind. It's nothing to do with you. Why did you come in here, anyway?'

She was not to be diverted. 'I never knew you'd a thing like that,' she said indignantly. 'It was just a little worm when we used to be bathed together in front of the fire.'

'You didn't have *them*, either,' he muttered, pointing to her budding bosom.

'They're my womanhood,' she informed him, repeating what her mother had told her when she'd asked why there were lumps growing out of her chest.

Donnie answered triumphantly. 'This is my manhood, then.'

'Does every man have a thing as big as that? I've never noticed it on any other man I've seen.'

'It's not big all the time – it's just because I was thinking about what Charlie did to Vena.'

'What did he do to her? Why's she here?' The fourteen-year-old was very curious to find out what had been going on.

'He put his thing inside her a while ago, and now she's going to have a baby.'

Ellie frowned in concentration for a moment. 'If you put your thing inside me, would I have a baby?'

'A man doesn't do it to his sister, you idiot.'

'Why not? And where inside her did he put it?'

'Oh, shut up, Ellie. You don't know anything.'

She was quite aware by now that she didn't know anything, but she meant to ask her mother at the first opportunity. 'But why's she here?' she persisted.

'Charlie'll have to marry her, didn't you even know that?'

'Of course I knew that.' She wasn't going to let him know the full extent of her ignorance.

'They're likely arranging the wedding now.'

Taking one last glance at Donnie's bulge, which was now subsiding, Ellie went downstairs with her knew-found knowledge.

'Are the girls in bed?' Bathie asked.

'Yes, Mother. Is it true Charlie has to marry Vena?'

Charlie looked shocked, Vena laughed, Albert glowered and Bathie was extremely embarrassed, but Ellie's candid gaze didn't falter.

'Yes, it's true.' Bathie knew that her daughter wouldn't be satisfied until she had an answer. 'Vena's going to have Charlie's baby, but don't tell anybody because it's a secret. Now, be a good girl and go and sit with Donnie for a while.'

'Donnie doesn't want me there, he's . . . ' It occurred to Ellie, then, that her brother might not want other people to know what he'd been doing, so she turned and went out.

Albert laughed fondly. 'She doesn't get any better, does

she? She never thinks twice about asking about anything.' His face sobered. 'You'll have to arrange things with the minister, Charlie, and set the date as soon as you can.'

'Yes, the sooner the better,' his son said, ruefully.

'Aye, Charlie, the sooner the better.'

There was something in the tone of Vena's voice, and the expression on her face, that troubled Bathie. This girl that Charlie claimed to have seduced had been no innocent, she thought, and the more she dwelt on it, the more certain she became. When Albert urged her, however, she agreed to go with Vena on Thursday to choose her white wedding gown. There was no point in arguing about it. Charlie had made up his mind, and any arguments would only make him more determined.

They spent the next hour discussing what would have to be done to the two attic rooms before the newly-weds moved in, then Charlie took Vena up to see them. They'd been unoccupied since Mary Wyness and Willie Dunbar left for New Zealand, ten years before, although Flo, Gracie and Hetty sometimes played there if it was raining.

Vena was shivering when they came back. 'It's awfu' cold up there, an' the rooms are nae very big, are they?'

'They're big enough.' Albert sounded angry.

Both the attic rooms were much larger than Mrs Bruce's filthy kitchen, Charlie thought, and felt rather disappointed in her for criticizing them.

When the young couple left, Albert glanced at his wife and shrugged his shoulders. 'She could've been worse, I suppose, but not much. I just can't understand Charlie, for she's not the sort of girl I'd have thought he'd even look at.'

'I don't like her,' Bathie said flatly. 'There's something about her . . . I don't know . . . she's forward and sly.'

'She was likely putting a face on because she was awkward at meeting us for the first time.'

'That's not what it was. I'm not happy about it at all.'

Albert grimaced. 'I'm not happy about it, either, but what can we do now Charlie's committed himself? If he

186

hadn't said he'd marry her, I could maybe have bought her off.'

'Can't you suggest it, yet?' Bathie sounded hopeful.

'Charlie'd be against it, and what's done can't be undone.'

But Bathie couldn't sleep that night, remembering the look on Vena Bruce's face when she said, 'The sooner the better.' Was the child going to be born sooner than they thought? If so, the question was – how much sooner? And was it possible that it wasn't Charlie's child at all?

Chapter Twenty

After the small wedding party came back from Greyfriars Church, Bathie and Ellie served up the meal in the dining room, while Albert tried to keep the conversation at a respectable level. He found it increasingly difficult, because the bride's mother became coarser and cruder in her speech as she downed glass after glass of whisky.

He'd been horrified when he met her. He'd been prepared for a common woman, but her strident voice grated on his ears, and the gaudy, creased dress covering her gross body offended his senses. He was glad that he hadn't invited either his or Bathie's parents, even though he knew they'd be annoyed at not seeing their grandson being married.

Charlie was thankful that the woman was at least clean, although her pendulous breasts, flopping over her uncorseted stomach, made him avert his eyes every time they fell on her.

The woman was enjoying herself, however. 'Vena's lucky. I thought she'd be landed the same as me, an' the bairn'd be left withoot a father, for I just ken't that Dutch . . . '

'Ma!'

Her daughter's warning flustered her momentarily, then, dropping one eyelid, she said, 'I hope the bed doesna creak an' let a'body in the hoose ken how often Charlie needs it.'

Bathie was furious at the woman's indelicacy, but knew that her previous suspicions about Vena had been justified. It hadn't even needed the mother's little slip to tell her that Charlie wasn't the father of the coming child. The straining seams and gaping buttons on the white gown showed that Vena was more than two months pregnant. Much more. Charlie was being used as a scapegoat.

Bathie couldn't trust herself to speak, so Albert had to step in to cover the confusion at his son 's mother-in-law's remarks.

'What did your husband work at, Mrs Bruce?'

Charlie drew in his breath. He'd prayed that his father wouldn't ask that, and felt sick as the woman threw back her head and bayed with laughter.

Wiping the tears of mirth from her eyes with her sleeve, she gasped, 'Oh, Mr Ogilvie. Did Charlie nae tell you I've never been wed? Mind, I had eight bairns a' thegither, though three o' them died o' the fever when they were infants.'

'Oh.' Albert was at a complete loss. He had heard of unmarried women having one or two children, for mistakes could happen, but eight? The father must have been married already.

'Nae ane o' the men would admit it was his bairn.' Self-pity passed fleetingly across the woman's sagging features, then she giggled. 'But naebody can say I've been neglected that way, an' they were a' named after their Das – as far as I could work oot.'

She waited, obviously hoping for a laugh, then added, 'I wasna sure about Ina's Da, but I didna want to forget George, for he'd a cock on him like a stallion.'

Bathie found her tongue at last. 'I must ask you to guard your tongue, Mrs . . . um . . . Bruce. That's not the kind of talk I like to hear in front of my children.'

'Oh, michty me.' The woman became heavily sarcastic, and adopted an exaggerated English accent. 'I beg your pardon, I'm sure.' She lapsed into offended silence.

Albert tried to ease the crackling tension. 'Vena, I'm sure your mother would like to see your two rooms.'

'Aye. Come on, Charlie.' Vena jumped up and pulled her bridegroom off his chair, then led the little procession out.

Because Ellie's eyes were wide with interest, Bathie and Albert could only exchange troubled glances, and were deeply grateful to Donnie when he stepped in to prevent his sister from coming up with any awkward questions. 'Ellie and me'll do the dishes. Flo and Gracie and Hetty, if you three lend a hand, we'll get them done all the quicker.'

There was a flurry of commotion for a few minutes, then Albert and Bathie were left completely on their own.

She looked at him tearfully. 'I'm sure it's not Charlie's child. Vena's too big. She's supposed to be nine weeks on, like me, and I'm not even started to show yet. And there's something about her . . . I just know she's up to no good.'

'Oh, Bathie.' Albert was rather annoyed at her for being so suspicious. 'She wouldn't marry Charlie if it wasn't his.'

'Yes, she would, if the real father wouldn't.'

Mrs Bruce's return silenced them. She came in on her own, her face disfigured by a leering grin. 'I've tell't them nae to bother comin' doon. I'll manage to see mysel' hame, an' maybe pick up a man on the road. A' that whisky's set my juices boilin', an' I saw for mysel' that Charlie's juices were boilin' an' all, an' he could hardly wait to get stuck in.'

Bathie was disgusted, but it came to her that this was a good opportunity to find out the truth, with the woman in such an inebriated state. 'I've forgotten how far on Vena is.'

Mrs Bruce tapped her nose. 'It's six month ony road, nearer seven, maybe. I mind on her comin' in an' tellin' me this Dutch sailor had ta'en her twice in the lobby, an' I just ken't she'd land up wi' a bairn in her belly.'

'So it's not Charlie's?' Bathie smiled and kept her voice light, hoping that the woman wouldn't see through her tactics.

'God, no. There was three or four after the Dutchman, but your Charlie was the only ane to believe her when she tell't him it was his.'

Bathie turned to her husband. 'See Mrs . . . er . . . Vena's mother down the outside stairs, Albert.'

When he returned, she was weeping, softly and hopelessly.

'I'll throw the bitch out right now,' he vowed.

'No, we'll tell Charlie in the morning, and we'll have to accept it if he still wants her, but everybody'll think the child's his, and it's going to be born in two or three months.'

Albert held her heaving body for a moment. 'I think you should go to bed, Bathie, and we'll see what tomorrow brings.'

When the newly-married couple came down for breakfast, Charlie looked embarrassed, but Vena winked at Albert, who was outraged but held his tongue for his wife's sake.

Bathie ate very little, and waited until her eldest son was finished. 'I want to speak to you in private, Charlie, so we'd better go through to the parlour.'

Vena frowned, and Albert was pleased to see a little touch of fear come into her eyes. He'd give all he possessed to see Charlie throwing her out on her ear.

Telling her beloved son the truth about his bride was the most difficult thing Bathie had ever undertaken, and she wasn't surprised that it took him some time to believe it.

'Your father's willing to pay her off,' she said, at last, 'and he'll give her whatever she asks for.' Charlie's silence worried her, and she stood, uncomfortably, waiting for him to say something.

A full sixty seconds passed before he said, very quietly, 'It's been a great shock to me, Mother, but I love Vena, no matter what she did before I met her, and I'm absolutely sure that she loves me.'

Her heart plummeted. She certainly hadn't expected this. She'd thought that Charlie would have been glad to see the back of this cheap whore. 'Shouldn't you at least think about it?'

His face was agonized, but his reply was firm. 'I don't need to think about it. I can't live without her.'

It was final, and Bathie bowed her head, while her son looked down on her helplessly. After a moment, he turned and went out, leaving her to weep out her frustration and anger. When she felt more composed, she stood up to return to the kitchen, but before she reached the door, Vena opened it and came in, eyeing her very apprehensively.

Knowing that she would have to accept this girl if she didn't want to lose her son, Bathie said, 'Did Charlie tell you why I wanted to speak to him?'

Vena nodded, then whispered, 'I'm sorry, Mrs Ogilvie. I ken you're disgusted at what I did, but I think the world o' Charlie, an' I'll be a good wife to him, I promise. I was desperate nae to be left wi' a fatherless bairn, that's why I did what I did, an' when Charlie said he'd stick by me, I could hardly believe it. As God's my witness, I'll never look at onybody else again, for he's a fine man.'

A fine man. The words reverberated in Bathie's head – he was still only a boy. 'As long as you keep your word, Vena, I'll never mention what you've done, and I'll think as much of your child as I'd have done if it really was Charlie's.'

'Thank you, Mrs Ogilvie. It's mair than I deserve.'

Seven weeks later, Charlie burst into his parents' room just before three o'clock one morning. 'It's Vena,' he said, urgently. 'She says she's started, and she's very bad.'

They both jumped out of bed, and Albert dressed and ran for Dr McKenzie, while Bathie climbed up to the attics to see what she could do to help Vena.

The sight of the girl's white, terrified face touched her deeply, and as she watched Charlie trying to comfort his wife, Bathie realized that there was no time to waste – Vena had already begun the strong pushing of imminent childbirth.

Thrusting her son aside with a curt, 'Get as much boiling water ready as you can,' she rolled up the sleeves of her thin kimono and prepared to do whatever was necessary. She couldn't leave the girl, even to get a rubber sheet, but it couldn't be helped, so she flung back the bedclothes.

'Pull up your knees and open your legs,' she ordered, and wasn't surprised, when Vena obeyed, to see the crown of the infant's head.

Soothing the girl and coaxing her to push regularly and rhythmically, Bathie delivered the tiny scrap of humanity on her own.

She was attempting to smack some sign of life into it when Gavin McKenzie rushed in, his dark hair tousled, so she laid it down beside Vena and stood aside to let him take over.

When Charlie carried in a steaming basin, she motioned to him to lay it down on the old chest of drawers, her eyes never leaving the bed, but her spirits were sinking at the serious expression on the doctor's face.

Gavin looked up suddenly. 'They're both in a dangerous condition, Charlie,' he said gravely. 'If you want me to try to save the baby, I'll do my best, but I'm very much afraid . . .'

It was Bathie who murmured, 'I think it's too late for that. Save his wife, please.'

Albert, who had come in behind the doctor, put one arm round her and the other round his son, who seemed to be quite unaware of what was happening.

'It's God's will, Charlie,' he said, gently, 'and it's maybe all for the best.'

Bathie began to weep softly.

Chapter Twenty-one

When Bathie's labour pains began, five months later, it was Vena who attended to her until the doctor arrived, Vena who volunteered to look after new-born Ishbel, as well as the other children, until Bathie was on her feet again.

This seventh birth had been even more gruelling than Hetty's, so Bathie was glad to let Vena run the household for several weeks, while she lay in bed thinking. She knew that she'd been very near death, and something kept bothering her, something that she couldn't quite remember.

When it did come to her, one quiet afternoon, she was still puzzled. Someone had murmured to her, during the time she'd been half delirious and hadn't known all that was going on, 'Don't slip away from me, dearest Bathie. I love you.'

It couldn't have been Albert – he hadn't been allowed in the room – yet the voice had been familiar. Had she imagined it, or had she sensed Albert's thoughts from the other side of a closed door? She drifted into an uneasy sleep, hearing the same words over and over again, until she awoke with a start.

It had been Gavin McKenzie's voice! But that was quite ridiculous. His wife had died from consumption nearly four years ago, but he would never say anything like that to her – another man's wife.

And yet he called every day to see how she was, although she'd assured him almost two weeks ago that there was no need.

'Why don't you call me Gavin?' he'd said then, very gently. 'I've known you for at least sixteen years now, Bathie, and if Albert can, I'm sure you could, if you tried.'

She'd smiled, a little embarrassed. 'I suppose I can . . . Gavin.' It had felt strange, but she'd thought nothing of his request. Now that she came to consider it, though, his voice had been tender, and was it possible that his grey eyes had been trying to tell her something at that time? Heavens, she knew his eyes were grey, but she'd never paid any attention to them, not consciously. She was being very foolish, and it just showed how weak she was. She must stop this madness before she started imagining herself in love with him.

As it drew near five o'clock, the time Gavin usually came, she was ashamed of the excitement building up in her. It was Albert she loved – she could never love anybody else. But in spite of herself, she couldn't stop her thoughts dwelling on Gavin McKenzie – his tightly-curled hair, grizzled now, his clean-shaven face, craggy and kind, his long, gentle fingers. Oh, what was she doing, thinking these things?

When he hadn't appeared by seven minutes past five, she was rather relieved, and glad that she'd calmed down, but her heart started beating wildly when Vena popped her head round the door a few moments later.

'Here's Dr McKenzie to see you, Mother,' she announced, and withdrew immediately.

Bathie felt her face flaming. 'I'm not an invalid now and there's no need for you to visit me, doctor.'

A little smile touched the edges of his mouth, making it even more attractive. 'So it's back to doctor, is it? Have you forgotten how to say Gavin?'

'N . . . no,' she stammered, realizing, as he lifted her hand, that he would feel how much her heart was racing, and wishing that Vena had remained in the room with them.

His fingers were cool on her wrist, but he looked up quite anxiously. 'Your pulse is far too rapid. I think you're worrying about something, Bathie, and it's not good for you. I strongly advise you to tell me about it, whatever it is.'

She wanted to snatch her hand away, but was frightened of offending him. 'It's nothing,' she whispered.

'It's not nothing. Your pulse is galloping and . . . ' He stopped suddenly, his eyes searching her face, making her look away hastily. 'I believe you've remembered what I said when I thought you were slipping away. I'm sorry, for I never meant you to know how I feel about you.'

A few seconds passed, during which he looked down at the hand he was holding, and Bathie tried desperately to think of something to say to prevent him from voicing what he was so obviously considering.

Her hand still in his, he sat down on the bed. 'Let me say this once, Bathie, and I'll never mention it again. The first time I attended you I thought you were very

194

attractive, but that was it. I loved my wife as much as Albert loved you.'

Squirming a little, Bathie prayed that he wouldn't go any further. It was indecent for a married woman to be sitting in bed waiting for another man's declaration of love.

Clearing his throat nervously, Gavin carried on. 'Even before Margaret died, I'd begun to love you, but it was a love which needed nothing in return.'

'I think you've said enough, Gavin.' She had to stop him. This wild pounding in her veins was definitely not good for her, however heart-warming it was to be told she was loved.

He seemed not to have heard. 'It was a different kind of love from what I had for my wife, but it grew stronger as time went past. I missed Margaret very much after she died, and my one comfort was to think of you.' His head dropped. 'I'd no right, Bathie, and I'm sorry if I've embarrassed you. I thought we were going to lose you, and I was feeling angry with Albert for making you pregnant again.'

Bathie felt absolutely helpless. How could she tell him – this man who professed to love her – of the loathsome way in which Ishbel had been conceived? Albert had made love to her many times since the night he'd practically raped her, but she was certain that the seed had been planted then.

Her sigh was half a sob, and Gavin raised his head. 'I'm sorry, my dear. I've been thoughtless and cruel. You're in no fit state to deal with this. I know you love Albert, and that's as it should be, but I hope we can still be friends.'

'Yes, of course we can.' The awkward moments were over, but she knew that their relationship could never be quite the same again.

'I don't know what we'd have done without Vena,' Bathie told her husband one night after they went to bed.

Albert grunted an agreement. 'It was just as well her bairn died, and there's nothing to remind us what she

195

used to be. You made the right decision that night, my love.'

'Somebody had to, and I think it's what Charlie himself would have wanted, though he was too shocked to say anything. You know, Albert, I'm glad he married her, though I was very angry about it at the time.'

'That mother of hers was a bad example, but she'll soon learn how to behave properly.'

'She's doing very well, and I'm very fond of her now, but I must admit I'm thankful that Donnie hasn't got involved with any girls. He doesn't seem to take any interest in them.'

'He will, Bathie, he will, but he'll maybe be like his father and take a long time until he meets the right one. If he finds as good a wife as I did, he'll be a very lucky man.'

Two days later, the house on the brow of the Gallowgate was shaken by the news of Wattie Ogilvie's death. Always so healthy, he had suffered a fatal heart attack when helping Nell to shift furniture for her spring cleaning.

Albert and Bathie, both very upset, dropped everything and went to Market Street with the woman who had been sent to tell them. Nell was white-faced, but dry-eyed, as she took them into the kitchen.

'I aye thought I'd go first, Albert,' she murmured sadly, 'an' I used to worry if your father would manage on his own. He never did a blessed hand's turn in the house, an' it was only me complainin' o' a sair back that made him shift the wardrobe himsel'. It's my fault he's awa'.'

Laying his hand on her shoulder, Albert tried to comfort her. 'It's not your fault, Mother, and you should be glad Father went so quick and didn't have to suffer.'

'Aye, I suppose I should. Albert, will you see to things for me? I got Beenie Reid to send a wire to Walter an' Jimmy afore she went for you, but they're that far awa', they'll nae be here in time for that, if they come at a'.'

'They'll come, I'm sure, but I'll make all the arrangements for you, Mother, so don't worry about it. I'll go right now, and Bathie'll stop with you till I come back.'

When he went out, Nell turned to her daughter-in-law. 'I'm happy Albert's got you, lass. You've been a good wife to him, an' I'll nae be feared to leave him when my time comes.'

'That won't be for a long time yet, Grandma.' Bathie felt rather inadequate. She'd loved Wattie and was heartbroken by his death, and she was finding it hard not to show her sorrow in front of his composed widow.

'Wattie wasna an auld man,' Nell observed, 'but he worked hard at the fishin', an' they went to sea come hail, wind or shine. He ken't nothing else, for his father went to the sea afore him, an' his father's father afore that. He was against him takin' me for a wife, Wattie's father. I was a country lassie workin' as a servant in the toon when we first met each other, an' he was a fine upstandin' lad, wi' his red hair an' his dark eyes . . . oh, he had my he'rt as soon's I looked at him. We walked oot for a good while afore he took me to meet his folk. They bade in auld Torry and they werena pleased. Fisher folk are close-knit, you see, an' I wasna a fisher lassie.'

A sad smile played across her lips. 'Auld Jeemsie – that was Wattie's father, an' a right devil he could be – said he'd put him oot if he didna stop seein' me, an' Wattie said he'd nae want to bide, ony road. They'd a real set-to, shoutin' an' sweirin' an' thumpin' on the table, an' I was feared they'd start thumpin' each other, they were baith that angry, an' their faces as red as turkey cocks.'

Bathie was surprised that Albert's father had had to battle to marry the girl he loved, the same as Albert had done for her, but she said nothing because it seemed almost as if the old woman was talking to herself.

Nell twisted her broad golden wedding band. 'It a' come right in the hinner-end, though, for auld Jeemsie started laughin', an' said Wattie was just as thrawn as himsel'. Wattie an' me had near fifty year thegither – fifty happy year, though we had our ups an' doons, an' I'd to learn how to be a fisher's wife.' She straightened up, her voice becoming stronger. 'Oh, I'm sorry, Bathie. I'd near forgot you were there.'

'It's all right, Grandma. I was very interested. It must have been a hard life for you as well as for Grandpa.'

'Aye, well, it was, I suppose, but I'd a good man an' three sons, an' I never regretted weddin' him. He wasna ane for the women, so I never had that to worry aboot, but I aye ken't the sea was his first love, an' I didna mind, though I was pleased when he gi'ed it up.' She got to her feet abruptly. 'We'd best ha'e a cuppie tea, afore I start feelin' sorry for mysel'.'

She was clearing up again when Albert returned.

'That's everything arranged, Mother,' he said, briskly. 'The undertaker'll be here as soon as he can, and the funeral's on Wednesday at two. I told them St Clement's kirkyard, seeing that's where his mother and father are buried, but if you want it somewhere else, I can change it.'

'No, no, St Clement's'll do fine.' Nell looked up at her son pathetically. 'What does it matter, ony road, when he'll never ken where he's laid?'

'He'll be nearer the sea,' Albert reminded her, gently.

'Aye, so he will. That would ha'e pleased him.'

'Will I stay tonight?' Bathie asked, thinking that she would hate to be alone with a corpse if it were her.

'No, no, you've your bairns to see to, Bathie, my dear, but thank you for offerin'. Beenie Reid, next door, said she'd come in an' bide wi' me the night, an' Walter an' Jimmy should be here by the morn, so aff you go, the pair o' ye.'

'We're not going until the undertakers have been,' Albert said, sitting down.

'She's taking it very well,' Bathie remarked, when they were walking up Market Street later. 'I'm sure I wouldn't want to go on living if anything happened to you.'

'I'd be the same if anything happened to you, Bathie, but we're different.'

'We're not different.' She repeated what Nell had told her about Wattie and his father, and Albert looked thoughtful.

'I never heard that before. You never think your mother and father had loved each other, or . . . anything like that.'

Bathie had never thought about it with regard to her own parents, either, and she wondered if her mother would have been so calm if *her* husband had just died.

She wasn't from the same mould as Nell Ogilvie, of course, and she'd never had to worry about what Arthur was doing if he wasn't at home – he was never away from home, except to go to the bank.

When they arrived back at the Gallowgate, Albert rejoined Charlie and Donnie in the shop, but the strain of the last few hours was telling on Bathie, so she went into the parlour to have a short rest. Wattie's death hit her with full force when she was on her own, and she gave way to the sorrow she had repressed in front of Nell, sobbing as if she would never stop.

Half an hour later, she climbed the stairs to the nursery, where Vena reported that everything was quiet.

Albert allowed himself no time to think – he even spent the evening stocking up shelves – so when he went to bed, his grief was all the deeper for having been held back for so long.

Bathie cradled him in her arms until his shuddering body stilled, then without a word, he mounted her, and fell asleep the minute he was satisfied.

He hadn't touched her since Ishbel had been born, eight months before, and she didn't blame him for not being careful. He'd been so upset about his father that there was an excuse for him, but she wondered ruefully – since his seed was potent and her body seemed to be receptive to it – if this was the planting of little J, boy or girl, whichever it might prove to be. She could only wait and see.

There was a large crowd at Wattie Ogilvie's funeral. His seafaring friends turned out in full force, young and old, and dozens of neighbours from Market Street, who had known and liked the bluff, kindly man for years. Arthur Johnstone also came to pay his last respects to his daughter's father-in-law, whom he had come to regard very highly.

It was difficult for Bathie to believe that Walter and Jimmy were Albert's brothers, they were so different from him, both in looks and manners. They had Nell's dark hair, but their sharp faces showed none of the kindness that hers always bore, and their eyes were hard and greedy. They seemed ill-at-ease with Albert's wife, and she was hurt when they ignored her as much as they decently could.

Feeling like an outsider, she wandered desolately over to the window, and stood for some time watching the carts going up the steep hill from the harbour.

She jumped when Nell touched her shoulder.

'Bathie, I ken how you must feel, for I felt the same wi' Wattie's folk when I met them first, but never mind the rest o' them. You were closer to him than Walter an' Jimmy ever were, or their useless wives. Wattie thought the world o' you, lass.'

It was too much for Bathie and she buried her head in the other woman's shoulder. 'I loved him,' she whispered. 'And you, too. I'm sorry . . . I'm sorry.'

'Aye, I ken.' Nell patted her back. 'But we havena lost him, for he'll aye be in oor he'rts.'

She regarded Bathie for a moment, then added, 'An' there's nae need for you to feel sorry for me, my dear, for I've got Albert an' you, an' my grandchildren, an' a' my friends roon aboot me, so I'll never be lonely. What's mair, I've got happy memories to dwell on if I feel doon. Come on, noo, lass, an' let folk see you're made o' stronger stuff than they think.' Bathie swallowed and tried to pull herself together, for Wattie's sake. He wouldn't like her to make a fool of herself, so she followed Nell across the room, and listened to murmurs of sympathy until everyone had gone except the family.

It was only then that her mother-in-law sat down by the fire. 'There's nothin' to divide oot,' she told her three sons, 'for we just made sure we had enough to see us buried decent. That's your father laid to rest, an' there's as much as see me laid beside him. We didna ha'e muckle, but we never owed a bawbee to a soul.'

Walter, the eldest, looked at her hopefully. 'You'll be giving up the house and selling your furniture, though, won't you, Mother?'

'It's my hame, an' I'll bide here till I go to join your father.' Nell was indignant.

Jimmy took over. 'We'll be going back tomorrow, but Albert and . . . his wife will make sure you're all right.'

'I can see to mysel',' his mother snapped.

'As long as you understand that me and Walter won't be able to come up again for a long time, and we've no room for you in any of our houses.'

'I understand perfectly.' Nell glared at him. 'I ken where I'm nae wanted.'

'Oh, Mother, it's not like . . . ' Walter was blustering now.

'An' I ken where I dinna want to go,' she interrupted. 'I've to make a new life for mysel' now, on my ain.'

Albert stood up, uncertainly. He was very angry with his brothers, but wanted to avoid a scene. 'Well, Bathie, we'd better be off.'

'I'll come to see you tomorrow afternoon,' Bathie said quietly to her mother-in-law. 'Just for a little while.'

'I'll be pleased to see you, but dinna feel obliged . . . '

'I want to.' Bathie turned to her other in-laws. 'Well, goodbye. It was nice meeting you.'

None of them stood up or offered to shake hands, so she followed her husband outside.

Taking her arm, he said, 'They're not worth bothering about, my love, and they'll be away tomorrow, so things'll be the same as they were before.'

No, Bathie thought, sadly, things would never be the same as they were before. There would be no Wattie Ogilvie to cheer them up with his droll sayings.

Chapter Twenty-two

Nell had known as soon as Bathie herself, if not sooner, that she was pregnant again, and had been furious at Albert.

'He's ower hot-blooded,' she'd declared, 'but he should ken better by this time, surely. Seven bairns is mair than enough for ony woman, an' you're nae as strong as some. You'll ha'e to say no to him, after this ane's born.'

Bathie knew that she could never refuse her husband, and she couldn't tell his mother that this one had been conceived on the day his father died, so she just gave a little smile.

Henrietta Johnstone took much longer to recognize what her daughter was trying to conceal. 'You are very pale,' she said, when she was paying a call one afternoon. 'Your face actually looks kind of pinched, almost as if . . . Oh, Bathia, it is not another child, is it?' Her nostrils flared in disgust and her thin lips compressed even more tightly.

'Yes, I'm afraid so.' Bathie waited, apprehensively.

'I would never have thought that Albert could be so . . . inconsiderate,' Henrietta stormed. 'Really! He should try to control himself, or better still, he should learn to leave you alone, and not expect you to . . . ' She paused, then carried on. 'You were quite ill when Ishbel was born, and if I remember correctly, you told me he had promised not to . . . '

'He did promise, but . . . ' Bathie lifted her shoulders briefly. What was the use of trying to explain? It made no difference how it had happened. It had happened and nothing could be done about it now.

'Your father must speak to him.'

'No, Mother, please. It'll only make things worse.'

'He must be told to control his . . . lust.'

'I don't want anybody to interfere. I knew you'd be upset about it, but it's my life, and I'm not complaining.'

'It is absolutely shameful.' Henrietta shook her head

as if that would dispose of the new life in her daughter's womb.

It was some time before Albert himself noticed. 'Have you put on weight?' he asked her one morning as he lay in bed and watched her dressing. 'If I didn't know better, I'd think you were . . . ' He frowned. 'How far on are you?'

'Seven months.' Her eyes were apologetic. 'I'm sorry.'

'It's me should be sorry.' His hand rose to his brow. 'It was the day my father died, for I've never . . . Oh, Bathie, I can't . . . touch you without . . . I can't pull out of you, I just can't, and I promised you. Oh, my God!' He raised his eyes. 'Why didn't you tell me as soon as you found out?'

'It wouldn't have made any difference, would it? I knew you'd be angry at yourself.' Her mouth twisted. 'I don't mind, Albert, and you'll maybe get your third son, after all.'

Jumping abruptly out of bed, he kissed her tenderly. 'My father was right. He once said you were too good for me.' His voice had a catch in it as he went on. 'I've made a machine out of you, a machine for producing the bairns I can't help making, and you're not fit to have any more. Oh, Bathie, why didn't you stop me?'

'Albert, I love you.' It was all she could say.

After suppertime that night, he waited until the younger children were in bed, then gathered Charlie, Vena, Donnie and Ellie together in the parlour. 'Your mother is going to have another child. She was scared to tell me before, for I'd sworn to her there would be no more, but it's my fault. I can't stop myself.'

He looked round their astonished faces. 'You're all old enough to understand what I mean, but now it's happened, I want you to make sure she doesn't do too much.'

'Oh, Albert.' Bathie was horrified at what he'd admitted to them, and glanced at her daughter-in-law to see how she was taking it. Vena, however, wasn't smiling, as she'd feared, but was regarding Albert as if she were seeing him properly for the first time.

Charlie was the first to speak after the shocked silence. 'You can depend on us, Father. Can't he, Vena?'

'We won't let her lift a finger.'

Although Ellie hadn't understood everything her father had said, she chimed in, 'And Donnie and me'll be the same.'

'Donnie and I,' Albert corrected, without thinking.

Ellie grinned wickedly. 'You, too, Father.' She was just teasing, of course, because she knew what he'd meant this time.

The following afternoon, Albert, having decided that he'd better get it over quickly, went to Froghall to tell the doctor that there would be another confinement to attend.

'I got the shock of my life,' he burst out when he got home. 'Gavin ranted and raved like a bloody madman. He even accused me of having no consideration for you, and then said he wished he could castrate me.'

Albert wouldn't have taken kindly to that, Bathie thought, and prayed that he hadn't said something he'd regret.

'I nearly told him to go to hell, but he's a good doctor and we're going to need him.' Albert thoughtfully stroked the cleft in his chin. 'It wasn't like Gavin, though.'

'He knew how ill I was last time.'

Grimacing, Albert muttered, 'Aye, that's true.'

Bathie couldn't help feeling guilty. On the night that Gavin had told her of his love, she'd lain awake imagining him taking her in his arms and kissing her, but that was when she was still weak from having Ishbel, and she had never allowed herself to think anything like that again. Nevertheless, she was very relieved that Albert had let the matter drop.

When Bathie's labour started, one Saturday morning, Vena noticed immediately, and ordered her straight back to bed, then despatched Ellie to fetch the doctor.

Two hours later, Bathie didn't care whether she lived or died. In fact, she'd have been quite happy to die, to drift peacefully away from the excruciating pains which were ripping through her, leaving her ashen-faced and gasping for breath. They were even worse than last time.

Gavin McKenzie had been at another confinement, so was late in coming, but he saw at once that his warnings to Albert had not been exaggerated. This dear woman's life was hanging in the balance.

Ellie was ordered to keep Albert out, should he come up from the shop, and to keep the rest of the family well away from the bedroom on the first floor. In tears, she passed his message on to her father at dinnertime, then carried the two kettles through to the bedroom.

'He can't keep me away from my wife,' Albert shouted, and marched to the door after her, but Charlie grabbed his sleeve. 'No, Father. I know how you feel, but you must let the man do his job without any interference.'

'Your mother needs me,' Albert roared, beside himself with fury at Gavin McKenzie and with deep fear for his wife, and it took the combined efforts of both his sons to keep him from bursting into the other room.

'I have to go to her. She might die and I . . . '

'You should have thought of that before.' Charlie's eyes were hard with scorn. 'God Almighty, Father, you've been married to her for nearly twenty years, and she's given you seven living children already. Surely you could have learned to control yourself by this time?' He jumped back as Albert's open hand hit the side of his face.

'The same as you control yourself? Or are you not man enough to father a bairn? You haven't had one of your own.'

'Father!' It came like the crack of a whip from Donnie. 'You've gone too far, and it's Mother you should be thinking about, not standing fighting like . . . '

An unearthly scream startled them, and Albert collapsed into a chair, shaking all over. Scream after scream followed with terrifying regularity, until the three men thought they could bear it no longer. It was like nothing any of them had ever heard in their whole lives before.

When at last the chilling, blood-curdling noise stopped, they looked at each other in alarm in the eerie silence which fell, then Charlie laid his hand over one of his father's and Donnie covered the other.

Albert's spine seemed to give way, and he slumped back in the chair, his chin resting on his chest. 'Bathie . . . Bathie,' he moaned. 'You can't leave me, for it would be the finish of me.' Conscious of the pressure on his hands, he was beyond comfort.

'Father.' Charlie spoke gently. 'If it's God's will . . . '

Albert lifted his tortured face. 'It can't be God's will. I swear to Him, in front of my sons, that I'll never touch her again if He spares her.'

They all looked up apprehensively when the door from the landing opened, but it was only Flo who came in.

'What's happened? We heard . . . ? Mother's not . . . ?'

Donnie scowled and waved his free hand to make her leave, but she advanced into the kitchen.

'Ellie made us take our dinner upstairs, but there was that awful screaming and I had to find out what it was.'

'Mother's having the baby,' Donnie told her. 'Go back, and keep the others up there, please.'

'But . . . '

'Flo.' Albert's voice broke. 'Just do what you're told.'

When Ellie returned with the empty kettles, three heads jerked up, three pairs of eyes asked the same silent question.

'Mother's having a terrible time,' she whispered, quite unnecessarily. 'She's unconscious just now, but the doctor's struggling to pull her through.' Going over to the sink, she turned on the water tap to fill the two kettles again.

Albert's face had turned as white as the cloth on the table. 'Oh, my God!' he muttered, looking at Charlie, but the red weal across his son's face reminded him of how he'd struck out, and he felt sickened by his own behaviour.

'I'm sorry, Charlie.' It came out as a faint whisper. 'I'd no right to hit you.'

'You'd every right. I was wrong in saying what I did, but we shouldn't have been fighting at a time like this.'

Ellie, having filled the kettles and placed them on the hob, swept past them carrying two steaming pots.

Charlie watched her going out, then said, in a low voice, 'We'd better go and open the shop, Donnie. Father can stay up here if he wants to.'

'I have to stay,' Albert muttered.

When his sons went out, he buried his head in his hands, and prayed that God wouldn't take his wife from him. All afternoon he sat, desperately wishing that he knew what was going on behind the bedroom door, but each time Ellie came through, she just said, 'She's still the same.'

His sons had come up for their supper before Ellie came through with her face wreathed in smiles. 'She's come round, Father, and the doctor says she's going to be all right.'

Albert's head had lifted fearfully at her entrance, and he breathed, 'Thank you, God.'

'And you've got another son, at last.' Ellie's laugh had a slight tremor in it. 'Vena got the baby breathing the time the doctor was working on Mother.'

'Good old Vena.' Donnie exuberantly slapped his brother on the back, and Charlie grinned proudly.

Albert regarded his eldest son earnestly. 'It's a good thing for us you were determined to take that girl for your wife, Charlie. Your mother and I weren't at all happy about it at the time, but she's been a godsend, more than once.'

'Mother wants to see you, Father,' Ellie remarked, 'and the doctor says you can go through, but just for a minute.'

He was on his feet at once. 'Why didn't you tell me?'

Although only Vena and Gavin McKenzie were there with Bathie, it seemed to Albert that the room was full of people. He crossed quickly to the bed. 'Oh, Bathie, my love, my dear, dear love.' He took her hand and lifted it to his lips, afraid to kiss her properly. There was a translucence about her face that alarmed him, and he glanced at the doctor.

'She's very weak, and it's going to take her a long time to get over this.' Gavin looked exhausted. 'We've all had a long struggle, but I'll leave your wife and child in this young lady's capable hands.' His eyes rested briefly on Vena, who coloured and looked away in confusion.

'I'll see you out, Gavin.' Albert led the way.

At the top of the outside stairs, the doctor breathed air deep into his lungs before he spoke. 'I'm sorry if I sound brutal, Albert, but if Bathie has another pregnancy, it'll kill her. This one almost did.'

'Gavin, I've sworn to my Maker I'll never touch her again.'

'It's the only way, Albert, I'm afraid, and I'm sorry.'

'You've nothing to be sorry for. If it hadn't been for you, I'd have lost her today.' He clasped the other man's hand. 'Thank you, Gavin, for everything.'

'There's one other thing, Albert. The child is alive, but I don't know for how much longer.'

In spite of Albert's gasp of dismay, he carried on. 'I want you to prepare Bathie, but try not to upset her too much.'

'I'll do my best. I don't care for myself, as long as I've still got my wife, but . . . Oh, my God! Poor Bathie.'

'It's only a matter of weeks, maybe just days, but it's inevitable.' The doctor went slowly down the iron stairs.

The tears were running down Albert's face now, but he made no attempt to wipe them away. He wasn't crying for the doomed infant, but for the heartache it would cause Bathie, when she'd come through so much to give him birth.

After almost five minutes, he drew a shuddering breath, ran his cuff over his face and turned to go inside.

Vena met him at the bedroom door. 'She's sleeping now, Father.'

'I'm going to sit with her all night. It's the only thing I can do to make up for . . . '

'Did the doctor say anything about the baby?'

'He said it wouldn't live long.'

'I was feared for that.' She shook her head mournfully.

Not by one word or gesture did Gavin do anything out of place, and Bathie looked forward to his visits. It wasn't until he told her that he wouldn't call again that she realized how far her gratitude to him had gone. Not gratitude any longer, but deep and lasting affection. It had been his tender care that had helped her to bear the death of little James, just ten days after he was born, although Albert had done his best.

It was on the tip of her tongue to ask the doctor not to stop visiting, but she managed to bite the words back.

At suppertime, Albert said, 'Gavin came into the shop to tell me he wouldn't be back, but we owe him such a lot, I asked him to come to supper on Sunday. I hope you don't mind.'

She swallowed – it would be difficult seeing him on a different footing from doctor and patient – but met her husband's eyes. 'I don't mind – it was good of you.'

By Sunday, she'd been on her feet for three days, and her anxiety about her hair, and if her figure was back to normal, made Vena remark, 'You look just fine, Mother. The doctor'll take a fancy to you if you're not careful.'

Bathie wondered if this was a warning, but didn't really care. She tried on her second-best dress – not the very best, in case Albert read something into it – and was pleased that it didn't look too tight, although it strained a little across the bust. Luckily, it fastened down the back.

When her husband returned from church with his two sons and his four eldest daughters, he exclaimed at the sight of her. 'My, Bathie, you're looking the picture of health again. Be careful not to overtire yourself.'

She laughed, but took a rest in the early afternoon to be sure she'd look her best at suppertime. When she heard the knock at half past four, she glanced at Albert and a stab of alarm shot through her when she saw his eyes fixed on her.

Ellie ran down to let the visitor in, but when she came back, she announced, 'It's Grandmother and Grandfather.'

Henrietta walked in first, and her eyebrows lifted above the top of her spectacles when she saw Bathie sitting by the fire. 'I am glad to see that you are up and about again. No one came to tell us how you were.'

209

Arthur stared at his son-in-law. 'Surely you could have sent Ellie or one of the others to let us know, if *you* could not tear yourself away from your wife?'

Recalling what Arthur had said, in his drunken ramblings on the day that Hetty was born, Albert was rather incensed by the man's sanctimonious sarcasm. Fortunately, Ellie saved him from having to reply.

'I'm sorry, Grandfather. We've all been busy.'

Recovered slightly after her disappointment that it wasn't Gavin who had come in, Bathie said, 'I'm fine, Mother. There was no need for you to worry about me.'

Another loud knock made her jump. 'That'll be the doctor this time.' Hoping that she sounded calm enough, she turned to her mother and added, 'Albert invited him to supper because he's been so attentive to me.'

'Your doctor?' Henrietta's brows met then parted slowly. 'He will tell us the truth about your state of health.'

A loud gasp from Arthur Johnstone made them all look at him as he staggered suddenly and collapsed across the couch, his face grey and beads of perspiration standing out on his high forehead.

'Is it the same pain again, Arthur?' exclaimed his wife.

Gavin McKenzie came in unnoticed, grasped the situation and strode over to the couch. Pushing Albert and Henrietta aside, he probed gently around the area Arthur was indicating until his fingers told him what he wanted to know, and the man's sharp cry only served to endorse his diagnosis.

'Appendicitis,' he said, tersely. 'It's acute, and needs to be operated on immediately. Can you give me a hand to get him downstairs, Albert? I'll have to take him to the Infirmary.'

Donnie and Ellie took their sisters upstairs out of the way, leaving Bathie and her mother alone in the parlour.

'He has been complaining several times of a pain there,' Henrietta said, 'but I never thought . . . you know your father. He is half dead when he has a cold. Your doctor seems to be a very capable man. What is his name?'

'It's McKenzie. Gavin McKenzie.' Her father's collapse had put an effective stop to Bathie's romantically-inclined thoughts towards him. There really had been nothing between them, but she felt as guilty as if they'd been carrying on an illicit love affair for years.

'Gavin?' Henrietta smiled. 'What a nice name for such a nice man. You know, Bathia, he is exactly the kind of man your father would have been happy to see you marrying. He is well educated, very handsome and mannerly.'

'Oh, Mother. Gavin's everything you say, but you know I love Albert.'

'How much does he love you, though? Do you think, if he really loved you for yourself, he would have saddled you with so many children? Ten, if they had all lived.'

What her mother was saying made Bathie wonder again if Albert had really meant to propose to her on that far-off day, or if it was the beast inside him that had wanted her for her body alone, as her father had said at the time.

'He does love me, Mother.' It sounded unconvincing.

'Do you remember how much your father was against you marrying him at first? I wonder now if he had recognized the same needs in Albert as he had himself. He only gave in when I threatened to leave him if he did not stop . . . er . . . ' She halted in confusion.

'Stop what?'

'I did not want you to know, Bathia, but I suppose I owe you an explanation. Some men have insatiable appetites for . . . that sort of thing, you know, and your father was no exception. When I refused him, he . . . er . . . went to my maids. That is all over now, of course.'

Bathie was shocked and angry at what her mother had said about Albert and her father, also worried about her own guilty confusion over Gavin McKenzie, and finding out the reason for the reversal of her father's decision about her marriage did nothing to ease the tumult in her brain.

They sat in silence until Vena tapped and came in. 'Will Grandmother be staying for supper? It's nearly ready.'

Bathie nodded. 'Yes, she'll be staying, and you can serve it now. There's no sense in all of us going hungry.'

When Vena went out, Henrietta leaned forward anxiously. 'Bathia, I am sorry, I never meant to tell you . . .'

'We all say things we don't mean, when we're upset.'

'But telling you that about your father, and saying those awful things about Albert. I really do like him, you know. He kept his word and paid me back every penny of the loan, with interest I did not want.'

'He's an honourable man, Mother, and please don't think it's all his fault. I agreed with him, from the very first, that we'd have a large family, and I'm very happy with all my beautiful children.'

Their tête-à-tête was brought to an end by the return of the two men from the Infirmary.

'They said we were just in time,' Albert informed them. 'They're going to operate as soon as they can.'

Bathie kept her voice as calm as she could with Gavin's eyes on her. 'It's a good thing you were here, Doctor.'

He smiled stiffly. 'Appendicitis is unusual in a man his age, but I was sure that it couldn't be anything else.'

At the table, while Henrietta was being profuse in her thanks to the doctor, Bathie turned to Albert.

'Are you sure my father will be all right? You're not keeping anything from me, are you?'

'I'm telling you everything I know, my love. They told Gavin there shouldn't be any problems, so don't worry.'

He squeezed her hand, but drew away hastily when he saw her glancing towards the other man.

Bathie was ashamed that she'd made him jealous, and took his hand again, very deliberately, keeping her voice at its normal pitch as she said, 'I love you, Albert.'

She was conscious that Gavin was looking at her across the table, and that all other eyes were also on her, but she kept her head turned towards her husband.

'It'll always be you I love, Albert,' she declared, 'no matter what happens.'

Chapter Twenty-three

'It gives you a funny feeling when the king dies, doesn't it? As if things are going to be different.'

Bathie Ogilvie had been listening to her husband reading out the front page of the *Aberdeen Journal*.

Albert nodded. 'Aye, everything changes when there's a new ruler to the country. Mind you, Edward was only king for nine years, and Victoria reigned for more than sixty. I wonder how long this George the Fifth'll have?'

'Edward would have had longer if his mother had let him. Fancy making him wait till he was sixty before he was King.'

Albert's eyes twinkled. 'She couldn't die just to please him, though. Not even a Queen can do that.'

Bathie was horrified. 'What a thing to say. You know what I mean. She could have abdicated, couldn't she?'

'Aye, she could, I suppose, but she didn't think Edward was fit to be king.'

'Neither he was. Carrying on with women the way he did. Poor Alexandra must have been heartbroken.'

'Royalty's different from ordinary folk, Bathie.'

'They're not when it comes to things like that. I tell you, Albert, I couldn't live with you if I thought you were carrying on with anybody else.'

Her serious face made him laugh. 'She's got appearances to think of, that's the difference. She was the queen, and the queen can't leave her husband, no matter what he's done.'

'More's the pity, then.'

Bathie looked up as their eldest daughter walked into the parlour with her coat on. 'You're not going out again, are you, Ellie? That's every night for about a fortnight.'

'I think our Ellie's got a steady lad.' Albert winked and the girl blushed to the roots of her deep chestnut hair. 'So I'm right, am I?' He smiled indulgently.

'I don't want any of the rest to know, they'll tease me.' Ellie's dark eyes pleaded with him.

'We won't tell them, but I'd like to know a bit about him.' Albert felt rather jealous of this unknown youth who seemed to have captured his favourite daughter's heart.

'His name's Jack Lornie, and he'll be nineteen in two weeks. He's very nice.' She blushed again, deeper than before. 'He's a conductor on the tramways, and I got to know him when I was coming home from Ferryhill one night.'

'How long have you been going with this one?' Bathie was quite surprised that Ellie had been keeping it to herself. She was usually so open about all the boys who took her out, and only went with them once, as a rule.

'Just over a month. I would have told you, Mother, but . . . I've always told you everything before. I never told you lies.'

Bathie had assumed that the girl was meeting some of the friends she'd made through the church. 'No,' she admitted, 'you never told any lies, but I'd have liked to know the truth.'

Ellie smiled mischievously. 'You know now.'

Her step was springy when she went out, making Albert say sadly, 'She's not old enough to be going steady with a lad. I hope she's not serious about him.'

'Don't act the heavy father,' Bathie laughed. 'She's eighteen, two years older than I was when I married you.'

'That was different.'

'No, it wasn't, and you can't hold on to her for ever, even if she is your pet.'

'She's not my pet.' Albert's indignant expression softened into a smile. 'Nothing goes past you, does it? I've always had a soft spot for Ellie, ever since she was born. Remember the trouble she used to get into when she was little?'

'She's always known her own mind, and, if she wants to, she'll marry this boy, whatever we say, though we could be reading more into it than there really is. Let her have her way, Albert. If you try to stop her seeing him, she'll just be more determined. You should know her by this time.'

'Aye.' He smiled crookedly. 'She's got a thrawn streak in her, the same as me.'

Chuckling, Bathie said, 'That's true, and if we don't interfere, she'll maybe tire of him in a week or so.'

Ellie didn't tire of Jack Lornie, however, and her initial attraction to him developed into something much deeper over the weeks, until eventually she confided in Flo. 'Don't tell any of the rest, but I'm in love.'

Flo's reaction was all that she'd feared. 'Oh, Ellie, you speak a lot of rubbish. You can't be in love, you never go out with any boy long enough.'

'That's all you know.' Ellie wished she hadn't mentioned it, but it was too late now.

'Father'll go mad if he finds out.'

'He knows, and Mother as well, for I told them about Jack ages ago, and they didn't·say anything.'

'Jack? Jack who? And how did you meet him? You never said anything about him before.'

Ellie told her all the details, then said, 'I do love him, Flo, and I think he loves me.'

'He must be daft, then.'

'He's not, he's really nice, and I'm sure he wants to marry me. He hasn't asked me yet, but I'll say yes if he does.'

'I bet he hasn't even kissed you.'

'He has so. Well, just little pecks when he takes me home, but he'll do it properly one of these nights.'

Flo sighed. 'I feel uncomfortable when any boy speaks to me, though I haven't met that many, really. I don't even think I'd go out with one if he did ask me.'

'You'll know the right one when you meet him. Jack just looked at me when he took my fare, and I could feel a spark of something between us, maybe love at first sight. You'll know what I mean when it happens to you.'

'I don't think it'll ever happen to me.' Flo screwed up her nose ruefully. 'But you never know, it might.'

Jack Lornie started a late shift the following night, so Ellie had to wait a full week before he took her out again. Luckily, it was a warm, dry evening, so they walked to the Bridge of Don, then along the beach, and while they strolled, Jack told her of his ambition to travel.

'I'd like to go to France, and Germany, and Spain, just to see how the people live there. I often look at folk on the tram and try to imagine what kind of houses they live in, what they work at. Oh, it must sound silly to you.'

'No, it doesn't sound silly.' Ellie had never thought along these lines herself, but it sounded interesting.

'After that,' his voice was high with excitement, 'I'd like to see the rest of the world – America, Australia . . . '

He stopped, the light going out of his eyes. 'Oh, Ellie, it's only a dream. I'd have to work my passage, but it would mean I'd be away for years.'

Ellie's face fell. Years? She could hardly bear it when she didn't see him for a week.

He was still talking. 'I don't want to leave you, though.'

'Take me with you.' All practicalities were forgotten.

'Oh, no!' He sounded shocked. 'It'd be bad enough for a man, but a girl . . . No, it's impossible, Ellie.'

Her racing thoughts halted. 'What did you mean, when you said you didn't want to leave me?'

'Just what I said. I think I love you.'

'Oh, Jack, I think I love you, too.'

At last Ellie received the proper kisses she longed for. She'd known that they'd be wonderful, but hadn't imagined that she could feel anything like this. Her hands slid up round his neck and she was aware of nothing but his body against hers.

'If you only knew how much I've wanted to do this,' he murmured. 'But I was scared I'd frighten you.'

'You wouldn't have frightened me, I wanted you to do it.'

His kisses became more passionate, and Ellie could hardly breathe for the thrill of them, so she wasn't conscious of his arms slipping downwards until his hands reached the small of her back. When he held her so close, she could feel something big and hard pressing into her at the front, and a picture of Donnie came into her mind.

216

She'd almost forgotten it. Donnie, panting and red faced, before he'd buttoned up his trousers to hide the huge thing she'd only caught a glimpse of.

Jack looked puzzled when she shoved him away. 'What's wrong, Ellie? Have I frightened you with my kisses, after all?'

'No, it's not that. I remembered something. I'll have to go home now, Jack, and don't bother coming with me.'

'All right, if that's how you feel.'

Her conscience pricked her at the hurt note in his voice, but she stalked off, still trying to come to grips with the memory he'd evoked. She'd never learned the truth of what Donnie had been doing that night, so how could she find out if it was right or wrong for it to happen? And why it happened at all?

She was about to cross Castle Street when she remembered one person who always answered her questions honestly. This was different, of course, but Grandma was her only hope.

Nell was quite surprised to see her at that time of night, but Ellie often surprised her. 'I was thinkin' aboot goin' to my bed, lass, but did you want to speak to me aboot somethin'?'

Ellie hesitated, then decided she may as well ask now she was there. 'Grandma, there's something about boys I just don't understand. I can't ask Mother or Flo, but if I tell you what it is, will you tell me the truth and not laugh at me?'

'I'll do my best, Ellie.' Nell smiled.

The girl told her everything, and ended up, 'So I want to know why their things grow big – Donnie wouldn't tell me.'

Her forthright attitude had alarmed Nell at first, but it proved how innocent Ellie was, so she did her best as she had promised, and explained the phenomenon as simply as she could.

Ellie listened intently, then remarked, 'So it's not wrong for a boy to be like that, is it?'

'It's nae wrong, lassie, it's very natural.'

'Would Jack have wanted to put it inside me, like Charlie did to Vena? Donnie said that's why they'd to get married.'

Stifling the amusement she felt, Nell said, 'If your Jack's a decent laddie, he'll nae do onything like that, even if he feels like it.'

Ellie frowned. 'It must be wrong if decent boys don't . . .'

'Oh, Ellie, you'd ask the breeks off a Heilan'man. It's how bairns are made.'

'Well, I wouldn't want a baby before I was married, but did you mean that Jack grew big because he loved me?'

Nell's amusement burst out at that. 'Oh, I'm sorry for laughin', Ellie, an', aye, I suppose that's what I did mean.' Her face straightened. 'But keep yoursel' pure, lassie. Dinna let him tak' his way wi' you, even if he wants to. Wait till you're wed, an' he'll respect you for it.'

Bouncing to her feet, Ellie cried, 'Thank you, Grandma. I feel better now I know. You won't tell Mother, will you?'

'It'll be oor secret.' She patted the girl's hand kindly. 'Now, off you go, an' let an auld woman get some peace.'

As Ellie neared the top of Market Street on her way home, she was astonished to see Jack Lornie standing at the corner.

'How did you know where I was?' she demanded.

He looked rather sheepish. 'I followed you, and I saw you turning down here, so I waited. I knew you'd be coming back.'

'I went to ask my Grandma something. Jack, I'm sorry for walking away from you like that, it was very rude of me.'

'If you'd told me you were going to see your Grandma, I'd have walked with you. I couldn't understand you going off so suddenly, and I thought you were annoyed at me for kissing you like that. I won't do it again, if you don't want me to.'

Ellie looked up at him frankly. 'I wasn't annoyed, and you can kiss me again, whenever you like.'

Jack needed no second invitation and pulled her into a doorway, but she was slightly disappointed that his kisses had lost their ardour, although they were still quite exciting.

When he released her, he said, 'You'll never walk away from me again, will you?'

'No, I promise. Will I see you again tomorrow night?'

'Tomorrow, and every other night I'm not working. Oh, Ellie, I love you an awful lot.'

'I love you an awful lot, too, Jack,' she whispered.

Her mother, alone in the parlour, regarded her daughter shrewdly when she went inside. 'Is it still Jack Lornie?'

The happiness inside the girl was too great to hide, and she burst out, 'He told me tonight he loved me.'

Bathie's eyes glinted in amusement. 'And I take it you love him, too, or you wouldn't be in such a state about it?'

'Oh, yes, Mother, I love him. More than I've ever loved anybody in my whole life, even Spanny.'

It was so incongruous, so like Ellie to compare the boy with their old dog, that Bathie couldn't stop the smile which spread across her face.

'It's not funny.'

'No, my dear, being in love's not funny.' Bathie's face sobered. 'It's the most wonderful thing in the whole world.'

Running across the room, Ellie knelt down on the rug in front of her mother's chair. 'Did you love Father?'

'Oh, yes. I felt like you do, at first, but that changes as time goes on, and becomes deeper and more enduring. I still love your father, Ellie, with all my heart.'

'Do you? I'd never thought about that, but I suppose you really have to love a man before you can live your whole life with him.' Pausing briefly, Ellie raised her frank blue eyes. 'Mother, did you keep yourself pure till you were married?'

Somewhat taken aback, Bathie returned her daughter's gaze steadily for a moment. 'Your father was a decent man and that problem never arose.' Wondering what had prompted Ellie to ask such a question, she said, 'Has your Jack tried to . . . ?'

'No, he hasn't. He's decent, too – I think. Mother, can I ask him to come to supper some time?'

'That's a good idea, then we can all meet him.'

'And you'll all like him, I'm sure.'

When Ellie took him into the parlour the following Sunday, his disarming smile won Bathie round at once, and she liked the way his brown wavy hair curled round his ears. They made a fine couple, Jack being a good bit taller than the five-feet-seven girl.

Albert saw a tall young man, whose eyes met his with appealing honesty. The oval face was finely proportioned, the mouth was strong and firm. He'd been rather afraid that the boy would be an easily-led, weak specimen who'd had no say in the matter, and was glad that he'd been wrong. Ellie wouldn't be able to order Jack Lornie around, but maybe she wouldn't even want to try.

Bathie tried to make the young man feel at home. It was obvious that he was deeply in love with Ellie, but just as obvious that he was uncomfortable at meeting her parents.

Albert let the others do the talking until he had sized Jack up properly. He seemed a bit shy, which was only right and proper, but he was soon chatting to Bathie quite naturally, his eyes resting on Ellie occasionally, with so much love in them that her father was satisfied. He'd have no objections to his favourite daughter marrying this man if she wanted to.

More introductions had to be made when Donnie came home, and again when Charlie and Vena came downstairs, and by the time they sat down to supper, Albert was treating Jack like an old acquaintance and the atmosphere was much more relaxed.

Gracie and Flo did all the dishing up, serving, offering second helpings and clearing away, while Hetty and Ishbel just looked at Ellie's 'lad' and wished they were older.

Waiting for the last course, Bathie leaned back and let her eyes rove round the table. It must be terrible for Jack, meeting the Ogilvie clan en masse, she reflected, and wished that things had been like this for Charlie and Vena, but they looked happy enough now. Who would be next to bring a loved one to meet the family? Donnie? Flo? A light touch on her arm broke into her thoughts.

'Are you feeling all right, my love?'

'I'm fine, Albert. Just thinking.'

He squeezed her hand under the table. 'Aye, it's times like this that make you think.'

Donnie excused himself as soon as the meal was over. 'I'm meeting somebody at seven, so I'll have to hurry.'

'A lassie?' Albert's eyes twinkled.

'No, just one of the lads. I've got more sense than Jack and Charlie, and I can't be bothered with girls.'

'Maybe they can't be bothered with you.' Charlie stood up. 'Nice to have met you, Jack, and we'll see you again, no doubt?' Turning to his mother, he said, 'We're going upstairs now.' He took Vena's hand and they followed Donnie out.

'Can we go up to our room, as well, Mother?' It was Hetty. 'Ishbel and me haven't finished playing Ludo.'

'Off you go.' Bathie laughed as they scampered off. 'They all disappear once they've been fed, you see, Jack. Now, we'll go back to the parlour to let Flo and Gracie clear up.'

After they moved, the young man seemed ill at ease, and when he rose abruptly a few minutes later, Ellie was shocked. Surely he wasn't leaving already? What had gone wrong?

'Mr Ogilvie.' Jack's voice was squeaky and had a slight tremor. 'Mr Ogilvie,' he repeated, more firmly, 'I haven't said anything to Ellie yet, but . . . ' He glanced at the girl, whose puzzled eyes made him carry on. 'We've been walking out for over three months now, and I've a good job, and we get on well together . . . I mean, we love each other . . . and what I'm trying to say is . . . I'm asking your permission to marry her, if she'll have me.'

Albert and Ellie both jumped to their feet.

'Yes, you have my permission,' Albert said.

'Yes, I'll have you,' Ellie cried out, at the same time.

In the laughter that followed, Bathie also stood up. 'We couldn't be happier, could we, Albert?'

He beamed. 'No, I'm very pleased. Sit down, for goodness sake, all of you, and we'll drink to this.' He stole a quick look at his wife. 'I promise I'll not have more than one, my love, but I must celebrate my oldest daughter's betrothal.'

Reseating herself, she smiled indulgently. 'Yes, of course you must, Albert.'

Jack found a small flat to let in Schoolhill, so Bathie's old sewing machine was put into use again, and Albert gave them enough money to buy all the furniture they needed.

Three and a half months after Jack's introduction to the family, Eleanor Ogilvie became Mrs John Lornie.

The old wedding dress – kept specifically for Ellie – had been much too short, but Bathie had cut the skirt and inserted a wide strip of matching lace.

It brought back memories to Henrietta. She had worn the same gown when she had been married, as had her daughter. Now, her granddaughter was wearing it, looking completely different from the tomboy she used to be.

'Ellie looks beautiful as a bride,' she whispered to Arthur, who turned round and looked at his wife for a moment.

'Nearly as beautiful as you were,' he murmured, at which his wife hastily dabbed her eyes.

Although she was happy for Ellie, Nell Ogilvie's thoughts were tinged with sadness. A large family gathering like this really brought it home to her how much she missed her husband. Dear Wattie, who had bought her wedding dress for her because she'd no money. Not a white gown, of course, he could never have afforded that, but it had still been lovely in her eyes – a blue crepe-de-Chine, which she'd kept as best for many years, until it almost fell apart at the seams.

With tears in her eyes, Bathie watched her daughter as she made her wedding vows, and prayed that Ellie and her Jack would always be as happy as they were that day. They would have their ups and downs – there wasn't a married couple who hadn't – but as long as they kept loving each other, they would surmount any difficulties.

Albert was very pleased that Jack's parents seemed to be decent folk, but he had to swallow several times during the ceremony to shift the lump in his throat. His darling Ellie, his little girl, belonged to another man now, and by God, Jack Lornie had better look after her for the rest of her life. If he didn't, he'd have his father-in-law to contend with.

PART THREE

Chapter Twenty-four

The murder of an Austrian Archduke couldn't affect her, Bathie Ogilvie had thought – these foreigners always seemed to be killing each other – so the declaration of war came as a great shock to her. Her sons were of an age when they might be expected to go to fight the Huns, and the only consolation she had was that Albert was too old, but it was small comfort.

She was scrubbing the kitchen table one morning just two months afterwards, when Vena came in.

'Mother, I want to tell you something.'

Bathie knew by her face that it must be important, and her low spirits sank even further. She loved her son's wife like a daughter, and hated to see her so serious.

'Charlie's made up his mind to enlist.'

'What?' It was the last thing on Bathie's mind, and she felt her blood slowly turning to ice. 'He can't do that. What about the shop? His father's often away on council business.'

'He says Donnie could manage, and Flo could help. I'll miss him, but he's twenty-four, and he thinks he's done nothing useful with his life, and I understand how he feels.'

Her legs turning to jelly, Bathie waited a moment before she spoke. 'If you both think he's doing the right thing, then who am I to argue?' Her heart reminded her that she was the woman who had borne him, the woman who loved him more than she loved any of her other children, but what could she do?

'He's going this afternoon, but I wanted you to be the first to know.'

'Thank you, Vena, dear. That was very considerate of you.' How could the girl remain so calm?

There was great excitement amongst the other members of the family when Charlie's patriotic urge was made known to them, and the clamour of questions was so loud that it was a few minutes before Donnie could make himself heard.

'I've been thinking of enlisting myself, and that settles it. I'll come with you, Charlie boy.'

'That's the spirit!' Albert cried, beaming at them.

Bathie was very angry that he was encouraging them, and when she tackled him about it in bed that night she hoped that he would at least sympathize with her, understand how she felt, but she was bitterly disappointed.

'Two sons fighting for their country?' he said proudly. 'What more could a father ask?'

'They might be killed.'

He smiled maddeningly. 'It'll only take a few months to sort this out, and then they'll be marching home with the rest of the soldiers – heroes, all of them.'

Praying that he'd be right, she wished that he'd taken her in his arms when he tried to reassure her, but he seemed to be afraid of any physical contact with her at all, these days. He'd even stopped kissing her goodnight.

Lying beside her unresponsive husband, she couldn't help wondering how it would feel to be kissed by Gavin McKenzie. He was a regular visitor now, ever since the day her father had been taken ill, but had given no further sign of his love, although she was almost sure that his feelings hadn't changed.

When Nell Ogilvie had met Gavin for the first time, she'd remarked to Bathie later, 'That doctor's got an eye for you, but he's a decent upstandin' man, an' he'll do nothin' aboot it. Just dinna let your feelin's for him get the better o' you, for they could easy get oot o' hand.'

Bathie had laughed. 'One man's enough for me, Grandma.'

After several weeks' training in Perthshire, Charlie and Donnie were sent to separate camps somewhere in France.

Flo and Gracie had taken their places in the shop – Albert saying that they were just as good as their brothers – and Hetty now helped her mother in the house.

Vena had joined the V.A.D., to do her bit for her country, and Ishbel, still at school, was hoping that the war would last until she was old enough to be a nurse, too.

It seemed to Bathie that she had no control over her life any more. Although she felt like an old woman sometimes, she was only forty-one and should be having time to relax, not being a drudge for those of her family still at home.

She was a wife in name only to Albert, who was hardly fifty and must still have urges to be satisfied. The more she thought about it, the stronger her fears became that he must be finding his pleasure with another woman.

It was over a year since he'd become a Town Councillor, so he was out quite a lot on his own, and Bathie began to view with suspicion his tales of late-night sittings on committee meetings. But there was no one she could turn to for advice. She could never approach her parents, nor tell Albert's own mother, however sympathetic Nell usually was. Vena was hardly ever there, and Ellie and Flo would be horrified if she said anything about it to either of them.

She lived in a constant state of tension, her suspicions becoming certainties in her mind, until they culminated, one afternoon, in a blinding headache which forced her to lie down for an hour. She did feel slightly better when she rose, but couldn't understand what had caused the attack, and worried about that, too.

A few days later, with the pains in her head growing so bad that she could hardly bear them, she sent Hetty to ask the doctor to call to see her, then undressed and went to bed, thankful that the house was quiet for a while.

Gavin McKenzie was there within fifteen minutes. 'Hetty said you were having very bad headaches.' He laid his hand on her brow for a moment, then pulled her lower eyelids down.

'They're really terrible,' she whispered. 'They're so bad, I can hardly see, sometimes.'

'I don't think there's anything physically wrong with you, Bathie. Have you been worrying about something?'

She hesitated, then it all came flooding out – her anxiety for her sons, Albert's absences, her belief that he was seeing another woman because he never even kissed her any more, her feeling of complete uselessness. He sat on a chair beside the bed, listening and nodding encouragingly, but actually studying her flushed face and nervous agitation.

At last, he said, 'Poor Bathie. You feel you've nothing to live for now your children can look after themselves?'

'Is it just nerves then?' She seemed ashamed.

'Whatever you like to call it, but it can cause real pain. Stop worrying about Charlie and Donnie, they're both grown men now. It will be difficult, but worrying doesn't help them, nor you. And don't think you're useless, because the rest of your family would be lost without you.'

'I suppose so,' she murmured, uncertainly, 'but Albert . . .'

'I'm sure Albert loves you as much as ever, he just can't show it without . . . It's the way he's made, Bathie, and I'm sure he would never take another woman, so put that fear right out of your head.'

'But . . .'

'No buts.' The appeal in her lovely blue eyes snapped his self-control. 'Do you think I'd say that if I didn't believe it was true?' he said passionately. 'I love you so much, I . . . ' He stopped, dismayed, then went on, gently, 'I didn't mean to bring that up again. I'm quite content to worship you from the sidelines as long as I know you're happy. But if you ever need me, Bathie, let me know. Will you promise?'

'Yes, I promise.' It was a shy whisper.

'Good. Now, stop worrying and that will be the end of your headaches. That's my promise to you.'

Gavin was on his way out of the bedroom when Albert came up the stairs. 'What's wrong, Bathie? Hetty said she'd had to get the doctor for you.'

His anxiety lifted when Bathie said, 'It's nothing, Albert. I've been having terrible headaches, but it's just nerves.'

'Thank God it's nothing serious.' Looking at the other man, he said, 'You're not keeping anything from me, are you?'

'No, Albert, that's all it is.'

The doctor made for the door. 'Remember what you promised, Bathie.'

'Yes, I will, and thank you, Gavin.'

'What did you promise him?' Albert was frowning.

'Oh, just to stop worrying about everything, especially about Charlie and Donnie.' It wasn't the whole truth, but it satisfied her husband.

Fortunately, her mind was taken off her own troubles when Ellie came to announce that she was four months pregnant.

'Why didn't you tell me as soon as you knew?' Bathie was rather hurt at her daughter's apparent thoughtlessness.

'You'd enough on your plate, Mother, with the boys away. I didn't want you to start worrying about me, too.'

'Worrying about you? Is there something wrong?'

'I didn't know how you'd feel about being a grandmother.'

'Oh, Ellie, I'd just love to be a grandmother. It's the best news I've had for ages.'

Knitting for her grandchild took up Bathie's spare time now, and her suspicions about Albert were forgotten. She tried not to worry about her sons, but still put up a nightly prayer for them, adding Vena's name when she, too, was sent abroad.

When Mary wrote from New Zealand that Will had joined the ANZAC forces, Bathie felt a great sympathy for her. Mothers all over the world were having to worry about their sons, so Bathia Ogilvie wasn't unique.

Chapter Twenty-five

Little Kathleen Lornie, born on the third day of May, 1915, gave Bathie something other than the war to think about. It was good to have a baby around the place again, even if it was only for one or two afternoons a week, and she was happy that Ellie and her husband were both besotted by the child, too, but who could help loving the tiny red-headed infant who was so like her mother?

She was all the more angry, therefore, when Ellie appeared one afternoon in late October, to tell her that Jack Lornie had enlisted in the army. 'What possessed him to do that? There's plenty of younger, single men who could go.'

'He felt he had to, Mother.' Ellie cradled her five-month-old baby in her arms. 'He says he only waited till Kathleen was born, and I was back on my feet properly, so he'd know I could cope on my own, but he thinks people are saying he's a coward. He's probably wrong, but there it is.'

'He's no business to leave his wife and child,' Bathie raged. 'He's got a responsibility to you both.'

Ellie shrugged in resignation. 'I knew he'd have held it against me if I'd tried to stop him, and he leaves next Friday. Don't worry, Mother, I'm not going to go into a decline, or anything like that.'

Her own anger evaporating in the face of her daughter's calm acceptance, Bathie said, gently, 'Maybe the war won't last much longer. It's been more than a year, already.'

'There's no sign of it stopping,' Ellie remarked, sadly. 'And I'm not the only wife who's had to let her husband go. Men want adventure, I suppose, and if I hadn't had Kathleen, I'd have joined the V.A.D. like Vena, for I'd have liked a bit of adventure myself.'

One Saturday evening in November, Bathie was knitting at the parlour fire, the hailstones battering against the

229

window and the wind howling down the chimney. Hetty and Ishbel were squabbling over their game of Ludo; Flo was laboriously sewing a button on to a blouse, stopping occasionally to suck blood from a pricked finger; Gracie was reading, her mousey head bent over her book, her legs curled under her on the couch.

Albert was out, and although she knew that it couldn't be council business, not on a Saturday night, his wife was so used to his absences that she accepted them as quite normal, having swept her previous suspicions to the back of her mind.

When a loud knock sounded on the outside door, Hetty ran down to open it, and returned with a broad, khaki-clad figure who was smiling shyly. Bathie stared blankly at the young man's tanned face for a moment, until the New Zealand flash on his sleeve made her realize who he was.

Jumping up and flinging her arms round him, much to the amazement of the four girls, she cried, 'Oh, Will! I didn't recognize you straight away, but it's good to see you again.'

When she stepped back, she saw that he was gazing at Flo, whose astonished face had turned a deep shade of pink at the sight of her old playmate. Turning to her younger daughters, who were either too young to remember, or hadn't been born when Mary and Willie had taken their son to the other side of the world with them, Bathie introduced him.

'It's Will Dunbar, girls, Mary Wyness's son. She used to be our nursemaid, and Will was born in this very house on the same day as Flo.'

Gracie and Hetty sat down again after they shook hands with him, but Ishbel plied him with questions about life in Wanganui, while Flo stood to the side, her eyes following his every gesture and blushing each time he looked at her.

At last, Bathie said, 'Leave the poor boy alone, Ishbel, you're an awful torment. And Will, take off that wet coat, for goodness sake, or you'll catch your death of cold.'

Laughing, he unbuttoned the heavy greatcoat, and slipped it off. 'Thanks, Flo,' he murmured, as the girl took it from him to spread over the back of one of the chairs.

'You'll be staying a while, of course?' Bathie motioned to him to sit down. 'We can easily put you up, because we've a few spare beds nowadays.'

Seating himself on Albert's chair, he said, 'Thank you very much, but I don't want to inconvenience you.'

'Its no inconvenience, and Albert'll be wanting to see you. How long leave do you have?'

'Ten days, but . . . '

'You're more than welcome, for ten days or a hundred and ten. Gracie, go and make something for Will to eat, ham and eggs or something. I'm sure he must be hungry.'

He chuckled. 'Does it show? To be honest, I haven't had anything since seven o'clock this morning.'

Remembering suddenly about Willie Dunbar's death, Bathie said, 'I was very sorry about your father, Will. It must have been a terrible shock to your mother.'

'She was heartbroken, but she took a job in a hotel, and Father's boss was very kind and gave her a pension, although he didn't need to, then he let me start as an apprentice joiner when I left school.'

While the young man ate what Gracie had cooked for him, Bathie asked more about his mother, about his Aunt Jeannie and Uncle Robbie, and he told her all she wanted to know while the girls listened eagerly.

Before very long, however, it became apparent to everyone in the room that something was building up between Will and Flo. They had eyes only for each other, and, watching them, Bathie couldn't make up her mind whether to be glad or sorry.

Flo had never taken an interest in boys – not like Ellie, who had hardly ever gone out with the same boy twice running until she met Jack Lornie – so could it be that she was going to turn out to be a one-man girl like her mother?

Flo and Will had been very close when they were children, of course, but this was different, and they didn't really know each other now. If it became serious, Flo would worry about Will when he went back to the fighting, and, if he came through the war, she'd want to marry him and go off to New Zealand.

This did make Bathie feel rather sad, but the happiness shining like a bright light from Flo's eyes made her decide that she wasn't really sorry about this possible new romance.

The younger girls, who had been allowed to stay up until ten o'clock in honour of the visitor, were in bed before their father came home. Bathie was shocked to notice that it was almost half past eleven, but kept her questions to herself.

Albert monopolized the young man for the next twenty-five minutes, then Bathie had to say, 'You can ask him everything in the morning, Albert. Flo, take Will up to Donnie's room.'

'Do you want me to come back and tidy up, Mother?'

Bathie stood up. 'No, we can leave it till tomorrow. It's nearly twelve o'clock, for goodness sake.'

When Flo took Will upstairs, Albert followed his wife through to their bedroom, slackening his tie as he went. 'What a surprise, young Will turning up like that.'

'Yes, I didn't think we'd ever see him again, not even after what Mary wrote last Christmas.'

'What was that?'

'She said Will was with the ANZACs, but I never dreamt that he'd turn up here.'

Holding the bedknob, Albert kicked off his shoes, then thumped down on the bed to remove his socks, but in the act of rubbing his feet, he looked up accusingly. 'I can't remember you ever telling me that young Will was in the army.'

Bathie's old suspicions had reared up again at the smug expression he'd worn on his face when he came home. It had changed quickly to surprise when he saw Will, but it had been there, that look of being satisfied – satiated, even. Now her anger boiled over. 'You're never here to tell you anything,' she snapped.

'I can't help it if the council meetings go on so late.'

'Till nearly midnight on a Saturday?' She couldn't keep the sarcasm out of her voice. 'I'm not a complete fool.'

When he couldn't meet her eyes, she knew for certain that what she'd suspected for so long had been true, after all.

'You've been seeing another woman.'

His breath came out slowly, but he didn't attempt to deny it, and she was astonished at her own calm. Now that she knew the truth, knew that he'd been unfaithful to her, she wasn't heartbroken as she'd thought she would be. She wasn't angry. She wasn't even hurt. She was just numb.

She did feel a grim satisfaction when she noticed his trembling hands. 'How long has it been going on?'

'I met her about two years ago. She was on a committee for the soup kitchen, and we . . . er . . . took to each other right away, so I walked her home to Queen's Road.'

'Queen's Road? The west end?' Her voice was harder now. 'You were aiming high, but then you always did. She's not just an ordinary whore, then?'

'Bathie, I didn't want you to find out, but I had to have a woman, and she was willing.'

'I'm sure she was. I was willing, too, Albert, but you . . . '

'You know why I couldn't touch you, Bathie.' His eyes were regarding her sadly now. 'She's different. She's a bit older than me, but she and her husband never had any children.'

'He is another blind fool like me, I take it?'

'He died a few years back. She's a lusty woman and since I knew there was no chance of putting her in the family way, I could let myself go. You're too . . . '

Bathie was silent. He'd used another woman to satisfy his needs because he was afraid of making his wife pregnant – but that didn't really excuse him. If he'd loved her, as he used to swear he did, he'd have forced himself to be careful. A knife turned in her heart when she thought that he couldn't have loved her for herself, right from the beginning, and that he'd only married her to gratify his own desires.

Looking penitent, he murmured, 'I'm sorry.'

'It's too late to be sorry,' she said, as she turned away from him, her voice as icy as the wintry elements outside. 'I understand, but I don't want you to share my bed again, ever.'

He paused for a moment, then muttered, 'I'll sleep in the attic till you cool down.'

'I told you once that I couldn't live with you if I knew you'd been carrying on with another woman, so you'd better go and live with that whore in Queen's Road for good.'

His face suffused with dark colour as he jumped to his feet. 'I worked hard to pay for this house, and it's you that can get out. Go to Gavin McKenzie. He's loved you for years, though he didn't think I suspected, and he could be the father of some of your children, for all I know.'

She whipped round to face him. 'Gavin has never . . . ' She bit her lip to keep from shouting. 'He told me he loved me, but that's all. I wouldn't have had anything to do with him, anyway, because it was you I loved. It was, Albert, but not any more. You've proved how worthless you are.'

She struggled to control her rising voice. 'Every single one is your child, because I, at least, remembered my marriage vows and remained faithful. Let me past.'

Albert had tried to block her from reaching the chair where her clothes were folded, but he dropped his arms at the look of contempt on her face, and watched her dressing.

She took longer than usual, her hands were shaking so much, but at last she opened the cupboard door to take out a valise. She had meant to pack some clothes to take with her, but he stepped in front of her.

'You'll go in what you stand up in,' he shouted, harshly. 'Gavin McKenzie can bloody well clothe and feed you, as I've had to do for more than twenty-six years.'

Without a word, Bathie went out and took her coat off one of the pegs on the landing. Closing the outside door softly behind her, she stood, breathing quickly, until she felt capable of carrying on. Her heart was thumping erratically and deep pains were shooting across her head. She had no idea of the time, but it must be after one, and she was glad that no one would see her in this state.

Turning up her coat collar, she went down the metal steps and through the close, but her feet were soon squelching inside her already saturated indoor shoes, the only pair that had been available to her. The sleety snow soaked through her clothes, too, before she had gone very far, but she carried on in a kind of daze, her teeth chattering, her whole body shivering in the freezing cold.

Barely conscious of what she was doing, she crossed to the other side of the street when she came to the foot of the Gallowgate, and had taken only a few short halting steps when something seemed to explode inside her head.

Chapter Twenty-six

After breakfast on Sunday, Flo and Will went out for a walk, having turned down Ellie's suggestion that they should accompany the family to church. The snow was crisp underfoot, but the girl and boy were happy to be on their own, and wouldn't really have minded if it had still been snowing. As it was, the sun was shining, but giving little warmth.

Flo glanced at her companion. 'Do you ever get snow in New Zealand?'

'Not often.' Will laughed suddenly. 'Our winter's your summer, of course. Um . . . Flo, I must ask you this. Is there a boy in your life?'

She was confused by the abrupt change of subject. 'I've never been out with any boys. Have you got a girlfriend?'

'I've had a few, but nothing serious. I always knew I'd come back to Aberdeen some day. I often thought about you, and was saving up so I could come home.'

'Come home? But Wanganui's your home, Will.'

'Nearly all the Scots over there talk about Scotland as home, and I was determined to come.'

'Was that why you joined the army? So you'd be able to come home to Scotland?'

'Not really. I enlisted without thinking, you see, so I could hardly believe it when they sent me to England for some extra training. I was near enough to come and see you.' He gripped her arm as she slipped on an icy patch.

Flo was pleased when he let his hand remain where it was. 'I often thought about you, too, but I never imagined I'd ever see you again. I'm really happy you're here, Will.'

'Are you, Flo?' His voice was serious.

'Yes. Truly happy.'

'We'll have nine whole days together.'

'I've to work in the shop, though, so I'll only see you in the evenings.'

'Won't your father let you have a few days off?'

'He's not there, most of the time. He's on the Council, you see, so there's just Gracie and me.'

'I'll come and help you. I used to serve in Uncle Robbie's store to help him out, before I started my apprenticeship.'

'Will you go back to being a joiner when the war's over?'

Their eyes met and held, then he whirled her round and hugged her. 'This might sound crazy, Flo, but I might not have another chance to come back to Aberdeen, so there's no time for a proper courtship. I'll only go back to New Zealand if you'll promise to come with me, my dearest.'

'Just try to stop me,' she laughed, surprised by her lack of shyness with him.

He hugged her again, but it was far too cold to stand in the street, and they walked on, with Will's arm tightly round Flo's waist now.

'Where will you have to go when you finish your training?'

'I don't know, but probably France or somewhere.'

'Will you write to me after you leave Aberdeen?'

He smiled down at her. 'I'll write as often as I can.'

'I'll write every day.' Flo's eyes suddenly clouded. 'I'll worry about you.'

'Don't worry about me, I'm indestructible.' Will hated to see her so sad. 'Being born the same day, in the same house, makes a bond between us. I always felt very close to you.'

She regarded him seriously. 'I feel closer to you than I do to my own brothers and sisters.'

'We were meant for each other, so nothing can ever come between us. Not even war.'

'Not even war,' she echoed.

They were silent for a moment, then Will said huskily, 'I love you with all my heart, Flo dearest. I always have, ever since I was a little boy.'

'I love you, too, Will.'

'I'll come back and marry you after the war, and we'll go to Wanganui as husband and wife.' Will pledged this with a kiss, then put his hand in his breast pocket and pulled out a small jeweller's box.

'It's my great-grandmother's engagement ring. My mother gave it to me when I left home. Do you know what she said, Flo? She told me she knew that I'd my heart set on you, and that I should take her grandmother's ring with me, just in case I was lucky enough to come to Scotland. I believe she thought it would bring me luck.'

'Dear Mary,' Flo murmured. 'What a wonderful thing to do.'

He lifted her hand, pulled off her glove and slid the ring on to the third finger of her left hand. 'I'll buy another one for you if you'd rather, but this one means quite a lot to me.'

After studying the heirloom sparkling on her finger, she whispered, 'It means a lot to me, too, Will, and I'll always wear it.'

He kissed her quickly, then said, 'I think we should go back now, to tell your parents we're engaged.'

'They'll be pleased about it, I'm sure.'

'I certainly hope so. I know my mother will.'

They'd been strolling aimlessly before, but turned with purpose in their steps, and even the flakes of snow which began to fall couldn't mar their happiness. When Flo saw Dr McKenzie's motor car coming towards them, she waved to him vigorously, so he braked carefully, and walked across the street to speak to them, surprised at seeing young Flo Ogilvie with a boy's arm round her waist. He hadn't known she had a young man, and it was easily seen that they were in love.

'This is Will Dunbar, Doctor.' Flo's voice was full of pride. 'Mary Wyness's son, remember, born the same day as me?'

As the two men shook hands, Will murmured, 'I don't expect you'll remember about that – it's more than twenty-one years ago.'

'Oh yes, I do remember.' Gavin McKenzie smiled broadly. 'That was a day I'll never forget. Your grandmother and I were kept very busy making sure that the two of you came into the world safely, and we had quite a lively time of it. I see you're in the army. Were you sent over here for training?'

'Yes, sir, and when I was given ten days' leave, I came to Aberdeen especially to see Flo.'

'We're engaged, Doctor.' Flo couldn't keep it in any longer, and held her hand up to show him. 'It's Mrs Wyness's mother's ring, and you're the very first to know.'

'That's a great honour, and congratulations to you both.'

'We're on our way to tell Flo's parents now,' Will told him. 'Wish us luck?'

'You'll need no luck. They'll be delighted about it.' He shook hands with them, then said, 'I'd better be getting on, though, before my housekeeper starts wondering where I am. How is your mother, Flo?'

'She's fine . . . I think. We didn't see her this morning, and Father just said she'd a bit of a headache.'

Gavin's cheery face sobered. 'I hope her headaches aren't starting again, but I'll see her this afternoon.'

Flo and Will watched him drive away, then carried on walking towards the Gallowgate, so wrapped up in each other that the world could have fallen about their ears and they would never have noticed.

Albert was sitting in the kitchen with his head bowed when they went in, and Gracie's frown, which accompanied a slight shake of her head, should have warned Flo that something was wrong, but she was too carried away with excitement to notice.

'I've just got engaged to Will. Look, he's given me his great-grandmother's ring.' She held up her left hand.

Albert's head swung up. 'Without asking my permission?'

Will stepped forward. 'I'm sorry, Mr Ogilvie. I did mean to ask you, before I asked Flo, but I love her and . . . '

'I will not allow my daughter to marry a bastard, Will whatever-your-name-is, for it's certainly not Dunbar.' Albert had risen to his feet and his face was now within two inches of the soldier's.

His eyes puzzled, Will backed away. 'I don't understand what you mean, Mr Ogilvie. You knew my father.'

Gracie tried to intervene, but Albert shook her off. 'Willie Dunbar married your mother out of pity, to give you a name. The man that fathered you refused to make an honest woman of her, though he'd been quick enough to put her in the family way in our wash-house. Of course, your mother must have been more than willing to let him lay her on her back.'

'Father!' Gracie placed herself between the two men as Will's hands came up aggressively. 'You're upset, and you don't know what you're saying.'

'I'm saying what's the truth, as he'll find out if he asks his mother.' Albert pushed her aside again. 'Go ahead and hit me if you like, lad. It'll not change anything.'

Will let his hands drop. 'I swear I knew nothing about this. If I'm a bastard, as you say, Mr Ogilvie, I'm not fit to marry Flo, and I apologize for the trouble I've caused.'

Flo had been standing open-mouthed, unable to speak, but now she burst into tears. 'Will,' she sobbed, 'I don't care who your father was, I'll marry you whenever you like. I love you.'

Albert turned a furious face to her. 'Go upstairs at once, Florence. I'll not have you marrying this man, so you can make up your mind to it.'

His use of her full name told her that it was useless to argue and she turned to leave, but Gracie held her arm.

'Wait, Flo. I'll tell you why Father's acting like this. He'd a terrible row with Mother last night, and she walked out. She told him she was going to live with Dr McKenzie.'

'She's not with the doctor.' Flo could scarcely think straight, but she knew that.

'We saw him,' Will said quietly. 'He asked Flo how her mother was, and said he hoped her headaches weren't starting again. He's calling this afternoon to see her.'

'He always comes to supper on Sundays.' Gracie eyed her father suspiciously. 'You told me Mother had gone to live with the doctor because she loved him, but I'm sure she never said that. Something's going on, and I wish I knew what it was.'

'I threw her out, damn you.' Albert glared at her. 'Gavin McKenzie has loved your mother for years.'

Gracie, the most docile of all his daughters, turned on him unexpectedly. 'Mother couldn't help that.' She returned his glare defiantly. 'What happened last night? And you'd better tell me the truth, for I won't rest till I find out.'

His eyes held hers then dropped. 'She found out I'd been . . . seeing another woman.'

This was the last thing she'd imagined, and her anger almost overpowered her. 'What? I thought you loved Mother?'

'I do love your mother,' he moaned. 'But, oh, I can't tell you, Gracie. I just can't.'

'Yes, you can. You owe it to Will and Flo.'

He lifted his head. 'I owe him nothing.'

Arthur Johnstone's purple face suddenly swam before his eyes, the clarity of it sickening him, and he breathed deeply to dispel it.

When he spoke, his voice was much calmer. 'Mary Wyness was a good friend to Bathie, so for her sake, and for Flo's, I'll try to explain what has happened between your mother and me.' Bowing his head, he cleared his throat.

'I loved her from the moment I saw her, but my . . . needs built up over the years. It was like I had a beast inside me. I kept it in check, most of the time, though, but sometimes I couldn't help myself, and let it have its head. Her body was receptive to me, and that's why we had so many children. After Hetty was born, Gavin McKenzie warned me that he was concerned about your mother's health, but I made her have Ishbel, and I almost lost her when she had James. Then he died, and . . . ' He was staring into space now, his eyes vacant, and he had obviously forgotten about his listeners. 'I couldn't be careful, I needed Bathie so much, so I'd to stop touching her, and that's not natural for any man.'

Flo and Gracie glanced at each other, their horror at what he was saying reflected in their faces, while poor Will carefully avoided looking at either of them. He was far too embarrassed by the man's coarse-honesty.

Quite unaware of their reactions, Albert moistened his lips and went on. 'It's nearly seven years since I laid a finger on her, but I still had needs that had to be satisfied, so about two years ago, I started seeing . . . this other woman. Jean was past the change, and I could let the beast in me have its way without having to worry about being careful.'

He halted, and Gracie's top lip curled up at what he was admitting, but he looked up and caught her, and his rather sensuous expression changed abruptly.

'Oh, my God, Gracie, I'm sorry. I'm saying things I should keep to myself, but I'm just trying to make you understand why I did what I did. Jean's body was what I needed, but it was your mother I loved. I never stopped loving her, though that's maybe hard for you to credit, and Jean Rust knew exactly why I went to bed with her.'

'But, Father, if it was you that betrayed Mother, why did you throw her out?' Gracie couldn't fathom that, although she could understand now why he'd turned to the other woman.

Her father groaned hopelessly. 'I was jealous of Gavin McKenzie, Gracie, and when she told me to get out, I saw red and told her to go to him.' He shook his head sadly. 'She swore there was never anything between them, and to be quite honest, I don't think there was, so I was punishing myself as much as her.'

'But Mother had eight children altogether,' Flo protested. 'She couldn't ever have . . . refused you?'

'She had eight children and two miscarriages, that's why I couldn't make her have any more. She never once refused me, and this is how I treat her.'

He buried his face in his hands. 'Oh, God, she's the best woman in the world, and I'll love her till my last breath.'

Gracie voiced the fear which had also beset her sister and the young soldier. 'If she didn't go to Dr McKenzie, where could she have gone?'

'She must have gone to him. Where else could she go? He'd been covering up for her when he spoke to Flo.'

Will had been standing silently for some time, but now he said, quietly, 'I'm quite sure he wasn't, Mr Ogilvie. He seemed very concerned about the headache you told us she had.'

After a long, rather ominous silence, Gracie said, 'We'd better take our dinner before it spoils, and we'll have to wait and ask him when he comes for supper.'

She set the table, then called to Hetty and Ishbel to come down, and while the younger girls were there, conversation was rather stilted. Gracie, Flo and Will were trying to hide their anxiety about Bathie, and Albert was bitterly regretting every word he'd uttered to her in his guilty anger.

Mercifully, the girls didn't sense anything wrong, and started to wash up after the meal, while Gracie led the others into the parlour. They said nothing, because each of them was fully occupied with his or her own thoughts, and, in any case, there was nothing more to be said.

When Hetty came in to say they were finished, Gracie told her, 'You two had better go back upstairs again. If you've any homework to do, Ishbel, get it done, but stay up there because the doctor's coming.'

It was the usual routine. Hetty and Ishbel hated sitting primly in the presence of the adults, and genuinely preferred to be out of the way as much as possible.

Will Dunbar, who was sitting on the couch with Flo, leaned forward. 'Do you want me to leave, Mr Ogilvie?'

'No, he doesn't,' Gracie answered, before her father could speak. 'You're engaged to Flo, Will, one of the family.'

He sat back and took Flo's hand. This was not the time to plead with her father to change his mind, because the man was incapable of reasoned thought at the present moment.

About an hour later, with nothing further being said, Gracie stood up, put some coal on the fire, then put a lighted taper to the mantle in the glass shade hanging down from the ceiling. The sudden plop as the hissing gas ignited, made them look at each other.

'He won't come.'

They didn't have to ask whom Albert meant, and not one of them answered. What was the point of saying anything?

The slam of a car door, about three quarters of an hour later, made Gracie jump to her feet and run to the window. 'It's the doctor.'

The four grim faces illuminated in the flickering light made Gavin assume that Albert had not been pleased about the engagement, so he glanced sympathetically at Flo and Will then said, 'I'd better take a look at Bathie before I sit down.'

'She's not here.' Albert sounded defeated. He'd made himself believe that his wife had found refuge with this man, and it was hard to accept that she hadn't.

It was left to Gracie to explain, which she did without any reservations as to the blackness of the picture she was painting of her father.

Gavin turned angrily to Albert. 'Good God, man. Have you lost all the sense you were born with? Throwing your wife out in weather like this? She didn't come to me, so where in God's name is she? And why the hell are you sitting here?'

Albert was unable to answer. His deep shame at his own conduct was almost as great as his anxiety for his wife, and having his two daughters knowing how low he'd sunk was almost unbearable. Furthermore, he'd slandered Mary Wyness without a thought as to how much he was hurting her son.

Gavin was still trying to think where Bathie might have sought help. 'Would she have gone to Ferryhill? I've got my car outside. Come on, Albert. Face up to it, man. You can't change what you did, but you could try to make it up to her.'

Albert stumbled to his feet like an old man. 'Aye, Gavin. I'll have to try to make it up to her.' He moved towards the door, then turned. 'Gracie, don't tell the girls.'

She looked at him coldly. 'If they ask where Mother is, I'll tell them you put her out. I despise you, Father.'

The doctor laid his hand on her shoulder. 'Try to forgive him, Gracie. He's being punished more than you know.'

'He'll never be punished enough.' She pulled away from him and he followed Albert down the stairs.

When they reached Ferryhill, Gavin said, 'Let me speak first, Albert. There's no need to alarm Mrs Johnstone.' He strode up the stone steps and knocked on the door loudly.

Inside, he smiled to Henrietta. 'Albert and I went for a run in my car, and he asked me to take him here to see how you were.' Luckily, he'd remembered Bathie telling him the week before that her mother had a bad bout of influenza.

Henrietta still looked somewhat pale, but she beamed at him. 'I am feeling much better.' She turned her eyes on her son-in-law. 'I hope Bathia is keeping well, Albert?'

He forced a smile. 'Yes, thank you. I'm sorry we can't stay, but we promised we wouldn't be out long.'

'Have you not even time for a cup of tea?'

'No, thank you. It'll soon be suppertime.'

'How do you find your automobile, Doctor?' Arthur sounded quite interested. 'Is it better than your pony and trap?'

Gavin smiled. 'It's warmer, but not much quicker, and sometimes not so reliable. I'm glad you're both keeping well.'

When they were inside the car again, he said, 'Bathie has never been there today, that's definite.'

'Her father would gloat if he knew what I've done.' What he'd done, he thought ruefully, was even worse than Arthur Johnstone had admitted to, years before, when he was under the influence of drink, and he didn't even have that excuse himself.

The doctor peered through the celluloid windscreen which was fast becoming obscured by snowflakes. 'You just made a human mistake, that's all.'

Albert groaned. 'A damned *in*human mistake, for I've hurt Bathie to the marrow.'

'If I had ever thought you'd been hurting her before, Albert, or abusing her, I'd have taken her from you years ago. I admit that I love her, but I knew she loved you, and I've been content just to be in her company every Sunday.'

'She should have married a man like you, Gavin, and she might end up coming to you yet.'

'She'll never come to me, I regret to say. Now, will we tell your mother the same as we told the Johnstones? We'll be in Market Street in a few minutes, so you'd better make your mind up quickly.'

Albert was extremely thankful to have Gavin McKenzie guiding him. The doctor had the common sense to see both of them through this awful nightmare. 'You'd better just say the same,' he muttered. 'I don't want my mother to know there's anything wrong.'

But Nell was more perceptive than Henrietta. She knew that their visit was no pleasure outing, not when there was a blizzard blowing, but she asked no questions. If Albert didn't want to tell her why he was so agitated, she'd not try to find out from him. Perhaps she'd get it out of Bathie some time.

Albert broke down when they were back in the car. 'Where in God's name can she be, Gavin? Where can we look now?'

The other man wished that he could show his grief, too, but forced himself to sound matter-of-fact. 'What about Ellie?'

'Bathie would never tell Ellie what I did.'

'Would she have gone to Maggie Lindsay, or Annie?'

'Dan Munro's a police sergeant in Huntly now, and Annie's man was promoted, as well, but I don't know where they are.'

The doctor ran his hand over his chin. 'Then we'd better go to Lodge Walk and report her missing.'

'Oh, God, do you think something's happened to her?'

'I hope not, but she can't have been walking the streets since one o'clock this morning.'

The calm voice had a steadying effect on Albert, who had been unfit to reason things out before, and during the short journey from Market Street to the Police Head-quarters, he did some clear thinking for the first time that day.

He'd made his wife miserable enough already, and if he found her, he wasn't going to force her to come back to him, even though it nearly broke his heart to contem-plate his life without her. He would do the decent thing, and tell her she belonged with Gavin McKenzie, who loved her and would care for her properly. It never crossed his mind that Bathie could still love him, not after what he'd done, and he felt easier now that he'd decided to give her up.

At Lodge Walk, the police sergeant told them that a lady had been found unconscious at the foot of the Gallowgate about five o'clock that morning. 'She was taken to the infirmary,' he went on. 'She wasn't the usual type we pick up after Saturday night, so she might be your wife, sir.'

'Thank you, Sergeant.' Gavin pulled at Albert's sleeve. 'Come on, man, there's no time to lose.'

Almost having to lift the other man into the car, Gavin set off again, but when they arrived at Woolmanhill Hospital, Albert remained seated. 'You go in,' he said. 'I'll wait here.'

Gavin turned to him angrily. 'You'll have to go in. If it is Bathie, she'll be critically ill, if she's still alive. If you want her back, you'll have to go in and see her.'

'No, I want you to find out how she is. Once I know she's still alive, I'll walk away and never enter her life again. She'll be far better with you, Gavin, you'll never hurt her like I've done. I know she thinks a lot of you, and she'll come to love you – if she doesn't already.'

The doctor's eyebrows rose. 'Self-sacrificing now, are you? I've known you for twenty-five years, Albert Ogilvie, but I didn't realize till now what a silly bugger you are. It's you Bathie loves. It's you she married, for better or worse, and by God, things couldn't be much worse. For Christ's sake, man, make them better for her. Go in and tell her you love her, and let her see you mean it.'

Albert's obstinate expression was fixed. 'I'll only go in if you come in with me. I want to see for myself which one of us she wants now. If it's you she turns to first, I'll leave and never bother her again.'

'You'd do that for her, would you? All right, Albert, we'll go together, but don't be disappointed if it's not Bathie.'

It was Bathie. Not the vital beautiful woman they both knew and loved, but a white, unconscious figure who couldn't turn to either of them. Her dark hair was lank, her alabaster skin was almost transparent, the bedclothes scarcely moved when she breathed, but she *was* breathing.

Albert's heart turned over. 'Are we too late?'

'I'll see if I can find a doctor.'

Tears trickled down Albert's haggard face. He didn't touch his wife nor go near her – that would have been unfair to the other man – but he could imagine his hands stroking her brow and her eyes opening to reveal love for him. Oh, dear God, would her eyes ever open again, and if they did, would they show the same hatred and disgust he'd seen in them last? What a mess he'd made of his life – and hers – and if Bathie still wanted him he'd be true to her supposing he had to let Gavin castrate him, as he'd once threatened to do.

He felt a hand on his shoulder and turned round.

'This is Dr Sangster.' Gavin indicated the tall grey-haired man who had come in behind him.

'She is your wife, I believe, Mr Ogilvie?'

'Yes, doctor. Is she . . . ?'

'She has been unconscious since she was brought in, and the likelihood of her pulling through is very slender.' He continued in spite of Albert's shuddering intake of breath. 'She was soaked through and stone cold, so there's the danger of pneumonia in addition to the shock her system has received. We haven't yet found out what caused her collapse, and she could slip away without regaining consciousness.'

Gavin stepped forward. 'She's had bad headaches for some time. I believed that they were caused by tension, but . . . '

The older doctor nodded gravely. 'It could be a tumour or a blood clot. On the other hand, it may have been hemicrania, a severe migraine, in which case, we will just have to worry about the effect of her exposure to the cold for so long. Four hours, you told me? I can tell you nothing more, meantime, Mr Ogilvie, so I suggest you go home.'

'No, I can't leave her, now I've found her.'

The doctor stroked his chin. 'I'll allow you half an hour, but I'm afraid you will have to leave then.'

'Dr McKenzie's an old friend – can he stay with me?'

'I hope he can persuade you to go when I come back, even if there's no change.'

Gavin gave a wry smile. 'I'll do my best, but he can be a stubborn devil when he likes.'

He looked mournfully at Albert when the other man left. 'There's nothing we can do, you know. You'd be better to let me drive you home, to tell the girls we've found their mother, and we can come back later on, in the evening some time.'

'I want both of us to be here when she comes out of it,' Albert said, doggedly, 'so she can tell us which one . . .'

'I wish you'd put that stupid idea out of your head, man. I've told you already, it's you she'll want.'

Albert shook his head, but said no more, and they sat on the chairs one of the nurses brought them. Their eyes were riveted on the woman in the bed, their bodies were tensed with the hope and fears inside them, but they watched for the next twenty minutes in silence.

Gavin stretched out his legs to ease them. 'We'll have to leave soon, Albert, even if I've got to knock you senseless and carry you out.'

'That's the only way I'll go.' Albert folded his arms without moving his eyes.

A few minutes later, they both sat up alertly, at a very faint movement of Bathie's fingers.

'She's coming round,' Albert breathed.

'Don't build your hopes up too high.'

When Bathie's eyes opened, two minutes later, they both leaned forward. Her eyes fell on Gavin, her mouth curving up slightly as she recognized him.

'Gavin.' It was the merest breath.

'Yes, Bathie, it's me.'

Albert leaned back, feeling as though he'd received a kick in the stomach. His suspicions had been proved correct, after all. It was Gavin she'd turned to first.

But her troubled eyes were moving restlessly, and he held his breath, hardly daring to hope that they were searching for him. He was longing to say, 'I'm here, my love,' but she had to make her own decision, without any prompting from him.

When she located him eventually, no sound came from her bloodless lips as she formed the words, 'Albert, I love you.'

Almost choked with love and relief, he bent towards her and lifted her icy hand. 'Thank you, my love.'

Her bewilderment reminded him that she couldn't possibly know what he was thanking her for, and he added hastily, 'I love you, Bathie, more than you'll ever know, and I'm thanking you for still loving me.'

Gavin touched his elbow. 'I'm happy for you both, Albert, and I mean that from the bottom of my heart. I'll go now, to let your family know we've found her. It's up to you, now, but don't tire her, she's very weak.'

Albert didn't move. Bathie's eyes had closed again, but he kept holding her hand – she was going to recover.

Dr Sangster came back, took one surprised look at the two hands clasped over the counterpane, and hurried forward.

'Did she come round?'

'She knows I'm here,' Albert murmured. 'She looked at me and told me . . . ' He choked and couldn't finish.

'How did your wife come to be wandering about outside in the middle of the night like that?'

Keeping his emotions under a tight rein, Albert told him the whole story, holding nothing back, although he was bitterly ashamed of the events before and after the quarrel.

Dr Sangster looked at him incredulously when he ended. 'If you believed that Dr McKenzie loved your wife, it wasn't very wise of you to tell her to go to him, was it?'

'Wisdom's not my strong point,' Albert said sadly. 'And she only got as far as the foot of the Gallowgate.'

'Where does Dr McKenzie live?'

'Froghall.'

There was a short pause, then Dr Sangster's mouth relaxed into a smile. 'She was found at the opposite end of the Gallowgate, Mr Ogilvie, near Broad Street, so she couldn't have been on her way to Froghall, not if your house is on the brow of the hill, as you told me earlier.'

Albert's face registered his astonishment. 'She was going in the wrong direction. Thank you for telling me that, it's made me feel much happier.'

The doctor's expression darkened suddenly. 'Don't feel too happy, Mr Ogilvie. Your wife's condition is critical.'

'I understand that, but my Bathie's got stamina, and I can feel in my heart that she's going to pull through.'

'I certainly hope so. You may stay for perhaps another thirty minutes, on condition that you don't talk to her.'

'I promise I won't do anything but pray for her,' Albert vowed. 'Thank you very much, Doctor.'

It might be weeks before Bathie came home – she would come home, he was certain – but from now on, his life would be centred on his wife. She meant everything to him, and he would never stray again, no matter what temptations came his way. He had almost lost her through his own folly, but he had learned his lesson, and it was a lesson he could never forget.

Let Gavin McKenzie keep on loving Bathie in his own quiet way. Let Flo marry her Will, if that was what she wanted. Let Gracie despise her father for the rest of his life, if she felt like it. Nothing else mattered, now he knew his wife still loved him, even after all he'd done.

That was true love. Love that passeth all understanding, as it said in the Bible.

Chapter Twenty-seven

'Albert, have you seen the *Journal* this morning?' Bathie's eyes were wide with alarm.

'Not yet. Why?'

'Read that.' She handed over the newspaper.

Fishing in his pocket for the spectacles he had to wear now for reading, Albert looked at the news splashed across the front page.

'"Gallipoli evacuated",' he read out. '"January nineteenth." Oh, that's not a very good start to 1916, is it?'

'Carry on.' Her voice was urgent.

'"After fierce fighting for weeks, British and ANZAC troops were forced to evacuate Gallipoli."'

'ANZACs, Albert. Will Dunbar could have been there.'

'Aye, I see what you mean. Well, we'd better not let Flo see this, or she'll worry herself sick.' He folded the sheets of paper and placed them in the top drawer of the big dresser, just before his daughters came downstairs.

The girls' chattering prevented any further discussion between Bathie and her husband, but when he went down to the shop with Flo and Gracie, and Hetty and Ishbel were clearing up the breakfast things, she opened the drawer, extracted the newspaper and took it into the parlour with her.

There was no mention of which section of the ANZACs had been involved, but an inner sense told her that Will had been there, and she prayed that he was still alive.

When Flo came upstairs at dinnertime, she already knew. 'A customer told me the ANZACs were at Gallipoli. Something's happened to Will, I know – I dreamt he was screaming.'

'He maybe wasn't even there, and I'm sure he's all right.' Bathie tried to reassure her daughter, but inside she wasn't so sure. Flo and Will had been like twins when they were small. Was it possible that one of them could tell if the other was in trouble? Were they telepathic?

'Dear Mother, I'm meeting Charlie in Paris next Tuesday, at long last. It took a bit of doing, but we've got leave at the same time, and I'm keeping my fingers crossed that we'll both be there. Sorry I haven't time to write more, and I wish I could see you again, Your loving Vena.'

Checking the date on the top of that day's morning paper, Bathie realized, with a sinking heart, that Charlie should have been meeting his wife last week, and it was too late to pray that they'd both kept the appointment.

Charlie's letter arrived next day. 'I'm spending a leave with Vena. It's the first time we'll have seen each other since I came here. I just wish all this business was over, and we were back home, for I'm heartsick of every damned thing here.'

Week after week went past with no word from Will, and Flo's face became pinched and white, her eyes staring out of deep, dark sockets with such hopelessness that Bathie longed to throw her arms round her to pet her like she used to. She held back only because she was afraid it would make Flo break down altogether.

Donnie hadn't written for some time, either, so his mother was concerned about him, too, but couldn't voice her fears in front of poor Flo, it didn't seem right.

Sometimes, sitting on her own, Bathie reflected sadly on what the war had done to her family. Charlie and Donnie had been first to go, then Vena, then Jack Lornie. Will Dunbar had come back and had taken Flo's heart with him when he left, and Gavin McKenzie had volunteered while she had still been so ill in hospital, and she'd never had the chance to say goodbye.

Flo was wasting away, Ellie was living for letters from her husband, Hetty, at sixteen, was going out with all kinds of servicemen, and causing her mother a great deal of anxiety. Thank goodness Gracie wasn't interested in boys and Ishbel was still too young to bother with them.

Donnie's letter, when it came, told her only that he was still alive, but there was still nothing from Will Dunbar. It was almost six months since Gallipoli, and poor Flo, who had steadfastly insisted that he couldn't have been killed, was slowly beginning to accept that he would never write again.

An unexpected letter from New Zealand made Bathie wonder why Mary was writing at this time, and she was almost afraid to open it. What would it do to Flo if Will was dead? Her fingers fumbled with the flap of the envelope and shook when she drew out the folded sheet of paper.

'Dear Mrs Ogilvie, Will was wounded at Gallipoli. He is home now, but he has lost an arm, and I haven't told him I'm writing, for he doesn't want Flo to know. He said it would be better for her if she thought he'd been killed, but I know he still loves her. If she writes to him, maybe he'll see how cruel he's been. That is, if she still loves him. We were delighted when he wrote to us that he'd fallen in love with her, and I don't want to see it finished like this. I hope you don't mind me writing this way, but I thought it was the only thing to do. Your friend, Mary Dunbar.'

Bathie's relief forced her to sit down, but after only a moment, she jumped to her feet again and shouted up the stairs. 'Flo, come down. This minute.'

When her daughter came running into the kitchen, her face puzzled, Bathie handed her the letter, and watched her as she read it, her pale face crumpling before she burst into tears – from happiness that Will was still alive, or with sorrow for his affliction, her mother couldn't be sure. Probably both.

'Will's alive, Flo, and it's not surprising that he didn't want you to know what had happened.'

When the girl stopped weeping, she said, 'I'm going to write to him this very minute, so I can catch the first post.'

Albert emerged from the bedroom as Flo ran upstairs. 'What's wrong? I heard you shouting to her to come down.' He spotted the envelope lying on the table and turned it over. 'A letter from Mary? Oh, Will hasn't been . . . ?'

'No,' Bathie said hastily. 'He's lost an arm, and he's back home, but he didn't want Flo to know anything about it. She's gone to write to him, so she'll be a bit late going to the shop. It'll be all right, won't it?'

'Aye, we're never that busy first thing. Poor Flo, but at least she knows he's still alive.'

'I hope he sees sense, though.' Bathie was rather worried about the boy's state of mind. She'd heard some rumours about amputees becoming changed personalities. 'It'll break Flo's heart if he doesn't answer her letter.'

Over the next few weeks, the post brought short scrawls from Vena, Charlie and Donnie.

'Up to my elbows in filth, as usual,' Vena wrote. 'The few days I had with Charlie in Paris were heaven, but it feels like years ago already.'

Charlie's letter told how tired he was of the fighting. 'The days go past, and nothing changes. I miss Vena, and the time we had together was so short and sweet, everything felt worse when I came back here.'

As he always did, Donnie had written only a few lines, but this was the shortest yet. 'Dear Mother and Father,

I am still well. Hope all of you are the same. Love, Donnie.'

Bathie was thankful that he'd written at all, but wished that he would tell them something about himself. It wasn't enough for his mother just to know he was well. What was he doing? What was he thinking? What was happening out there, wherever he was?

Will didn't answer Flo's letter, so she wrote again, after waiting for almost two months. Her mother was pleased that the girl looked happier than she'd been before Mary's letter came – her hollow, sunken cheeks had filled out again, her dark brown hair had recovered its sheen, her blue eyes smiled along with her lips when she laughed.

'I'm just as determined as Will is,' Flo told her mother after she posted the second letter. 'If he doesn't answer this time, I'll keep on writing till the war's finished, then I'll go to New Zealand myself. He can't brush me off so easily.'

Bathie's eyebrows went up. 'It's you he's thinking of, Flo. He doesn't want to tie you to a man with only one arm.'

The big eyes clouded a little. 'It must be terrible for him, but I'd marry him even if he'd no arms at all.'

'I know you would.' Bathie's laugh was somewhat sad.

'If he doesn't write soon,' Flo remarked, when there was still no letter from Will, 'I'm going to stow away on a boat and go to him. Let him try telling me to my face that he's stopped loving me and doesn't want me any more.'

'You know that's not why he doesn't write, and you can't stow away in wartime.' Bathie tried to make her see reason, but she couldn't help smiling at the senseless things girls said when they were in love.

A sailor friend of Hetty's had taken some photographs of her and her sisters, so when he presented them to Hetty one night, she ran upstairs in great excitement.

'He says he loves this one of me,' she burst out, and he's going to get another one off it, and keep it with him when he goes back to sea. But Flo, there's a really good one of you, so why don't you send it to Will and . . . '

'Oh, Hetty! That's the very thing.' Flo caused much amusement amongst the others when all she wrote on the back, in large letters, was, 'I love you, Will'.

When she ran to find an envelope for it, Bathie picked it up and studied it. As Hetty had said, it was a really good likeness of Flo. Her eyes were pensive and appealing, her mouth was slightly open and attractive fronds of dark hair framed her oval face. She looked beautiful, and Will Dunbar would surely fall in love with her all over again when he saw it. If this didn't melt his heart, nothing would.

All the next forenoon, Bathie felt in good spirits, and was very pleased when Ellie came in that afternoon carrying Kathleen.

'Flo's sent a pho . . . ' She stopped, dismayed by the glazed look in her eldest daughter's eyes. 'What's wrong?'

Ellie took a yellow envelope out of her pocket, and handed it mutely to her mother whose heart contracted. She knew what the telegram would say before she read it.

'Oh, no! Oh, Ellie! My poor, poor Ellie.' Bathie moved quickly to embrace the young widow, then took the fatherless child in her own arms. 'And poor little Kathleen,' she crooned, 'but Grandma'll look after you both.'

Jack Lornie's death affected the household for weeks; it brought home to every one of them the dangers being faced daily by Charlie, Donnie and Vena, serving their country just as Jack had done.

Shocked as Albert was when he was told about it, he was quite unable to find the proper words to tell his favourite daughter how much his heart ached for her. But he lay in bed at nights cursing the enemy for taking her husband away, and wishing that there was something he could do.

Ellie had been persuaded to stay at the Gallowgate for one night, but, no matter how much her parents tried to coax her, had firmly refused to remain any longer.

'I'll have to go home some time,' she'd said quietly. 'And the longer I put it off, the worse it'll be.'

'Gracie or Hetty could come and sleep with you for a few nights, if you like?' Bathie suggested, hopefully.

'No, there's no need, Mother. I'll have to get used to being on my own, and I've got Kathleen.'

Once they left, it came to Bathie that she'd coped very well herself, under the circumstances. There had been no heart pains, no headaches, just a dull sensation, a void, in the pit of her stomach.

She visited Ellie every day for two weeks, and wasn't altogether surprised when the young woman put her foot down.

'There's no need for you to trail down here every day. It'll take me a little while to adjust, but Jack's been away for so long now, anyway, I'm used to doing everything for myself.'

Her voice broke suddenly. 'It's just the thought that he'll never come back that hits me now and then.'

'I know, my dear,' Bathie soothed. 'It must be awful.'

Ellie nodded her head, then said, 'I don't suppose you ever realized this, Mother, but Jack and I were intending to carry on from where you left off.'

Puzzled, Bathie said, 'I don't know what you mean.'

'You were trying to go through the alphabet with our names, weren't you?'

Bathie gave a faint smile. 'That was your father's idea.'

'We all knew what you were doing, and you'd got as far as J, though poor little James didn't live. That's why Kathleen was called Kathleen, if you see what I mean. K was the next letter, but now . . . Ellie blinked a few times.

'I didn't realize.' Bathie gave a little sniff.

'We thought it would please you.'

'It does, and I'm sure your father'll be pleased, too.'

When she told Albert, he said sadly, 'Kathleen's not an Ogilvie. She's a Lornie, and it doesn't count.'

'She's half Ogilvie,' Bathie reminded him.

'It's still not the same, but my dream'll maybe be carried out some day. There's Charl . . . Donnie's children to come yet.'

'Yes.' Bathie had noted him correcting himself, and it hurt her as much as Albert to remember that Gavin McKenzie had told them, some time after Vena's baby died, that she would be unable to have any more.

When at last a letter arrived from Will, Bathie yelled the good news upstairs. All her daughters came running down, and the others placed themselves expectantly round Flo.

She ripped the envelope open, saying, 'I'll read it out, to save you all wondering. "My dear Flo, All I want to say is I love you, and I'm sorry I hurt you. Your photograph was enough to make me realize how stupid I was, but I still have several things to sort out in my mind."'

She raised her eyes suddenly. 'What things has he got to sort out, for goodness sake?'

'He'll have to face up to only having one arm,' Bathie observed, softly. 'He probably feels he's no use for anything, but if he wants you to go out there to marry him after the war, he'll have to be able to support you. I'm sure he'll get a job of some kind, though. Somebody must be willing to employ a man who's been disabled in the war.'

'What else does he say?' Albert was worried in case Will Dunbar was going to tell Flo to forget about him.

Flo carried on from where she'd left off. '" . . . things to sort out in my mind. I will write again when I get my other feelings under control, but I promise I'll never try to shut you out of my life again. Your devoted Will."'

A babble of congratulations broke out, but in the midst of it all, Flo sat down and burst into tears.

'There's no need to cry, when he's told you he still loves you.' Albert was smiling.

Flo lifted her head. 'I've felt like crying for so long,' she gulped, 'it had to come out. I kept up a pretence of being strong, but underneath it all I was terrified he'd be changed by what had happened to him and didn't love me any more. Now I'm so happy, I don't really know what to do.'

Nine-year-old Ishbel remarked, rather disdainfully, 'You shouldn't be crying if you're happy, though. That's stupid.'

Her father ruffled her red hair. 'People sometimes cry when they're happy, as well as when they're sad. You won't understand about it till you're older.'

'That's what everybody's been telling me for as long as I can remember.' Ishbel pulled a rueful face. 'How old do I have to be before I can understand things, for goodness sake? A hundred?'

Chapter Twenty-eight

Donnie's letter threw Bathie into such a turmoil that she ran through to the bedroom to show it to Albert.

After he'd read it, he remarked, kindly, 'It's just a passing phase, my love. I'm sure there's hundreds of wounded soldiers all falling in love with their nurses.'

'Donnie's never been one for the girls,' she protested, but left her husband to finish dressing.

Over the war's three years, there had been so many lives lost that Bathie had almost felt glad when Donnie was wounded – it had taken him out of the battlefield for a while.

She sat down at the kitchen table to read this latest letter once again, the letter which had agitated her so much.

'Dear Mother and Father, My leg is healing up very well. I'll be fit to join my unit in another two weeks at the most. I'm not looking forward to going back to the trenches, but "say la gerr" as the Frenchies put it.

'Now for the best news. At twenty-seven, I've fallen in love. She's a nurse, and her name is Helene Lowell. Her father is a grocer in Croydon, so that's a coincidence, isn't it? I haven't said anything to her yet, but I'll have to pluck up my courage very soon, before I leave the hospital, so wish me luck. Your ever loving son, Donnie.'

Bathie folded the thin sheets of paper carefully and slid them into the envelope. Maybe Albert was right. Nearly all soldiers fell in love – or thought it was love – with the girl who nursed them, and Donnie hadn't told this Helene how he felt yet. She might just laugh at him, for it must have happened to her lots of times before.

Sighing, Bathie laid the letter on the dresser, to let the rest of the family read it when they had the chance. She knew the girls would be interested, if Albert wasn't.

Ellie would be pleased for Donnie, she'd always been closer to him than to Charlie. She was still in Schoolhill with Kathleen, of course, but visited quite a lot. Hetty, at seventeen, was making munitions now and having the time of her life with the men who were either too young or not fit enough to be in the forces, but she'd be delighted about this.

Gracie, too, would be happy for her brother, she always asked what he and Charlie had written. She was rather serious and quiet, and, as well as serving in the shop, had taken over most of the heavy cleaning in the house since her mother's serious illness, almost two years ago.

Remembering those eight weeks in the infirmary, Bathie thanked God again for sparing her life. Albert had spent hours sitting at her bedside, willing her to pull through. He'd given up his council work and had been so contrite about what he'd done to her that she'd forgiven him completely.

Gavin McKenzie had been gone before she came home from hospital, but he wrote, now and then, from some unspecified medical field station, short friendly scrawls in which he asked after her health, and that of all her family, but telling them little about himself.

The slam of the outside door broke into her reverie, but she assumed that it was Ishbel home for dinner.

'You're a bit early,' she said, without looking round.

'I thought I was a few years late, myself.'

The deep voice made her spin round and jump to her feet. 'Oh, Donnie, Donnie.'

She ran to her son, then realized that he hadn't come in alone. A black-haired girl was standing shyly in the doorway, her large eyes slightly apprehensive.

Donnie held out his hand to pull her forward. 'Mother, I'd like you to meet Helene – my wife.'

'Your wife?' Her breath almost taken away, Bathie stared at him in amazement. 'But I only got your letter this morning, saying you hadn't told her how you felt.'

'That was written about three weeks ago. I told her just after that, and she said she loved me, too. We asked the padre to marry us, and as from two days ago, she is now Mrs Donald Ogilvie.' His shining eyes looked lovingly at his young bride.

The girl held out her hand. 'It must be a shock, having it sprung on you like this, Mrs Ogilvie.'

Bathie took the proffered hand, and laid her other hand on Helene's shoulder as she kissed her cheek. 'It has been a shock, my dear, but a very pleasant one, and I hope you'll both be very, very happy.' Her eyes suddenly filled with tears. 'Oh, don't mind me,' she begged. 'I'm just a silly old woman and it's all been so sudden, and seeing Donnie again. I'm overcome with happiness.'

The outside door banged again, and Gracie came running up the stairs. 'Father says he won't be long, he's . . . ' She stopped. 'Donnie? Mother didn't tell us you were coming home.'

'I didn't know.' Bathie wiped her eyes. 'Gracie, this is Helene. They were married two days ago.'

'Married? Donnie?' Gracie stood for a moment, flustered by the presence of the stranger, then ran to her brother and pumped his hand. 'Congratulations, Donnie, and you, Helene.' The second handshake was just as vigorous.

Bathie had recovered her equilibrium. 'Gracie, would you go back and tell your father that I want him to come up right now. Tell him nothing's wrong, but don't say anything else.'

When Albert came up, his perplexed face broke out in a huge grin on seeing his son. 'Donnie! Gracie never said . . . ' He crossed the room, and was thumping his son's back when he spotted the girl. 'Oh! I didn't notice . . . '

Donnie grinned. 'Meet my wife, Father. Helene, as you'll have gathered, this is the head of the family.'

Like Bathie, Albert had no reservations about welcoming this new member, and in the hubbub of all the explanations and congratulations, Bathie's legs gave way. She held on to the table for a minute, then sank down on a chair, her face grey, her heart pounding and an uncontrollable agony spreading right across her chest and down her arm.

Helene noticed first. 'Is something wrong, Mrs Ogilvie?'

As her new daughter-in-law moved across anxiously, Bathie whispered, 'It's . . . here.' She pointed to her chest.

Helene felt her pulse, then laid a cool hand on her brow. 'You should be in bed, and you must get a doctor at once.'

Her voice was crisp and authoritative, and Albert said, 'I'll go for him.'

Helene helped Bathie into bed, and by the time old Dr Proctor arrived, in the car he'd taken over from Gavin McKenzie along with the practice, she was feeling slightly easier.

'It's her heart, Doctor,' Helene told him.

He examined Bathie thoroughly, and agreed with the girl's diagnosis. 'I'll leave a prescription for tablets, so make sure she takes one every four hours for the rest of today, then two a day for the next two days, then maybe she could stop. But keep them handy in case she has another attack.'

When Albert went out to the street with him, the doctor said, 'Your wife's heart is not in very good condition, Mr Ogilvie, and she'll have to avoid any exertion or excitement.'

'That's what's done it, then.' Albert explained about his son arriving unexpectedly with a wife.

The old man nodded sadly. 'That's certainly what did it, so try to cushion her from shocks in future, if you can.'

'I'll do my best.'

Having to swing the starting handle several times before the engine coughed into action, the doctor muttered, 'This damned car needs to be retired, the same as me.'

Helene made Bathie stay in bed, although she protested that she was feeling perfectly well again, but after Gracie removed her dinner tray, she lay back exhausted, admitting that she did need to rest, after all.

She knew herself that it was all the excitement of seeing Donnie with a wife which had affected her, and thought, with wry amusement, that it was a good thing she wasn't presented with an unexpected daughter-in-law every day of the week.

She'd taken to Helene straight away, not like when she met Vena. But her first impressions had been wrong there, and Bathie loved her now like she loved her own daughters. It had been the girl's background that had been at fault. For the umpteenth time, Bathie prayed that Vena would come through the war unscathed, also Charlie, Donnie and his new wife. Thank goodness she only had two sons, and it was a blessing that Ellie had Kathleen, otherwise she'd have wanted to go to France as a nurse, like Vena, as she'd once said.

As it was, she seemed quite content to remain at home to look after her daughter. It would have been much better for her to have come home to the Gallowgate to live after Jack Lornie was killed, but Ellie was independent, like Albert.

Helene made sure that her mother-in-law spent the next few days in bed, in spite of her protests, and while Donnie and his wife were there, it was as though new life had been pumped into the whole household. The place rang with laughter again, and it did Bathie good to hear them all teasing each other. If only it could be like this all the time, she thought, but that day would come.

Too soon, for all of them, it was time for the young couple to leave.

'Look after yourself, Mother Ogilvie,' Helene said. 'I don't want to hear of any more turns.'

'I'll make sure she looks after herself,' Albert declared.

'I can look after myself,' Bathie said, rather tearfully, because she was going to miss them.

'The house feels empty now,' she told Albert next day.

'There's still six of us here, isn't that enough for you? When they all come back, there won't be room for everybody.'

'When they all come back,' she whispered. 'Oh, Albert, it'll be absolute heaven to have them all home again, supposing the two of us have to sleep on the kitchen floor.'

Chapter Twenty-nine

In the spring of 1918, another unexpected visitor turned up on the brow of the Gallowgate one afternoon.

Bathie was resting in the parlour when Hetty brought in a tall, dark-haired young man, with a New Zealand flash on his arm. Her first thought was that he must be Jeannie Wyness's son, but Hetty's introduction disproved that.

'Mother, this is Martin Potter, and he's from Wanganui, the same as Will. I'll go and make us a cup of tea.'

Bathie smiled a welcome, presuming him to be one of Will Dunbar's friends. 'Sit down, Martin. Please excuse me for not getting up, but I'm supposed to rest a while every day.'

'I'm sorry if I have disturbed you, Mrs Ogilvie, but my mother made me promise to call on you if ever I had the chance to come to Aberdeen.'

Racking her brain, she tried to place him. He couldn't be Jeannie's son if his name was Potter, so whose son was he?

'Your mother?' she began, uncertainly, then a horrifying sickness clutched at the pit of her stomach. Potter? Surely he couldn't be . . . ?

'I believe she worked for you for a time, before she went to New Zealand.' The young man smiled engagingly. 'She told me to ask if you remembered Bella Wyness?'

Bathie tried to still her thumping heart. How could she ever forget Bella Wyness? That slut? That insolent, filthy, perverted slut? 'Yes, I remember your mother,' she managed to get out.

'Thank goodness!' Martin grinned as he leaned back in the couch. 'It would have been awkward for me if you hadn't.'

A tightness started in her chest. 'How is she?' It went against the grain having to ask, but it was only polite.

'She's very well, thank you, but my father died last year. You wouldn't have known him, of course.'

'No, but I'm sorry to hear of his death.' Keep speaking, she told herself. Don't let this cause another heart attack.

'Mother often used to tell me how happy she was here.'

'I'm glad.' Her voice faltered.

'Are you all right?' Martin stood up in alarm. 'You look very pale. Can I get you anything?'

'My tablets,' she gasped. 'Top . . . drawer . . . kitch . . . ' She was unable to finish, her breath being cut off by the agonizing, excruciating pains shooting in all directions in her chest.

Martin rushed out, and almost immediately, Hetty came in, a round pillbox in one hand, a glass of water in the other. The boy hovered behind her.

'Will I get Father to come upstairs?' the girl asked with deep concern, when she saw her mother's grey face.

Bathie nodded, swilled down a tablet with a mouthful of water, and leaned back to wait until it took effect.

Left alone with her, Martin looked at her apprehensively, obviously hoping that she wouldn't get any worse.

When Albert came in, he strode straight across the room to his wife, scarcely noticing the stranger. 'Is it the same pain, my love? Have you taken a tablet?'

She nodded once more, and waited a few minutes before she took a small, cautious breath and sat up. 'I'm easier now, it was just a little turn. Albert, this is Martin Potter, Bella Wyness's son.' She lay back, glad to leave him to deal with the visitor. It wasn't the boy's fault he had Bella Wyness for a mother, but was she to be plagued by that trollop for the rest of her days?

'I've often wondered about the family in the Gallow-gate,' Martin said. 'I'm pleased to meet you, at last, Mr Ogilvie.'

Albert smiled. 'You look too young to be a soldier.'

'I'm eighteen now, but I lied about my age.' Martin grinned mischievously, but Bathie was dismayed to see that his eyes followed Hetty when she came in with the tea tray.

Her heart began to flutter again, as another appalling thought struck her. *Please God*, she prayed silently, *don't let a romance start between my daughter and Bella Wyness's son*. She felt sick when she noticed Hetty taking a long lingering look at the tanned, handsome boy as she went out.

Oh no! This couldn't be happening. But it couldn't come to anything, anyway, because he was only here on an afternoon's visit, and they'd never meet again. She was being stupid, worrying about things that could never materialize.

Her blood ran cold the next minute, when she heard Albert playing the genial host. 'If you haven't got anything planned, lad, you're welcome to spend your leave here.'

Martin's face lit up with joy. 'That's great! I was going to ask if you could tell me where I'd get a bed for a few . . .'

'We've plenty of room here, haven't we, Bathie?'

His wife's pinched, haunted face made Albert regret his unthinking hospitality. The young soldier had made such a good impression on him that he'd forgotten, for the minute, who the boy's mother was, and he couldn't retract the invitation now. Looking at Bathie, he waited for her to say something.

'We've plenty of room,' she agreed quietly. What was the good of trying to fight this? If it was ordained that Martin and Hetty would fall in love, there was nothing she could do to prevent it, however much she hated the idea.

'You're welcome to stay,' she added.

'Thank you, Mrs Ogilvie,' Martin beamed. 'You know, my mother always said you'd a heart of gold. She thinks

266

highly of you, and so do my Aunt Mary and my Aunt Jeannie.'

This last was a topic Bathie felt she could safely follow, so she said, 'How are your aunts?'

'They were both very well, the last time I saw them. I visited them just before I left Wanganui, and Will was looking much better than he did when he went home first.'

'Yes, he seems cheerful enough when he writes to Flo.'

Albert asked about Martin's training, so Bathie sat back and let her mind return to Bella, the rotten apple in the Wyness barrel. She'd only been sixteen when she did that vile thing to Charlie, and Mary had said in her letters that Bella had carried on with a lot of men before she was married – like Vena had done before she married Charlie.

But Vena had changed completely and had been a good wife. Was it possible that Bella might have changed, too? Could a decent man have succeeded in reforming her?

Looking across at Martin's animated face as he described his army life to Albert, it occurred to her that his mother must have changed, since she'd produced such a fine boy, for he was a fine boy, there was no getting away from that.

Hetty, who had seated herself on the couch next to him when she brought in the teapot, evidently thought so, too. Her face was bright and her eyes never left him. She was eighteen, like he was, but still a child. No, Bathie corrected herself. Hetty was two years older than she herself had been, when she fell in love with Albert.

Waiting until the boy came to a halt, she said, 'You'd better go upstairs and air Donnie's bed for Martin, Hetty.'

'Yes, Mother.' Hetty rose rather reluctantly, but Martin jumped to his feet.

'I'll help you.'

A becoming blush stole over Hetty's cheeks as they went out, and Bathie's sigh was long and shuddering. 'Do you see what's happening, Albert?'

'What's happening?' It was a moment before he realized what his wife meant, then he smiled reassuringly. 'Hetty never keeps a lad for very long, it'll blow past. Anyway, it'll be easy enough to put a stop to it if we have to.'

'You can't stop them falling in love,' she said sadly. 'And it's too late to do anything about it, for I think they're in love already.'

'I'm sorry, Bathie. I should never have asked him to stay. It was out before I thought, and I couldn't back down.' He frowned a little. 'You don't honestly think they're in love already, do you? They've just met.'

How little her husband knew about the human heart, she reflected, or how much he'd forgotten. 'They maybe don't know it themselves, yet,' she said, 'but I'm quite sure they are.'

When Hetty and Martin returned to the house after their third evening out, Bathie could tell that they'd kissed for the first time. There was just that much more awareness between them, holding each other's eyes, a tendency to make contact.

'They know themselves now,' she told her husband, later.

'I could see that for myself,' he retorted.

'I told you it was too late to do anything about it,' she said sadly. 'We'll have to accept it.'

Pushing his lower lip out as he thought the matter over, he said, 'I can accept it, Bathie, but can you? Can you ever forget what Bella Wyness did to Charlie?'

No, she thought. She would never be able to forget that, nor could she forget how Albert had been tempted by the girl, as Bella had been then. But that was all in the past. Could she forgive after all this time, and welcome Bella's boy as a son-in-law if it ever came to that?

Ellie brought little Kathleen to visit the following afternoon. 'Hetty took Martin to see me last night,' she told her mother. 'I couldn't believe he was Bella Wyness's son. Not that I remember much about her, but I know there was something queer about the way she left. Why did you give her the sack?'

Bathie rubbed the tip of her nose with her forefinger then said, somewhat coldly, 'She wasn't suitable as a nursemaid, Ellie. Just leave it at that.'

'But . . . ' Ellie stopped suddenly. The expression on her mother's face told her that it was no use asking.

'How's my little Kathie today?' Bathie turned to her granddaughter, steering the talk away from the distasteful subject of Bella Wyness.

'Her name's Kathleen,' Ellie snapped, still smarting from her mother's rebuke. 'It's a lovely name, that's why Jack and I chose it, and I don't want anybody calling her Kathie.'

'I'm sorry. It's a bad habit I have, making up pet names, and I did it with all of you, except Ishbel, and there's not a pet name for that. But Kathleen *is* a lovely name.' The toddler was moving around, occasionally putting out a hand to touch something and, as Bathie watched, a lump came into her throat because Kathleen was so like Ellie. The curly red head, the deep blue eyes, the sturdy little body, were exactly as Ellie's had been. Even the mischievous grin when the child asked the same awkward questions.

'Mother, there's something else you should know.' Ellie broke into Bathie's thoughts.

She transferred her gaze to her daughter, now fiddling nervously with her handbag. Ellie's words had sounded rather ominous, as if she knew that what she was about to say would distress her mother.

'I thought it would be best to warn you,' Ellie continued, 'so you won't get a shock when they tell you, but I think Hetty and Martin are falling in love.'

Bathie's relief came out as a giggle. 'I don't *think* they are. I *know* they are.'

'Don't you mind? I thought you'd be upset about it.'

'I was, at first, but what could I do?'

'Nothing, I suppose, and there's a bright side to it, you know. If Hetty wants to marry Martin, she'll be going to New Zealand after the war, too, so you won't have to worry about Flo. They'll be company for each other on the journey, and Mary and Jeannie'll keep an eye on them once they arrive.'

That was true enough, Bathie told herself, but what about Bella? Would Bella Wyness keep an eye on Hetty, or would she make the girl's life a misery out of spite? Had she planned this, so she'd have a chance for revenge?

'Mother, is anything wrong?'

With a start, Bathie focused her eyes on her daughter. 'I was just thinking. It's going to be hard if they both want to go, but, as you say, they'll be together, so that'll be a comfort. Anyway, I'll still have you, and Gracie, and Ishbel.'

Her rather serious expression changed suddenly. 'Unless another New Zealander turns up and takes Gracie away, too.'

Ellie giggled. 'I shouldn't think there's much chance of that. She'd run a mile if a boy ever spoke to her.'

Bathie noticed that Kathleen was struggling to fasten a shoelace that had come undone. 'Let Ga-Ga do it, my pet.'

'Oh, you're as bad as Jack's mother.' Ellie sounded exasperated. 'She'll never learn to speak properly if you both use baby words to her.'

Stifling a pang of jealousy at the other grandmother, Bathie defended herself. 'It's what Kathleen calls me.'

'That's only because she couldn't say Grandma.' Ellie turned to the toddler. 'Kathleen, it's Grandma. Let me hear you saying it. Grandma.'

The little girl smiled impishly. 'Gran-ny,' she said.

'Oh, that's nice.' Bathie beamed with delight. 'Let her call me Granny, Ellie. I'd really like that.'

'Well, I suppose it's not so bad as Ga-Ga, and she could call Jack's mother Grandma, instead of Grandmother.' Ellie smiled. 'Granny. It's quite sweet, really.'

'Come to Granny, Kathleen.' Bathie held out her hand, and was delighted when the child repeated, 'Granny' as she obeyed.

'You'll spoil her.' But Ellie's smile was fond as she looked at her mother.

After her visitors left, Bathie sat thinking. Poor Ellie, losing Jack Lornie like that. What a pity she couldn't find another man, but she'd no chance to meet anybody, though maybe she'd take a job once Kathleen started school.

When Hetty and Martin returned from their stroll, shortly afterwards, Martin kept Bathie company while Hetty disappeared into the kitchen to prepare the tea.

'Did you have a nice walk?' Bathie asked.

'Yes, we went to the Bridge of Don, then came back along the beach, and sat for a while watching the boats . . . Er, Mrs Ogilvie, I wanted to talk to you alone.' Martin's hand fidgeted in the same way as Ellie's had done.

'Yes?' Bathie had a good idea of what he was plucking up courage to say, and she was glad she was prepared for it.

'I suppose you've realized by now how I feel about Hetty,' he began, tentatively.

Bathie smiled and nodded encouragingly.

'She's the only girl I'll ever love,' he carried on, 'and I think she feels the same about me.'

'I know she does.'

'I can't ask her to be serious while the war's still on.'

'You haven't asked her yet, then?'

'No, and I think Hetty's hurt that I haven't, but . . . Oh, it's not just the war. We're a bit too young for marriage.'

'I was only sixteen when I married her father,' Bathie murmured. 'Albert was twenty-four, of course.'

'A man should be older than eighteen before he commits himself. And I might not survive the war – that was another reason I've held back.'

Bathie's heart turned over. He had too old a head on his broad young shoulders. 'Martin, I can't guarantee your safety,' she said, sadly, 'but I think you should tell her how you feel. When the war's over, if you still love each other, you can be married then. If you've changed your minds . . . ' She shrugged expressively. 'That'll be that, and no harm done.'

'I'll never change my mind about Hetty, but do you think your husband will be agreeable to what you've suggested?'

His earnest young eyes were so blue, so darkly fringed, that Bathie could see why her daughter loved him.

'Albert'll want what's best for Hetty. Now, go through and tell her everything you've said to me.'

'Thank you, Mrs Ogilvie. Mother was right. You always know what to do for the best.' Martin rose to his feet, hesitated briefly, then said, in a low voice, 'I may as well tell you this, too. I know what my mother did to your oldest son when he was a small boy, and I know she tried to tempt Mr Ogilvie to be unfaithful to you, and that she didn't succeed.'

Bathie was speechless for a moment. 'Who told you that?' she whispered at last.

'She told me herself, just after Father died.'

'I can't get over her telling you.' Bathie licked her dry lips. 'You know, when I first saw that you were attracted to Hetty, I wondered if your mother had planned it for revenge on me for dismissing her.'

'She holds no grudge against you for that,' Martin assured her. 'She regretted what she did and always spoke very highly of you. She says herself that she was almost past redemption when Father took her in hand and tried to lick her into shape, although I often had the feeling that he seemed disappointed in her, but she's always been a genuine, caring mother to me.'

He gave a boyish grin. 'If things work out for me, I'll also have a genuine, caring, mother-in-law.'

Bathie laughed in spite of herself. 'Get on with you and your New Zealand flattery. Go and try it on Hetty, she'll be a lot more receptive to it than me.'

He winked and hurried out, leaving Bathie to lean back in her chair, quite weak after what he'd just told her. And fancy Bella Wyness being described as a genuine and caring mother. It was unbelievable, after what she'd been before. But it wasn't impossible – just look at the change in Vena.

Martin Potter's father must have been an exceptionally good man, and Martin himself was thoughtful and honest. Hetty would be a lucky girl if she did eventually marry him, and Flo, too, when she married Will Dunbar.

A tear trickled out of the corner of Bathie's eye, and she wiped it away with her finger. Jack Lornie had also been a fine boy. *Please God, look after the rest of my boys.*

Her troubled mind rambled on. Would Donnie and his wife settle down after the war and raise a family? Gracie seemed scared of men, so it was unlikely that she'd ever fall in love, but what a lot she'd miss. Love could cause doubts, jealousies and heartaches, but as the old saying went, ' 'Tis better to have loved and lost, than never to have loved at all.'

What would her own life have been like without Albert and her children? The worries and sleepless nights they'd caused her had been more than compensated for by the love and pleasure they'd given her over the years.

When Albert came in, he was surprised by the warmth of her greeting, and touched by the kiss she rose to plant on his cheek – so touched that he put his arm round her waist and hugged her tightly. 'Bathie, my love,' he said, softly.

It had been so long since he'd embraced her, or spoken to her so tenderly, that her eyes filled with tears.

'Is anything wrong?' he asked anxiously.

Stretching her hands up, she pulled his head down and kissed him. 'That's what's wrong,' she whispered. 'Why don't you ever tell me . . . ?' She couldn't finish, because his lips came down hard on hers and her heartbeats quickened as though she were a young girl again.

Drawing away, he stroked her cheek with his finger. 'You know how much I love you, Bathie.'

'Why don't you tell me sometimes, then? You never say it, Albert. You haven't said it for a long time.'

'I didn't think I needed to, but I love you more than my own life.' He stepped back and looked at her with raised eyebrows. 'What brought this on?'

'I'll tell you when we go to bed. The girls'll be up in a minute, and Martin and Hetty are in the kitchen, so there's no time now. It was just something that made me want to be sure you still loved me, nothing bad.'

They moved further apart when Flo and Gracie came in.

'Did Hetty come back in time?' Gracie demanded.

'Yes, she's in the kitchen with Martin, so you'd better knock before you go through.' Bathie gave a small chuckle.

'Why should I? They shouldn't be doing anything, anyway, except making the supper.' Gracie disappeared and they heard her barging straight into the other room.

'She's jealous,' remarked Flo. 'She's the only one of us who hasn't got a lad, except Ishbel, and she doesn't count.'

'Poor Gracie.' Bathie could understand what the girl was feeling. It hadn't been so bad when Flo was engaged, because she was one year older than Gracie, but Hetty was three years younger, so she must feel it more.

And both Flo and Hetty would be impatiently waiting for the war to come to an end so that they could go to Wanganui to marry their sweethearts. When that time came, she would have to make Gracie understand how grateful she was that one of her grown-up daughters would be remaining at home.

When Martin Potter was leaving, he shook hands with all the girls except Hetty – who was going to the railway station with him – then turned shyly to Bathie and Albert.

'Thank you both for your hospitality, and, Mrs Ogilvie, thank you for your advice. I'll be writing to Hetty, once I'm sent to wherever it is.'

'Take care of yourself, lad.' Albert's voice was gruff.

Bathie kissed the boy's cheek. 'You'll be in my prayers.'

'Thank you.' Martin's voice broke, and he turned away rather abruptly, Hetty following him as he went out.

'It's a crying shame that lads of his age have to leave their homes and go and fight,' Albert said vehemently. 'Though, if it hadn't been for the war, Hetty would never have met him, so even that cloud had a silver lining.'

Bathie's heart was too full to allow her to answer. If it hadn't been for the war, all her children would still be here with her. Donnie and Helene would never have met, either, of course, nor Flo and Will, and she felt so confused about that, she gave up trying to think about it.

Charlie and Donnie would be home when the fighting was over, and she'd have to look on Vena and Helene as replacements for the two daughters she would lose. Heaving a sigh, Bathie went into the kitchen to fortify herself with a cup of tea.

Chapter Thirty

When the newspaper headlines shouted, *ARMISTICE SIGNED AND HOSTILITIES CEASE*, Albert could hardly contain himself.

'On the eleventh hour of the eleventh day of the eleventh month,' he marvelled, 'but it says underneath, "Resumption practically impossible for Germans". We should have made damned sure it was impossible for them to start a war again.'

'Calm yourself, Albert.' Bathie was deeply thankful that it was over at last. 'There'll never be another war. There were so many casualties on both sides, no country's going to let that happen again. Not even Germany.' Her blue eyes, slightly jaded of late, had brightened up considerably at the good news. The rest of her family would be coming home soon, and they'd all be together again. A stab of pain shot through her as she remembered that they wouldn't all be together. She was happy that Flo and Hetty had found true love, but part of her wished fervently that Will and Martin had been Aberdeen boys, though the two New Zealanders seemed to be decent and honest, and would be good husbands.

Will Dunbar had been fitted with an artificial arm, and his affliction no longer seemed to worry him unduly. A month ago, he'd told Flo that he'd been promoted to office manager of the building firm he worked for, and was saving up to buy a house.

Martin Potter was still writing love letters to Hetty, and their attachment seemed to be as strong as ever.

275

She'd have to let both her daughters fly the coop when the time came, Bathie mused, sadly. Gavin McKenzie had once said they'd be lost without her, but she knew that Flo and Hetty could stand on their own feet now, without any help from her, and she'd always be here if they ever needed her.

She let her thoughts turn to Gavin, and although it was some time since she'd heard from him, she was quite sure that he was still alive and would be coming home soon. She hadn't seen him for three years, and she wondered how she would feel when she met him again. And how Albert would feel.

Of course, Gavin might not want to return to Aberdeen, but he still owned the house in Froghall – old Dr Proctor had only taken it over while he was acting locum tenens – so he'd have to come back to sell his property.

Bathie considered her feelings carefully. She'd thought very fondly of him at one time, affectionately, as she'd have done with any old family friend. Knowing that he loved her had made her more aware of him, that was all. She'd never loved him, not in the deepest sense of the word.

It was always Albert she had loved, for better or worse, as she'd vowed on their wedding day. It had been mostly for the better, she decided, for the good times had far outweighed the bad, and he was only human, after all.

That night, Gracie approached her mother after suppertime. 'Can I go down to the Castlegate later on to see the Armistice celebrations?'

'By yourself?' Bathie was astonished. Gracie was so shy that this was a most unusual request.

'I asked Flo and Hetty, but they didn't want to go, and it's something I'll never see again.' The girl's eyes were more animated than usual, and a few strands of her mousey locks had escaped from their hairpins, curling round her rather long face and making it look rounder and more attractive.

Bathie hadn't the heart to disappoint her. 'All right, but don't stay out late. There'll be a lot of drinking, I expect, and drunk men don't care what they do.'

'I can look after myself, Mother. I'm twenty-one.'

Even at that age, Bathie reflected, morosely, the girl was naive and innocent, but she couldn't say so.

When she came out of Broad Street into the Castlegate, Gracie felt the excitement mounting inside her at the joyful sound of celebration. In a minute, she was engulfed in the milling throng, and was amused to see some servicemen kissing any girl who let them, laughing all the while at the giggling squeals they let out. A hefty Gordon Highlander grabbed her suddenly and gave her a quick kiss before he let her go and turned away to do the same to someone else.

Never having been kissed before, Gracie found that she quite enjoyed it, and mingled with the soldiers hopefully, giggling like the other girls each time any of them put an arm round her, but the boys always moved away afterwards. It would be much better if she had a lad of her own, she thought, but . . .

Her hand was seized roughly by a tall sailor who dragged her into a huge circle of people, all singing 'It's a long way to Tipperary' at the top of their voices.

The heady atmosphere made her lose her shyness, and she felt quite exhilarated, laughing delightedly when the sailor broke hands with the person at his other side and pulled her away with him. He placed his hands on her waist to lift her high in the air, then let her down slowly until she was held tightly against him.

'You're as light as a feather,' he told her, looking down at her with great admiration.

She'd to strain her ears to hear what he said above the renewed singing that had broken out. 'There's a long, long trail a-winding . . . '

As she held her laughing face up to his, his head came down abruptly. His kiss was different from the others she'd received, and within a second, Gracie had fallen in love with an absolute stranger.

When their lips parted, the sailor sighed. 'You were made for kissing. Did you have anybody in the war?'

'My two brothers,' she whispered. 'They're in France.'

'Nobody else?' His voice was urgent.

'Nobody else.'

'Some boy in Aberdeen, then?'

'Nobody.' Her heart was pounding so quickly that she was sure he must hear it, but she didn't care.

'What's your name, Miss Nobody?'

'Grace Ogilvie.' She'd always hated being called Gracie, it sounded so common.

'Grace? That's a lovely name. I'm John Trevelyan.'

'Trevelyan? That's unusual.'

'Not where I come from. Falmouth, in Cornwall.'

Her heart sank. 'That's hundreds of miles away.'

'About eight hundred, I'd say. Grace, may I see you home? This crowd's getting a bit rowdy now.'

She hadn't been aware of it, but she allowed him to tuck her arm through his. He pushed his way through the rabble, and although many of the men, and women, were drunk, they stood aside, grinning lewdly, to let them pass.

'Up here,' Gracie told him, when they reached Broad Street, also thronged with people making their way home.

The Town House clock struck several times and John jumped as the loud booms sounded, almost in his ear. Gracie had no idea what time it was, and in any case, she wasn't bothered in the slightest.

Some of the university students were holding their own celebrations outside Marischal College, and one of them shouted across the street to the young sailor, 'You're all right for tonight, Jack, I see.'

'You bet,' he called back.

'Are you called Jack sometimes?' Gracie wondered how on earth the student had known.

'Every sailor's called Jack. Jack Tar, I suppose.'

'Oh.' She laughed at herself for not realizing. There was so much she didn't know.

Going up the Gallowgate, he glanced into several of the closes, so she wasn't surprised when he drew her inside one.

'This is better.' He pulled her towards him and his kiss was long and tender. 'Beautiful Grace,' he murmured, before his lips found hers again, demanding and passionate.

Gracie was transported away from the damp smell of the brick-lined close, away from the bitter November night air, away from her mundane life, to a heaven she'd never dreamt existed. John Trevelyan was steadily draining her of all emotion except love, and she prayed that he would go on kissing her for ever.

As his hands caressed her back, the faint stirrings of awakening sexual desire grew stronger inside her and she gasped with the ecstasy of them, until he drew away from her with a jerk. 'Have you ever been with a man before?'

'No, never.'

'Oh, God, why did I have to pick on you?' he groaned. 'I haven't had a girl for months, and I thought . . . '

Her sudden, unconscious, wriggle inflamed him, and he kissed her so fiercely that she didn't even try to resist what he did next, and shy, mousey, man-hating Gracie was deflowered in a dirty close-mouth a matter of yards away from her own.

It was over before she came to her senses, pushing down her skirts in confusion. 'I shouldn't have let you do that.'

'I shouldn't have done it, but I couldn't help it,' he told her, adjusting his trousers. 'I'd better take you home now.'

All she wanted was to be alone, to ponder over why this terrible thing, this wonderful thing, had happened. 'It's only a little way, I'll easily manage, thank you.' She swept past him with her head in the air, but her legs shook and her heart was burdened down with remorse.

Aware that he was watching her, she waited until she turned into her own close out of sight before she gave way to tears. How could she have been so stupid? She'd always agreed with the women customers who said that a girl had been asking for it before she landed in trouble.

Had she been asking for it? She supposed she had, in a way, which made her feel even worse. Oh, God! What would happen to her if she was left to bring an illegitimate child into the world? What a disgrace that would be, but she'd have to face it as a penance for the sin she'd committed. A shuddering deep sob burst from her as she walked across to the iron staircase. Her parents would see that she'd been crying – what could she tell them? Her hand was on the rail, her foot on the bottom step, when a movement behind her made her turn her head.

'Grace.'

The soft, seductive voice created new thrills deep down inside her, but she remained where she was, still weeping.

'I'm sorry.' John came close and laid his hand over hers. 'I'd been at sea for a long time. Please say you forgive me.'

Her sobs became louder. 'It wasn't all your fault. It was me that made you . . . I asked for it, but I'm scared to think what my mother'll say if . . . if anything has happened.'

He hesitated, then put his arm round her slim waist. 'If anything's happened, I promise I'll see you all right.'

She cried out in relief and they didn't hear the house door opening above them, their kiss was so ardent.

'Is that you, Gracie?' Bathie's voice was shrill with anxiety, and she was halfway down the stairs before she saw them properly. They had jumped apart, but she could see, in the light streaming down from the doorway, that Gracie had been crying. 'Is something wrong with you?'

'Nothing's wrong. John took me home from the Castlegate.'

'It's half past midnight, Gracie, and I was worried about you.' Bathie ignored the sailor. 'Come inside this minute, before you waken your father.'

The young man looked up at her apologetically. 'I kept her out because . . . I was enjoying her company.'

His brief pause was significant to Bathie – enjoying her body was more like it, she thought – but she let it go. 'Thank you for bringing her home, then, and good night.'

Leaning towards Gracie, he whispered, 'We sail tomorrow morning, my pretty Grace, but I'll write to you.' He walked quickly round the corner, and Gracie climbed the stairs behind her mother, desperately searching for an explanation to give if she was asked why she'd been so upset.

Inside, Bathie gave her daughter a searching look. 'What did that sailor do to you to make you cry?'

'Nothing.' Gracie tried to meet her mother's eyes and failed. 'We were just speaking . . . and kissing.'

'Look at me, Gracie. It's written all over you what you've been up to. Did he force himself on you?'

'No, he didn't. I wanted him to do it. I asked for it.'

Bathie's eyebrows shot up so quickly, they almost touched her hairline. 'You asked for it? Oh, God, Gracie!'

'I didn't ask him outright. I just wanted him to do it.'

'Didn't you realize it was wrong? I thought you'd have had more sense, and I only hope . . . ' Bathie didn't finish.

She was very angry at what had happened, but she should have known that Gracie hadn't the experience to deal with such a situation when it arose. 'Go to bed, Gracie, for goodness sake,' she said, gently, for the girl was upset enough already, 'and I won't tell your father anything about it.'

Standing for a moment, she tried to calm herself before going into the bedroom. Her quiet daughter's behaviour had shocked and upset her, but if Albert found out, he would be so angry there was no telling what he might do.

Time would tell if there were to be any consequences from Gracie's misdemeanour, and there was no good in upsetting her father unless it became necessary.

Chapter Thirty-one

It was almost the end of March 1919 before Flo and Hetty were permitted to sail to New Zealand, and their parents saw them off on the first leg of their journey.

'I'll write every week once we're there,' Flo promised her mother, somewhat unsteadily.

Hardly able to speak for weeping, Hetty added, 'Me, too.' She flung herself at Bathie when the guard blew his whistle. 'Oh, Mother, I'm going to miss you.'

Not wanting to reveal her true feelings, Bathie answered lightly. 'You'll have a husband to look after you.'

'Aye, just think of the grand new life you'll be having.' Albert's voice was gruff with emotion, as he kissed them both.

This last farewell was too much for Bathie. She'd tried to keep up, so that their last memory of her would be cheerful, but now her tears mingled with theirs as she hugged them.

'God bless you, my daughters.'

Albert put his arm round Bathie, and they waved until the train was out of sight. 'They're going to be with the men they love,' he reminded her gently. 'Always remember that.'

'It's the only way I could let them go,' she sniffed.

Rather subdued, Gracie and Ishbel were sitting in front of the fire in the parlour when their parents returned home.

'Did they get away all right?' There was a slight catch in Gracie's voice – she was going to miss her two sisters.

Albert nodded. 'Yes, they're away, but now we can look forward to the boys coming home.'

This thought cheered them all up. Greatly relieved that Gracie had not become pregnant through her rash behaviour on Armistice Night, Bathie reflected that nothing bad could happen to her family now.

She was wrong, however. When she went to see Albert's mother the following day, Nell looked so ill that Bathie said, 'How long have you been like this? You should be in bed.'

'Ach, bed's for invalids, an' I've just got the flu.'

Her voice didn't have the usual bite in it, and she made no further protest.

Bathie made a little thin porridge for her, then said, 'I'll stay with you till you get over this.'

'What a fuss.' But Nell didn't argue.

The old lady's condition worsened so quickly that Albert took to visiting every evening.

'My time's come, Albert,' Nell said weakly, when he arrived after the shop closed on the fourth night.

'Nothing of the kind.' Although he was trying to reassure her, he felt alarmed. His mother was seventy-eight, and there was usually some kind of deterioration at that age, but surely not as quickly as this?

He drew his wife aside when Nell dozed off. 'Would you like me to stop here all night, just in case . . . ?'

'Maybe you'd better,' Bathie said, after a pause.

When Nell's breathing became rapid and shallow, her son decided that it was time to have her doctor in. It was after eleven o'clock, but the man returned with Albert, knowing that he wouldn't have been sent for unless it was urgent.

'She's very frail,' the doctor informed Bathie at the door when he was leaving. 'Old age comes to all of us, you know, and she has no reserves of strength to fight. I'm afraid she could go at any time, so be prepared.'

When Bathie went inside, Nell looked up into her drawn face and whispered, 'Dinna fret for me, lass. I'm ready to go.'

Holding her mother-in-law's hand until she fell asleep, Bathie dozed off herself, but Albert sat straight up in the old armchair, anxious about his mother, and thankful that his wife was there to look after her, until he, too, succumbed to sleep.

It was almost twenty minutes to two when Bathie woke up with a vague sense of disquiet. She leaned forward, but Nell had peacefully slipped away to join her husband, without her son or his wife being aware of it.

The ordeal of the funeral, and the clearing of the rented house, was made all the worse by interference from Walter and Jimmy, Albert's elder brothers, when they arrived from Grimsby.

Urged on by their wives, they insisted on removing those of Nell's belongings which they considered to be of any value, or to which they had taken a fancy.

'You always admired that vase,' Albert remarked to Bathie when Walter was about to pack it into a box with several other items he was taking away. 'Do you want me to get it for you?'

'No, Albert.' Bathie was sickened by the greed that was being displayed, and wanted no part of it. 'I don't want to cause ill feeling between you and your brothers.'

'I don't give a damn about them. If you want it, I'll . . . '

'No, let Walter have it.'

The only thing Bathie took as a keepsake was an old china plaque, which hung in the kitchen. The glaze was a little cracked, but the sentiment on it had always appealed to Bathie.

To forgive and forget is a maxim of old,
Though I've learned but one half of it yet.
The theft of my heart I can freely forgive,
But the thief I can never forget.

'Wattie gi'ed me that afore we were wed,' Nell had told her once, and had often glanced at it after her husband died.

'Are you sure you wanted that old plate?' Albert asked his wife, when she was hanging the plaque up in their parlour.

'Yes, I'm sure. It's true what it says, Albert. If you love somebody, you'll never forget them. I'm sure your mother found comfort from it after your father died.'

Bathie knew better than to tempt fate again by assuming that nothing else bad could happen, and began to fear for her own parents. Nell's death had brought it home to her that they, too, were growing old and frail. Her mother was seventy-one, and her father was seventy-three. Neither of them had ever had to work so hard as Wattie and Nell, but they didn't have Albert's mother's resilience, either.

Bathie's main concern, however, was the state of Gracie's mind. For over five months, the girl had been looking for a letter from the sailor, and had grown more and more despondent as time went past without any word from him.

'The war's over, so nothing could have happened to John,' she said, pathetically, one day in June.

284

Her mother hadn't the heart to tell her that the boy had probably never had any intention of writing. He'd got what he was after, and sailors usually had a girl in every port, so she was really better off without him.

The next outstanding event was more joyful. Albert, his wife and daughters were sitting in the parlour, one evening in August, when they heard feet pounding up the outside stairs. Bathie sat up in alarm, imagining it to be someone coming to tell her that one of her parents had been taken ill, and she could hardly believe her eyes when the door opened. 'Charlie!'

Jumping to her feet, she flung her arms round her son, then saw that Vena was just behind him. 'You're both home, thank God.' She smiled tremulously through tears she couldn't hold back, and sat down with a thump.

Something good was happening for a change, she thought, happily. Charlie and Vena were home at last, and soon Donnie would be back, with Helene. She'd have to buy a double bed for Donnie's room – they couldn't sleep in the old single – but what did anything matter when she'd have her family round her once again? It wouldn't be complete without Flo and Hetty, of course, but it was all the family there would be from now on.

It came to her suddenly that she had a duty as a mother. 'Gracie, go up and set a match to the fires in the attics. I've had them lit once every week, to keep the place aired,' she told Vena, 'so the rooms shouldn't be damp.'

Vena laughed. 'After the places we've been in, Mother, the attics'll be heaven.'

When Albert bombarded them with questions, they seemed reluctant to talk about their experiences, but were willing to recall some of the humorous situations which had relieved the starkness of war for them.

While they chattered, Bathie studied them. Charlie's face was much thinner, his dark hair was sprinkled with white, and his eyes gave the impression that they'd seen terrible things. Maybe one day he'd tell her about them, but she'd never ask.

Turning her attention to Vena, she saw the same sorrow in her eyes, even though she was laughing at something Charlie had said. Her face, too, was thinner, her cheekbones standing out gauntly, her fair hair hanging lank and dry. They would probably never forget the things they'd seen, but good food and cheerful company should improve their health.

When their stories ran out, a little silence fell, then Charlie said, 'Is Donnie back yet?'

'No, but he should be home any day now, with his wife.' Bathie beamed with pleasure.

Charlie grinned. 'You could've knocked me down with a feather when I got your letter telling me he was married.'

'We could all have been knocked down with the very same feather.' Albert chuckled at the memory. 'He took Helene to meet us, and she's a very nice girl. She practically saved your mother's life when she had that heart attack.'

Charlie turned to his mother accusingly. 'You didn't tell me you'd had a heart attack.'

'I didn't want to worry you, and anyway, it was nothing.'

They sat until the early hours of the morning, discussing everything that had happened since Charlie went away. He had never come home on leave – there was no point when his wife wasn't there – so there was five years to catch up on.

Finally, Albert rose stiffly from his chair. 'We'll all be like washed out dish-clouts in the morning.'

Lying in bed beside him, Bathie said, 'It's good to have them home, and it's not surprising they look tired, considering what they've been through.'

Albert let out a long sigh. 'They'll not want to stop in the attics when the excitement wears off.'

'Oh.' Bathie couldn't hide her disappointment. She hadn't thought beyond the homecoming. 'Well, if they don't, Donnie and his wife can have them when they come home.'

'Don't plan for them, Bathie. They've their own lives to lead, the same as we had, remember?'

286

'If they both want houses of their own, we can always go to visit them, but it won't be the same as having them here.'

She snuggled against him and he threw his arm over her. 'There'll come a day when it'll just be you and me in this big house, Bathie. How will you feel about that?'

'That'll never happen. Gracie'll be here, and Ishbel's only twelve, so it'll be a long time before she thinks about leaving us.' Her slight frown cleared. 'Anyway, even if they both take husbands, Gracie could have the middle floor and Ishbel could have the attics, so we'd never really be on our own, would we?'

'You're making plans for them again.' Albert surprised her by kissing her. 'Bathie, my dear, I haven't told you this for a while, but I love you. Now, go to sleep, or else be quiet so I can get peace to shut my own eyes.'

Chapter Thirty-two

Mary ran out of her house as soon as the car drew up at the gate.

'Flo, my little Flo,' she crooned, rocking her old charge in her arms. 'I never thought to see you again, an' I canna tell you how pleased I was that my Will found you again.'

She had retained much of her native dialect, but Flo found it amusing to hear a touch of the New Zealand drawl in it.

'I was very pleased he found me again, too,' she laughed, having got over the shock of seeing him with a leather glove on his left hand.

'An' this is Hetty?' Mary turned to the younger sister who was still inside the car. 'You werena born when I left, but your mother kept me up-to-date wi' what happened. Martin's a fine laddie, an' you'll like Wanganui, though it's littler than Aberdeen and you'll be bidin' a good bit oot.'

'I'm sure I'll like it,' Hetty murmured.

'I'd better be going.' Robbie Park had driven Will and Martin to Wellington to meet the two girls, and didn't want to be away from his business for longer than he could help.

'Righto, then, but, Martin, mind and take Hetty back to see me as soon as you can.'

'Yes, Aunt Mary, I promise.'

The woman waved as the car edged away, then she turned. 'Come inside, Flo, I'm sure you must be famished.'

Mary's house was cosy and homely, and Flo sat down, with Will, to eat the huge meal Mary had prepared, smilingly refusing second helpings when they were offered.

As soon as they were finished, Will stood up. 'I can see you're tired, my dear, but come and sit by the fire for a while. I'm sure Mother has dozens of things she wants to ask you.'

After kissing her son's intended bride, Bella Potter stood in front of her, her face wreathed in smiles. 'I was really pleased that Martin fell in love with you, Hetty. I often used to wish that I was part of the Ogilvie family, in the old days, but I never for a moment dreamed it would ever happen. I thought a lot of your mother and father, when I worked in the Gallowgate, but you weren't born when I came to New Zealand to be with my sisters. You've met Mary, of course, and no doubt you will be meeting Jeannie soon.'

She transferred her attention to her son. 'Take Hetty's cases upstairs to her room, Martin, then we can eat.'

When he went out, she turned to Hetty again. 'Is your brother Charlie home from the war yet?'

'Not when we left.' Hetty wished that she could go to bed right now, but it wouldn't be polite. 'Nor Donnie,' she added, recalling that Bella would have known him, too.

'It's Charlie I remember best.' Bella's blue eyes held a peculiar glint. 'A fine big boy, with a sturdy body on him.'

'Yes, Charlie was always tall for his age, so Mother said. Donnie's a bit shorter, and broader.'

'They shared a room, you know, and little Donnie was quite a sound sleeper, but Charlie always heard me when I looked in.'

The expression on the woman's face made Hetty shiver – she couldn't understand why. 'Charlie and Donnie are both married now,' she said, as brightly as she could.

'Yes, I know. Ah, here's Martin. He'll keep you company until I dish up. I let my little maid go, you see, when I knew you were coming. It'll be better with just the two of us, when Martin's away all week at university.' Bella swept out.

Hetty smiled as Martin sat down beside her. 'It seems funny that your mother knew my parents before I was born, and Charlie and Donnie, as well, though you never met them when you were in Aberdeen.'

'I met the only Ogilvie that matters to me.'

Her heart leapt at the love in his eyes, and he'd told her, as soon as she came off the boat, that he'd set the date of their wedding. In only five weeks, she'd be his wife.

Will and Flo were married first – he'd had the wedding arranged for the week after she arrived – and Bella ordered Martin to hire a car to take them to the small church.

Hetty was in tears when she saw Flo so radiantly happy, after all the months of worry she'd had when Will refused to write to her, but the ceremony went smoothly and Mary had laid on a wedding feast fit for the King himself.

When she was in bed that night, it occurred to Hetty that there had been a reserve between the three Wyness sisters, although Mary and Jeannie had been quite friendly and very polite to Bella. Too polite, Hetty realized now. There had been no warmth in their manner towards her, nor was there an easy-going relationship between the three of them like there had been between the Ogilvie girls, who'd all teased each other unmercifully, but affectionately.

It seemed almost as if Mary and Jeannie had some grudge against their youngest sister. She must have offended them in some way, or was it only jealousy on their part because she was now a wealthy widow? Anyway, Hetty thought, it was none of her business, and she'd take Bella as she found her.

Her thoughts bounded on, past her wedding to Martin, past the lonely nights he'd be away from her, to the time they'd be husband and wife, seven days a week, fifty-two weeks a year.

Hetty found that she got on very well with Bella, in spite of the difference in their ages. There were no signs of the peculiar expression which had caused the girl to shiver on her first evening in the house, and she came to believe that she'd imagined it because she'd been so tired.

Apart from the rough work, which was done by a woman who came in once a week, they shared the tidying up and cleaning of the house, and by lunchtime, everything was spotless. They usually went out for a walk in the afternoon, if the weather was clement, or sat by the fire, talking, if it wasn't.

Very occasionally, they went into Wanganui in a hired car to do some shopping, Bella showing the girl which were the best places, and introducing her to the shopkeepers, although, strangely enough, she never went near Robbie Park's store.

In the evenings, they just sat and talked, and Bella told Hetty, one night, how she'd met her husband, describing him as a forceful man with a sound head for business.

'Martin's not like him in temperament,' she added, smiling a little. 'He's too easy-going, but he has a big heart. He was a godsend to me when his father died, I don't know how I'd have coped without him. But I didn't stop him when he chose to enlist. He wouldn't have listened anyway – he's got his father's determination, if nothing else.'

'I'd never have met him if he hadn't enlisted.'

'That's true.' Bella's hand went up to pat her hair, which was obviously her great pride, the blonde tresses swept up in a smooth swirl on the crown of her head. 'I don't know why I gave him your mother's address, and it came as quite a shock when he wrote to tell me that he'd actually been to Aberdeen, and had fallen in love with one of the Ogilvie girls.'

'It was love at first sight for both of us.' A shy smile crossed Hetty's lips, then, remembering the parlour in the Gallowgate where she'd had her first meeting with Martin, a sudden twinge of longing for her own mother made her thankful that his mother would always be with her while he was away.

Bella's eyebrows lifted a little. 'I was surprised that your mother encouraged Martin to declare his love to you, especially after such a short time, and that your father was agreeable to the match, but I suppose war makes a difference to people's attitudes.'

The following evening, Bella spoke of her behaviour when she came to Wanganui first. 'My sisters were married to good men, and I felt very much left out. I was working in a hotel, and I went out with any man that looked at me twice.' She gave a rueful laugh. 'My sisters thought I was awful, for I behaved like a tart, pickin' up men an' boozin' like there was nae tomorrow.' She had lapsed into her natural tongue without realizing it. 'Ma was boilin' mad at me, an' said she shoulda shoved me aff the boat comin' over, but I was havin' a good time an' I didna listen.' She stopped, looking slightly bewildered, then patted the side of her head again, although not a hair was out of place. 'My mother died about six months after we arrived, so it was Mary who criticized me after that, but I paid no attention to her, either. I was very headstrong, you see.'

Noticing that she had recovered from her lapse, it struck Hetty that Martin's mother was not so sophisticated as she appeared. The unconscious slip into the broad Aberdeen accent, and the unnecessary patting of her hair, showed her insecurity.

After a long pause, Bella went on. 'All I was interested in was having a good time. Single men, married men, they were all the same to me as long as they bought me drinks and gave me a bit of loving. No, that's not quite true. I actually preferred the married men, because it gave me a bigger thrill knowing they belonged to someone else.' Sighing, she screwed up her mouth in self-disgust. 'Then I met Matt – Martin's father. I don't know what he saw in me, but he was determined to have me. He was older, and didn't approve of my drinking. He reformed me, would you believe?'

The girl laughed along with her. 'If you hadn't told me, I'd never have believed you could have behaved like that.'

'Ah, well. It took me a while to realize I'd been stupid, but I accepted his proposal eventually. He was a good husband, and I came to care very deeply for him.'

'I'm sure you were a good wife to him,' Hetty said softly.

'Yes, I was.' It was said without boasting. 'I kept on the straight and narrow for the whole seventeen years we were married, and when he died, I was broken-hearted, and I've never looked at another man since. I'd always be afraid that they were only after me for what Matt left me.'

In bed, Hetty mused over what she'd been told. She was grateful to Bella for being honest, but perhaps she'd done it to explain why Mary and Jeannie had been so distant with her. They hadn't been able to forgive her for carrying on the way she had at first, or possibly they'd been rather put out that she'd found a rich husband at the end of it.

Now that she knew, Hetty felt better, and determined to be a model daughter-in-law to Bella Potter.

On Martin's first weekend home, he asked Hetty how she was getting on with his mother, and was delighted when she said, 'I love her, Martin. She's like my own mother to me.'

'She has her ups and downs,' he admitted, 'but, on the whole, she's not too bad.'

Later, when they were all seated round the fire, Bella said, 'I've been thinking.'

Martin squeezed Hetty's hand. 'And what profound thought did you come up with?'

'It's only four weeks now until your wedding, and I feel it's not fair to Hetty to expect her to live here after you are married. She'll want her own house, where she can have you all to herself when you come home. I'm prepared to lend you enough to buy a decent house, Martin, and I won't expect you to start paying me back until you finish your studies and are earning a decent salary. I trust that sounds fair enough to you both?'

'It's very kind of you, Mother, but I couldn't allow you to do that, not when you're seeing me through university as well.' Martin looked troubled.

'I'd have made you a gift of it, but I knew you wouldn't have agreed to that, though all I possess will come to you when I die.'

'You'll live until you're ninety, I hope.'

'I might, so that's why I want to give you something now. We'll make it a loan, if you prefer it, but I won't take no for an answer, so start looking for a house.' Bella smiled, and seemed surprised when Hetty stood up and kissed her cheek.

'You're very kind, and I love you,' the girl whispered.

'I have to make sure that you're properly looked after. I owe that to your mother and father.'

Even through Hetty's happy excitement, she was conscious of a trace of the same chill which had swept over her on her first evening in the house, but she dismissed it once again as imagination. Martin's mother could never wish her any ill.

Chapter Thirty-three

The letter was postmarked 'Croydon', so Bathie had thought that Donnie was having a short holiday with his in-laws before coming to Aberdeen, but it proved to be no holiday.

'I've talked it over with Helene,' he'd written, 'and we both agree that it would be better for us to live down here. I'm sorry if this upsets you, Mother, but I promise we'll come to see you as soon as we can afford it.'

She had no interest in the remainder of the letter, this part was a dreadful blow, and so unexpected. It would be better to tell Charlie about it now – she'd heard him talking with Vena about looking for a house, to leave the attics free for Donnie – so she went out on to the landing.

'Vena! Charlie!' she shouted. 'Come down a minute.'

She handed them Donnie's letter without a word, and after they'd read it, Charlie said, 'You must be very disappointed, Mother.'

Noticing that their faces had fallen, it came to Bathie that they'd be disappointed, too, and she remembered Albert telling her that she should let them lead their own lives.

'I don't want you to feel you'll have to stop here because Donnie's not coming back. I'll be glad if you did, it's not that, but if you want a house . . . '

Charlie glanced at his wife. 'We *have* found a house we like. It's for rent, and it won't be vacant for a few months. But we can't leave you now.'

'Why not?' Bathie felt that her life, and her family, was disintegrating around her, but she kept herself well under control. 'Your father and I will still have Gracie and Ishbel, so you won't be leaving us on our own. Just be sure it's what you want before you sign anything.'

Charlie kissed her icy brow self-consciously. 'Thank you, Mother, I should have known you'd understand.'

Before long, Vena took a job in the Ladies' Department of a large store. 'I can't just sit at home twiddling my thumbs,' she told her mother-in-law, when Bathie expressed disapproval at married women going out to work. 'And, anyway, we'll need all the money we can get, if we're going to furnish a house.'

Bathie would have been happy to give them something from her grandmother's inheritance, but when she said as much to Albert, later, he ordered her not to.

'Let them ask for money, if they need it.'

'They'll never do that,' she protested, 'and you gave Ellie and Jack enough money to buy their furniture.'

'Times were different then,' he excused himself.

Recalling old Joseph Duthie saying, years ago, that young people shouldn't get things too easily, he added, firmly, 'They shouldn't have everything handed to them on a plate.'

The tone of his voice, and his challenging stare, defied her to argue, but she was hurt that he'd provided for Ellie, his favourite, and not for Charlie, who was hers. Still, she thought, afterwards, things could be a lot worse. Charlie and Vena would always be in Aberdeen, Helene would make sure that Donnie kept writing home, Flo and Hetty sent letters every week, as they had promised.

Gracie was spending less time in the shop now that her brother was back, and the warm summer days seemed to have had an uplifting effect on her. Her face broke into smiles more often, and she took more care with her appearance. Her mother didn't think there was any special reason for it, and was just glad that the girl had got over that sailor.

Ishbel was outgrowing her clothes, width-wise as well as lengthwise. She'd only be twelve on her next birthday, so goodness knows when she would stop. She was almost the same height as Ellie, and like Ellie used to do, she always asked about things she didn't fully understand.

Ellie visited every Wednesday and Sunday with four-year-old Kathleen, who, in spite of Ellie's earlier fears, spoke beautifully, with no trace of baby-talk. Ellie, herself, was more reserved nowadays, and carried her slim figure with an erectness which made her seem even taller than she was. Her deep blue eyes were quite unfathomable at times, but she seemed to be happy enough.

Everything seemed to be going well with her family, but a vague sense of foreboding touched Bathie now and then. She usually managed to shrug it off, though, and scolded herself for always imagining trouble to be lurking round the corner.

Washing down a shelf one forenoon in September, Bathie was quite unaware that anyone had come up the outside stairs until a deep voice said, 'Hello, Bathie.'

She dried her shaking hands on her apron, almost afraid to turn round, and her insides turned a somersault when she did. The familiar face was still craggy, the hair still tightly curled although it was white now, the grey eyes still tender.

'It's good to see you again, Gavin,' she said cautiously. 'You haven't changed a bit.'

'Neither have you. You're still as bonnie as ever.'

The compliment flustered her. 'My hair's grey.'

'Only a few more silver strands, and it suits you.' He looked at her for a moment as if he were drinking in her whole appearance, then said, softly, 'I expected a warmer welcome than this.'

There was still something in her heart for him, although it wasn't love, so she went to him and kissed his cheek. His hands came up and, holding her face firmly, he kissed her full on her mouth, then stepped back, smiling at the alarm in her eyes. 'Don't worry, Bathie,' he assured her. 'I'm not going to say anything out of place.'

'I'm glad about that. Sit down there, Gavin, and tell me everything that's been happening to you, and I'll finish the shelf and start getting the dinner ready.'

Like Charlie and Vena at first, he seemed reluctant to tell her anything, but described some of the places he'd seen.

He then asked about her family, so she brought him up to date.

'You knew about Flo and Will Dunbar getting engaged – that was before you went away – but Hetty fell in love with Bella Wyness's son, when he came here in 1918.'

'Bella Wyness? She was the one you dismissed rather abruptly, wasn't she? How did you feel about that?'

Bathie was glad that he didn't know the real reason for Bella's dismissal. 'Martin's a very nice lad, and they were deeply in love. Anyway, Flo and Hetty sailed for Wanganui in March, and they're both married now, and in their own houses. They write every week. Donnie's married and works with his father-in-law in Croydon, though he's speaking about starting up on his own, but I don't know if it'll ever come off.'

'He's got his head screwed on the right way, so he should make a go of it. What about his wife?'

'Helene was a nurse during the war, and she's a really sensible girl, so she'd be able to help him quite a bit.'

Recognizing that Bathie was in her element discussing her children, Gavin asked, 'Is Ellie's husband out of the army yet?'

Her face sobered. 'Jack Lornie was killed in 1917.'

'Oh, poor Ellie. How did she take it?'

'She's much quieter than she used to be.'

He smiled. 'I can hardly picture Ellie being quiet.'

'She's got her little girl, of course, so that keeps her busy, though Kathleen isn't the handful that Ellie was herself when she was small.'

They were still laughing about Ellie's childish exploits when Albert and his two assistants came upstairs. Charlie and Gracie soon let their old doctor know how pleased they were to see him, but their father stood back thoughtfully.

Bathie flushed, then was annoyed at herself. There was no need to feel uncomfortable, but she couldn't help glancing at Gavin, who stepped forward with his hand held out.

'Hello, Albert, it's good to see you again.'

To his wife's great relief, Albert's face broke out in a large grin. 'Welcome back, Gavin.' He took the outstretched hand and shook it with genuine pleasure. 'How long is it?'

'More than three years.'

'A lot's happened in that time. You'll be staying for a bite of dinner?'

Gavin glanced at Bathie, who nodded. 'There's plenty, and you're very welcome.'

Before he went back to the shop, Albert said, 'Stay and keep Bathie company for a while, Gavin. She needs somebody to speak to, somebody nearer her own age than the girls.'

'Will you be needing me this afternoon, Father?' Gracie looked at him hopefully. 'If you don't, I'll clear up here then I want to go to Broad Street to buy some embroidery threads to finish the tablecloth I'm sewing.'

'For your bottom drawer?' Albert regretted teasing her when he saw the look of pain in her eyes. 'Aye, it's all right, Gracie lass. Charlie and I'll manage fine.'

Turning to their visitor, Bathie said, 'Come through to the parlour, Gavin, out of Gracie's way. She doesn't like anybody standing over her when she's doing the dishes.'

She felt much more at ease with him since her husband had shown his pleasure at welcoming him. 'I suppose you'll be taking over again shortly. Dr Proctor's quite good, but I've a suspicion he's beginning to feel his age a bit.'

'Aren't we all?' Gavin grinned then screwed up his face. 'I don't know if I *should* take over again, Bathie. It might be better if I started a practice somewhere else. I'll have to find a younger man for this one, of course, so I'll probably be in Aberdeen for a while yet.'

She looked away hastily as his eyes held hers once more. He could still affect her, she mused, and he knew it. Perhaps that was why he was going away.

Fortunately, Ellie came in at that moment with Kathleen, who regarded the stranger curiously for a minute and then ran straight across to Bathie.

Ellie paused on the threshold, not recognizing Gavin until he said, 'Don't you remember me, Ellie?'

'Dr McKenzie!'

He stood up and took her hand. 'I was very sorry to hear about your husband, my dear. So many fine men were killed.'

'Thank you, but I'm getting over it now.'

'Yes, time heals everything, although one never forgets. You've got a sturdy wee girl there, and she's very like you.'

'She's dying to start school, but she's only four.'

'Already? How time flies. It doesn't seem all that long since I attended at her birth.'

From the safety of Bathie's lap, Kathleen announced, 'My Granny's going to buy me a school bag when I go to school.'

The man's eyes crinkled up. 'How do you like being a Granny, Bathie?' he chuckled.

'I love it.'

They talked about the old days until Ellie went to make a pot of tea, and Kathleen followed her mother into the kitchen.

Gavin's smile was touched with sadness. 'Ellie's a fine-looking woman, but what else could anyone expect, with you for a mother? She has Albert's hair, but she reminds me of you, when you were younger. The set of her head, the way she looks up sometimes, I don't know, but it's something.'

'I just wish she'd meet another man. She's only twenty-seven and she must be lonely. All her love goes on Kathleen.'

'It's good that she *has* Kathleen,' Gavin reminded her.

When Gracie came in, a few minutes later, she said, 'I hurried back to make you a fly-cup, but Ellie's doing it.'

'Sit down for a while, Gracie. Did you get your thread?'

'Yes, thank you.'

The girl was shy in Gavin's presence, but when Ellie came through with the tea-tray, conversation began to flow again.

Bathie couldn't help comparing her two daughters: Gracie listening but not joining in; Ellie joking and laughing, her blue eyes dancing, her cheeks pink and tendrils of her auburn hair swinging gently round her face when she moved her head. She hadn't looked so happy for a long time.

Transferring her gaze to Gavin, Bathie saw that he, too, was much more animated than before. His thin face was scored with lines now, but that wasn't what made him appear older, nor was it his white hair. She couldn't pin it down until she realized that it was an expression in his eyes at times, the same as in Charlie's and Vena's when they came home first.

At four o'clock, Ellie stood up. 'Well, Kathleen Lornie, it's time we were going home.'

'You could have your supper here,' Bathie offered. 'And you, too, Gavin, there's always more than enough.'

'No, thank you, Mother.'

'No, thank you, Bathie.'

They spoke in unison then laughed hilariously.

'It's very kind of you,' Gavin went on, 'but I told John Proctor that I'd be back, and Mrs Main, the housekeeper, will likely have prepared supper for the three of us.'

He rose to his feet. 'I'll walk home with you, Ellie, if you don't live too far away. My legs need a stretch. I'm not as fit as I used to be.'

'No, no. It's all right, Doctor,' Ellie said quickly. 'I'm still in Schoolhill, and it's no distance at all.'

'That settles it. It'll be a little constitutional for me.' He turned to Bathie. 'I'll come to see you again, if I may?'

'Of course, Gavin. You're welcome any time.' She kissed her granddaughter and stood at the top of the outside stairs until they went into the close, out of sight.

'I can see what's going to happen next,' Gracie observed, rather mournfully, when her mother went into the kitchen.

Puzzled, Bathie said, 'What do you mean?'

'Ellie's going to fall in love with Dr McKenzie.'

'Oh, no!' Bathie's heart turned over. She'd wished that Ellie would find somebody, but . . . not Gavin?

'Her eyes never left him, and I wouldn't be surprised if she's in love with him already. He's the only man who's paid any attention to her for years.'

A small sigh escaped from Bathie. She'd been too pleased that Ellie and Gavin had been getting on so well together to notice anything else, and felt slightly irritated now.

'Oh, Gracie, that's nonsense.'

Gracie turned away with a shrug. 'If Ellie makes up her mind to something, that's it. You know her.'

'He's only a year younger than your father, that makes him fifty-two, and she's only twenty-seven, just half his age.'

'You can't count, Mother,' Gracie remarked dryly. 'But have it your own way.'

Bathie wandered through to the parlour to think. If Ellie had set her heart on Gavin, he stood no chance against her. But it was ridiculous – Gracie's mind must be twisted. She must still feel bitter about the sailor.

A dozen times, Bathie convinced herself of this, and a dozen times she wavered. What if it was true? Even if they did fall in love, what was wrong with that? She'd made it clear to Gavin, years ago, that it was Albert she loved, so he was free to love whomever he pleased . . . but surely not *Ellie*?

But she was being selfish. She didn't want Gavin herself, but she was begrudging him her daughter. It was laughable, in a way, but she didn't feel like laughing. Could this be the trouble she'd thought was lurking round the corner?

When Albert came in, he said, 'I thought you'd have asked Gavin to stay for supper. He was looking very well, wasn't he? He'll maybe meet a nice woman and settle down now he's home.'

'I hope so.' As long as it isn't Ellie, Bathie thought, and despised herself for it.

Ellie made sure that her daughter was tucked up in bed properly, then went into her kitchen to ponder over what had happened that afternoon. She'd known Dr McKenzie for as long as she could remember, and had never thought twice about him, so why should she start now? He'd only walked her home out of politeness, and he was old enough to be her father. Of course, she hadn't seen him for a long time, but there had been something about him today that hadn't been there before. A sadness in his eyes? A difference in his voice?

Whatever it was, it had set her pulses racing as she'd thought they would never do again. His eyes had been tender when he'd bidden her goodbye, she was sure, and his hand had held hers for longer than was necessary.

She used to think that he was in love with her mother, but that had been silly. He liked her mother, anyone could see that, and her mother liked him, but there couldn't have been anything more in it. Gavin was too decent to let himself fall in love with another man's wife, but . . . another man's widow?

She jerked up, angry at herself, and stifled all thoughts of him over the next two days. She had no control over her dreams at night, however, and wove fantasies in which he took her in his arms and declared his love. When she went to the Gallowgate on Sunday afternoon, therefore, she couldn't help being disappointed that he wasn't there.

On the way home, she told herself that she was behaving like a love-struck schoolgirl. A woman could read more into a man's attentions than there really was, especially a woman who had been a widow for years.

When Bathie and her husband were making ready for bed, she could see that there was something on Albert's mind, and waited for him to come out with it. They had been lying in the darkness for a few minutes before he did.

'I thought you would have invited Gavin to start coming to supper on Sundays again.'

She'd been afraid he'd be jealous if she did that, but it seemed he was doubting her because she hadn't. 'I didn't know how you'd feel about it,' she said, carefully.

Turning towards her, he lay silently for a moment. 'I'm not jealous of him now, and I always got on well with him.'

Bathie didn't really believe what Gracie had said about Ellie, but she wondered if it would be storing up trouble to have her and Gavin here every Sunday. Still, she'd have to invite him, or tell Albert why she wouldn't, and he'd just laugh at her for being stupid.

It became a habit for Gavin to see Ellie and Kathleen home on Sunday evenings, until even Albert remarked on it. 'I don't know if it's a good thing, you know.'

Bathie was so troubled that she couldn't keep her fears to herself any longer. 'I'm sure it's not a good thing – Gracie thinks Ellie's falling in love with him.'

'Has Ellie said anything to you?'

'No, but I think she could be. Haven't you noticed the way she looks at him sometimes?'

'How would you feel about it if it's true?'

She evaded the issue. 'He's far too old for her.'

'Age makes no difference when you're in love, but I didn't mean that. I suppose I should have asked how you would feel if Gavin fell in love with her?'

'If you're worried that I'd be jealous, you needn't be. I've always liked him, liked him a lot, but it was never love, as you very well know, Albert Ogilvie.'

His smile was smug. 'Well, then. There's no need for you to be upset, is there?'

Bathie gave up. Albert would never understand how she felt. She could hardly understand it herself, come to that.

Ellie could never bring herself to invite Gavin in when he saw her home. That would be like throwing herself at him, and she didn't want to give him that impression. If it had been anyone else, she'd have told him how she felt, and made sure he felt the same way, but not Gavin.

As the weeks went past, then the months, she lived only for Sundays, just to see him again, to have him walk beside her for a little while, to hear his soft voice, although it never spoke words of endearment. It was enough that she was in his company, and she would never ask for anything more.

Bathie was sure now. Ellie *was* in love with Gavin, but it was difficult to tell how he felt. Did he still look on Ellie as a child, to be seen home out of a sense of duty, or did he see her as a desirable woman? Was their relationship still innocent? Shaking her head, she reminded herself that it was none of her business – they were both free, and old enough to please themselves.

One cold, February evening, Ellie was darning one of her little girl's stockings, when someone knocked at her door. Heaving a resigned sigh, she laid her sewing basket down on the table, expecting her caller to be Ishbel, who could be rather wearing on the nerves sometimes, and Ellie wasn't in the mood for dealing with her young sister.

When she opened the door, however, it wasn't Ishbel who stood on the landing. 'Gavin!' she exclaimed, involuntarily showing her delight. 'Oh, I'm sorry – Doctor.'

'I don't see why you shouldn't call me Gavin,' he smiled. 'You've known me long enough. May I come in?'

'Oh, yes, of course.' She held the door open for him. Removing his felt hat, he sat down, looking rather ill-at-ease. 'You'll be wondering why I've come?'

She nodded, not trusting herself to speak.

'I'm wondering myself, now I'm here.' He smiled wryly. 'You'll probably think I'm an old fool, but . . . you've been on my mind an awful lot lately, Ellie. Before I say anything else, though, I have to tell you that when I came back to Aberdeen that morning, it was your mother who was the first person I wanted to see after I'd dropped my things at Froghall.'

Unable, and unwilling, to tear her eyes away from his, which were regarding her somewhat mournfully now, she forced herself to speak. 'I know you and Mother have always been very good friends.'

'It was more than that, Ellie. I've loved your mother for years, since the first time I attended her – when Donnie was born, so you'll know exactly how long – but I didn't admit to myself that it was love for a long time after that.'

His eyes dropped to his hands as they twirled his hat, and Ellie's heart sank. She'd hoped that he'd been going to say that he loved *her*, but it was her mother, after all, and what had gone on between them, over all those years?

After a few seconds, he raised his head. 'Please don't think badly of your mother, Ellie. She never returned my love, though I believe she does feel some affection for me.'

'How can you be sure she doesn't love you?'

He pursed his lips. 'I can't tell you everything, Ellie, not yet, but she once had to decide between your father and me, and she chose your father.'

Her innate curiosity was aroused, wanting to know all the details of what had happened, and when, but she bit back her questions. She would find out one day.

'I was content just to love her, and it was always Bathie I thought of during the war.'

He leaned forward to take Ellie's hand. 'I wanted to make you understand about that before . . . When I saw you that first afternoon, I thought you had grown very attractive since I'd been away, but that was all. I walked home with you, and found I enjoyed your company, but again, that was all.'

He hesitated, looking at her earnestly. 'Ellie, over the weeks, something happened to me. I still love your mother, but in a different way now. I've been puzzling about it, trying to assess my feelings, and last night I came to a conclusion.'

She held her breath when he paused again, with her hand still in both of his. 'You'll maybe laugh, Ellie, and I wouldn't blame you if you did, but I think – no, I'm sure – I love you.'

'Oh.' It was a long, drawn-out sigh, as if it had been squeezed out of her gradually.

'I don't mind if you say you don't love me – I'm quite used to that reaction.'

'I do love you.'

Jumping to his feet, he kissed her, slowly and lovingly, then said, quietly, 'Ellie, will you marry me?'

Tears came to her eyes. 'I can't marry you, Gavin. How would my mother feel about it? If she's known for years that you loved her, she's bound to be jealous.'

'Not my Bathie. And you're not jealous of her, are you?'

'I don't think so, not really, but it'll take a while to get used to – you having been in love with my mother.'

He pulled her to her feet and enveloped her in a bear hug. 'Your mother was my whole life for so long, Ellie, and I'll always love her, but not in the same way any more. You and Kathleen will be my life from now on, and I'll love you as a husband should, if you'll only say yes.'

She surrendered, instantly and irrevocably. 'Yes, yes, yes.' Her eyes clouded. 'But how will we tell her?'

'Let me tell her, Ellie. It's my duty to her.'

As soon as Gavin asked Gracie if she'd please leave him alone with her mother, Bathie knew what he was going to say, and she waited, rather nervously, for him to get it over.

'This will probably come as a shock to you,' he began, 'but I wanted to tell you myself. I've always been honest with you, Bathie, as you were with me, so I hope you can understand. I still feel a deep devotion for you, but people change.'

'Yes, people change.'

'I want more from life now. I want to settle down with a wife and family . . . '

'A ready-made family?' she said, gently.

He hesitated. 'You know? Has Ellie been here?'

'No, she hasn't, I just knew, and I'm pleased she's found somebody to love at last, but I'd like you to tell me one thing. Do you really love her enough to make her your wife?'

'Yes, Bathie, God help me, I do. I was hardly aware of it at first, but I was certain of it before I asked her.'

'You've asked her already? What did she say?'

'She said yes. I didn't want to hurt you, but I know you never loved me, and I didn't think you'd mind.'

'I don't mind, not in the way you mean, but you're so much older than she is, and she's so vulnerable.'

'I agree, but she's not committing herself to a man old enough to be her father without being sure she wants to.'

A sad smile crossed Bathie's lips. 'No, Ellie knows what she wants, she always has, but does she truly love you?'

'She says she does, and I believe her. I told you before that I should leave Aberdeen – that was because I didn't want Albert to get any more wrong ideas – but that's

306

what I'm going to do. I understand how you must feel about this, Bathie, and I can't put you in a position where you'll always be reminded that the man who loved you has married your daughter.'

Her composure crumpled. 'Albert couldn't understand that,' she gulped. 'Thank God you do.'

'You've discussed this with Albert? You knew what I was going to do, before I knew it myself?' He gave a little laugh then looked at her earnestly. 'Tell me you're happy for me, Bathie. I need your blessing.'

'I'm very happy for both of you, but leave now, before I make a proper fool of myself.'

When he brushed her lips with his, she stretched up her hand to touch his cheek. 'You have my blessing, Gavin, dear, and Ellie's very lucky to be marrying such a good man.'

'Thank you.' His voice broke as he turned away. 'Now it's me who's making a proper fool of myself.'

When she accompanied him to the outside door, he said, 'Do you want me to come back to tell Albert?'

'No, I'll do it. Goodbye, Gavin, and you'll let us know about the wedding arangements?'

'It won't be for quite a while, but I'll keep you informed. Goodbye, Bathie, and thank you, for everything.'

Climbing the stairs, she reflected, rather sadly, that this was the end of a relationship which had seen her through some very bad times, but surely she and Gavin would always remain good friends? Her step lightened, and she ran on to the landing as Gracie appeared from the middle floor, having heard the visitor leave.

'What did the doctor have to say that he couldn't say in front of me?' the girl asked, curiously.

'He was telling me that he's going to marry Ellie.'

'Is that all? I told you that would happen.'

Bathie's tension released into a gale of hearty laughter, and it was a moment before she spluttered, 'So you did.'

Albert took it much better than his wife had expected. 'Ellie needs a man like Gavin, and he'll make a good husband.'

Looking at her speculatively, he asked, 'How do you feel about it, though, now that it's actually happened?'

'I'm very pleased,' she assured him, truthfully. 'He's been a good friend to us for years, and that won't change, even if he's going to start a practice away from Aberdeen.'

'So that'll be another one of our daughters going away,' he mused, sounding sorrowful in spite of himself.

Coming through from the kitchen just in time to hear his last remark, Gracie said, ruefully, 'Don't worry, Father, you'll always have me.'

'Aye, that's one God's blessing.'

The sudden glistening in the girl's eyes made Bathie wish, from the bottom of her heart, that Gracie, too, could find a man to love – a man who would love her – as long as whoever it was didn't whisk her off to the other end of the earth.

Chapter Thirty-four

Charlie made his startling announcement one morning in June.

'Vena and I are thinking of going to Wanganui,' he stated, baldly, then glanced at his mother, whose face had turned a ghastly white.

'Not you, too, Charlie,' she whispered.

'I know you wanted me to take over the shop eventually, Father,' he rushed on, 'but I want to . . . oh, I don't know. Try myself out, I suppose. We've been discussing it for a while, and from what Flo and Hetty say in their letters, there seems to be more opportunity out there.'

Albert sighed. He'd told Bathie so many times that their children had their own lives to lead, but it was hard to let them go, one by one – or two by two – like this. 'You'll have to do what you feel's best for you, Charlie, and I'll not stand in your way, whatever you've decided.'

Charlie appealed to the silent Bathie. 'Mother?'

Nodding, she said, 'If that's what you want.'

She felt frozen. This was different from letting her two daughters go. This was Charlie, her first-born, her favourite. How could he do this to her when Ellie would be leaving for Edinburgh immediately after her wedding? It was too much.

Looking sadly at his father as Bathie ran out, Charlie murmured, 'I knew she'd be upset – will I go through to her?'

Albert shook his head. 'No, leave her to cry. She'll get over it. It's a big blow to her, Charlie, and to me, I can't say it isn't, but parents must expect their children to make their own way in life.'

After breakfast, Albert went through to the bedroom, where Bathie was sitting on the edge of the bed, not crying now, but her eyes still swollen and red-rimmed.

Sitting down beside her, he put his arm round her. 'I know how you feel, my love.'

She brought her face up and laid her head against his shoulder. 'Oh, Albert, it's awful. It's my Charlie, this time.'

She started to weep softly, hopelessly, and he stroked her hair gently. 'We brought them into the world and raised them to grown men and women, but that was our duty, and we shouldn't expect them to owe us anything. We have to let them go.'

'I know, I know.' She clung to him desperately, her whole body racked with sobs. 'Hold me, Albert, for I need you now, and I'll need you even more when it's time for him to leave.'

He took her in his arms then, whispering, 'Bathie, Bathie,' and let his lips touch her brow, her eyes, her nose, until the weeping stopped and she was at peace.

At last, she lifted her head. 'I don't know what I'd do without you, my dearest, dearest, Albert.'

His grip tightened, but she broke away from him. 'No, go down to the shop now. I've got over the shock of it.'

He kissed her again before he went out, and she waited a few minutes before she went through to the kitchen.

Gracie and Vena looked at her quickly when she went in, then carried on with the washing-up. Ishbel was clearing the table, so Bathie said, 'You'd better be getting yourself ready.'

When Ishbel left to go to school, Gracie went upstairs to make her own bed and her sister's, and Vena sat down beside Bathie, looking quite concerned. 'I'm sorry, Mother. It must have been an awful shock to you, Charlie springing it on you like that, but we've thought about it for weeks. That's why we didn't rent that house.'

Bathie swallowed. 'It's not your fault, Vena.'

'We both want to go. We've never felt settled since we came home, and New Zealand's the best place to go.'

'There'll soon be more of my family in Wanganui than there is here.' Bathie managed a light laugh.

It took Bathie several weeks to come to terms with it, and she reached a rueful conclusion. If it was meant to be that all her children would leave the family home and find new lives for themselves in other countries – or in Ellie's case, a different city in the same country – it was meant to be, and there was nothing she could do about it.

She had given birth to eight children, but very shortly, there would be only two left – Ishbel, who would likely fall in love as soon as she left school, and poor Gracie, who seemed destined to remain single. Well, at least she and Albert would have one daughter to look after them in their old age.

Ellie had asked if she could be married in the house on the brow of the Gallowgate, so for weeks preparations for the wedding took up most of Bathie's time. She baked and cooked – assisted by Gracie and Vena, when they could spare the time – and cleaned and polished until everything sparkled.

Her parents had been invited, but Arthur Johnstone was recovering from a bad bout of bronchitis, and Henrietta said she couldn't leave him. Donnie had written to say he couldn't afford the fares, so only those of the family who were still at home would be attending.

On the 20th November, 1920, Gavin McKenzie took Ellie as his wife, in the parlour of her childhood home, with Charlie acting as best man, and Gracie as bridesmaid, although she'd said that she would rather Vena took on the duty. But Ellie had insisted, so she'd given in, slightly ungraciously.

Albert, in a stiff new suit – he'd put on too much weight to wear his old best one – held his wife's hand throughout the short ceremony, thinking that she didn't look old enough to have a son of thirty, and certainly not old enough to be a grandmother, even to a six-year-old.

When Gavin placed the ring on his bride's finger, Bathie couldn't help remembering that other ceremony, in Greyfriars Church, where she had watched this same daughter being married in the white wedding gown, but the navy tailor-made costume suited Ellie very well. She looked mature but subdued, and Bathie wondered if she, too, was recalling the day she'd been joined in matrimony to poor Jack Lornie.

Gavin was also serious, although his responses were made in a clear, firm voice. He looked most distinguished in his dark grey suit, and Bathie felt a tiny twinge of regret that he was lost to her for ever. Not lost, she corrected herself. He was part of her family now, her son-in-law, although he was seven years older than she was.

Her throat tightened when the newly-wed couple kissed, the love they had for each other plain for all to see, but, when Albert gave her hand a sympathetic squeeze, she returned it to show him that she felt no jealousy. In the dining room, Albert set himself out to create a party spirit, while Bathie worried in case Gracie was brooding about being single and Charlie about leaving Aberdeen.

But the gaiety wasn't forced, Bathie felt, letting her eyes rove round. Love and happiness radiated from Ellie and Gavin, while genuine pleasure and approval was reflected in the faces of Charlie, Vena, even Gracie. Albert was joking with the minister, so she turned her attention to her granddaughter.

'Do you still like school, Kathleen?'

'Oh, yes, Granny, and d'you know what Miss Murray told us? She said that Edinburgh was the capital of Scotland, and . . . '

Bathie listened contentedly to the girl for a few minutes, then asked, 'Will you be sorry to leave Miss Murray when you go to Edinburgh?'

'Just a little bit, but my new Daddy told me the teacher there will be just as nice as Miss Murray.'

Dear Gavin, Bathie thought, happily. He was so kind and considerate. She wouldn't have to worry about this branch of her family when they left Aberdeen.

The Reverend Steele made the first move, standing up and beaming at them all. 'Before I go, I must thank everyone who was concerned in the preparation of this delicious meal. The best chef in the world couldn't have done better.'

His voice grew serious now. 'Next, my best wishes go with Charles and his wife when they emigrate to New Zealand.' Murmurs of agreement interrupted him momentarily, and he smiled again as his eyes rested on the bride and groom. 'Most importantly, as this is really their day, I wish long life and prosperity to Eleanor and Gavin. May they always be as happy, and as much in love, as they are today.'

A round of hearty applause, and some table-thumping from Charlie, made the man smile as they all lifted their glasses in a toast.

Gavin rose, grinning bashfully. 'My wife and I, and our daughter, thank you all for your good wishes.'

Bathie felt her heart filling with gratitude to him for remembering to include Kathleen in his little speech, and she dabbed her eyes with her handkerchief.

'Good luck in your new life, Charlie and Vena,' Gavin continued, 'and give my kindest regards to Flo and Hetty when you get to Wanganui, also to Mary and Jeannie Wyness. Tell them I remember them both very well.'

When the minister stood up to leave, Albert went to the door to see him out, and came back smiling. 'Now we can all relax. Does anybody want another drink?'

'No, thank you, Albert.' Gavin got to his feet. 'We'll have to go, too, because we still have a few odds and ends to attend to before we leave in the morning.'

'Oh, it's early yet,' Albert began, then caught Bathie's eye, and stopped.

'It's true, we do have to finish packing, Father.' Ellie laughed and rose out of her chair. 'Come on, Kathleen.'

Gavin turned to his two sisters-in-law now. 'Gracie and Ishbel, you will be welcome to spend a holiday with us any time, and that goes for you, too, Albert and Bathie. I've known you for so long, it doesn't feel strange to be a real part of your family at last, though I never dreamt I'd end up by being your son-in-law.'

Bathie felt choked, but Albert said, in a somewhat husky voice, 'And we're very pleased to welcome you into our family, Gavin. Good luck in your new practice, and, Ellie, you'll write to let us know how you all settle in?'

His favourite daughter ran round the table to kiss him warmly. 'I'll write every week, and thank you, Father, for all you've done for me.'

Bathie stood up to hug Kathleen, while Gavin shook hands with Albert, and Ellie embraced her brother and his wife then her five sisters. When Gavin came towards her, Bathie, already perilously near to breaking down, couldn't hold back her tears, and he held her shoulder as his eyes searched hers.

'No tears today, Bathie. I'm happier than I've been for many a long year, and I'll always think fondly of you . . . and Albert.' His hold tightened for a second.

'Good luck, Gavin,' she whispered, acutely conscious that they were the focus of all attention, especially Albert's. 'We'll always think of you fondly, too.' Her voice growing stronger, she went on, 'But we're being silly. This isn't a final goodbye – you'll all come back to see us, very soon.'

When Gavin took Kathleen's hand and went out, Ellie held back and went over to her mother.

'I promise to look after him – I do love him, you know.'

Bathie gulped, but her eyes didn't waver. 'I know that, Ellie, and he's a very lucky man. Just keep him happy.'

'I mean to.' Ellie hesitated briefly. 'He told me how he felt about you, so I hope you're not . . . '

'I've always had a great affection for Gavin,' Bathie said, quietly. 'That's all. Affection, so always remember that.'

They joined the others, who were waiting at the foot of the outside steps, then Gavin took one of Kathleen's hands, Ellie took the other, and goodbyes and good wishes were called after them as they walked into the close. Bathie was last to go inside, feeling that all emotion had been drained out of her as she put one foot past the other automatically.

She was glad when Gracie said, 'Vena's going to help me with the clearing up, Mother, so you go and sit down. Ishbel, don't bother sneaking off upstairs. You can help, too.'

'I'm sneaking off upstairs, at any rate,' Charlie remarked, which made them all smile.

Alone in the parlour, Bathie was hit by reaction to all the days of preparation and the strain of that day, so she was weeping silently when Albert joined her.

'Bathie.' He stood in front of her, looking down at her solicitously. 'Are you sure you don't mind about Gavin and Ellie? I know how you felt about him.'

Anger and exasperation swept through her. 'No, you don't know how I felt about him. It was never love. I tried and tried to make you understand that, but you wouldn't listen. You were too . . . ' She stopped, searching for a word.

'Thrawn?' he suggested, with a smile.

It was the best thing he could have said, and she burst out laughing, the tears still running down her face. 'That's it, exactly. You're as stubborn as an old mule. As I told Ellie before they left, I'll always have a great affection for him, but I'm honestly glad he's found true love at last. They both deserve all the happiness they can get.'

314

Satisfied, he changed the subject. 'I've been considering employing a man for the shop. Once Charlie goes, there'll just be Gracie to help you and me both, till Ishbel leaves school.'

'She's old enough to do a bit more in the house now.'

'Aye, well, but I need somebody to help me.'

'Whatever you think, then, Albert.'

He picked up the morning paper, which he'd had no chance to look at before, and read until his two daughters came in, Ishbel looking somewhat aggrieved.

'That's everything washed and put away, Mother,' she said. 'Can I go upstairs now?'

Bathie smiled. 'Yes, off you go, and Gracie, I think you should have a seat for a while. You deserve it.'

The girl flopped down on the couch with a grunt. 'Thank goodness there's not a wedding in this house every day.'

Both Bathie and Albert agreed wholeheartedly with that sentiment.

Chapter Thirty-five

The excitement of Ellie's wedding had barely faded when Charlie received notification that they would be sailing on 3rd January, 1921. That unsettled everyone, but it was nothing compared with what occurred three weeks before Christmas.

Henrietta Johnstone fell downstairs and her husband had struggled in vain to lift her. Their doctor told Bathie later that her mother had suffered a seizure and so had felt nothing when she fell, and that her father's heart – much weakened by another bout of bronchitis – had given out with the exertion.

Not only horrified and devastated by their deaths, Bathie was burdened down with guilt. She'd been so involved with her own life that she'd paid little attention to her parents recently.

315

She'd sent Gracie or Ishbel to Ferryhill occasionally to find out how they were, but it was her duty to have gone, and she should have made the effort.

They'd always come regularly to see her before her father became too feeble to leave the house. Her mother must have worn herself out looking after him, when Bathie could quite easily have installed them in her house. There had only been one spare room since Charlie and Vena came back, but Gracie and Ishbel could have doubled up to give their grandparents a sitting room and a bedroom on the middle floor.

Over the three days leading up to their funeral, Bathie retreated further and further into herself, and her movements became more and more mechanical. Albert was left to arrrange everything, even to detailing Gracie and Vena to organize the funeral tea. Vena had also taken it on herself to soothe the Johnstones' young maid, who had found her master and mistress lifeless when she'd run downstairs to find out what had caused the noise she'd heard.

Most of Arthur's banking contemporaries had either died before him, or moved away from Aberdeen when they retired, so the funeral was quite small, but Bathie wouldn't have taken in who was there and who wasn't, in any case.

Albert, Gracie and Vena were still in the process of clearing out the house when it was time for Charlie and his wife to leave. Fortunately, in a way, Bathie's senses were so numb that their departure hardly registered with her.

Gradually, however, she came back to life, mourning the sudden deaths of her mother and father in a natural manner, and facing up to the fact that her eldest son and his wife had also vanished from her life, possibly for ever.

It was Gracie who sank into despondency then. She took no interest in anything, her face became haggard, her eyes stared pathetically out of deep, dark sockets and her clothes hung on her almost-emaciated body. But she assured everyone who asked that there was nothing wrong.

Bathie was extremely thankful when the girl came upstairs one day at the beginning of April, and said that Joe Ferris, Albert's young assistant, had asked her out. Surely this would take her out of her depression and bring her back to health?

When Gracie came down after dressing that evening, she already looked different – her eyes shining incongruously out of their deep hollows, her face less drawn and her walk with some purpose to it.

'Does this skirt look all right, Mother?' She twirled round to let Bathie see the full effect.

'You look fine, dear. Just go out and enjoy yourself, it's a lovely night for it.'

'I don't see why you didn't help with the dishes,' Ishbel grumbled. 'You know I don't like drying.'

'You should have told me,' Bathie said, quickly. 'I'd have let you wash them.'

Gracie's laugh was a tonic to her mother. 'She doesn't like washing them, either. She doesn't like doing dishes at all.' She walked to the window with a spring in her step that had been missing for months.

'Have you any home lessons, Ishbel?' Bathie asked. 'If you have, you'd better go and do them, right now.'

The lanky schoolgirl tossed her auburn curls and pulled a face, but did as she was told, and Albert laughed, fondly.

'She's another Ellie.'

'Here's Joe, now.' Gracie whirled round from watching the street, and hurried out to meet the young man. Excitement made her skip down the outside stairs, but she was sure of one thing. She wouldn't allow Joe to do anything like that sailor had done on Armistice Night, it was too easy for emotions to get out of control. The guilt of it had come back to haunt her a few weeks ago, eating away at her until today – when Joe had asked her out so shyly.

Gracie had known him for weeks – her father had employed him before Charlie left – and she'd worked alongside him when they were busy, so she didn't consider him a stranger. She had talked to him easily in the shop, and was soon laughing and joking with him while they walked down the street together, surprising herself as much as the young man.

At last, he stopped and turned to her seriously. 'You know, Gracie, I've wanted to ask you out for quite a while, but you always looked . . . a bit proud. I felt you wouldn't want to be seen walking out with an ordinary grocer's assistant.'

'My father was just a grocer's assistant when he married my mother,' she told him. 'There's nothing wrong with that. I'm sorry if I made you think I was looking down on you, I didn't mean to. I suppose I've been a bit unhappy for a long time, but I feel much better now.' Glancing sideways at him, she smiled. 'I was being stupid about a boy, you see.'

'Oh.' Joe sounded rather dismayed. 'I didn't know you were going out with anybody else.'

'It was just somebody I met once. He promised to write, but he didn't. We were ships that passed in the night.' She gave a wry grin. 'It was a long time ago, Joe.'

'How would you feel about going steady with me?'

She held her head on one side, pretending to consider, then laughed. 'I wouldn't mind.'

They started meeting two or three evenings a week, and Albert and Bathie were very pleased that the girl was acting normally at long last. Ishbel teased her, of course, but Gracie could take it now.

'You're only fourteen,' she admonished her sister one day. 'You'll have to wait till you're older before you know what you're speaking about.'

'Wait till you're older, that's all I'm ever told.' Ishbel stamped upstairs, leaving Gracie and their parents laughing.

Hardly a day went past that there was no letter from one or other of Bathie's far-flung family, and answering them all was a labour of pure love for her.

When Flo told her that Will's boss was going to retire, and had offered Will a partnership in the building firm, she was delighted for them, especially when she read the postscript Flo had added. 'I'm expecting a baby at the beginning of November, so I bet you'll be pleased about that.'

Bathie was delighted, and hoped that her other daughter in New Zealand would be telling her the same thing in a short time. Hetty's letters were usually filled with descriptions of the modernizations they were having carried out in their house, but the letter which arrived a few days later made Bathie uneasy.

'We're getting rid of the old furniture we bought at first, and buying new. Martin's mother has been a great help, for she advised me where to go, and what to buy. She lent Martin the money to buy the house in the first place, because she was left very well off when her husband died, and she says we can take our time about paying her back. It's really kind of her.

'I can't understand why Mary and Jeannie are so distant with her, she *is* their sister, after all. I'm sure Martin knows why, but he won't tell me. It must have been something she did long ago, maybe before she left Aberdeen, even, so you might know what it was, Mother.'

Yes, Bathie thought, she knew. It had almost slipped her mind who Hetty's mother-in-law was, but she would never forget what Bella Wyness had done. It was best that Hetty knew nothing about that dreadful business, and there was no cause to warn her to be on her guard against the woman – not yet. Bathie couldn't even mention her resurrected fears to Albert. He'd only laugh at her for worrying about nothing.

She cheered up a little when Ellie wrote that she, too, was going to have a baby, due about the end of November.

'Gavin's nearly jumping his own height, and Kathleen's absolutely up in the clouds about it. I'm keeping quite well, apart from a touch of morning sickness, and we're going to come to see you before I grow too big to travel comfortably. Gavin's arranging for a locum for the first three weeks in July, so I hope that's suitable for you.'

Bathie laid the letter down. Yes, she decided, she was every bit as pleased about Ellie's coming child as she was about Flo's, and, boy or girl, it couldn't have a better father than Gavin McKenzie.

After Albert read the letter, she said, 'That's two grand-children on the way, and they say everything comes in threes. I wonder who's going to be next? Helene or Hetty?'

His eyes were soft as he looked at her. The excitement had made her eyes sparkle and brought the colour back to her cheeks. She looked like his old Bathie, the sixteen-year-old who had captivated his heart, and she was only three years short of fifty.

'As long as it's not Gracie,' he smiled.

Each letter now was opened with feverish haste, and, when no more pregnancies were announced, Bathie watched Gracie's face apprehensively for signs of morning sickness.

The days went past uneventfully. The girl looked happy, her face and body had filled out since she'd started keeping company with Joe. She was blooming with health – so different from the pathetic, thin creature her mother had feared was sinking into a decline a few weeks earlier. Bathie was certain that Gracie was not pregnant.

It was Charlie who surprised her, the first paragraph of his next letter going straight to his important information.

'Dear Mother, We're going to have a baby in December!! After all these years of thinking it was impossible, Vena had a small operation, and the next thing was she was expecting. I can't tell you how happy we both are, and I'm sure you'll be pleased for us.' His letter carried on, 'I've started working on a sheep station a good bit out of Wanganui, and there's a house along with the job, so things are looking up for us.'

Bathie was pleased that they were settled, but his other news was more important to her. Vena would make a wonderful mother – look how she'd coped at the time of Ishbel's birth, and James's – and Charlie would be a good father.

She was content now that she knew the third mother-to-be. The babies' births would all be fairly close, Flo's in early November, Ellie's in late November, Vena's into

December, so there would be plenty to celebrate at Christmas, 1921. But, first, there was Ellie's visit to look forward to.

Albert was amused at first to see his wife cleaning rooms and sorting out bedclothes, but began to worry that she was doing too much, too quickly. 'Slow down, Bathie,' he told her, one dinnertime. 'There's still two weeks to go. You'll wear yourself out before they come.'

'No, I feel good. Waiting to be made a Granny three times within a month is wonderful medicine, better than a tonic.'

He covered her hand as she laid a plate down in front of him. 'It does my heart good to see you so happy, my love.'

'You haven't called me that for a long time, Albert.'

'Bathie, you've always been my love, no matter what I did to make you think otherwise, and you'll always be my love till the day I die.'

She laughed at his earnestness. 'Maybe I'll die first.'

Frowning, he said, 'It's nothing to joke about. My life would be empty without you, Bathie.'

She pulled her hand away from his, but bent to kiss his forehead. 'And mine would be meaningless without you, but we can't choose who's going to go first, so eat your dinner and stop arguing.'

On the day that the McKenzies were coming, Bathie rose early. Ellie and her husband were to sleep in one of the attics, and Kathleen was to be in the room next-door to them, so she lit the fires in both rooms and ran over the furniture with a duster before making breakfast.

A letter from Donnie made her sit down for a minute, but it was just the usual chat about how he and Helene were coping in their small newsagent/tobacconist's shop in South Norwood.

'It's going to take a bit of time till we're established,' he wrote, 'but things are coming on not too bad. Hope all at the Gallowgate are keeping well, and that you are still hearing from the folk in New Zealand. What a surprise we got when you told us Flo and Vena and Ellie were all expecting about the same time. We're not thinking of starting a family yet, not till we're on our feet, but mistakes can happen. Ha, ha!!'

Bathie smiled as she laid the letter down. She had no time to waste today. Her visitors would be arriving about half past twelve, so everything would have to be ready in good time.

She started to watch for them at twenty past, and when the car drew up outside at quarter to one, she ran down to meet them, so excited that she kissed them all, even Gavin.

In the parlour, she had only time to ask how Ellie was keeping and how Kathleen was liking her school, when Albert and Gracie came up from the shop, so there were more rapturous greetings. Then Ishbel called them through to the dining room.

Seeing seven people sitting down for the meal, instead of four as there had been for the past few months, made a warm glow start deep inside Bathie, and she sighed with pleasure as Gavin answered Albert's questions, Ellie laughed with Gracie, and Ishbel and Kathleen chattered together.

It wasn't until the second course that any mention was made of the three expected babies.

'I can't get over the coincidence,' Ellie smiled. 'First Flo, then me, then Vena, it's unbelievable.'

'Aye,' remarked Albert, dryly. 'The stork'll have to put his skates on, to get from New Zealand to Edinburgh and back to New Zealand again within a month.'

This made them all double up with mirth, and Gavin waited for them to quieten down before he said, 'It was the happiest day of my life when Ellie told me, though I suppose I'm a bit old to be a father for the first time.'

Albert smiled. 'A man's never too old to be a father.'

His fleeting expression of sadness made Bathie sure that he was disappointed at not having had more children. She was feeling so well, now, surely there was no reason for her not to have another one? It was thirteen years since little James had died, so her reproductive system must be recovered by this time, and she was only forty-eight. She'd heard about women having babies right into their fifties, so it wasn't impossible. She'd ask Gavin's advice when she got the chance – he was a doctor, after all.

It was two days before she had the opportunity to talk to him on his own. Ellie had taken Kathleen out to buy some new clothes for going back to school, so Bathie told Gavin to sit down, laughing at his rather wary eyes. 'It's nothing I shouldn't be saying. I only want to know if it would be safe for me to have another child.'

This was the last thing he'd been expecting, and he looked horrified. 'You must be mad. How can you think of having more when you almost died with the last one?'

'It surely wouldn't affect me the same, not after all this time?' The hope she felt was shining from her eyes.

He stroked his chin thoughtfully. 'I don't know, Bathie. If you're willing to take the risk . . . but, you're forty-eight, so you probably wouldn't conceive, anyway. Have you . . . ?'

He was so embarrassed that she leaned forward. 'Have we tried, is that what you mean? The answer's no. Albert and I haven't . . . been intimate for a few years now.'

He looked away. 'That wasn't what I was going to ask. Are you still . . . menstruating regularly? Forgive me, but I have to ask that. If you are, there is a very faint chance that you may conceive, but if you've stopped, there's no chance at all.'

'I haven't stopped,' she murmured, hope rising again. 'I'm irregular, but I still . . . '

'But maybe . . . ' He groaned. 'Oh, Bathie, I can't discuss this with you any longer. I'm not your doctor now. You're my mother-in-law, and it doesn't seem proper.'

'I'm sorry, Gavin. I put you in a terrible position, and I'm a stupid old fool, being broody because of all the babies that are on the way.'

'You're not stupid, and you're not old,' he said, so quietly that she had to strain to hear. 'You're one of those fortunate women who keep their youthful looks till they're . . . '

'Would you like a cup of tea?' A change of subject seemed called for. That night, she astonished her husband by telling him, as soon as they were in bed, 'Gavin says it might be all right if I had another child, Albert.'

'Gavin says?' His dark eyes narrowed. 'Don't tell me you discussed a thing like that with Gavin McKenzie?'

Angry at herself for her insensitivity, she went on, hastily. 'I didn't think of him as a man, I thought of him as a doctor. I want to give you another son before I'm too old.'

She waited, wondering if she'd reawakened his jealousy of Gavin, then stretched out and ran her fingers over his cheek.

'I love you, Albert, dear, can't you . . . ?' His shrug of irritation made her drop her hand in dismay.

Closing her eyes wearily, quite sure she that she wouldn't sleep, she heaved a loud sigh. Maybe she *was* mad, like Gavin had said. Maybe she *was* just being broody because Flo and Ellie and Vena were expecting. Maybe she *was* too old to produce any more children, even if Albert did get over his jealousy and put his seed inside her.

When his hand cupped her breast, she drew her breath in sharply. 'Albert, don't do anything if you don't want to.'

His eyes flashed in the darkness. 'I wouldn't do anything I didn't want to,' he said, softly. 'You're nothing but a wicked witch, Bathie Ogilvie.'

His hold tightened, and she turned gladly to face him, but in a moment he took his hand away and groaned. 'It's no use.'

She couldn't understand. 'What's wrong, Albert?'

'Nothing's wrong.' His voice was curt. 'I just can't.'

He rolled round, facing away from her, and she lay, far into the night, wishing that she'd had the common sense to leave things as they'd been before.

The McKenzies took Bathie out in the car several times before they went back to Edinburgh, and she enjoyed every minute of the outings. Kathleen, sitting in the back seat with her, kept giving little squeals of delight every time they passed something interesting, and Bathie followed her pointing finger, feeling every bit as excited as her granddaughter. Occasionally, Gavin would give a little snippet of the history of the place they were passing through, and Bathie asked as many questions as the child did. If only it could always be like this, she thought.

On the first full Saturday, Gavin and Ellie took Ishbel with them instead, there being room for only one extra, and on the Sunday, Albert had his turn. Gracie didn't mind not being included, being with Joe more than made up for it.

On their last Saturday evening, Gavin and Ellie were sitting with Bathie and Albert in the parlour when Gracie brought in her young man. She was ecstatically flushed, and her mother's spirits hovered, unsure of whether to be glad or sorry at what the girl was obviously going to tell them.

It was Joe who came forward. 'Mr Ogilvie,' he began, shyly, 'I've come to ask your permission to marry Gracie.'

In the confusion of good wishes and congratulations that broke out, Albert was left sitting with his mouth open. He'd had no chance to say yea or nay, for the decision seemed to have been taken out of his hands, and he remained seated for a few more minutes before jumping up to join the excited group.

He pushed his way to Joe, who looked at him ruefully. 'I'm sorry, Mr Ogilvie . . . '

Albert grasped his hand. 'I haven't had a chance to say it yet, but you've got my permission, and my blessing.'

'Thank you.' The young man's face, round and red-cheeked, reflected his happiness, and when he turned to look at Gracie, his shining eyes proved to them all how much he loved her.

She laughed with delight. 'I'd a feeling Joe was going to ask me some time soon, and I was wishing he'd hurry up and do it before you went home, Ellie, for I wanted to let all of you know at the same time, and he did.'

Going back to his seat, Gavin remarked, 'You've given us a grand finale to our holiday, Gracie.'

'When are you getting married, Auntie Gracie?' Kathleen looked up hopefully. 'Can I be flower girl?'

'Oh, Kathleen,' Ellie reprimanded her, 'give them time. They haven't planned it yet, and I'm sure Auntie Gracie'll let you know if she wants you.'

'Yes, Kathleen.' Gracie wanted the little girl to be as happy as everyone else. 'Of course I'll want you to be my flower girl, and I'll give you plenty warning, so you can have another beautiful dress made.'

Ishbel's face fell now. 'What about me, Gracie? Do you not want me to be your flower . . . ?'

Gracie turned to Bathie. 'Would she be old enough to be my bridesmaid, Mother?'

'She'll be fifteen in a couple of months, so I suppose she'd be old enough. You're not thinking of having your wedding sooner than that, are you?' Bathie wasn't looking forward to losing another daughter.

'No, no. It'll be a good while yet.'

Joe butted in. 'I want to find a house first.'

'But you don't need to look for a house,' Bathie burst out, then recalled Albert's warnings about planning her children's lives for them, and stopped in confusion.

Looking at Joe, Albert said quietly, 'There's plenty of room for you here, if you want to come. There's two attics, and there'll be two rooms spare on the middle floor, but it's up to you, lad. We're not forcing you into anything.' Gracie made the decision before Joe could answer. 'We want our own house, Father.' Looking at Bathie, she added, 'I hope you're not disappointed, Mother.'

'No, of course not. It's only natural.'

Later, Bathie thought mournfully that in another couple of years, Ishbel would want to leave the house on the brow of the Gallowgate, too, the house Albert had been so taken with over thirty years ago, the house which had once been filled with their children, and which she'd hoped would be filled with their children's children some day.

Joe would leave Albert and get a better job with higher wages – who could blame him? In no time at all, they'd be left on their own in nine rooms, with no help.

Worse than any of that, there would be no more children for them now. Since she'd tried to kindle his desire again, Albert had given her a light peck on the cheek every night, then turned over and gone to sleep. She hadn't had the courage to ask Gavin why her husband had stopped when he'd seemed so aroused, and believed that her body had repelled him.

Next morning, when Ellie went upstairs to pack the things she'd just ironed, Bathie felt the need for a reviving cup of tea. After the activity of the last two weeks, she was going to miss the McKenzies after they went home.

When Gavin came in and sat down with his bushy eyebrows raised, she knew what he was silently asking her.

'Albert couldn't,' she whispered. 'I thought he was going to, but he stopped and said it was no use.'

'I thought that might happen.' Gavin was totally the doctor now, as she fully realized. 'He's probably impotent.'

'Impotent?'

'Not able to carry out his sexual urges.' The words came out casually. 'He'll have all the signs that he's roused, but when it comes to the act, everything fades.'

'Oh.' Bathie breathed out slowly. 'I thought he didn't want to. I thought he must be disgusted at me being older.'

The man's professional smile didn't reassure her much. 'He might get over it. He probably will, if you give him time and don't say anything about it.'

She couldn't really understand, but nodded as if she did, and his smile became natural again.

'Now, Bathie, one more word to you. You're going to have a bit of stress when all your grandchildren are being born, and also when Gracie gets married, so take it easy. You don't want another heart attack or any of those old headaches.'

'I certainly don't. I'll try to keep calm and not do too much, though it's going to be difficult. You know how I am.'

'That's why I'm warning you, and don't start fretting that there'll soon only be you and Albert left. All mothers have to face that some time, and it doesn't make them useless. They've a role to play as grandmothers, too. Remember that, Bathie.'

Leaning back in his chair, his face softened. 'Ellie'll need you for a while after the baby's born, you know, so you'll have to come and stay with us for a few weeks when the nurse leaves. I've only booked her for one week.'

Kathleen poked her head round the door at that moment. 'Daddy, Mummy says will you go up and give her a hand to shut the cases. She's tried everything, but she can't do it.'

When he stood up, the little girl placed her hand in his, to pull him through the door, and he winked to Bathie over his shoulder as they went out.

She poured herself another cup. She certainly didn't want any more headaches, nor heart pains, so she'd have to keep calm about everything, and just pray that her husband would stop being impotent.

The house was quiet after Ellie and her family left in the early afternoon, until Ishbel came stamping down the stairs, her face a study in exasperation.

'I've been thinking. How can I be a bridesmaid when I'm still at school? You should have let me leave in June.'

'You're better to take the chance of a good education when you can,' her father told her, firmly.

'Why? You'll just make me work in the house and the shop when I do leave.'

'If you pass the Higher Day School Leaving exam, I might think about letting you take a proper job.'

'You'd better remember your promise when the time comes,' she muttered darkly, as she went out.

'We'll never be weary as long as we've got Ishbel,' Albert observed. 'I know you're feeling downhearted about Gracie not wanting to live here after she's married, but it's up to them, for they've . . . '

' . . . their own lives to lead,' Bathie finished for him, despondently. 'But all our children seem to want to get as far away from us as they can. Gracie and Joe'll want to go in a while, no doubt, and Ishbel, as well, when she gets married.'

Her husband chuckled loudly. 'You're really down in the dumps, aren't you? Don't meet trouble halfway, Bathie.'

328

Offended by his laughter, she sat in silence, but she knew he was right. She *was* down in the dumps, and was it any wonder, with what was happening in her life? It didn't make it any easier, Albert laughing at her like that. He could at least have tried to be a bit sympathetic.

That night, to her great joy, he cradled her in his arms. 'I'm sorry for laughing at you today, my love, but if I hadn't, you'd have ended up in tears. Remember, you'll always have me, and I'll be happy having you all to myself again.'

'Yes,' she gulped. 'We'll always have each other.'

He overcame his earlier impotence in a few minutes, and a delighted Bathie was left to wonder, when it was over, whether or not another Ogilvie had been planted.

Chapter Thirty-six

'Flo's had a boy, Albert.'

When Bathie ran into the shop, the cable flapping in her hand, both men looked up and grinned, and, because Albert had told all his customers about the triple expected happy events, the two women they were serving listened with interest as he read the message out.

'Handed in at 8.15 a.m. on 4th November, 1921. Mother and son both doing well. One-armed father still in shock.'

There was no sender's name, but they all had a good laugh at the last six words, and Bathie felt very relieved that Will Dunbar could joke so easily about his disability.

She climbed the stairs much more slowly than when she'd gone down, and Gracie turned round from the table in alarm at the sound of her mother's laboured breathing.

'You shouldn't have run down,' she chided, gently. 'You're not so young as you used to be, you know.'

'I'm not a decrepit old woman, either,' Bathie answered sharply, then sat down heavily on the nearest chair.

Reassured by the quick retort, Gracie turned away. 'I wonder if Flo'll carry on down the alphabet?'

'So you all knew we were doing that, did you?' Although Bathie was smiling, her hand was on her heaving chest.

'Ellie pointed it out when Kathleen was born, so Will and Flo's will have to be L, if they're going to do it.'

'He's my first grandson, Gracie, whatever his name is, and I'll never see him,' Bathie said, her misery made worse by the knowledge that her attempts to produce another son had failed.

'Once Will's been a partner for a few years, they'll maybe manage to come home for a holiday.'

'I should be grateful I'll be able to see Ellie's baby when it comes. It'll be the only one of the three, though.'

'Gavin asked you to go to Edinburgh after the baby's born, didn't he? You won't have long to wait.'

'I don't know if I should go, Gracie – it's a long way to travel on my own.'

'Don't be silly. It won't be a holiday for you, but it'll be a change.' Gracie looked up from mixing a sponge pudding. 'Have you ever had a holiday?'

'Not since I married your father. Where could we have gone with all you children?'

'You'll soon only have one left, so you can go away any time you like,' Gracie reminded her.

At one o'clock, Albert brought up a bottle of wine. 'We'll have a little drink with our dinner, to wet the baby's head,' he said, and laughed when Bathie stipulated, 'Just one, remember.'

Hetty's letter, which arrived the following day, had been written before her sister's baby was born.

'Flo's looking like a healthy hippopotamus, and Will's like a cat with two tails. I just hope everything goes all right for Vena, but she was quite well the last time I saw her, which was quite a while ago, but Charlie would have let us know if anything was wrong. I feel a bit jealous, but my turn will come once Martin pays his mother back what she lent him.

330

'I wasn't going to tell you, but she's been a bit funny lately. It started the last time we invited Charlie and Vena here for an evening, and Mother-in-Law turned up as well. I don't know if Martin had told her we'd invited them, I don't think so, and I didn't really mind her coming, because she'd never met Vena before, and it was the first time she'd seen Charlie since they came here, but a queer thing happened.

'She shook hands with Vena, but she gave Charlie a long kiss on the mouth. I didn't think anything much about it at first, but she went on and on, like he was her lover, and we were all embarrassed.'

Bathie's chest felt tight, afraid of what might be coming, but she had to read on.

'When she stopped, she said, "That's just to remind you, Charlie", and he went red as a beetroot. I don't know what she meant. He must have been quite young when she left Aberdeen, so they couldn't have been having a love affair, but she kept looking at him the whole evening. I could tell he was very uncomfortable about it, and he hasn't been here since.

'I've been trying to puzzle it out, and I think she must have done something to him when he was a boy, something he doesn't want to remember. Is that why you sacked her? I can't ask Martin, for he wouldn't know, but he was very angry at her that night. I'm sorry to pour it out to you, Mother, but there was nobody else, and I feel a lot better now I've written it all down. Lots of love, Hetty.'

Bathie let the last page slip from her shaking fingers. It shouldn't have come as such a shock. She'd known all along that Bella Wyness could never change, but it had been Hetty she'd been afraid for, and she'd forgotten about her fears by the time Charlie went over there.

Thankful that Gracie had gone upstairs, she folded the letter and returned it to its envelope, then went through to the bedroom and put it under her pillow. By good luck, a letter from Donnie had arrived by the same post, so she could say it was the only one the postman had delivered.

She read Donnie's scrawl, then went over to the fireplace, but the warmth did nothing to thaw the icy fury that gripped her. If thoughts could kill, Bella Wyness would be dropping dead that very minute at the other side of the world.

At dinnertime, she couldn't give Albert any indication that anything was wrong, not while Gracie and Ishbel were at the table with them, but she meant to tell him in bed, if she didn't get a chance before that.

Scanning Donnie's letter quickly, Albert said, 'He never tells us much, does he?' His eyes narrowed when he glanced at his wife. 'You look a bit peaky, my love. The excitement of Flo having her baby has been too much for you. If you don't watch, you'll be having one of your headaches again.'

She realized then that she already had a bad headache. She'd been concentrating so much on what Hetty had written that she hadn't noticed before. Now she became aware that her whole body was aching, her very thoughts were aching, with the worry and alarm churning inside her.

'Bathie?' Albert half rose from his seat in concern.

'I do have a bit of a headache,' she admitted, 'but it's nothing at all.'

'Put your feet up and take things easy,' he ordered, then turned to Gracie. 'Stay with your mother this afternoon.'

'Stop fussing,' Bathie snapped. 'I don't need Gracie, or anybody else.' How could she face the girl all afternoon with this on her mind?

When they went out, she let her thoughts drift back to the day she'd dismissed Bella Wyness. She could still see the sneering face and untrammelled breasts as the girl stood in front of her, laughing, and, remembering how guilty eight-year-old Charlie had been when he admitted what Bella had made him do, she could imagine his shame when it had been recalled to him in that vile manner in Hetty's house.

With a sickening lurch of her stomach, it came back to her that Albert had been involved with Bella, too, although that hadn't come out until much later. He'd said that he had only 'tickled her up' and had 'stopped short of going all the way', but she couldn't believe, now, that he had held back if he'd been roused enough to make advances in the first place.

She was certain that he'd betrayed her just as fully with Bella Wyness as he'd done years later with the widow in Queen's Road, and God knows how many others in between that she knew nothing about.

She struggled out of her half-doze, and tried to sit up, but her head was throbbing so painfully that she abandoned the attempt. Calm down, she told herself. She'd be bringing on another heart attack as well if she wasn't careful. Albert's philanderings were over and done with, and Charlie was old enough to deal with his own problem. In any case, that evil woman could do nothing more to hurt him.

At quarter to five, when she came up to start preparing the supper, Gracie was pleased to find her mother sleeping peacefully, and didn't disturb her. During the evening, Bathie found Albert's anxious eyes on her several times, and smiled to reassure him. She couldn't say anything with Gracie in the room, and was dreading what he'd say when she gave him Hetty's letter to read. Maybe she shouldn't let him see it, after all.

Her headache was growing fiercer by the minute, so she decided to take two aspirins before she went to bed, and not to tell Albert anything. She couldn't cope with his anger as well as her own.

Hetty's next letter, which Bathie opened with trembling fingers, just enthused about Flo's baby, so a great tide of relief washed over her. Charlie had seemed his usual self in the letter which had arrived a few days before, and it must have all been a storm in a teacup.

The new grandchild had been named Leonard – L, as Gracie had predicted – and Bathie, thankful that her headache had not recurred, looked forward to the coming of Ellie's baby.

A few nights later, however, she was dismayed by a sharp pain which started at her temple when Joe Ferris told her he'd rented a house in George Street. She'd known that Gracie would be leaving, and it was stupid to be so upset.

'We can go ahead with our wedding plans,' Joe was telling Albert. 'Now we've got the house, there's nothing to wait for.'

'Mother's not fit to have the wedding here,' Gracie said, hastily, 'so we thought maybe one of Wiseman's Rooms – I've heard they do a lovely meal, and we don't need anywhere big, there's not that many people.'

'Just my mother and father, and my young sister,' Joe put in. 'That's all on my side.'

'We'll invite Donnie and Helene, if they'll come,' Gracie went on, 'and Ellie and Gavin and Kathleen. It won't be till after her baby's born, so they should manage, and there'll be plenty of us to take turns in looking after it. Then there's Mother and Father, and Ishbel, that's eleven, plus Joe and me.'

'But that makes thirteen,' Bathie pointed out anxiously. 'It's an unlucky number.'

Gracie laughed. 'That's superstition, Mother, and Donnie and Helene likely won't come, so that's only eleven.'

Joe found that Wiseman's Rooms were fully booked until well after the New Year, so the wedding was set for the 18th January, 1922, still more than eight weeks away.

When a telegram boy delivered a telegram the following morning, Bathie was extremely flustered.

'Ellie's had another daughter,' she told Gracie. 'And that means I'll have to go to Edinburgh.'

Her agitation made Gracie giggle. 'Not for a week yet, and you'll be in your element fussing over Ellie and the baby. Will I go and tell Father, or do you want to do it?'

'You can go. I'm still shaking.'

Picking up the telegram, Gracie took a quick glance at it. 'You didn't tell me the rest. "Ellie fine, Morag perfect".'

She looked up, beaming broadly. 'Morag McKenzie. What a lovely name. It's exciting, isn't it, seeing the names the babies get. Vena's one'll have to be N.'

Vena, Bathie thought, as Gracie went out. It was Vena and Charlie who were the cause of her worrying, not the journey to Edinburgh, although she'd been fooling herself it was that. Would Vena's body be capable of producing a healthy child, or would there be a repetition of the first time? Had she been jealous when Bella Wyness kissed Charlie, and had she found out what had happened between them years and years ago?

And what about Charlie, himself? Would he be content to ignore what Bella had done to him recently, or was he planning some horrible revenge on her for what she did to him when he was a child? He was so quiet, but he could be very deep at times, and God knows what desperate measures he might take if he was driven to it.

Her headache had started again, and she put her hands up on each side of her forehead, as though her fingers could massage away the inner torture. Bewildered by the suddenness of the onset, and how quickly it gathered momentum, she also became aware of a paralysing pain spreading across her chest.

She'd have to do something – get an aspirin – shout for Gracie to get the doctor. Closing her eyes, she dug her fingers into her temples. She doubted if she could move, but had to get something to relieve the agony, for she couldn't bear it much longer. She staggered blindly to her feet, found she was unable to stand and grabbed at the table for support, but her fingers, like her legs, had lost their power.

Gracie heard the muffled thud as she was coming up the stairs, and ran panic-stricken into the kitchen where she found her mother sprawled on the floor. She struggled vainly to lift the unconscious woman, then raced down to fetch her father.

'Mother's fainted, or something,' she shouted as she opened the side door of the shop, and Albert sped past her.

His gut twisted when he saw his wife lying so still, but he gathered her up in his arms to carry her through to the bedroom, pushing Gracie aside as she reached the landing. 'Get the doctor! Quick!'

Laying his wife down gently on the unmade bed, he pulled the blankets up over her, then ran back to the kitchen for the smelling salts. The glass stopper seemed to be jammed, and he muttered, 'Come out, damn you', his trembling fingers fumbling, fumbling. At last, he waved the dark green bottle under her nose, but there was no reaction.

'Oh, God!' he moaned. 'Come on, Bathie! Please?'

After a minute, he flung the bottle aside, and began to rub her limp hand, but still there was no response. What else could he do? Brandy! That should bring her round. But when he tried to force the glass between Bathie's white lips, the liquid just dribbled down her chin.

Sinking to his knees, he laid his head on the bed, great shuddering sobs breaking from his throat, hot tears falling on his dead wife's hands.

PART FOUR

Chapter Thirty-seven

On the morning after the funeral, Gracie still hadn't made up her mind. Should she tell, or shouldn't she?

The letter she'd found in her mother's drawer had shocked her almost as much as her mother's death. She'd thought that the jet brooch would be ideal to fasten the neck of her blouse, and had gone into her parents' bedroom about an hour before the service was due to begin. She knew exactly where to look for it – in the polished wooden jewellery box which was kept in the top drawer of the nearest chest – but she'd opened the lid rather guiltily.

She'd found the brooch – a slim, figured gold bar set with lovely glistening black stones – and noticed an envelope tucked in against the velvet padding. Not really thinking what she was doing, she'd taken it out and recognized Hetty's hand-writing. On an impulse, she slipped it into the pocket of her skirt, then went up to her room.

What she read mystified her at first, then understanding came, and she felt so sick that she had to grasp the bedpost.

She couldn't remember Bella Wyness, but Mother and Father had spoken guardedly about her after Martin Potter had been here in 1918, and she'd gathered that there was some mystery about why his mother had left the Gallowgate. If she'd been interfering with Charlie when he was a boy, it was no wonder she'd been sacked.

Several times, after the funeral, she'd been on the point of producing the letter, but something had held her back. Then Gavin had driven back to Edinburgh and Donnie had gone to bed early, and she hadn't had the courage to tell her father on her own. She needed someone as a buffer in case he lost his head, but she still wasn't sure if she should say anything.

Her father had been a broken man, and had wept all that first day, and it had been Joe who had sent the telegrams and cable she had drafted out. He'd even offered to keep her company if she wanted to sit up all night with her father, but Albert had brusquely told them that he wanted to be on his own. She hadn't been able to sleep herself, and heard him pacing the floor all night like a caged lion.

Gavin had arrived the next day – Ellie was still too weak – and the two men had disappeared into the bedroom together. It had been some time before they came out, but her father had seemed more in control of his grief.

When Donnie made his appearance that night, it had been Albert who comforted him, and Gavin had taken Gracie through to the kitchen to leave them alone for a while.

She had been amazed at how well her father had kept up yesterday, though he'd needed Donnie's and Gavin's support to follow the hearse to St Peter's Cemetery, so it would be awful if this letter upset him again. But she couldn't keep it to herself. She had to know the truth . . . and so did he.

Donnie heard Gracie going downstairs. He still hadn't decided if he should ask his father to lend him money, but he was going back on the night train, so it would have to be done today if he wanted his business to survive.

It was funny how nobody ever wanted to admit defeat, and it had been hanging over him for a long time, but he'd ignored it until his creditors started clamouring.

They'd both been to blame, of course, himself as much as Helene. She'd always been buying new clothes and gadgets for the house, but he shouldn't have bought that Armstrong-Siddeley when he knew they couldn't afford it. It had been superior to the Fords which were ten-a-penny now, but he'd had to sell it eventually, at a great loss. Their biggest mistake had been the house – it was the repayments of their mortgage which took most of his profits, but neither he nor his wife wanted to part with it now.

He heaved a deep sigh. They wouldn't have to, if his father coughed up, and the little newsagent/tobacconist would be coming into its own shortly, with all the new houses being built round about. He'd been too ambitious, starting up in Norwood, where most of the men worked in the City and brought their *Financial Times* and their cigars home with them, but it should work out in the end. The new council scheme would bring increased business, and he'd be able to repay any loan.

Having convinced himself of this, Donnie rose and dressed, then went downstairs.

Albert turned over, his arm automatically reaching out for his wife, until an agonizing pang in his heart reminded him that she wasn't there. How could he go on without her? It was only days since she died, but already his life was barren.

That was Gracie coming down. Poor Gracie, she'd worked like a Trojan, preparing for the funeral tea, but something about her yesterday had worried him – had made him feel that another calamity was hanging over them.

It had started when she'd come through here for Bathie's jet brooch. She'd gone straight up to her room afterwards, and her face had been ravaged by grief again when she came down, much later. He'd thought that she was upset at looking through her mother's jewellery, but there had been something else there. Puzzlement? Anger? Even apprehension?

He'd been angry and puzzled himself about Bathie's death, and also because Charlie hadn't answered the cable Gracie had asked Joe to send. Neither Flo nor Hetty had acknowledged it, either, and that must be what was troubling Gracie.

It was good of Gavin to come – his wife still recovering from childbirth – but he'd always loved Bathie. After the war, of course, he'd fallen in love with Ellie, but he'd still been deeply attached to her mother. Gavin hadn't made him feel jealous yesterday, though. The gnawing jealousy that he'd felt for years had been laid to rest when Bathie regained consciousness in the Infirmary, on that terrible day in 1915. He'd been told, later, that a blood clot must have passed across her brain, and that she'd contracted pneumonia, too, but had fought for weeks. She hadn't wanted to leave him then, but this time she'd had no choice.

Another set of feet on the stairs? They were too heavy for Ishbel – it must be Donnie. Poor lad. He must feel guilty at not having come to see his mother before she died.

Albert stretched himself. He'd better rise, too, another day to get through. That was all he would ever do now.

While Gracie and Ishbel were tidying up after breakfast, Albert and Donnie went into the parlour. They were slightly ill-at-ease with each other, and sat looking sadly into the fire which Gracie had kindled when she rose.

At last, feeling obliged to make conversation, Albert remarked, 'You've a long journey in front of you tonight.'

Donnie nodded, then looked directly at him. 'I don't like having to ask this, Father, but . . . ' His head went down again.

'Out with it. The worst that could ever happen to me happened four days ago. Nothing can affect me now.'

Albert studied his son as he struggled to form the words he needed. Donnie's red hair was brighter than his own, which had dulled down to a sandy-greyish colour. The young man's face and body had filled out, and he looked much older than the twenty-three-year-old who had gone off so blithely to war seven years before. Was his temperament changed, too?

Lifting his head, Donnie caught his father's gaze. 'Do I look like a successful business man?'

Considering briefly, Albert said, 'Aye, I suppose you do, but there's something . . . '

'Yes, there's something.' Donnie gave a rueful smile. 'I may as well tell you – I'm up to my ears in debt.'

Comprehension came to Albert. The lad was just trying to pluck up courage to ask for a loan. Well, his father knew all about that, and how it felt to be beholden to somebody. 'Have you been declared bankrupt? Is that what you're telling me?'

'Not yet, but unless I can pay something soon, I will be. The ironic thing is, in a few months I'll have dozens of new customers from the council houses they're building.'

Remembering Henrietta Johnstone's kindness to him, Albert said, quietly, 'How much do you need?'

'Four or five hundred would help, if you could manage.'

Albert felt a slight irritation. An outright request for money was not the same as asking for a loan. It wasn't that he couldn't afford to hand over what Donnie wanted, but he didn't like beggars. If it was unavoidable, he'd give his son what he'd asked, but, if he didn't offer to pay it back, that would be the finish.

They regarded each other warily for a moment, Donnie's eyes pleading and Albert's calculating, then the younger man burst out, 'I'm not asking for a gift, Father. I intend to pay you back as soon as I get on my feet again. It might take a while, but I give you my word I'll repay you as soon as I can.'

Albert's breath came out slowly with relief. 'I'll have five hundred transferred from my bank to yours tomorrow. It's not a loan, so you won't have to worry about paying me back.'

'I won't take it. I was asking for a loan, but maybe I didn't make myself clear.'

'It's a loan then.' Albert paused. 'You'll get your share of your mother's money once her estate's settled. When she was young, her grandmother left her two thousand, which I never let her touch, and she inherited quite a lot when her mother and father died, so with interest on it, I'd say the seven of you'll get quite a tidy sum. Maybe two or three thousand each.'

'My luck must be turning.' As soon as he said it, a look of horror came over Donnie's face. 'Oh, I'm sorry,

Father. I didn't mean that, not when it's because Mother died, but . . . '

Smiling, Albert said, 'I'm sure your mother would be glad her money was helping you, but don't use it to repay me.'

When Gracie joined them, Albert was saying, 'Always keep something behind you in case of emergencies.'

She walked over and handed him an envelope. 'I found this in Mother's jewellery box. It's not Hetty's latest letter, but when you read it, you'll understand why Mother kept it. I hope you'll tell me why Bella Wyness left here, because we all have a right to know.'

Albert's frown deepened as he read it. 'God Almighty!' he exploded, as he passed it to Donnie. 'The worry of this must have been the reason for the massive heart attack the doctor said she'd died from. She aye said Bella Wyness would take her revenge, and, by Christ, she's done it. She murdered my Bathie just as sure as if she'd plunged a knife into her.'

Curling his hands into fists, he moved his crazed eyes wildly from his son to his daughter.

'But what did she do to Charlie?' Gracie's voice held curiosity as well as alarm.

Donnie said, 'I was too young to realize what was going on, but Charlie's only a year older than me, so he couldn't have raped her?' He looked helplessly at his father.

'He didn't, and what he did do, wasn't done willingly. He was only about eight, and he didn't know any better.'

Baring his teeth, Albert went on. 'She made him do it, touching him and . . . oh, Bella Wyness was a trollop, as your mother always said. She even tried to get me to serve her.'

Gracie's eyes widened in horror. 'Oh, Father, you didn't commit adultery with her, as well, did you?' She hadn't forgotten about the woman in Queen's Road, but the pain in his eyes made her sorry for reminding him. 'No, Gracie, I didn't. I know you've a poor opinion of my faithfulness to your mother, but it was only that one woman, and I've regretted it bitterly ever since. I never

342

bedded Bella Wyness, and she must have turned to Charlie out of spite.'

'What I can't understand,' Donnie said, thoughtfully, 'is why he went to Wanganui. Bella was Hetty's mother-in-law, and he must have known he'd be bound to meet her.'

'I don't think that even crossed your mother's mind. I know she was worried, when the girls went out first, in case Bella would take her spite out on Hetty, but I'm sure her mind was at ease by the time Charlie went.' Albert sat up suddenly. 'This letter was written a while ago, and there's been nothing in any of Hetty's other letters, or Charlie's or Flo's, so maybe we're making a mountain out of a molehill.' He turned to Gracie hopefully. 'We'd have heard if something else had happened, wouldn't we?'

'I'm sorry, Father, but I'm sure something else has happened,' Gracie said, slowly. 'Charlie didn't answer the cable about Mother's death, and he couldn't have told Flo or Hetty, or surely one of them would have replied. I think he's had to leave Wanganui and our cable never reached him.'

They mulled over this supposition for a few moments, then Donnie said, 'The next letter from New Zealand might give you a clue, whoever it's from.'

'That's right.' Gracie sat up. 'It shouldn't be that long before one of them writes, then we'll know.'

Both his son and his daughter sympathized with Albert when he remarked, sadly, 'I don't think I want to know. I've had enough misfortune to do me for the rest of my days.'

Flo's letter came first, and reading 'Mrs A. Ogilvie' on the envelope made Gracie's stomach lurch uncontrollably. She was reluctant to open it, but had to find out what it said so that she could shield her father from any more bad news, if necessary.

'Dear Mother,' Flo had written, 'I don't really know what's been going on, but Charlie's disappeared, then Vena was put out of their house, it went with his job,

343

and we don't know where she's gone. They haven't got in touch with any of us, and I don't think they're together. We're very worried, especially about Vena, because it's not long till her baby's due.

'Leonard's growing fast, I wish you could see his podgy little arms and legs, you'd just love him, I know. He's not taking notice of anything yet, but another few weeks should make a difference.

'Will sends his love to you all, and so do I. Please try not to worry too much about Charlie and Vena, and I promise to let you know as soon as there's any news of them. Your loving daughter, Flo. P.S. Love and kisses to Granny from Leonard.'

Gracie decided that she might as well let her father see the letter. It explained why there had been no answer to the cable she'd sent to Charlie, but it told them nothing, really. She wished now that she'd sent one to Flo, as well, but she'd thought that he would tell his sisters.

There was something far wrong somewhere, and she wished she knew what it was. Or had Charlie quarrelled with Vena and walked out? It must have been bad before he would have left his wife in her condition.

Gracie was still puzzling over it when her father came up for his dinner, so she gave him the letter and stood beside him while he read it.

His frown grew deeper and deeper, and when he looked up, his eyes were almost hidden by his eyebrows. 'They must have had a fight, Gracie, and Charlie had just left. If he'd been upset, it wouldn't have struck him that the house went with his job and Vena would be put out.'

'But why did she disappear, as well? Flo or Hetty would have taken her in, or even Mary or Jeannie, come to that.'

He twirled one end of his moustache, then ran his thumb down the cleft in his chin. 'Maybe she went to look for him. I'm near sure it's got nothing to do with . . . Bella Wyness, if that's what you're worrying about.'

Considering briefly, Gracie said, 'Do you really think that, Father, or are you just trying to make me feel better?'

Albert looked at her sadly. 'I'm trying to make us both feel better, lass.'

She felt more and more uneasy, however. She had written to Flo, Hetty and Charlie after the funeral, so her sisters should get her letters any day now, even if Charlie didn't, and there was nothing she could do except wait for their replies.

Next morning, at breakfast, Albert looked so gaunt that Gracie decided to tell him what she'd been discussing with Joe Ferris the previous evening. Her father couldn't carry on like this, or he'd worry himself into his grave.

'Joe was saying, last night, that we should give up the house in George Street,' she began carefully.

'Oh? A touch of hope brightened his eyes.

'Well, you need somebody to look after you, and . . . '

'I need nobody to look after me.' He glowered at her for a moment, then his eyes softened. 'I've always got Ishbel, and the two of us can manage fine.'

'No, you can't, and it seems silly to have just two of you in this big house, and us being all that distance away. Joe says it would be handier for him if he was here.'

She'd struck the right note this time, and Albert agreed that it would be much better for Joe if he was living on the premises, but he knew that she'd only used that as an excuse, for the house in George Street wasn't more than seven minutes' walk away.

Ishbel was upset at first that Gracie and Joe meant to take over the entire middle floor, but when she learned that she was to have the two attic rooms to herself, there was no more grumbling. She'd have a bedroom and a room to study in.

Furniture was shifted, wallpaper and curtains were hung, new linoleum was laid on the floors. A new double bed was delivered and the unneeded single beds were shifted down to one of the stores at the back. Albert let them please themselves. As long as he was left in peace, he didn't mind what Gracie and Joe did with the rest of the house.

Mary's annual letter arrived on the morning of Hogmanay, addressed to Bathie, but Gracie opened it with no qualms. It told her nothing she didn't know already. Only the last part made tears come to her eyes.

'It's funny to think me and you are both grandmothers to the same child, Mrs Ogilvie, I just wish you could see him. Your old friend, Mary.'

At dinnertime, Albert read out a cable which had been delivered as he was coming up from the shop.

'Arriving 1st February. Hetty.'

'Oh,' Gracie moaned, 'there must have been a terrible row among them all. I hope she hasn't left Martin.'

'That Bella Wyness has something to do with this, anyway, I'm bloody sure,' her father exploded. 'She's waited a long time, but she's got her revenge a thousandfold, on me, on your mother and on Charlie, but why the hell did she pick on Hetty? The poor lassie wasn't even born at the time. It's a good thing Mary's there to protect Flo.'

They had no time to discuss it further, Hogmanay being the busiest day of the year for Albert. As usual, the shop was open until eleven o'clock, women always running in for things they'd forgotten to buy, and Gracie sat down thankfully after she'd washed her face. She'd asked Joe to stay in the house all night, in case her father broke down on this the first New Year after his wife's death, so there were four of them sitting round the parlour fire when midnight came.

'1922.' Albert shook his head in disbelief as the Town House clock started to strike. 'It's twenty-two years exactly since Hetty was born and Gavin warned me that your mother wasn't fit to . . . ' As he stopped, overcome with grief, Joe stood up and held out his hand.

'I wish you a happier New Year, Albert, and I hope . . . ' He floundered awkwardly, trying to think of something suitable to say. 'I hope you get better news from New Zealand soon.'

Albert nodded his head gravely. 'I hope so.'

Pulling a half-bottle of whisky from his pocket, Joe said, 'You'll have a dram with me?'

Gracie jumped up and kissed her father. 'I know you don't feel happy, but please have a drink with Joe, to wish us . . . '

Running his hand over his eyes, Albert lumbered to his feet. 'I'm sorry, lass, I forgot you and Joe were on the threshold of marriage. The eighteenth, isn't it?'

He accepted a small glass of whisky. 'I promised Bathie, once, that I'd never touch another drop, but she didn't object as long as I kept it to one, on special occasions.'

Holding the glass up, he made his toast. 'Here's to your future, Gracie and Joe. May it be long and fruitful. I hope you'll be as happy as I was with my wife, Joe, and Gracie, I hope to God you never have to put up with the anguish I made your mother suffer.'

She knew what he was meaning, and, in an unexpected flood of tenderness towards him, forgave her father at last.

Chapter Thirty-eight

On the last night of January, 1922, Albert Ogilvie hardly slept at all. He was excited about seeing Hetty the next day, after almost three years, but he was hoping against hope that she and Martin hadn't separated altogether.

He'd even made up his mind to pay her fare back if she'd left her husband over a little tiff, although he couldn't really believe she'd do anything so drastic unless it was serious. The more he thought about it, the more he was convinced that Bella Wyness was at the root of it. Somehow, the bitch must have come between her son and his wife, and Hetty was safer out of her clutches.

When, at last, he dozed off, he dreamt of the young Bella Wyness – fair hair, blue eyes looking at him invitingly, full lips slightly parted – bending over him with only her nightshift on. She'd wanted him to bed her before, and he'd roused a diabolical anger in her by refusing, but now she'd returned, determined that *she* would bed *him*.

She pulled back the blankets, laying her hand on his shoulder to steady herself as she made to lie down beside him, but he thrust her away. He couldn't let her go into Bathie's place. He didn't want her to go into Bathie's place.

'No! No!' he shouted.

His flailing hands knocked against the tray which Gracie was holding. 'Oh, Father, be careful.' She noticed his wild eyes then, and said, gently, 'Were you having a nightmare?'

'Aye.' He was trembling, not with passion but with anger, anger that the trollop had dared to . . . no, it was a nightmare, it was only a nightmare.

Gracie laid the tray down across his knees. 'If Hetty's on the night train from London, she'll be here any minute.'

'I'm going to the station to meet her.'

'You won't have time, you're not washed or dressed.'

He drank the tea in one long draught, scalding his mouth and gullet in the process, then swung his feet to the floor. 'I'll not take long to get myself ready.'

He was pulling his shirt over his head when a few loud knocks sounded on the outside door, but by the time he drew on his trousers and ran out on to the landing, Hetty and Gracie were weeping on each other's shoulders at the foot of the stairs. Then he noticed another figure standing behind them, and his heart leapt with relief that Martin was there with his wife. At least their marriage had survived whatever had happened.

The hugs, handshakes and introductions to Joe kept all their minds occupied for the next few minutes, until Hetty said, 'Where's Mother? Is she still in Edinburgh with Ellie?'

It was Albert who said, quietly, 'Your mother died on the twenty-second of November. Did you not get Gracie's letter?'

His voice broke when Hetty burst into tears, and Martin Potter drew her close to him, his eyes wide with shock.

348

Albert turned to his other son-in-law. 'Joe, will you go down and open the shop? I'd better stay here with Hetty.'

When Joe went out, Gracie told them how Bathie had died, and waited until her younger sister stopped weeping before she said, 'Now, tell us why you're here. What happened in Wanganui that made you come away like that?'

Hetty sent a glance of appeal to her husband, who began the explanation. 'Did you know that Charlie went away?'

Gracie nodded. 'Yes, Flo and Mary both wrote and told us, but we didn't know why.'

Martin hesitated then squared his shoulders. 'I've a strange feeling that it was my mother's fault, though I don't really know what drove him to it. She laughed to me about what she did to him in our house . . . '

'I told Mother about that in a letter,' Hetty interrupted. Albert couldn't reprimand her for sending that letter to Bathie, having known Bathie's weak condition, not now. 'We've read it.'

'Well,' Martin went on, 'she said that her revenge on the Ogilvies wasn't over yet.'

He looked earnestly at Albert. 'I thought she'd gone out of her mind, and I believed she meant to do some harm to Hetty. I was so angry, I told her I couldn't look on her as my mother any longer, and she . . . ' He swallowed noisily.

'She demanded the money back she'd lent us.' Hetty's eyes were full of cold fury. 'She wouldn't let us have any time, so we'd to sell the house and nearly everything else to pay her, and we'd just enough left to pay our passage home.'

Silence fell – an uncomfortable, brooding silence, while all of them harboured evil thoughts about the woman who had caused them so much heartache.

Finally, Albert said, brokenly, 'You've heard nothing about Charlie? Or Vena?'

Hetty's eyes flooded with tears again. 'Vena's dead. She died in childbirth in Wellington. She hadn't been eating, and we never found out where she'd been.'

349

Martin took over again. 'The police notified us because they'd found an address book in her bag, and we were nearest. I had to go to identify her. The baby was dead, too.'

'Why didn't you write and tell us?'

'I couldn't.' Hetty looked at him pathetically through tear-filled eyes. 'Everything was in a mess, and I didn't want to upset Mother any more than I'd done already. I didn't know she had . . . died. Why didn't you let us know?'

Before Gracie could explain, Martin burst out, 'Mr Ogilvie, I'm very sorry for what . . . my mother did to you and your family.' His earnest face was scarlet with embarrassment, but his eyes met Albert's squarely. 'I know that won't change anything – I only wish it could – but it's all I can say.'

'It's not your fault,' Albert said, sharply. 'Bathie always said Bella's mind was twisted.' He sat up abruptly. 'I'm glad she didn't live to hear about Vena.'

He looked apologetic for saying it, and Gracie laid her hand over his. 'We understand what you mean, Father, and we're glad, too.' She turned to her sister. 'I think that's enough, just now. Do you want to go up to your room? You'll have some unpacking to do. Where's your luggage?'

'We've a trunk with clothes and little odds and ends,' Martin told her. 'It's at the station, all we have in the world, so I'll have to arrange for it to be collected.'

Albert got to his feet. 'Come down to the shop, and Joe can take you in the van.' He was very proud of the vehicle which Gracie's husband had persuaded him to buy a few weeks earlier. 'The two of you'll manage to lift the trunk?'

'Oh, easily, and thanks.'

Hetty turned to her sister when the men went out. 'I can't understand why you didn't cable to let us know about Mother. I feel quite hurt about it.'

'I sent the cable to Charlie,' Gracie felt just as upset. 'I thought he'd tell you and Flo, and I wondered why none of you answered it.' She gulped.

'Oh, I'm sorry, I should have thought. Oh, God, Gracie, I've been thinking that we went through hell, but I suppose it wasn't much better for you here?'

Gracie smiled wryly. 'No, it was pretty awful here, too, and I was glad I'd Joe for support.'

'I like him, and I'm very happy for you both. Where will we be sleeping, what's the arrangements?'

'I didn't know you'd have Martin with you, but we can take up another single bed from the store. You'll be in Ishbel's old room, for she's gone up to the attics.'

'I hope we haven't made her give up her . . .'

'No, no. She's been up there for weeks, and she calls the extra room a sitting room now. It used to be a study, but she left school at Christmas, and has a job in an office in Union Street.' Gracie hadn't the heart to tell Hetty that it was Joe and she who were giving up one of their rooms.

When Ishbel came down there were more excited, tearful, greetings, but at last, Hetty stood back. 'Goodness, you've shot up since I saw you. I believe you're going to be taller than any of the rest of us, even Ellie.'

'I'm half an inch bigger than Ellie already, and I'm only fifteen.' Ishbel beamed proudly.

'Eat your breakfast or you'll be late,' Gracie scolded.

But Ishbel wasn't quite ready to eat. 'Why have you come back from New Zealand, Hetty?' Catching the troubled look that passed between her sisters, she added, sarcastically, 'Or am I still too young to understand things?'

Gracie gave her a little push. 'Yes, you are. Get on.'

'It's no fun being youngest. I'm always treated like a baby.' Still grumbling, Ishbel sat down at the table.

When Martin and Joe staggered up with the trunk, some twenty minutes later, the New Zealander was shaking his head and smiling. 'That Ishbel. She took one look at me as she passed just now, and said she thought you'd walked out on me, Hetty. What have you been saying to her?'

'Nothing, but I didn't remember she hadn't seen you today. I suppose she must have thought I was here on my own.'

The two men laughed, but Hetty looked thoughtful. 'It must be awkward for her. Maybe we *should* tell her everything.'

Gracie frowned. 'Oh, no. That would only make her want to know all the whys and wherefores, and she'd just be a pest.'

At the beginning of April, when Gracie and Hetty both announced that they were going to be mothers, it wasn't only Joe and Martin who were pleased. Ishbel was so excited that she couldn't stop speaking about it, until Gracie had to tell her to be quiet.

Albert thought it over in bed. It was good to have one more of his family at home, and the prospect of children running about again, prattling and wanting to know things, made him happier than he'd been since Gracie's wedding. The house would soon be full, like it used to be, like he and Bathie had wanted it from the very start.

'I can picture our children and our children's children here,' she'd said, when he'd taken her to look at it first.

All seven of their children had grown up here. Most of them had left for what they hoped were greener pastures, but Hetty had come back. It would serve Bella Wyness right if her vindictive shennanigans drove all the young Ogilvies home to the Gallowgate. No, Albert checked himself. He didn't want Flo and Charlie to be driven out of their adopted country.

His thoughts turned to the house again, for he'd improved it a bit since he and Bathie moved in. He'd had water plumbed in, and gas installed, and now Joe and Martin were doing their best to persuade him to put in a bathroom.

'We managed fine with one outside lavvy for nine of us,' he'd told them, when they suggested it first. 'And a tin bath in front of the kitchen range.'

'Once you've had a bathroom,' Hetty had said, caustically, 'this seems very primitive.'

She'd been right, and he should have thought about it years ago. He'd go and see about it tomorrow, but the plumber would have to figure out where to put it.

His mind jumped again to Flo, who knew about her mother now and wrote once a fortnight to Gracie. Leonard was 'quite a handful', as she put it, but he was only six months old. Wait till he was toddling about, poking his fingers everywhere he shouldn't, then Flo would really have her hands full. Hetty and her husband had settled down quickly, thank goodness. Martin helped out sometimes in the shop, but he'd applied to the University and had been accepted to begin after the summer break, to continue his Law studies.

If only he knew where Charlie was, Albert thought sadly, he'd feel happier.

Preparations for their expected infants took up much of Gracie's and Hetty's time, and Ishbel grew quite irritated.

'I'm sick and tired of seeing knitting needles and wool all over the place,' she declared one evening, when they were clearing up after supper. She watched them squeezing past each other and giggling as their bulky fronts collided. 'Oh, you two!' she burst out, at last. 'You're like a couple of elephants. All you need are tusks.'

'Wait till you're having a baby,' Hetty laughed. 'Then we'll see who looks like an elephant.'

As Ishbel's figure was rather a sore point with her, she subsided into hurt silence, and turned to the sink, muttering, sourly, 'It's all right for you to laugh.'

Gracie felt sorry for her, but Ishbel asked for all she got. They'd thought she would stop her complaining once she left school, but she was bored with her job and took it out on her family. They all teased her. However, it wasn't really fair to taunt her about her weight, because she was very sensitive about it, though it was only puppy fat.

Apart from Ishbel's occasional outbursts, the house was running smoothly, Gracie and Hetty were well organized. The new bathroom had been installed between Albert's bedroom and the dining room, although it had meant sacrificing a part of both. It had sounded terrible when the builder had suggested it, but now that it was finished, the reduction in the size of these rooms was scarcely noticeable.

Albert, however, had insisted that the large double bed was too big for his bedroom now, and had made his two sons-in-law dismantle it and take it up to the middle floor for Hetty and Martin. He used one of their single beds now, and the other was in the store again.

Martin had asked if he and Hetty could live in the house until his studies were finished and he was making a decent living as a solicitor, and Albert had been quite happy to agree. It was really much better for Hetty and Gracie to be together in their delicate condition.

Both confinements were to be in November, Gracie's about ten days before Hetty's, if all went according to plan, and they looked forward to comparing the progress of their infants once they arrived.

A close friendship had sprung up between Joe and Martin, and they took Albert out for a drink on Saturday nights, but he always specified, 'Just one, mind,' before they left the house. On Sunday afternoons, the three men usually went for a walk, if the weather was favourable, and left Hetty and Gracie to discuss their pregnancies.

Taken all in all, and apart from Bathie not being there, life on the brow of the Gallowgate was fairly satisfactory, Albert decided one night, before he closed his eyes and fell into a dreamless sleep.

Chapter Thirty-nine

It was extremely hot, even for November, and Flo Dunbar let herself into her bungalow with great relief. Pushing the go-car to the shops had taken much more out of her than she'd thought, and Leonard was being fractious, which hadn't helped.

She kicked off her shoes and put the kettle on. Thank goodness the kitchen was at the back, and didn't catch the sun until afternoon. Thank goodness, too, that Leonard had fallen asleep. She'd have peace to enjoy her cup of tea.

After she filled her cup, she sat down, put her silk-clad feet up on the other chair, then pulled her handbag across the table to take out her cigarettes. Will didn't approve of women smoking, but he didn't have to put up with Leonard all day, and a cigarette was the only thing to steady her nerves.

When the doorbell rang, she frowned, afraid that it would wake her son, but swung her legs down quickly to save whoever it was ringing again. She stared blankly at the tall figure on her doorstep for a moment before she recognized him.

'Charlie!' Flinging her arms round his neck, she burst into tears.

'Steady on.' He glanced round in embarrassment, in case anyone should see, but the dirt road was empty and he patted her back until she stopped crying.

Standing away from him, she said, 'Come in, Charlie, but if you waken Leonard, you'll be sorry.'

'Leonard?' A hint of a smile softened his rather grim mouth. 'So you and Will have carried on the Ogilvie tradition, have you? It had to be L after Ellie's Kathleen, of course.'

Flo nodded, feeling shy with him, but she had to find out more about this brother who had been gone for two years.

'Where did you go, Charlie? We were all so worried.'

He sat down and spread his hands out on his knees, palms up, then raised his eyes. 'First of all, how's Vena, and you'd better tell me if I have a son or a daughter?'

She almost choked on the nervous ball which filled her throat. 'Oh, God, Charlie!' She began to weep again.

His face blanched under his tan. 'What's wrong? What happened, Flo? For God's sake, tell me.'

'I'm sorry, Charlie,' she gulped. 'The baby was still-born and Vena . . . died giving it birth.'

He stared at her in disbelief for a few seconds, then dropped his head and broke into harsh, loud sobs.

When at last he looked up, his crumpled face had eased a little. 'Flo, had you any idea why I went away?'

'No. Was it something to do with . . . Bella?'

'It was everything to do with Bella.' His low voice was bitter. 'I may as well tell you from the very beginning, so you'll understand and not blame me too much.'

She listened, appalled, to his account of his experience as a child, but, each time she opened her mouth to speak, he held up his hand to prevent her uttering a word.

'You'll maybe find this hard to believe, Flo, but when Vena and I first spoke about coming to New Zealand, I forgot Bella was here. I fancied coming to Wanganui, we'd have you and Hetty, and Mary and Jeannie, so we wouldn't feel so lost. It seemed ideal, but, oh God, I wish we'd gone to Australia or Canada, or any bloody place but here.'

Stopping to pull out his handkerchief, he wiped his eyes and blew his nose. 'Everything was going so well for us, for I got the job – I'd always wanted to work in the open air – and the house, and Vena was expecting, after we thought she would never have any more. Then Hetty invited us that night.'

'But you'd been to see her and Martin before, hadn't you?'

'A good few times, but Bella once told Martin what she'd done, God knows why, so he'd made sure she was never asked at the same time as us. The bitch must have found out that we'd be there that night, and she turned up out of the blue.' Charlie's haunted eyes darted away. 'I felt sick at the very sight of her, but when she kissed me that way, it was a thousand times worse. I could have killed her when she said it was to remind me. I needed no reminding, for it had all come flooding back the minute I saw her sneering at me – the touching, the kissing, the . . . '

Shuddering, he drew in his mouth then blew his lips out noisily. 'I could feel the same guilt, the same terror, I'd had when I was eight years old. I made up my mind never to take the chance of meeting her again, but she came to our house a week or so after that, and told Vena a pack of lies. I was so mad, I went to tell her to leave us alone, but she just laughed and said she was having her revenge.'

'For being sacked all that time ago?' Flo couldn't believe that anyone could be so vindictive.

'Well, I thought it was because I'd told Mother what she'd done to me, but she said it wasn't only that. It turned out that Father wouldn't go to bed with her when she'd asked him.'

'I wouldn't think so.' Flo was heatedly indignant.

'You don't know how evil she is, Flo. She told Vena that I'd been unfaithful – with her, mind – and that I'd been going to her house steady and making love to her. All lies, but Vena believed her, and we'd a blazing row.'

'I've heard Mary and Jeannie saying they wouldn't believe a word Bella said. Couldn't you have made Vena understand?'

'I tried, but she was out of her senses with anger and jealousy, and that's when I walked out. I couldn't take any more, but I felt like killing that woman for what she'd done.' His hands clenched until the knuckles showed white.

'Charlie, did you know that Vena was put out of the house after you left?

'God almighty! No, I didn't realize. I was in such a state, I couldn't think straight. Where did she go?'

'I don't know, Charlie. We thought she might have gone to look for you, but she was in Wellington when . . . They found Hetty's address in her bag, and Martin had to identify her.'

'Christ, Flo! It's all my fault.' Charlie jumped to his feet. 'Mine and that bitch's.'

'Where are you going?' Flo stood up in panic.

'Where do you think?' His voice was rough.

Clutching him, she shouted, 'What good would it do now?'

'It would give me the utmost satisfaction.' His words rang round the room and seemed to echo for a moment.

'It would give her more satisfaction.'

'Not if I do what I intend doing.'

Their raised voices unfortunately, or perhaps fortunately, woke little Leonard, and Flo ran to pick him up.

Charlie's murderous intentions ebbed away as he watched his sister trying to pacify her child. 'Give him to me.'

The small boy stopped howling and looked at the stranger with huge round eyes as his mother handed him over.

'Come to Uncle Charlie,' the man crooned.

When Leonard echoed, 'Unca Charrie,' the laughter of the two adults became slightly hysterical, but the drama was over, thanks to the two-year-old who bounced gaily up and down on his uncle's knee when he sat down.

'He's a sturdy little devil,' Charlie observed, ruefully, as the little feet pounded against him.

When Will came home at teatime, he could hardly believe what he saw. Charlie Ogilvie, who hadn't been heard of for two years, was crawling about on the floor, with Leonard, chortling in delight, astride his back.

Flo signalled to him to say nothing about her brother's absence, so he just said, 'It's good to see you again, Charlie.'

Leonard jumped down and ran to his father, and Charlie pulled himself upright, flexing his legs. 'He's a great wee lad. You're a very lucky man, Will.'

'I know that.'

After tea, it was Charlie who suggested that he and his brother-in-law should take a walk. 'Will wants to know why I left like that, and I want to tell him.'

When Will heard the story – more graphic details added to what Flo had been told – he shook his head sadly. 'I don't know how you can be so calm about it. After what Bella did, I'd feel like strangling her, if it was me.'

'I did for a while, and the feeling came back when I was telling Flo what had happened, but, as she said, what good would it do? I'd only end up being hanged – though my life's no good to me now with Vena gone. I wish to God I'd never come back and learned that.'

'Why did you come back?' Will asked, gently.

'I meant to make it up with my wife, but I wanted to hear what Flo said before I went to Vena. Christ, Will, I'd give my right arm to undo . . . ' He stopped, appalled at what he was saying to a man who had lost his left arm in the war, but Will was smiling.

'I understand, Charlie.'

There was a long silence, then Will said, 'You were at the end of your tether, and you couldn't help what happened after you left, or before you left, for that matter, and you'll have to try to forget. Make a fresh start somewhere. Go back to wherever you've been for the last two years.'

'I was drifting, just drifting. Working a few days here, a few days there. I was all over North Island, nearly, for I couldn't settle, longing for Vena and wanting to see my child.' He gulped but carried on. 'Then I decided to come home. What happened wasn't Vena's fault.'

'No, it wasn't,' Will agreed. 'You know, Charlie, I felt really angry at you for leaving her. I didn't know what had made you do it, but it was only a month before the baby was due, and I thought you were the lowest of the low. I couldn't understand then, but I do now, and I don't blame you any more.'

They walked the next hundred yards without speaking, then Will said, 'It might be as well if you went home to Aberdeen. Away from New Zealand altogether.'

'My mother wouldn't forgive me for what I did to Vena.'

Hesitating for a fraction of a second, Will said, quietly, 'Flo didn't tell you? Your mother died two years ago.'

'God! Oh, God!' Charlie stopped walking, his anguished eyes squeezed up, his lips pulled back. 'Not Mother, too?'

Will touched his arm gently. 'We'd better turn back, Charlie. I can't tell you how sorry I am, about everything. It's a bloody awful homecoming for you.'

As soon as they went into the house, Flo could see that Charlie was more upset than ever. 'I've laid out some blankets for you,' she told him. 'I hope you don't mind sleeping on the sofa, but we never thought we'd need a spare bed.'

'I won't sleep, anyway, Flo, but thanks for bothering.'

When he was left alone, Charlie sat down, his face dark with his tormented thoughts. Everything had happened about two years ago. Flo or Hetty must have told Mother what he'd done, and she had died from the shock. And it was his fault Vena had died, too, and the baby. There was nothing for him to live for now, but . . . he could make atonement.

'Will, Charlie's not here!'

Flo's excited, anxious voice early next morning brought her husband rudely out of his slumber, and his eyes were still full of sleep when he jumped out of bed. She buckled on his artificial arm, and he pulled on a shirt and trousers before hurrying after her into the other room.

Her face was pale, her eyes wide with concern. 'There's no sign of him at all. Where could he have gone?'

Although he had a horrible suspicion of where Charlie had gone, and why, Will said, 'He could have gone for a walk. I'll take the car and go and look for him if you like?'

'Yes, please. He didn't seem very well last night when you came back, and he shouldn't be wandering about on his own in the state he's in.'

Her eyes brightened. 'Maybe he's gone to see if he can get his old job back. That could be it, couldn't it?'

'Could be. I'll go that way first.'

Will was outside before he remembered that he was only wearing slippers. What the hell? There was no time to change into shoes. He had to stop Charlie before . . .

When he reached the main road, he turned in the direction of Bella Potter's house, which was about eight and a half miles away, his eyes searching feverishly for his brother-in-law. He was almost sure that Charlie was on his way to have it out with the woman, but when had he set out? It could have been any time between about midnight and six o'clock.

Will cursed his old car, but this Morris-Cowley was all he'd been able to afford on top of paying for his bungalow. If only he'd asked Flo to give him some of her mother's legacy to buy a newer model, he'd have been at his destination by now, but he hadn't foreseen an emergency like this.

When Bella's rather pretentious-looking house came in sight, he slowed down. There had been no sign of Charlie on the way, and he wondered if he'd jumped to the wrong conclusion. He'd look a proper fool if he burst in and she was still asleep. It was only coming on for seven, after all.

Turning into the gateway, he drove cautiously up to the front door, and as he got out of his car, he tried to plan his tactics. If the door was locked, he'd go away without even knocking, but if it wasn't, he'd go straight in, because it would mean that Charlie had got there first.

He went straight in.

Chapter Forty

Even with all the stir of six adults and two one-year-old babies in the house, Albert Ogilvie didn't forget the second anniversary of Bathie's death.

Not that he'd forgotten the first one, but Gracie had gone into labour on this date a year ago, and there hadn't been much peace for him to think about anything until he went to bed, around two in the morning. It was funny that he'd worried so much about Gracie during her confinement – almost as much as he'd worried about his wife – and he'd felt really sorry for Hetty, who was only days away from hers. It hadn't upset her, though, and she'd produced a beautiful baby girl a week later.

This anniversary was different. Neil Ferris, Gracie's son, and Olive Potter, Hetty's girl, let themselves be heard if they were hungry, or wet, or both, and it seemed to remind him more of Bathie – though he didn't need any reminding. Her sweet face and bonnie blue eyes still came into his mind at any odd time; and when anything out of the ordinary happened, he still thought, wait till Bathie hears this.

It was perfectly natural, of course. They'd been married for thirty-two years when she died, and no man could easily forget the woman who'd shared his life for so long. If only they could have had longer together, but it wasn't meant to be.

It was hard to think she would never know about the two new grandchildren, but she *had* known about Leonard Dunbar and Morag McKenzie. No, he was being silly. Of course she'd know about these two as well. She'd be smiling down on them all right now, pleased that they were coping so easily without her.

Of course, it was Gracie who had done most of the coping. He wouldn't have come through, two years ago, if it hadn't been for Gracie, and she'd been the mainstay of the house ever since – dishing out advice to anyone who needed it.

Flo still wrote giving her all the news, Donnie and Ellie, too. They all kept in touch, except Charlie. He seemed to have vanished off the face of the earth, and not one of them, in Aberdeen, Edinburgh, London or Wanganui, had ever found out what had happened to him, or why he'd left Vena.

Remembering how sure Bathie had been that Bella Wyness would take revenge on them one day, and that Martin had told them his mother had said she wasn't finished yet, Albert was absolutely certain that the woman had been responsible in some way for whatever it was that had happened to Charlie.

Albert had a sudden feeling that it wasn't over yet. Some further calamity was hanging over the Ogilvie family. He could feel the dread of it sweeping right through him. He'd always comforted himself by supposing that Mary would watch out for Flo, but he had no doubt now that Bella could outwit both her sisters – and anyone else. Flo could be her next target.

Before he could become morbid about this, he was jolted out of his thoughts by Ishbel.

'It's all right for you, sitting here in peace on your own,' she complained, when she came into the parlour, 'but just imagine what it's like for me. It doesn't matter where I sit, somebody comes and tells me to do something for them. Tells me, mind, not asks. It's "Ishbel, take in the clothes from the wash-house" or "Heat up that pan of custard" or "Run up to the nursery for the zinc and castor oil ointment". It never ends, and I'm sick of it, Father.'

'Wait till you've got a baby,' he said, trying not to laugh, 'and it'll be your turn to order them about.'

'Huh! By the time I have a baby, Hetty'll likely have gone back to New Zealand, and Gracie'll have gone with her.'

His amusement evaporated quickly. 'No, Ishbel. I'm sure Hetty will never go back to New Zealand.'

'Well, they'll have gone away somewhere. I'm always left to do everything.' Ishbel went out, shaking her head.

Albert looked up at the mantelpiece. Ten o'clock already. Levering himself off his chair, he went through to the kitchen, where Hetty was ironing and Gracie was stitching a button on one of Joe's shirts.

'I think I'll go to bed,' he said. 'I feel a bit tired.'

Gracie laid down her sewing. 'I'll make some tea.'

'No, thanks, I don't want anything.'

He did feel tired. His legs ached as he walked through to his room, and when he took off his clothes, his arms felt like they were made of lead. It was because he hadn't been moving about enough, he thought. He'd been in the parlour since suppertime, and it wasn't good for man nor beast to sit about so much.

He hadn't had any significant dreams since the morning Hetty and Martin had arrived back in Aberdeen, but that night he saw his eldest son standing at his bedside, as clear as day.

Charlie looked tired, too, but there was an aura of peace about him, as though he'd achieved something he'd been wanting to do for a long time, something that made up for the terrible way he'd treated his wife.

'You don't need to worry any more, Father.' Charlie's voice sounded different, deeper, yet somehow from a distance. 'Bella Wyness can never hurt any of our family again.'

Waking up in a cold sweat, Albert couldn't get it out of his mind. What had Charlie been trying to tell him? What had he done now?

Albert knew it had been a nightmare, but still . . .

Chapter Forty-one

1924 came in cold and blustery, but, for all the adult inhabitants of the house, it was quite a merry occasion.

Ishbel had been to the Picture House earlier on Hogmanay evening, and had brought her current young man back with her, to see the New Year in at the Gallowgate. One of Joe's friends called with his wife just after midnight to first-foot them, and it was Hetty's twenty-fourth birthday, which made it all the more of a celebration.

Albert, who had been rather morose for some time, cheered up with the extra company, but took only his usual one drink. He'd been dreading the New Year, but found himself enjoying it, after all, and it was almost five o'clock in the morning when he locked the outside door behind the last of their guests.

Needless to say, he was the brightest of the three men later in the day. Hetty and Gracie, who had risen at eight to attend to their children – to whom the New Year was just another day – laughed heartlessly when their husbands came into the kitchen just before dinnertime. Martin and Joe had imbibed somewhat too freely the night before, and their pasty faces and hang-dog expressions revealed exactly how they felt.

Albert grinned. 'You're like a couple of sunny beasties, as my mother used to say.'

Ishbel thought this sounded very comical, although she hadn't the slightest idea of what it meant, but when she asked her father to explain, he couldn't.

'I know it means they've got a morning-after-the-night-before look about them, but I don't know why she said sunny beasties. Maybe it's because there's some little beasties that only come out when it's sunny and then get affected by too much heat.'

'That'll be it,' she exclaimed, gleefully. 'Joe and Martin don't drink much as a rule, so they got drunk when they took too much for the New Year, and it's affected them like the sun affects the little beasties.'

Joe regarded her with jaundiced eyes. 'You've always got to find an answer to everything, haven't you? Why can't you just sit down and keep quiet?'

'I wish you'd all be quiet,' Martin muttered. 'My head's banging like a drum.'

'Serves you right!' Hetty glared at him. 'I lost count of the number of whiskies you had.'

'So did I,' he groaned. 'Never again.'

'Who wants second day's broth?' Gracie glanced round them hopefully, her cheery voice making two of the men cringe.

'Not for me, thanks.' Joe rolled his eyes, to indicate that the mere mention of food was more than enough for him.

'Nor for me.' Martin's grimace was very expressive.

'I'll have some,' Albert smiled.

'Me, too.' Ishbel giggled at her brothers-in-law.

'That's four of us, then, and the children.' Gracie drew some cutlery out of the dresser drawer.

'There's a hen for supper,' Hetty said tartly, to Joe and Martin. 'And if you two still don't feel like eating, there'll be all the more for the rest of us.'

'Is there stuffing, as well?' Ishbel rubbed her hands in happy anticipation. 'And roast tatties?'

'And peas and sprouts,' Gracie added.

Hetty kept the punishment going. 'And there's trifle for pudding, with double cream and . . . '

'Excuse me.' Martin rushed out with his hand over his mouth, and the women laughed when they heard him going into the bathroom.

'All right, Hetty.' Joe glowered at her. 'You've made your point.' His face whitened, and he, too, ran out.

'He'll have to go to the outside lavvy,' Ishbel remarked, with great satisfaction.

Thinking that the teasing had gone on long enough, Albert said, 'They've learned their lesson, so leave it be, now. And, Gracie and Hetty, you'll have enough work preparing the hen and everything, so Ishbel and me'll do the dishes at suppertime.'

'Why does it always have to be me?' came the expected grumble from his youngest daughter.

Three days later, with things back to normal, Hetty and Gracie were having a quick cup of tea at midday, when they heard the postman.

'I'll go.' Hetty ran out, but handed her sister the letter as soon as she came back. 'It's from Flo.'

When Albert came up at one o'clock, he was aware of an unnatural silence, and as soon as Gracie told them all to sit down to listen to Flo's letter, he knew that something terrible must have happened in Wanganui.

Waiting until they were all settled and she felt more composed herself, Gracie said, gravely, 'Before I read this out, I'd better tell you that Charlie's dead, because Flo left it till near the end, and it'll save you building up your hopes.'

There was a confusion of gasps and moans, and she looked round their faces, each showing varying degrees of shock. She let her eyes rest longest on her father, and decided that she could safely read out the whole letter.

'"Dear Gracie, I'm writing to let you know that Charlie turned up yesterday without any warning, and he nearly went out of his mind when I told him about Vena and the baby. He was in a terrible state for a while, and he told us he'd walked out because Vena believed the lies that Bella told about him, and he couldn't take any more. He'd been working all over the place the time he was away, but he had suddenly made up his mind to come home and try to patch things up with Vena.

'"Maybe he had been ill before, maybe that's why he came back, I don't know, and he didn't look very well when we went to bed, but I was very surprised when I went through in the morning and he wasn't there. Will went to look for him in the car, and found him lying at the side of the road, about ten miles away, and I think he must have been making for the place he used to work, to see if he could get his old job back.

'"He was unconscious, and he died just after Will got him to the hospital in Wellington. If we'd known he was ill, we'd have looked after him, but he went away without telling us, and it must have been his heart. We're going to bury him beside Vena and the baby, we thought it was only right. Will says we shouldn't blame ourselves, for nobody could have done anything.

'"I still haven't got over the shock, though it's nearly six hours since Will told me. My thoughts are with you all at this sad time. Your loving sister, Flo."'

After a long pause, Albert said, 'Poor Charlie, and it's all that bloody Bella . . . ' He stopped and glanced at Martin, remembering, too late, that he was Bella Wyness's son.

'You're quite right, Albert.' Martin nodded grimly. 'I believe it was all my mother's fault, and I'm just as angry about it as you.'

Drawing herself to her feet, Gracie said, sadly, 'Well, we won't have to wonder where Charlie is now, and in a way, I'm glad he's at rest.'

They all agreed, Ishbel adding, with youthful romanticism, 'Vena and Charlie are together again, at last. It's a tragic love story, really, isn't it?'

Flo's account hadn't satisfied Martin. His intuition told him there was more to be told, so he wrote that afternoon to Will Dunbar, putting forward a theory which had formed in his own mind, and begging him to confirm or refute it.

They were all subdued and rather edgy, so Martin's silent brooding went virtually unnoticed. Only Hetty, closer to him than the others, recognized it, but assumed that he felt guilty about his mother's part in Charlie's quarrel with his wife.

Exactly a week later, her husband's vague suspicions about how Charlie had died were strengthened when he received a note from his Aunt Mary.

'Dear Martin, I know you broke away from your mother, but I felt you should know she fell down the stairs and died from the knock on her head. One of her neighbours found her, for she'd sacked her maid a while ago and couldn't get another one, and the doctor said she must have lain there for days.

'Me and Jeannie were never very close to her, as you know, but we arranged for her funeral and buried her beside your father, so I hope that was the right thing to do. We found her will, and she had changed it after you left, so everything goes to charity. I'm sorry for you, but there it is. From your loving aunt, Mary.'

It seemed to Martin to be too great a coincidence that his mother and Charlie Ogilvie had died within days of each other, and he was almost sure that Will hadn't told Flo the whole truth, but he trusted that his cousin would give him an honest reply to the letter he'd sent.

When Albert learned of Bella's death, his only remark was, 'What a pity Charlie didn't live to know about this.'

Martin Potter, however, was sure that Charlie *had* known.

It was the end of February before the letter came, and Martin removed it apprehensively from his pigeonhole in the University's common room.

'Dear Martin, you guessed right. I never told anybody, not even Flo, and I arranged things so nobody would suspect, but I wish I'd got there sooner. Charlie had good reason to do what I think he did, and he has paid the penalty.

'I can't say any more, but I beg you not to tell Hetty, or any of the family, and please destroy this, in case any of them find it. Sincerely, Will.'

Drawing a deep breath, Martin tore the letter into small pieces, and flushed them down the nearest lavatory.

Bella Wyness, as Albert always called her, must have gone completely mad in her obsession for vengeance, but it seemed that Charlie Ogilvie had somehow wreaked the ultimate revenge on her, and her own son blessed him for it.

Chapter Forty-two

Neil Ferris and Olive Potter were almost one and a half when Patricia Ferris made her appearance, and Gracie joked that Hetty had better get a move on, because she'd fallen behind.

Ishbel was going out now with a young man she'd met at a dance in the Trades' Hall, and the banter between his three daughters reminded Albert of the days when Flo, Charlie and Donnie had teased Ellie about her lads.

It was in the sanctuary of Albert's truncated bedroom that a sickening, gnawing suspicion had started to grow inside him. It was uncanny that Bella Wyness had died so soon after Charlie, so could the two deaths be connected?

Fortunately, his thoughts were diverted when Donnie wrote asking if he and Helene could come on holiday for two weeks in July, but Gracie didn't seem too pleased about it.

'There's no room for them,' she said, distractedly.

His displeasure showing on his face, Albert turned on her quite angrily. 'There's always room for my son and his wife in this house. It's only for two weeks, for God's sake.'

'The three rooms on the middle floor are all occupied,' Hetty pointed out. 'Martin and me in one, Joe and Gracie in one, and the children have the nursery. The only place would be Ishbel's sitting room, and she won't want to give that up.'

'She'll have no choice,' Albert thundered. 'She's hardly ever in these nights, anyway, to be needing anywhere to sit.'

Gracie passed his order on to Ishbel. 'Father says you'll have to give up your sitting room when Donnie and Helene come, and don't bother to argue, there's nowhere else for them.'

Ishbel couldn't deny this, but felt duty bound to give a token protest. 'It's always me. Why do they have to come at all, that's what I'd like to know.'

Sighing, Gracie said, 'Donnie hasn't been home since Mother's funeral, and this is his home, after all.'

'It's supposed to be mine, too.'

Two of the old single beds had to be taken out of the store, and the mattresses were hung over the outside stair railing. Blankets, bedspreads, sheets and pillows were aired in front of the kitchen fire, and all of them, except Albert, became irritated by the inconvenience of not being able to move about freely.

'They could have gone to a hotel,' Ishbel remarked one day, after being at the sharp end of Gracie's tongue. 'I'm sure they could easily afford it, and it would be a lot better for them and everybody else.'

Everything was ready by the time Donnie and Helene arrived, and they said they were delighted with their attic room.

'I'm sorry it's not a double bed,' Gracie apologized, 'but we only had the old singles spare.'

'We could have managed on one single, we only use half our bed at home.' Donnie winked at Helene, who blushed.

'Pay no attention to him,' she laughed. 'He can never be serious about anything.'

Albert was very pleased that they looked so happy, and he was even more pleased when Donnie came through to his room when he was making ready for bed that night.

'Here's the last of what I owe you, Father. I wanted to put it into your hand myself, so I can hold up my head.'

Casting a cursory glance at the wad of notes, Albert said, 'There's too much here.'

'I've added on interest, and don't say you don't want it.'

Albert didn't argue. He had done the same with Bathie's mother, after all. 'How did you manage to leave the shop long enough to take a holiday up here?'

'I took on an assistant a couple of months ago, and her brother's going to be giving her a hand the time we're away.'

'Are you sure you can trust them?'

'Oh, Father.' Donnie sounded exasperated. 'Of course I can trust them, they're Helene's cousins.'

'That's all right, then. Goodnight, Donnie.'

'Goodnight.' As he went out, Donnie was smiling at his father's canny Aberdonian outlook.

Helene made a great fuss of all the children, especially baby Patricia, or Patsy, as they all called her.

'Are you not thinking of having one yourself?' Gracie asked. 'You've been married for a good few years now.'

'Seven, but we wanted the shop to be on its feet first. I would like to start a family before I'm too old, though.'

Hetty giggled. 'Now's your chance, then. The air at the top of the Gallowgate has always been good for breeding.'

Helene coloured, but joined in the hilarity.

The two weeks passed very quickly, but this time, Donnie proudly escorted his wife round his native city, because she'd seen very little of it the only other time she'd been there. She'd been too busy looking after his mother at the time of her heart attack.

Their walks took them through Old Aberdeen to the chosen bend of the river where St Machar built his cathedral in the sixth century; to the bustle of the Fish Market early one morning; along the golden beach one lovely evening; into the West End. Helene was suitably impressed by them all.

Most of their evenings, however, were spent getting to know the family again, and the parlour was crammed with the extra chairs. The four men often ended up by talking together, while the three wives chattered on amongst themselves, but there was still a companionable atmosphere in the room.

The time flew past, their two weeks at an end before they knew it, and Martin, on holiday from the law firm where he was employed, saw them off from the railway station.

'The house seems quiet with them away,' Albert remarked, when he came up from the shop at dinner-time.

A squabble between Neil and Olive broke out just then, making baby Patsy open her eyes and scream, so Gracie threw him a quick look. 'Quiet? What's that?'

In September, Gracie read out Helene's letter with delight.

'I'm pregnant, folks. It must have been the Gallowgate air, like Hetty said, so she'd better be careful.'

'Too late,' Hetty remarked, dryly.

Once she stopped laughing, Gracie said, 'I wonder who's going to be first? Helene or you?'

'Does it matter?'

'Yes, it matters.' Gracie's eyes twinkled as she looked at her sister. 'What letter comes next?'

'Oh, no!' Hetty's chin dropped. 'We're at Q.'

'You'd better pray that Helene's before you, then.'

Shortly after that, Martin announced that he and Hetty had decided to buy a house of their own. 'I have quite a decent salary now,' he went on, 'and our family's increasing. It'll leave room for your family to increase, too, Gracie.'

'Two of my kind's enough.' Gracie leaned across the table to administer a gentle slap to Neil's hand, which had been edging towards a plate of biscuits. 'I've told you before, bread first, my lad.' Little Olive glared at her aunt, and put her arm round her cousin protectively. 'Me love you, Neil.'

'That two remind me of Flo and Will,' Albert observed, smiling. 'They were always sticking up for each other when they were bairns, as well.' A look of sadness came to his eyes. 'I'm going to miss the three of you when you leave.'

'We'll be visiting,' Hetty said quickly, 'and you can come and see us any time you like.'

He brightened up considerably. 'You'll maybe wish you hadn't said that, once I keep turning up on your doorstep.'

The housewarming took place on a Sunday afternoon just before Christmas, to enable Gracie and Joe to be there with Neil and Patsy. They were all most impressed by the dwelling Martin Potter had chosen, Ishbel included, and Albert secretly thought it surpassed even the mansion the Johnstones had lived in at Ferryhill. The house in Rubislaw Den was very large – a beautiful granite building, sparkling in the sunlight, with quite a big garden at the front, and a huge one at the back with an ornamental fish pond in it.

Martin had erected a wooden swing for his daughter, and as soon as Neil saw it from one of the windows, he rushed out to inspect it, Olive trotting behind him. They happily took turns to push each other, and were no bother for the rest of the afternoon.

When Hetty said that she'd be glad of some advice about the rooms which were still unfurnished, the women embarked on a loud, animated discussion, and Martin stood up, smiling to Albert and Joe. 'We don't want to be listening to this, so come through to my study and we'll have a quiet drink.'

Once they were seated again, Albert remarked, 'Like you, I only furnished the first floor in the Gallowgate to start with, and the nursery, but, of course, we had the old stuff from our tenement house that we put up in the attics.'

'We'll get round to the rest of the house,' Martin said. 'There's no rush yet.'

'Not yet.' Albert grinned. 'But if you're anything like Bathie and me were, the bairns'll come one after the other, and before you know it, your house'll be absolutely full.'

Martin exploded with laughter. 'What a prospect!'

When they were walking home, Joe said, 'Martin and Hetty have a lovely house, and I'm very happy for them.'

Gracie pulled a rather tired Neil by the hand. 'So am I. They deserve it, for they'd a bad time in New Zealand.'

There was a short silence, each of them remembering why Hetty and Martin had sold up and come to Aberdeen, then Albert shrugged his shoulders. 'They're on their feet now, and that's all that matters. I just hope you two don't decide to buy a house of your own now, and go off and leave me.'

'We can't afford it,' Gracie said, without thinking.

Joe shook his head at her, then, to change the subject, he said, 'Let me carry Patsy now, Ishbel, she's quite heavy.'

Gracie had made Albert think, however, and that night, he lay in bed recalling his frustration at being an underpaid assistant to Joseph Duthie for so long. He'd never heard from the old man after he went to London, and he must have passed on by this time.

Albert gave himself a mental shake; he'd almost forgotten what he'd been thinking about – old age must be creeping up on him. He wasn't being fair to Joe Ferris, that's what it was, and he'd have to do something about it.

In the morning, he told Gracie and Joe what he'd decided. 'We need another man in the shop. It's getting too much for me and I could be doing with a holiday.'

Ignoring the quick frown which Joe directed at his wife, Albert continued, 'The trouble is, somebody's got to take the responsibilities, so I'm employing a manager.'

The naked disappointment in Joe's face spurred him on to say, 'Gracie, meet my new manager – Joseph Ferris, Esquire.'

She jumped up in excitement, making a startled Neil miss his mouth with his egg-spoon and gaze at her with thin yellow rivulets running down his chin.

'Thank you very much, Albert.' Joe leaned across to shake his hand fervently. 'But I hope you didn't think Gracie was hinting at anything like this last night?'

'No, I'm glad she said it, for it made me think. I should have done this long ago, and I'm not expecting you to do it for the same wages, so would half as much again suit you?'

Gracie kissed her father first, then her husband, and they all burst out laughing when Neil piped up, 'Me, too.'

When their mirth subsided, she said, 'We're not going to buy a house, Father. We're very happy here.'

Albert leaned back against his chair with a look of deep satisfaction. 'Now we've got everything settled, would it be too much for me to ask for another cup of tea?'

Albert found it difficult not to interfere, but allowed Joe to find his own assistant before announcing himself officially retired. He felt like a lost sheep after he stopped going down to the shop, and his days dragged until he recalled that he'd mentioned taking a holiday.

It had been said on the spur of the moment, but he mulled over the idea for days, reflecting that there was no reason why he shouldn't go away somewhere for a while, he'd worked hard enough all his life.

Reaching this conclusion one afternoon in March, he sat down at the dining room table to write a letter.

Chapter Forty-three

'Hetty, Helene's had her baby.'

Gracie smiled as her sister walked in one afternoon in April, her expected child low down in her womb. 'You'd better sit down and look at her letter.'

She giggled with glee when Hetty started to read, waiting for the reaction she knew would come.

'Queenie!' Hetty let out a relieved squeal, as her face broke into a broad smile. 'They did carry it on, after all. Well, thank goodness! I've been worrying myself sick trying to think of names that began with Q.'

Albert was also delighted that his latest grandchild was carrying on his tradition, although Queenie was an outlandish kind of name. But at least this one was an Ogilvie.

He was happier when Hetty's son came into the world four days later – Raymond Potter sounded more civilized, and this was his eighth grandchild. Ellie and Gracie and Hetty all had two each now. Flo and Donnie still only had one apiece, but they were young yet, and maybe Ishbel would get married and have the next one. It kept him going, wondering about it, which was a relief from waiting for a reply to the letter he'd written weeks ago.

When it did eventually arrive, he kept Gracie in suspense for a few minutes after he'd read it, until his excitement got the better of him.

'I can see you're dying to know why Flo's written to me this time. Well, I wrote to her, a few weeks back, to ask if I could go there for a holiday.'

Gracie's mousey head jerked up, and her blueish-grey eyes flew open. 'To New Zealand? Oh, Father, what a good idea, but why didn't you say anything? What does Flo think about it?'

He handed her the letter, doubtful, suddenly, about undertaking such a journey at his age.

As soon as Ishbel heard what her father planned to do, she suggested that she should go with him, and was offended when her offer was turned down. 'I never get to go anywhere.'

'This is the first time in over sixty years that I've ever had a holiday,' Albert declared. 'So you've a long way to go before you catch up on me.'

'I'll save up and go somewhere myself, then,' she said pettishly. 'It wouldn't cost all that much to go to Edinburgh, would it?'

No one paid any attention to her. Gracie was too busy mashing up little Patsy's egg for her and keeping an eye on Neil, Joe's head was buried in the morning paper and Ishbel herself had diverted her father's mind to Ellie, whom he hadn't seen since Gracie's wedding.

There had been no room for anyone else after Hetty and Martin arrived from New Zealand, but they had their own place now and there was no reason why he shouldn't write to Ellie and ask her and her family to come for another holiday before he went away himself.

By one of life's strange coincidences, a letter came from Ellie with the second post, saying that Hetty had invited them to Rubislaw Den, and that Gavin was arranging a locum for two weeks in August.

'They should be coming here,' Albert lamented. 'We could easily make room for them.'

'Hetty's got more room than we have,' Gracie pointed out. 'It's not that I don't want them here, but it would be better for little Morag to be where there's a garden for her to play in. There's nowhere here for her.'

'Aye, I suppose you're right.' He screwed up his face for a moment, considering what this did to his plans. 'Well, I don't want to miss seeing Ellie and Gavin and the bairns, so I suppose I'd better leave my trip off until they've had their holiday. I'll book it for September or October.'

Gracie studied him as he drank his tea. His hair had thinned out, but there was a red tinge through the sandy-grey, making him look younger than Ellie's husband, who was pure white though he was a year younger. Father's thick moustache was still gingery, but he'd stopped waxing it a few years ago, and clipped it every Saturday morning.

He had developed a paunch, and his figure wasn't quite so erect as it had once been, but he wasn't at all bowed, and his face was fresh and unlined. There was no need to worry about him, she decided. He had all his faculties, and had a good Scots tongue in his head if he had to ask about anything, but she couldn't help worrying about him going so far away on his own. It would be awful if he took ill, or had a seizure.

When she voiced her fears to Joe, he smiled. 'Your father is built up on going, Gracie, and a holiday like that'll do him the world of good. He's at a loose end without the shop.'

'I know, but he goes out for walks with Neil, sometimes.'

'It's no life for a man who's been accustomed to working all hours of the day. Once he's seen Flo, he'll maybe settle down and take up a hobby, bowling, or something like that.'

Although the McKenzies weren't sleeping at the Gallowgate, they spent a lot of their time with Albert, and he was very surprised to see how tall Kathleen had grown. At ten, there was every sign that she was going to be as tall as Ellie and Ishbel. The three of them took after him, of course, their height as well as their red hair. Morag, four come November, was dark and petite, very like Bathie, with her big blue eyes and sweet little face, but she was a proper wee chatterbox, with Ellie's nature, and being a year older, ordered both Neil and Olive around. Ellie had put on a little weight, but with her height she could carry it, and her hair, dark auburn now, suited her in that earphone style she had it. Gavin was rather quieter than he used to be, but he was still very good company. Thank goodness their marriage had worked out well, even with the difference in their ages. Albert had wondered, at first, if Gavin had taken Ellie as a substitute for Bathie, but he was quite convinced now that he'd been wrong. Gavin loved Ellie for herself, not for reminding him of the woman he could never have, and that was as it should be.

'I hear you're going to New Zealand to see Flo,' Gavin remarked one afternoon when they were out walking together.

Albert hesitated. Should he confide in his old friend and tell him his reason for going? Almost immediately, he decided against it. There was no point in planting doubt in Gavin's mind about Charlie's death, because, knowing Ellie, she would find out, sure as anything.

'Aye,' he said, 'I thought it would be a good idea to see my other grandchild, before I was too old to travel.'

Gavin laughed. 'You've years ahead of you yet, man, but it is a good idea, and you'll have to come to Edinburgh some time, too. It would make Ellie very happy to have you visit her.'

A twinkle came into Albert's eyes. 'I'll maybe do that when I come back, for the wanderlust might be on me after I've been halfway round the world.'

They studiously avoided any mention of the old days – it was safer not to – and their talk was confined to comparing the children, discussing the family and Gavin's intention of taking a partner into his practice.

'Father and Gavin seem to get on well,' Gracie said, one day when the two men went out.

'They've always enjoyed each other's company.' Ellie was glad that her husband was looking much better over the past week. His work was taking its toll on him, but she hadn't the heart to suggest to him that he give it up.

Albert's excitement about his coming journey prevented him from being upset when Ellie and her family went back to Edinburgh. He had judged it right, just giving himself enough time to recover from their visit.

When the great day arrived, Joe took him to the station in the van, and waited with him until the train pulled out, and Albert waved from the window for as long as he could see the platform. Then he sat down, his stomach churning, and opened the magazine which Joe had bought for him.

He laid it down in a few minutes, unable to concentrate. In fourteen hours he'd be in King's Cross station, where Donnie was to meet him and see him on to the train for Southampton. Not one member of his family would be there to wave him off on the liner, he mused, but no doubt he'd survive.

As he watched the countryside flashing past, he wished that he could have taken Bathie away somewhere before all the children came on the go, but they hadn't been able to afford holidays. She'd never complained, but he sometimes wondered if she'd ever regretted marrying him and having so many bairns.

A pleasant surprise awaited him at Edinburgh. Ellie had come to Waverley Station to wish him bon voyage, and although they had only just over ten minutes to talk, it made him feel that she loved him as much as ever, and his heart was full.

When the guard blew his whistle, she grasped his hand. 'I want your promise that you'll come to visit me for a while, after you come back from seeing Flo. You've no excuse now.'

Albert laughed. 'No, I suppose I haven't, and I promise.'

Two other passengers had joined him in the carriage, so he settled back to speak to them, cheered by his favourite daughter's thoughtfulness. Newcastle was the next stop, with the porters all jabbering away in a strange accent, then the stations flew past, York, Grantham, Peter-borough, and it was no time before Donnie was shaking his hand in King's Cross.

'I'll take you round the corner to have some breakfast, Father, I bet you could be doing with something to eat.'

'Aye, I'm a bit peckish.'

It was only a small workmen's café, but the ham and eggs tasted delicious to Albert, and he had three slices of toast and two cups of tea, while Donnie smiled indulgently.

'We could easily get a bus to Waterloo, Father, it isn't far, but with your suitcase, I think we'll take a cab.'

As soon as he finished his breakfast, Albert was hustled outside, and before he got his breath back, he was installed in another train, on his way to Southampton.

'Give my love to Flo and Will,' Donnie called out, when the train moved off.

'I'll do that.' If he ever got there, Albert thought nervously, as he sank down in the corner next the window. It was the last bit of his journey that worried him. Out on the open sea for so long, with no land in sight, and what if the boat sprang a leak, or something? Look at the *Titanic*, back in 1912. It was supposed to be unsinkable, but it had sunk, just the same. He felt lost and alone, and rather frightened, but there were no icebergs between here and New Zealand, as far as he knew, so that was something to be thankful for.

Chapter Forty-four

The sight of Flo and her husband waving on the quayside made Albert's heart overflow with emotion.

Flo, whom he hadn't seen for more than six years, and Will Dunbar – looking every inch a businessman, although the glove on his left hand would never let anyone forget that he was a disabled ex-soldier – had driven to Wellington to meet him, and when he stepped cautiously off the gangway on to New Zealand soil, they greeted him ecstatically.

Dashing away the tears with his sleeve, he muttered, 'I must be getting old, carrying on like this.'

Flo dried her own eyes. 'I'm less than half your age, Father, and I'm having a good cry, too. Oh, it's great to see you, and to have you here for a while.'

'Only for a month, mind.'

The long drive to Wanganui tired them all, but Will and Flo were rather alarmed by her father's pallor and his dull, deep-set eyes, which brightened up a little when his grandson came running out of the bungalow to meet them.

Flo's mother-in-law – Mary Wyness as Albert would always think of her – followed Leonard out, having been left in charge of him while his parents were away, and looked embarrassed when her ex-employer embraced her warmly.

'Oh, if only you could have ta'en Mrs Ogilvie wi' you, an' all,' she whispered as she stepped back.

His voice deepened. 'Aye. Bathie would have loved to see you again, Mary.'

'I'll run you home now, Mother,' Will said briskly. 'But I'll bring Flo's father to see you in a day or two, when he recovers from his journey.'

'Aye, the poor man must be fair dead beat with all his stravaigin' aboot.'

Albert did take a day or two to recover, but he was happy enough to sit with Flo through the day, and to get to know the little grandson he'd never seen before. Leonard was almost four now, and chattered to him non-stop, his accent fascinating his grandfather, being twangy New Zealand interspersed with an occasional word in flat Aberdeen, picked up, no doubt, from his grandmother, who still retained a lot of her native tongue.

At breakfast time on the third day, Will had a suggestion to make. 'I don't know if you're ready yet, Father, but . . . '

'Call me Albert, lad, Joe and Martin always do now.'

'Thanks. I was going to say I could drive you to my Aunt Jeannie's house on my way to work. My mother's going to be there, too, and I'd pick you up on my way home.'

'That's a grand idea, Will.' Albert rubbed his hands with glee, then glanced at his daughter. 'You'll be coming, too, of course? And Leonard?'

She shook her head. 'No, Father. You'll all be speaking about things that happened before I was born.'

'Aye, right enough.' He disappeared into the room he was sharing with Leonard, who was thrilled with the temporary camp bed that had been put up for him, and came back a moment later carrying his jacket and a pullover.

Will's eyebrows shot up. 'You won't need them, Albert, it's hot already, and it'll get worse as the day goes on.'

Laying the jacket down, Albert said, 'I'll have to wear my pullover. I can't let Mary and Jeannie see me in my galluses.'

'Galluses?' Will looked at his wife, puzzled by the word.

'Braces,' she explained. 'He doesn't trust belts.'

Within ten minutes, Albert was hugging Jeannie just as eagerly as he'd greeted Mary two days before.

'I'm right glad I can offer you a cup of tea in *my* house, at last, Mr Ogilvie, for many's the sly cuppie I had off you when I was workin' at the Gallowgate.'

'You'll be owing me some yet, then,' he joked.

The next few hours were taken up with, 'D'you remember when . . . ?' and his family's early history was brought vividly back to him – Charlie's baby croup, Ellie's fall on the day of Mary's wedding, the day when Flo and Will were born and the closeness which had developed between them even when they were small, and a hundred and one other incidents which had almost slipped his memory.

Through it all, however, there was an underlying sad awareness that the most important person was missing from the reunion, but Albert, who could speak about

Bathie quite calmly now with only an ache in his heart, was determined that there would be no tears. Each time either of the sisters appeared to be bordering on sentimentality, he would skilfully remind them of one of Ellie's sayings and have them laughing again.

When he mentioned the Sunday that Charlie had been lost, Mary said, 'That must ha'e been terrible for you, right enough. Jeannie an' me were away by that time, but Mrs Ogilvie wrote an' told us all about it.'

She paused and regarded him sorrowfully. 'Mr Ogilvie, I'm awful sorry about what happened to Charlie. We still can't get over it, him dyin' like that on the very mornin' after he came back. It was like he knew he hadn't long to go, an' he'd come back to die among his own folk.'

Albert had been so involved in the distant past that it took a minute for his mind to adjust to this. Neither Flo nor Will had brought up the subject of Charlie's death, and he'd almost forgotten why he'd made this pilgrimage. His suspicion reared up again, stronger than ever, but he could say nothing about it to Bella Wyness's sisters.

'Aye,' he murmured, at last. 'It was a terrible business, and I don't suppose I'll ever get to the bottom of why he left his wife like he did.'

The two women exchanged glances, then Mary said, 'Jeannie an' me spoke a lot about it at the time, an' we came to think Bella had something to do with that.'

Lowering his head, he rubbed his hand across his chin. 'It's what I thought myself, but we'll never be sure.'

'I went an' asked her,' Mary continued. 'But she just laughed an' said she always knew Charlie Ogilvie wasn't normal. It was her that wasn't normal, though, spinning lies without battin' an eyelid. She even tried to tell me, on the very day o' Willie's funeral, that he'd been . . . takin' up with her before she wed Matthew Potter, an' that wasn't true.'

Jeannie nodded vigorously. 'She would have swore black was white an' have you believin' it, but we all knew she'd been jealous that Matt had offered to give Mary and Will a home.'

Albert's heart had sunk as he recalled how he'd lashed out at young Will that terrible day when he'd been out of his mind with worry about Bathie. 'I'm sure what Bella said wasn't true, Mary, but . . . did Will ever say anything about what I told him about you?'

'That he wasna Willie's bairn? Aye, he came out with that one day when he come back first, an' he was as low as ever I've seen anybody in my life. He doesna hold that against you, Mr Ogilvie, an' neither do I, for we understand you werena in your right mind at the time. It was only the truth you told him, when all's said an' done.'

'I should never have said it, though, and I can't tell you how much I regret it.'

'It's all forgotten about long ago, an' I'm sure . . . '

What Mary was sure about was never disclosed, because the door opened at that moment and Robbie Park walked in, so the two women left them to talk, while they dished up the lunch which Jeannie had prepared earlier.

Albert's old employee shook hands with him. 'I thought I'd better let you have a while on your own with them, for they were dying to get you to themselves. They're still a great pair for letting their tongues wag.'

Albert grinned. 'Aye, we've had a right good blether.'

'Fine. I'd a few little things to attend to. You see, I'd a bit of heart trouble a few years back, and the doctor advised me to take things easier. So I put a manager into the store, a good man and very capable, but I can't keep away altogether.'

Albert smiled ruefully. 'I know, Robbie, I'm the same myself. I let Gracie's man take charge, and I've to bite my tongue to keep from saying things I shouldn't, but they come out in spite of me, sometimes.'

After their meal, Albert and Robbie recalled some of the awkward customers they'd had to deal with so long ago, then Robbie described how his own business had grown, while Mary and Jeannie sat back, pleased that

Albert had a man to talk to, as a change from their female company.

Robbie beamed when a young man walked in, about two hours later. 'This is Ab,' he explained. 'You see, Albert, I didn't forget my promise to you. His full name's Albert Robert, but we call him Ab for short, though he'll be thirty in a few years.'

The young man shook hands, obviously embarrassed by the meeting. His parents had often told him that it was Albert Ogilvie who had paid their passage to Wanganui, and as a boy he'd pictured some sort of god, so he was very relieved when the man grasped his hand and said, 'You haven't disgraced the name, at any rate, for you're a fine upstanding lad.'

'My daughter, Jean, is working in Wellington,' Robbie said, 'but you'll maybe meet her another day.'

Jeannie would have liked Albert to stay for supper, but Will turned up to collect him, so they all shook hands with him and made him promise to come to see them again.

The weekdays were usually spent quite quietly, shopping with Flo occasionally, taking Leonard out, having a stroll in the evenings with Will. Albert found it all very relaxing.

At the weekends, Will took him farther afield. They went to see the hot springs at Rotorua, where Albert marvelled at the seething waters leaping high into the air, also to Mount Ruapehu, the dormant volcano which they told him was twice as high as Vesuvius.

Albert was intrigued the first time he saw a family of Maoris, but on the trips Will took him, they often passed a group of their shanties and he became accustomed to them as part of the attraction of the area.

Flo was pleased to see the gradual change in her father. By the third week, his step was sprightlier, his eyes were brighter and a smile came much readier to his lips.

'I wish he would stay for a bit longer than a month,' she observed to Will one night, when they were in their own room. 'He's looking a lot healthier now. Couldn't we find out if he can change the time for him going back?'

After considering it briefly, Will said, 'Leave it, Flo. I expect he'll be glad to be going home when the time comes.'

Sometimes, before they went to bed, Albert spoke about Bathie, and the sadness returned to his eyes. Flo longed to comfort him then, but felt it was better to avoid showing too much emotion. She'd been dreading him asking about Charlie – in case both of them broke down – and was very relieved that he hadn't, not yet.

Will drove him to Mary's occasionally, or to Jeannie's, where he did once meet Jean Park, a younger, quieter edition of her mother. The weeks seemed to fly past until Albert realized that his holiday was almost over and he hadn't done the one thing he'd come all this way to do. It wasn't going to be easy, and it would have to be done diplomatically.

He had the idea that Flo knew no more than she'd written in her letter, so it was Will he'd have to approach. He'd been on the point of tackling his son-in-law several times when they were out walking, but his courage had failed him at the last minute, and he began to wonder if it would be better just to leave it. But he knew he would never be content until he knew the truth, however much it might distress him.

On his second last evening, Albert was silent and morose. Flo tried to draw him into a light-hearted conversation, but he continued to sit looking despondently into the fireplace.

At eight o'clock, she said, 'I'll have to put Leonard to bed. Do you want to have a walk with Will, Father, or do you not feel up to it tonight?'

His mournful eyes turned towards her slowly. 'I'm sorry, I was remembering it's four years since your mother . . . '

'Oh, I'd forgotten the date.' Flo felt ashamed.

'That's all right, lass, but I'd like just to sit here, if you don't mind. I'm a bit over-tired with all the excitement I've had lately, and I'll have to be fit for my journey home.'

'I'll just go and give Leonard his bath and you can sit and talk to Will. If you're good, he'll maybe give you a beer.'

He raised a faint smile as she took the little boy out, then resumed his study of the unlit fire.

Waiting for a moment, Will got to his feet. 'What'll it be, Albert? Beer or whisky?'

'A beer, please. It'll help to cool me down. I can't get over how hot it is here, and it's nearly December.'

'It's our summer,' Will reminded him.

When he accepted the tall glass, Albert braced himself to look at his son-in-law. 'Can I ask you something, Will?'

'Sure, go ahead.'

'It's about Charlie.'

'Oh.' The younger man's smile was quickly replaced by a very guarded expression.

Albert hesitated, then began to speak quietly. 'You didn't tell Flo everything, did you? Since I retired, I've had time to think, and I can't help feeling it's queer that . . . Bella Wyness died . . . nearly the same time as Charlie, by what I figured.'

Will moistened his dry lips. He had anticipated that this would crop up some time, from one source or another, but had never been able to decide how to handle it. 'What are you getting at, Albert?' he hedged.

'I'm asking if Charlie killed Bella Wyness, or if it was the other way round.' It was out now, and there was no holding back. 'I'd be obliged if you didn't hide anything from me.'

Looking at his father-in-law's tormented eyes, then at the hands clenching convulsively, Will sat down heavily on the seat at the opposite side of the fireplace and took a draught of his beer. 'I haven't told anybody what really happened,' he said, at last. 'Not even my own wife.'

'I'm his father and I've a right to know.'

As if it were the most important thing in the world to him at that minute, Will kept his eyes riveted on his tankard. 'I should have told you before, but . . . ' He was obviously wondering where to start, even if he *should* start, but when he glanced up, Albert's commanding stare made him go on.

He repeated the reason Charlie had given for his abrupt departure, looking at Albert now and then to see how he was taking it, then said, 'He felt he had to get away from it all, what Bella was trying to do to him as much as what Vena was doing. I don't know why Vena didn't come here when she was put out of the house, or to Hetty, or my mother, that's one thing I can't understand – unless she wanted to put an end to herself, thinking Charlie didn't want her.'

'Poor lassie. She must have been heartbroken. Martin said he'd to go to identify her body.' Albert was silent for a few moments, then he said, quietly, 'But what about Charlie, when he came back? What happened after that?'

'I think he was beginning to accept things until I told him to go back to Aberdeen. He said his mother would never forgive him for what he'd done to Vena, and I had to tell him his mother was dead, too. I thought Flo would have told him, but she must have forgotten he didn't know.'

'Bathie would have forgiven Charlie for anything,' Albert observed mournfully. 'He was the apple of her eye.'

'He thought the world of her, too, I know, and I believe that learning she was dead was what put him over the edge. When Flo and I went to bed, he seemed quiet enough. He said he wouldn't sleep, but we thought he'd be resting anyway.' Will halted again. 'I shouldn't have left him. I should have known what he had in his mind.'

'Don't blame yourself, lad. Whatever was in his mind, he'd have found a way, in spite of anything you did. If he hadn't done it that day, he'd have waited, but I'm sure he'd have done it, sooner or later.'

Albert's firm low voice reassured his son-in-law. 'He was gone in the morning and I knew where, though I didn't tell Flo. I drove to Bella's house and found her lying behind the front door. The back of her head was smashed in, and there was nothing I could do for her, but I wanted to do something about Charlie. I didn't know if he'd still be there, but I searched the house and found him lying in the bathroom, with an empty bottle of sleeping tablets beside him.'

Albert gave a soft groan, but Will carried on. 'He was in a bad way, but I managed to get a little bit out of him. He'd left our house about three in the morning, and walked straight there, and banged on her door until she came down. He said she just laughed at him and went back upstairs, but he followed her, shouting that it was her fault that Vena and the baby were dead. When he was on the landing beside her, she . . . ' Will sucked in his breath, then let it out slowly through his teeth. 'She told him she didn't know he was so desperate to get into bed with her again. That's when he hit her.'

There was a prolonged silence, during which both men pictured the scene, then Will said, 'She overbalanced and fell down the stairs. Charlie said that she struck her head on the metal umbrella stand at the door, and when he ran down, she was dead. He sat on the bottom step for a long time to think, he told me, then he felt sick and went to the bathroom. That's where he found the sleeping tablets – nearly a full bottle.'

Albert found his tongue again. 'It was maybe the best thing he could have done. Given all the circumstances, nobody would have believed he didn't mean to kill her.'

Will's head jerked up. 'That's what I thought. He lost consciousness after I got him in the car, so when I reached the hospital, I told them he'd been depressed about his wife's death and had taken the tablets at my house. They couldn't do anything for him and he died shortly afterwards.' There was still much to be explained, and Albert waited.

'I arranged for the funeral, and I told Flo, when I went home, that I'd found Charlie lying at the side of the road about ten miles away, in the opposite direction from Bella's house. She believed that he'd gone to get his old job back, and that he'd had a heart attack after finding out about Vena and the baby, so I didn't disillusion her.'

'And you left Bella Wyness lying on the floor?'

Will couldn't tell what Albert was thinking, so he said, quickly, 'She was dead anyway, and the longer it was till she was found, the less chance there was of anybody connecting it with Charlie.'

'I see. It seems I owe you a lot, Will.'

'Oh, no. I did it without thinking, and it was nine days before anybody went to her house, so it turned out better than I'd hoped. The coroner thought she'd only been dead for a week. She was lying in the shade, you see, and he couldn't have taken that into consideration, and there was nothing to suggest to the police that her fall hadn't been an accident.'

He heaved a great sigh. 'I was on tenterhooks that whole nine days, wondering if I'd missed something that would lead them to find out Charlie had been there, and I couldn't relax until the verdict at the inquest was accidental death.'

'Aye, it must have been a great strain on you, Will, and I can't tell you how grateful I am for what you did.'

'I'd like to try to forget about it now, and I needn't ask you not to tell anyone else.'

'I'll not do that. The fewer people that know about it, the better.' Albert looked at Will with his eyebrows raised. 'There's one more thing I'd like to ask you, though. Would it be too much to ask that you show me where Charlie and Vena and the bairn are buried?'

'I'll take you tomorrow night, if you like. That's the last chance you'll have, anyway.'

Sitting back, Albert allowed himself to smile. 'I'll have that whisky now, if the offer still stands.'

While he was waiting for it to be poured, he said, 'You've told nobody else what you've just told me?'

Will concentrated on filling the small glass. 'Martin Potter wrote and asked me to tell him the truth, because he'd more or less guessed what had happened, so I wrote back, care of the University. All I said was that his suspicions were correct. Martin was Bella's son, remember, and I felt I had to let him know.'

'And Charlie was my son.' Albert regarded him sadly. 'Why didn't you let me know?'

390

'I should have.' Will turned round to hand Albert his whisky. 'I thought it would be too painful for you, on top of hearing about his death.'

Twirling the glass thoughtfully in his fingers, Albert said, 'Aye. I'm sorry. You had the best of intentions, and I know now. You took an awful risk, but it worked, thank God.'

He said little when Will drove him to the little cemetery the following night, although his heart almost broke when he read the two inscriptions on the memorial stone.

'In loving memory of Vena Bruce, born 1890, died 1921. Beloved wife of Charles Ogilvie of Aberdeen, Scotland.'

This had been Hetty's doing, but it had been Flo who had arranged for what was inscribed underneath.

'Also the above Charles Ogilvie, born 1890, died 1923.'

On the plinth were three words. 'Together for ever.'

Standing there, his felt hat in his hand, Albert's heart filled with relief until a frightening memory came back to him. It returned with sickening clarity – the nightmare he'd had about Charlie, even before he'd known his son was dead.

He could see him yet, standing by the bed, saying, 'Bella Wyness can never hurt any of our family again', and suddenly he doubted if it had been an accident at all. Charlie had gone to Bella's house with the intention of killing her, and he had succeeded – by chance or design.

Bowing his head, Albert put up a silent prayer that his eldest son had not been condemned to everlasting purgatory for what he'd done, but that he was, indeed, together again with Vena for ever, in a place where Bella Wyness would certainly never be accepted.

He was aware of Will's hand on his arm, and raised his head to smile at him. 'I'm all right, lad. I've seen what I wanted to see, and I'm glad he's at rest.'

When they returned to the bungalow, Albert said that he'd better have an early night, and Flo was rather relieved. He'd been too calm when he came in, but no doubt he'd been grieving for Charlie, and a good night's sleep should help him.

Her father couldn't sleep, however. It was just as well that he hadn't learned the truth until his second last night, for he couldn't have hidden his torment from Flo for any length of time.

Charlie had sacrificed his own life to rid the Ogilvies of Bella Wyness, who must have nurtured a hatred for them so deep that it was bound to end in tragedy. Her death was the only good thing to come out of the whole sorry business, and Albert thanked God once again for Will Dunbar's quick thinking on that early morning.

If he hadn't been so perceptive, Charles Ogilvie would have been publicly branded a murderer, alive or dead.

Chapter Forty-five

It was a great wrench for Albert to leave Flo and Will and his small grandson, but at last the liner steamed out of Wellington harbour and he went down to his cabin.

He knew he would probably never see them again, but cheered up at the thought that he could spend some time with Ellie in the not too distant future, and with Donnie, as well. Gracie and Joe deserved some time to themselves, that's why Hetty had taken Ishbel to Rubislaw Den while he was away. Her youngest sister could be a bit wearing at times.

Inclined to feel rather unsociable, Albert remained in his cabin all that first day, having his meals brought to him, but he awoke the next morning feeling that a great weight had been lifted from his shoulders. Nothing else could happen to his family now, barring illnesses, and as he'd told Bathie often enough, they'd their own lives to lead.

On his outward voyage, he'd spent most of his time in his cabin, content to wallow in his own morbid inner world. But what had happened two years ago couldn't be altered, he thought now, and he had still some of his own life to lead.

Making his way up to the promenade deck the next morning, he took a walk round in the bracing air, then went down to the dining room for breakfast.

There were six people altogether at his table, and the other five had got to know each other the day before, but they welcomed him warmly into their company. Mr and Mrs Foster, from Kent, had been in New Zealand visiting their son, and the Smiths from Waverley, not very far from Wanganui, were on their way to the husband's parents in Devon.

Sitting next to Albert was a lady who introduced herself as Mrs Benton, a widow from Bristol, and when the meal was over, she accompanied him out.

'My husband was in shipping,' she told him as they walked up a flight of wide steps and came out into the open air. 'We meant to take a world cruise when he retired, but, sadly, he died before that day ever came.'

'I'm sorry.' Albert thought that she wouldn't remain a widow for very long, she was far too attractive.

'I was heartbroken, but . . . ' She gave a wry smile. 'Life has to go on, hasn't it?'

Albert nodded. 'That's true. My wife died four years ago, so I know how you must have felt. How long is it since . . . ?'

'Almost eighteen months.'

Her blue eyes were so like Bathie's that his heart missed a beat, but she was completely unaware of his discomposure.

'For over a year I refused to go out, then I realized how stupid I'd been. My sons thought I was mad when I decided to come to New Zealand to see my sister and her family.'

Her tinkly laugh reminded Albert once again of Bathie, but this time, Mrs Benton did notice the quick flicker of pain which passed across his eyes. 'Am I upsetting you by talking like this, Mr Ogilvie?'

'No,' he said, hastily. 'It's not that. You laugh exactly like my wife, and your eyes are the same as hers – deep blue, with sooty-black lashes – and it gave me a bit of a turn.'

'Would you like to sit down and tell me about her?'

They had reached a row of deckchairs, mostly unoccupied, and she sat down without waiting for his reply.

Lowering himself on to the unfamiliar-shaped seat, Albert wondered if he could tell an absolute stranger about his wife, and began slowly. 'I met Bathie when she was sixteen.'

'Bathie? What an unusual name.'

'It was really Bathia, but Bathie suited her better. She was lovely, full of life, and I loved her with all my heart.'

Completely at ease with her now, he told her the story of his courtship, and she smiled encouragingly several times, although he wasn't conscious of it, his eyes being fixed on the horizon as he recalled those far-off happy days.

'She wasn't even fifty when she died,' he ended sadly, as he turned towards his companion. 'I'm sorry, Mrs Benton. I've been going on and on, and you can't have been interested.'

'I've been very interested, and my name is Rose.'

'Rose? That describes you perfectly. Mine's Albert.'

She gave another little trill of laughter. 'That's quite a coincidence. My second name is Victoria.'

Laughing with her, Albert felt as free as the seabirds wheeling overhead. It was an exhilarating sensation, and he made up his mind to enjoy this woman's company as often as he could. 'What about your husband?' he asked, after a short, but quite comfortable silence.

'Mine is not such a romantic story,' she smiled. 'John and I grew up together, and did everything together. Both our families took it for granted that we would marry, so we did. We had a great affection for each other, of course, and we were quite happy on our wedding day.'

Her pause enabled Albert to study her. Her dark hair had, perhaps, a little less silver running through it, and was in a different style, but even the tilt of her head reminded him of Bathie. She was a few inches taller,

394

nearly the same height as he was, but he felt the same sense of protection towards her as he'd often felt for his wife, and he was amazed at himself.

She smiled and carried on. 'We went to Paris for our honeymoon, lovely romantic Paris, and it was there that we discovered how much we really did care for each other. Love had crept up on us without our knowing, until it exploded in our hearts one wonderful, wonderful night.'

She turned her head, her eyes dreamy. 'Oh, Albert, I was wrong. Mine was a romantic story, too, wasn't it?'

Albert and Rose spent all their time together from then on. Her cheery good humour made him forget, for a time, the terrible things Will Dunbar had told him, and which he'd been agonizing over in his cabin that first day. And when he was with her, he could think of Bathie without the old dull pain gnawing at his innards.

Rose encouraged him to try the deck quoits, and to take part in all the other games and entertainments which the crew laid on for them, and even when they had lifeboat drill, she took his mind off the true purpose of the practice by joking.

'I feel like a whale with this life-jacket on. I'm far too well built for anything like this.'

'No, no,' Albert protested. 'You have a perfect figure. You're a full-blown rose, not overblown.' His face reddened at his unplanned familiarity, but she chuckled with delight.

'You're so gallant, Albert, I wish . . . '

Her eyes, which had seemed so wistful a moment before, filled with merriment again as she tucked her arm through his and pulled him to watch a game of tennis. Standing beside her, he wondered if she'd been about to wish, like he did, that the voyage would never end, that they could be together always.

Every morning now, he looked forward to the day ahead, and laughed at himself for acting like a young lad again. He could hardly wait until it was time to meet Rose on deck.

They spent all their days together, separating only when it was time to dress for dinner in the evenings. Then they danced until the ballroom emptied, and he saw her to the door of her cabin before making for his. Their enjoyment of each other's company was literally that, innocent enjoyment.

It was almost the last night of the voyage before Albert admitted to himself that he had begun to think very fondly of Rose Benton, but there was no harm in that. They were only shipboard acquaintances, and he'd have their friendship to look back on as the crowning glory of his first-ever holiday.

She was perhaps a year or two older than Bathie, it was difficult to tell, but with the same zest for life and the same appealing quality about her. Such a woman was meant to have a man, but if she ever married again, it would be to some wealthy aristocrat, not anyone like Albert Ogilvie.

After the dancing was over on the last evening, he saw her to the door of her cabin as usual, and sensed that she was every bit as reluctant to say goodnight as he was.

'Won't you come in for a few minutes?'

Her voice was husky, inviting, so he followed her inside – they were both free agents, after all. She melted against him with a gentle sigh as soon as he put his arms round her, and responded to his kisses so eagerly that desire for her almost swamped him, and he stepped back hastily in dismay. He hadn't foreseen such a reaction.

Her eyes, deep pools of blue in her flushed face, changed to hurt surprise, then to guilty shame, before she moved away from him, and he murmured, 'I'm sorry, Rose. I shouldn't have kissed you like that.'

She kept her eyes lowered now. 'Why not?'

'It's made me want to . . . ' Albert hesitated.

'I wanted you to.' Her colour deepened.

He was about to take a step towards her when a picture of Bathie flashed into his mind. Bathie, lying limp in his arms, four years ago, as he carried her to their bedroom, not knowing that she was already lifeless.

He couldn't desecrate her memory, not with Rose or any other woman. In his whole life, he'd been unfaithful to his wife only once, and every time he thought about it, he was bitterly ashamed. He'd found out, much later, that Jean Rust was a whore, as Bathie had said, and that a number of other men had shared her bed in Queen's Road. But Rose Benton wasn't a woman like that. She was a decent person, just lonely, like he was. Would it be so wrong for them to find solace together?

He'd almost convinced himself that he should give way to his emotions, when Rose broke the silence.

'It would have been a mistake, without love . . . although I came nearer to loving you than any man I've known, except John. Your wife was a very lucky woman. Goodnight, Albert.'

The dismissal came as rather a relief, and he left without saying a word. It wasn't love he felt for her, and he could return home with a clear conscience.

There was no opportunity for them to talk at breakfast, with so many farewells being made, and the Smiths detained him to ask for Flo's address, so they could go to see her when they went home to Waverley. By the time he'd written it out for them, Rose was gone, and his disappointment hit him like a douche of water. He would never see her again, and he hadn't even said goodbye properly.

Going down to his cabin to make sure that his luggage was ready for collection, he remembered the problem he'd been struggling with on his first day on board. Should he tell his family how Charlie had died? Or should he keep the truth to himself?

The sickness that had swept over him in New Zealand, when he found out what had happened, surged up in him again, as it did every time he remembered. Was it fair to place the remainder of his family under that same stress?

In any case, could he trust himself to speak about it rationally? Could he sit down, when he went home to Aberdeen, and tell his children that Bella Wyness had taken her terrible revenge on the Ogilvies at last?

Thank God – and God forgive him for even thinking it – that Bathie hadn't lived to see her prediction coming true.

He sat on for hours, reliving his whole life once again – the joys, the worries, the sorrows – and Rose Benton was completely forgotten as each chapter unfolded in his mind.

At last, he stood up, reflecting wryly that spending so much time in the past was usually considered to be a sign of approaching senility. Listlessly, he went up to the promenade deck to watch as Southampton loomed nearer and nearer, and had been gazing out to sea for some ten minutes when he sensed her presence and looked round.

'Oh, Rose, I'm glad we didn't part in anger.'

'I wasn't angry, Albert.' She took his hand and kept her eyes on it. 'I was ashamed at placing you in such a situation.'

'I went into it willingly,' he said, quietly.

'We were carried away by the circumstances, and because it was our last night. I'm really very grateful to you for stopping when you did.'

Releasing his hand, she raised her eyes. 'What will you be doing when you go home to Aberdeen?'

'I'm going to retire properly.' Albert laughed now, the cold light of day having made him see how stupid he'd been the previous night. 'I've a grocer's shop, you see, and I pretended to retire before, but I couldn't, not altogether. I've made up my mind not to interfere whatever Gracie and Joe – that's my daughter and her husband – want to do to change things. It's only fair to them, but it'll be difficult for me.'

'It *is* difficult to let your family go their own way,' she agreed. 'I've been through it, so I know. And it's just as difficult for them if their parents start leading a different life. My sons are learning to let me go my own way now, and your children will, too, however you fill up your time.'

Albert stroked his moustache. 'I haven't made up my mind what I'll do.' He screwed up his face. 'Do you know, I've often had a fancy to keep homing pigeons, and there's nothing to stop me, now. There's stores in our yard that would convert into pigeon lofts and I'd have something to work for, training them to come back and entering them into competitions.'

'That seems a good idea.'

'But first of all, I was thinking of having electricity put in, and we could get a wireless and a telephone . . . ' He stopped, rather put out by Rose's obvious amusement. 'Have I said something funny?'

'I'm sorry.' Her hand flew up to cover her mouth, rather like a child caught doing something wrong, but her eyes were dancing. 'One minute you were saying you didn't intend to interfere if your daughter and her husband made changes, and in the next, you're planning all these changes yourself. Let *them* make the changes, Albert, electricity if they want, wireless if they want, telephone if they want. Let them decide.'

'Oh.' His sigh of despair became a chuckle. 'I forgot. I'll leave everything to them, and I'll keep quiet, I promise.'

'You don't have to promise me anything, just make sure you keep faith with yourself.'

'Aye, and I can always take myself off to my daughter in Edinburgh if I get frustrated. She told me I could go for a holiday, and my son in London will likely do the same, when he knows I've coped so well this time. And I've another married daughter in Aberdeen, so I won't be short of places to go.'

'You are welcome to spend a week or two in Bristol with me, any time you like.'

Her invitation unsettled him again, and he looked at her seriously. 'Thank you, but I don't think I should.'

Her silvery laugh rang out. 'I have no designs on you, Albert, but perhaps you're wise. If we leave things as they are, we will always have happy memories of this voyage.'

A sudden surging forward among the other passengers told them that the liner was docking. 'Goodbye, then, Albert.'

'Goodbye, Rose.'

Her fingers touched her own lips then rested briefly on his before she walked quickly away.

He turned towards the rail again, looking down on the smiling faces of those who had come to welcome the travellers. Not that there would be anybody to welcome him. He was going to have to depend on some stranger to show him how to get to the station, but Donnie should be waiting at Waterloo to see him on to the Aberdeen train at King's Cross.

Idly, he let his eyes travel over the sea of hands below until an insistent waving, which seemed to be directed at him, made him half close his eyes to concentrate on that part of the crowd. He could almost have sworn it was Donnie, but he laughed off the idea. Donnie couldn't leave his shop for so long on a Saturday. He lost sight of the man for a time, then spotted him again, and this time he was sure. It was Donnie. His bright head was bobbing up and down now, in his efforts to attract his father's attention, so Albert gave an excited wave in return. He turned round and joined the moving line of passengers making their way to disembark, his step lighter because his heart was lighter. His only surviving son had cared enough to come and meet him.

It struck Albert, then, like a kick in the stomach, that he had fathered eight children, although poor wee James hadn't lived long, but not one of his grandchildren was an Ogilvie. There were Potters, Ferrises, McKenzies, a Dunbar . . . No, he was wrong. There was one Ogilvie among them, but Donnie's Queenie would become Mrs Something-Else when she was older, and his male line would be lost for ever.

The discordant hooting of the ship's sirens caused him to frown a little, but he was being swept along by the surging crowd around him, most of them anxious to set foot on the soil of their homeland again.

The message on one of the many plaques which had hung in his mother's kitchen came into his head. It had been similar to the one Bathie had chosen when his mother died, but all it said was, 'East, west, hame's best.'

400

He'd never understood its meaning when he was a boy, and had forgotten about it – probably a willing forget, because he'd been the one who had accidentally broken it – but it was true, he knew that now, and he couldn't wait to hear the broad Aberdeen tongue again, once he was home properly.

Stumbling as his foot met the gangway, he caught hold of the rope to steady himself. The sudden physical movement made him come to an equally sudden decision. He wouldn't tell his son and daughters anything. Let them carry on thinking that Charlie had died a natural death. There was no need to put them through any more distress.

His final decision made, he lifted his head, squared his shoulders and walked firmly downwards to where Donnie was waiting to welcome him back.

1939

The funeral tea was over. The young Ferrises (Neil and Patsy), Potters (Olive and Raymond), McKenzies (Kathleen and Morag), Lawrences (Ishbel's Simon, Thomas and Ursula), Queenie Ogilvie and Leonard Dunbar had all gone off to the pictures.

This had been Will Dunbar's suggestion, to get them out of the way, and the rest of the family were looking at him now, wondering why he seemed so nervous.

Clearing his throat, he said, 'I've decided to tell you something you should all have known years ago.'

Most of the faces remained blank, only Martin Potter frowned. 'If it's what I think it is, I don't think you should . . . '

'They should be told,' Will said firmly. 'It happened a long time ago, and . . . ' He stopped for a moment, then launched into the story he'd kept to himself, with one exception, for sixteen years.

They listened, their faces reflecting disbelief, sorrow, pain, horror, as the facts, both before and after Charlie's death, were disclosed. When Will came to an end, there was a stunned silence.

Gracie, with Joe's hand over hers, was the first to break it. 'Did Father know?'

Will nodded. 'Before he left Wanganui in 1925, he asked me to tell him everything, and I did.'

Hetty turned to Martin now. 'If that's what you thought Will was going to tell us, how did *you* know?'

'I didn't know the whole story, but I wrote to Will at the time and told him I'd guessed what had happened.'

'*I* didn't even know the whole story.' Flo sounded most annoyed. 'Will, why didn't you . . . ?'

'I couldn't tell you, Flo, not then, and I only told your father because he demanded to know the truth. But today, even as I was watching his coffin being lowered into the grave, I had the feeling that Albert was standing beside me, urging me to let you all know how your brother died.'

They discussed it for the next few hours, and although they were shocked, no one condemned Charlie, even if what had happened wasn't an accident. None of them had much sleep that night, each couple going over and over every detail in bed.

Gracie turned round as Joe came through for breakfast. He had filled out over the years; he was not fat, exactly, but wearing that way, and his hair was receding at the temples, but she still felt her heart stir each time she looked at him, and still loved every firm inch of him.

'I'll have to go back to the shop today,' he said, looking apologetic. 'That's three days I've been off, and everything's settled now, anyway, isn't it?'

'Yes, I knew you'd have to go in today.' She ladled out some porridge for him, to keep out the February chill, then sat down at the other side of the kitchen table.

'I can hardly believe it's twenty years since we saw Flo.'

Joe lifted a spoonful to his mouth and blew on it. 'Aye, the years fly past when you grow older.'

'You maybe feel old,' Gracie said sharply, 'but I don't.' She jumped up when she heard the postman pushing a letter through the door, and added, as she went out, 'Just sometimes, when Neil and Patsy start arguing.'

Her face was puzzled when she came back, turning a large envelope over in her hands. 'It's addressed to Father, and it's from the Council. What on earth . . . ?'

'Open it and see,' Joe said, dryly. 'It can't be anything very important, and you're the one that attends to everything.'

He watched her sliding her thumb carefully along the flap, then slipping a sheet of paper out and unfolding it.

'Oh, my God, Joe,' she whispered suddenly. 'Read that.'

'I've been half expecting this,' he said, when he laid it down beside his plate. 'The last time the Health

Inspector came round, he said he wouldn't be surprised if the property was condemned, but I never thought it would come so quick.'

'You never said anything about it to me.'

'I did tell your father that the place needed a lot of work done to it to keep it safe, I've been telling him for years, but he was always too taken up with his damned pigeons to pay any attention.'

'They kept him occupied, Joe, and he hadn't thought it was as bad as this, but they're pulling it down to make way for improvements to the Gallowgate. They can't do that. We'll have to fight it.'

He shook his head. 'We haven't a leg to stand on. God knows how long these buildings had been up before your father bought this property in 1890, nearly fifty years ago. But if you like, I'll ask if anybody else has got the same letter.'

The Council's communication was just as upsetting for the other members of the family when they learned about it.

Ellie looked angry. 'This would have broken Father's heart if it had come a week earlier.'

He'd have died from the shock of that instead of from the pneumonia, Gracie thought, slightly hysterically.

Hetty was still holding the Council's letter, frowning in concentration, but now she glanced enquiringly at Gracie. 'Should we let Flo and Donnie and Ellie take what they want before they have to go back? You don't have to be out until July, that's five months yet, so Ishbel and you and I can wait a while before we take ours.'

Flo looked indignant. 'I don't want anything. We can't start splitting up things . . . it doesn't seem proper, with Father not cold in his grave.'

Donnie stepped in, as the senior member of the family. 'I think Hetty's right. I don't mean we should divide things out, but I think we should all take something small as a keepsake, and let it stop there. Gracie's been the backbone of this family for years now, and she's looked after Father ever since Mother died, so she should have everything else.'

This proposal being agreed, they each picked a memento before Donnie and Helene left to catch the London train, his eyes moist because he was leaving the Gallowgate for ever.

Hetty and Martin went home shortly afterwards, also Ishbel and Peter Lawrence, the solicitor she'd met at Hetty's house when Albert was in New Zealand.

Albert had been delighted that she'd insisted on carrying on his tradition. 'Ursula,' he'd crowed, when her youngest child was born. 'I might see the end of the alphabet yet.'

The McKenzies had packed all their luggage in the car before they left Hetty's, and weren't leaving until later.

Gracie could see that Ellie's husband had been affected very badly by the funeral and by what Will had said. His face was grey, his eyes, when he did look up, were full of pain, and he'd been slumped back in one of the armchairs in the parlour since Donnie and Helene left.

'You shouldn't have let Gavin come,' she told her sister, when they were in the kitchen making another pot of tea. 'He doesn't look a bit well.'

Ellie grimaced. 'That's why I wouldn't let him drive, but I couldn't keep him away. He was determined to attend Father's funeral, even though I pretended to scold him by saying that it would be his turn next if he did.'

Gracie looked shocked. 'Oh, Ellie, how could you? That wasn't a very nice thing to say.'

'I'm not sure it isn't true, though. He looks really ghastly, and I'd better go through to see if he's all right. Flo and Will have gone upstairs to write to Mary, to let her know how the funeral went, and he's through there by himself.'

In the parlour, Gavin McKenzie lifted his white, balding head and smiled faintly to his wife, so she went across to him, and took his blue-veined hand in hers.

'Gavin, dear, I think you should have a rest for a while, before we set off. It's all been too much for you.'

He nodded slowly. 'I'm afraid it has, Ellie, but I had to come. Your father was a very good friend, and I loved him like a brother. And your mother . . . ' He faltered, then looked up at her. 'You've always known how much

I cared for Bathie, my dear, and my love for you was different. It was a husband's love for his wife, and what I felt for her was . . . oh, I don't know how to describe it, for it wasn't physical.'

'I know that, dear.'

'I was quite happy to know that it was Albert she loved, but now they're both gone, this house will soon be gone and I'll soon be gone myself.'

'Don't say that, Gavin.' Ellie felt a stab of apprehension shoot through her.

'I'm nearly seventy-three, Ellie – an old man, with an old man's memories.'

'You're just tired. Lie down for an hour or two.' She helped him up and steered him into her father's bedroom.

Noticing that he took a look around him, she said, 'Gracie changed the bedding, so there's no need . . . '

'I remember this room,' he mused. 'It's here I delivered all Bathie's babies.'

Ellie pushed him gently on to the bed and knelt down to remove his shoes. 'Yes, I know, Gavin.'

He giggled suddenly. 'I delivered you, Ellie, and a bonnie scrap of a thing you were, even then. Little did I think, when I held you up to smack the breath into you, that I'd fall in love with you one day and marry you.' He allowed her to lift his legs up, then lay back against the pillows, his mind still on the past. 'My first wife was still alive, and I should have had no thoughts of anything except making sure the infant was sound in wind and limb, but I felt attracted to Bathie. I couldn't help myself.'

Ellie let him ramble on. She couldn't do anything else.

'It was after Margaret died that I let myself fall in love with her, but it wasn't until Hetty was born . . . or maybe it was Ishbel? I can't remember, but that's when I told her. She wasn't fully conscious at the time, but it must have penetrated somehow. It was a few weeks afterwards, though, before I knew she'd heard me, and I told her straight out then, but I let her know I was quite happy to leave things the way they were.'

He fell silent, and in a moment his even breathing told her that he was asleep, but she stayed on for a little while, reflecting that it felt strange to hear her husband talking about attending at her birth. It was even stranger that he'd spoken about his love for her mother, for he'd never mentioned that once since they were married.

At last, she tiptoed out, closing the door softly behind her, and returned to the kitchen, where Flo and Will were now sitting with Gracie.

'Is Gavin all right?' Gracie was quite concerned.

'He's sleeping in Father's bed.'

'He's failing, you know,' Will said, sadly.

'I know, but he's not that old, and he's still got plenty of spirit left in him . . . well, usually.' Making a face, Ellie sat down beside Flo and poured herself a cup of tea. 'It's been good to see you two again. It's just a pity that it took Father's death to bring us all together.'

'We couldn't afford to come home before.' Flo was on the defensive. 'We weren't at Mother's funeral, and I felt I had to be at Father's, so we used some of the money Mother left us to pay our air fares.'

'I wasn't criticizing you,' Ellie said. 'I know you'd have come before if you could.'

Gracie turned to Will. 'Tell your mother to keep writing. I don't actually remember her, but I've got to know her, and like her, through her letters.'

'She looks forward to yours, too.'

'It's funny how much the Ogilvies have been affected by the Wynesses . . . ,' Ellie began, then turned red, remembering the terrible extent to which they had been affected. 'I mean,' she blustered, 'Flo marrying Mary's son, and Hetty . . . ' Her voice petered out at the thought of Martin's mother.

'We'll all have to forget about that,' Gracie declared. 'I'm very grateful to Will for telling us the truth at last, because we should have known about it, but it happened so long ago, and Martin couldn't help what his mother did any more than any of the rest of us.'

She broke off and sighed. 'Now it's goodbye to the house, goodbye to the shop, goodbye to everything that could remind us of Mother and Father.'

'We don't need the house to help us to remember them,' Ellie said quietly.

They spent the next hour and a half reminiscing about their childhood, then Ellie stood up. 'I'll have to go and waken Gavin. It'll take him a little while to come to himself, and we'll have to leave shortly. Thank goodness it isn't freezing, for I don't like driving on icy roads, especially when it comes down dark.' As she walked through to the bedroom, she felt a sense of foreboding, a tightness in her chest and lungs, and she wasn't altogether surprised when Gavin failed to respond to her gentle prodding, nor to the vigorous shaking she gave him as panic struck her. There wasn't the faintest movement of the blankets, so she sat down on the bedcover and took his hand. It wasn't cold, but she was quite certain that he was dead.

'Oh, Gavin,' she whispered, 'I know you loved me just as much as I loved you, but I'm glad you died here in this room, thinking of Mother. It just seems . . . right, somehow.'

Gracie forced herself to decide what to do about all the things in the house. The furniture was fifty years old, some of it a lot older, and wasn't worth moving to their new home, wherever it might be.

The best of Grandmother Johnstone's figurines had been taken by her brother and sisters. Ellie, strangely enough, had chosen the only item which had belonged to Grandma Ogilvie – the old chipped plaque.

'This meant a lot to Mother,' she had said when they all told her it was worthless. 'And she once told me it had meant a lot to Grandma, as well.'

The glazing on the gold-rimmed plate was cracked, and the gold paint itself was wearing off, but the words had still been quite readable.

To forget and forgive is a maxim of old,
Though I've learned but one half of it yet.
The theft of my heart I can freely forgive,
But the thief I can never forget.

It must have meant a lot to Ellie, too, Gracie had thought at the time, and had wondered if it was because of Jack Lornie, who had been killed in the war. It came to her now that Ellie had taken it to remind Gavin of their mother. Gavin had died just after that, of course, and everything else had gone clean out of her head.

Neither Flo nor Hetty had thought it strange that Ellie insisted on having Gavin buried in their parents' grave, he was family, after all, but Gracie had been surprised. She hadn't said anything while the others were there, but she'd tackled Ellie about it when they were alone.

'Why didn't you bury Gavin in Edinburgh?'

Her sister's white face had regarded her piteously. 'It would have been better for me, I suppose, but it wouldn't have been right for Gavin.'

'I can't see why not.'

'Gracie, you don't understand. He spent a big part of his life loving Mother, and . . . '

'That was long ago, Ellie, before he fell in love with you, you know that. He'd only been friends with Mother for years, there was nothing more than that, I'm positive. You've been torturing yourself over nothing.'

The tears had come to Ellie's eyes then, the first since her husband's death. 'I know he loved me, but he still felt something for Mother. He was speaking about how much he used to love her when he . . . fell asleep, and I know she always felt something for him. That's why I had him buried here. Father's closest to Mother, but Gavin comes next, and that's how it should be. That's how it always was.'

Remembering, Gracie sighed. That's how it always was, and that's how it would always be now, till the end of time.

Her heart ached for her sister . . . and for Gavin McKenzie.

Epilogue

Ironically, Albert's property, like all its neighbours, remained standing – empty, neglected and crumbling – for many years after Gracie and her family moved out in the middle of July, 1939, the outbreak of the Second World War having put an effective stop to the Council's plans where all entreaties from the residents had failed.

This part of the ancient thoroughfare was eventually demolished and rebuilt, however, and where there had once been dozens of shops and quaint old dwelling places, there now tower two rather unfriendly concrete masses – a Technical College and an eighteen-storey block of flats – externally and internally a thousand times more modern, but with nothing like the subtle appeal of the Ogilvies' house, which had stood tall – but not quite so tall – on the brow of the Gallowgate before them.